***ASSASSINS . . . WITH CROSSBOWS,
DRAGONBANE. . . .***

The dragon's warning mind-call had sent Karl and
Tennetty racing off on their horses, intent on stopping
the invaders before they could penetrate too deeply past
Home's defenses.

Now, the two stood outside the shack near which the
assassins had been sighted.

"Work your way around to the front," Karl said. "Then
make some noise. I'll move when you do. If I need
your help, I'll call out—otherwise, stay outside. But if I
kick anyone out the front door or window, they're
yours."

Karl grasped Tennetty's shoulder as she started to move.
"Watch your back—they may not be inside."

Waiting next to the rear window, Karl thought about
how easily the shack could become a trap for him. What
was taking Tennetty so long, he wondered. She should
be making some—

The snap of a twig sent him into action; he kicked open
the rear door and then moved to one side and dove
through the greased parchment window. He landed on
his shoulder on the dirt floor and bounced to his feet,
his sword at the ready. . . .

BOOK THREE OF GUARDIANS OF THE FLAME

THE SILVER CROWN

A FANTASY NOVEL BY

JOEL ROSENBERG

A SIGNET BOOK

NEW AMERICAN LIBRARY

Copyright © 1985 by Joel Rosenberg

Cover art by Segrelles

SIGNET TRADEMARK REG. U.S. PAT. OFF. AND FOREIGN COUNTRIES
REGISTERED TRADEMARK—MARCA REGISTRADA
HECHO EN CHICAGO. U.S.A.

SIGNET, SIGNET CLASSIC, MENTOR, ONYX, PLUME, MERIDIAN
and NAL BOOKS are published by NAL PENGUIN INC.,
1633 Broadway, New York, New York 10019

First Printing, April, 1985

5   6   7   8   9   10   11   12   13

PRINTED IN THE UNITED STATES OF AMERICA

For Tim Daniels
in memoriam, *dammit*

ACKNOWLEDGMENTS

I'd like to thank Mary Kittredge, Mark J. McGarry, and most particularly Harry F. Leonard, all of whom helped to make this a better book than it otherwise would have been. This is both my fourth book and the fourth time I've thanked all of them in print; that isn't coincidental.

I'd be more than a little remiss if I didn't also thank my agent, Richard Curtis; my editor, Sheila Gilbert, for her advice, support, and patience; my favorite policeman, Officer William T. Badger, NHPD/VSU, for creating the quiet; and Felicia, for the usual—and more.

There is nothing more difficult to take in hand, more perilous to conduct, or more uncertain in its success, than to take the lead in the introduction of a new order of things.

—*Niccolò Machiavelli*

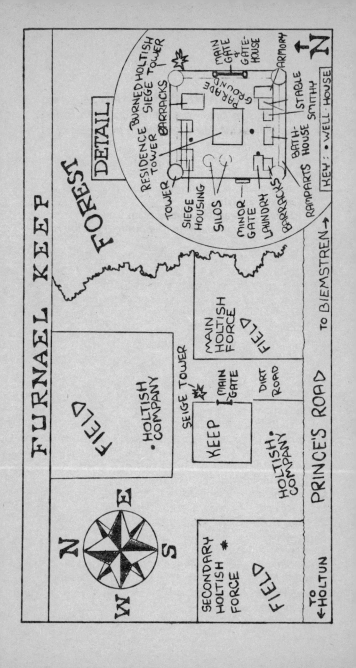

DRAMATIS PERSONAE

Ahrmin—master slaver
Fenrius, Danared—journeyman slavers
The Matriarch of the Healing Hand Society
Doria—Hand acolyte
Karl Cullinane—warrior, raiding-team leader
Tennetty, Ch'akresarkandyn ip Katharhdn, Piell ip Yratha—squad leaders in Karl Cullinane's raiding team
Walter Slovotsky—Karl Cullinane's second-in-command; thief, warrior, smartass
Wellem, Erek, Therol, Donidge, Hervean, Firkh, Restius—warriors, members of Karl Cullinane's raiding team
Gwellin, Gerrin, Daherrin—dwarf warriors, members of Karl Cullinane's raiding team
Sternius—master slaver
Jilla, Danni—slaves
Ellegon—a young dragon
Henrad—novice wizard; Andrea's apprentice
Andrea Andropolous Cullinane—wizard, teacher, Karl Cullinane's wife
Jason Cullinane—Karl and Andrea's son
Aeia Eriksen Cullinane—Karl and Andrea's adopted daughter, teacher
Mikyn—freed slave
Alezyn—Mikyn's father
Ahira Bandylegs—Home Mayor
Louis Riccetti—ex-wizard, the Engineer
Ranella, Bast—apprentice Engineers
U'len—cook
Thellaren—Spidersect cleric
Kirah Slovotsky—Walter Slovotsky's wife
Jane Michele Slovotsky—Walter and Kirah's daughter
Ihryk—farmer, houseman
Pendrill—stableman

Werthan—farmer

Anna Major—Werthan's wife

Anna Minor—Werthan and Anna Major's daughter

Afbee—assassin

Nehera—dwarf blacksmith

Daven—warrior, raiding-team leader

Wraveth, Taren—warriors, members of Daven's raiding team

Jherant ip Therranj—elf warrior

Dhara ip Therranj—emissary from Lord Khoral of Therranj

Beralyn, Lady Furnael

Thomen Furnael—heir to barony Furnael

Chton—farmer, leader of Joiner faction

Petros—farmer, of sorts

Harwen, Ternius—farmers

Valeran—guard captain in the service of Lord Gyren of Enkiar

Halvin—Valeran's second-in-command

Norfan—one of Valeran's warriors

Prince Harffen Pirondael—ruler of Bieme

Aveneer—warrior, raiding-team leader

Frandred—Aveneer's second-in-command

Theren, Thermen, Migdal—warriors, members of Aveneer's raiding team

Zherr, Baron Furnael

Garavar—a captain of the House Guard

Taren—warrior of the House Guard

Arthur Simpson Deighton/Arta Myrdhyn—lecturer in philosophy, master wizard

Introduction

It had long since ceased being a game. Friends didn't really die in a game.

But . . . it had been just a game, years before. Professor Arthur Simpson Deighton was the gamemaster. Karl Cullinane, Jason Parker, James Michael Finnegan, Doria Perlstein, Walter Slovotsky, Andrea Andropolous, and Lou Riccetti had sat down for an evening of fantasy gaming. The game suddenly, without warning, became real: James Michael became Ahira Bandylegs, a powerful dwarf; skinny Karl Cullinane turned into Barak, a massive warrior; Lou Riccetti became Aristobulus, wielder of powerful magicks; Andrea became Lotana, novice wizard.

It had become real, every bit as real as the pain Jason Parker felt in his last moments kicking on the end of a bloody spear, every bit as real as Ahira's fiery death, and his resurrection by the Matriarch of the Healing Hand Society.

But there was a price to be paid for that resurrection: Karl and the others promised to fight to end slavery. They declared war on the Pandathaway-based Slavers' Guild, the dealers in human flesh who traveled across the Eren regions, securing and selling their cargo.

Attacking the slavers was one thing—but what to do with the freed slaves? Some could be sent home, but some had no home to go back to. That was easily solved: They built Home, a new kind of society for the world they found themselves in.

Aeia Eriksen did have a home to go back to, a village in

Melawei. While returning her there, Karl discovered evidence
that Professor Deighton was actually the almost legendary
wizard Arta Myrdhyn, who had left a magical sword in a
cave, clutched in fingers of light, waiting.

Waiting for whom? For Karl's son, it seemed; Deighton/Arta
Myrdhyn had plans for Karl's son. . . .

Not my son, Karl said. He left the sword of Arta Myrdhyn
in Melawei and returned Home, continuing to venture out and
attack Slavers' Guild caravans wherever they could be found.

It had long since ceased being a game.

A revolution is never a game; it is, in more senses than one,
a bloody mess.

PROLOGUE:

Ahrmin

"You may enter, Ahrmin," the acolyte said. She was a slim woman, dressed in the long white robes of the Healing Hand Society. Her long blond hair shimmered in the sunlight as she stared coolly at him out of the yellow-irised eyes set exotically but not unpleasantly far apart in her high-cheekboned face.

Idly, Ahrmin estimated that she was easily worth thirty gold; he could remove that air of superiority within a tenday, perhaps less. Perhaps much less.

She shook her head as though in response to his unvoiced comment. "You, and you alone. The others shall remain outside. It is unpleasant enough to tolerate their presence on the preserve; I will not have their breath fouling the air of the tabernacle itself."

She stared to turn away, but spun back as Fenrius growled and started toward her. Fenrius towered menacingly over her slim form, but the huge man froze in place as the acolyte raised her hand, all the while murmuring soft words that Ahrmin could hear clearly, but never recall. As always, he tried to remember them, but he couldn't; they vanished as the sounds touched his ears.

As the spell ended, the cleric gripped the air in front of her; Fenrius' arms flew down to his sides, his leather tunic wrinkling as though he were in the grip of a giant invisible hand. Muscles stood out cordlike on his unshaven cheeks; his mouth worked silently, lips drawn wide in a soundless gasp as sweat beaded on his forehead.

"No," she said, smiling gently, almost affectionately. "Not here. Here, you are within the grasp of the Hand. In more senses than one." She began to tighten the grip of her straining fingers. Leather squealed in protest; Fenrius' breath whooshed out of his lungs.

His mouth worked frantically, but no sound escaped.

Ahrmin's five other men stood stock-still, Danared shaking his head in sympathy. But even he was not foolish enough to make a move toward the acolyte.

Just as Ahrmin was sure that Fenrius' chest would cave in beneath the pressure, the acolyte stopped, cocking her head to one side, as though listening to a distant voice.

"Yes, Mother," she said, with a deep sigh. She raised her hand and twitched her wrist; Fenrius tumbled end over end through the air, landing on the grass with a thump.

"You may follow me, Ahrmin," she said.

Ahrmin limped after the acolyte down dark corridors to a vast, high-ceilinged hall, the drag-slap of his sandals a counterpoint to her even steps. They walked through a high arch and into the hall, halting in unison before the high-backed throne, as though obeying an unspoken command. Later, he couldn't recall whether the room was crowded or empty; his eyes were drawn to the woman on the throne.

If the acolyte was thin, this woman was positively skeletal. He always remembered the tissue-thin skin on the back of her hands, skin as white as a dead man's, unmarked save for the bulges caused by underlying bones and sinews.

But despite the funereal slimness of her form, she radiated a sense of power as she sat there, her face hidden by the upswept cowl of her faintly glowing white robes.

"*Greetings, Ahrmin, son of Ohlmin,*" she said. "*I have been expecting you.*"

Her voice was like nothing he had ever heard. Though she seemed to speak softly, her words rattled his teeth.

"Then you know what I want."

"What you . . . want is obvious," the acolyte hissed. "Karl wrecked your body—he should have killed you. He should have—"

The Matriarch raised a hand. "*Be still, daughter. We shall take no side in this matter.*" She turned back to Ahrmin.

"*Which is precisely the point. You were injured in combat with Karl Cullinane—*"

"Injured?" He raised a fire-twisted hand. "You call this *injured?*" Had it not been for the bottle of healing draughts he had drunk while the ship burned around him, Ahrmin would have died. As it was, he had never fully recovered from the burns or the long trip over the mountains from Melawei to Ehvenor.

"*Yes. Would you not agree?*" She gestured, her long fingers twitching spastically as she spoke words that could only be heard and forgotten.

The air to one side of the Matriarch shimmered, solidifying into a mirror.

"*Look at yourself,*" she commanded.

He did, forcing his shoulders back and standing tall.

It wasn't a pretty sight; it was never a pretty sight. The hair on the right side of his head was gone, the skin permanently browned and puckered, save for the few fleshy spots where his trembling hand had splashed enough of the healing potion to restore those patches to normal health.

The left side of his face was normal enough; the fire had only singed him there, and the healing draughts, combined with his body's natural healing ability, had brought that back to normal.

But the right side of his face was a horror. The flames had seared away his ear and most of his lips; it had burned his cheeks down to the bone. While the draughts had healed what remained, their power was not great enough to bring flesh back from ashes.

Surely, the Matriarch was powerful enough to do that; she was said to be able to raise the dead. Surely—

"*No.*" She dismissed the thought and the mirror with a wave of her hand. "*I do not expect that you will understand this, but there are forces involved here that even I would not wish to involve myself with again. I have done so three times. Once, many years ago, to protect the tabernacle and its preserve, and twice again,*" she said, laying a gentle hand on the acolyte's arm, "*for reasons that do not concern you. I will not do so now.*"

"But I've brought gold." He waved a hand toward the door. "Sacks of it."

"Gold?" The acolyte sniffed. "Bring a mountain of gold, and we still won't help you. Right now, you wouldn't have a chance against Karl. But if we healed you—"

"I'll hunt the bastard down and kill him. He murdered my father—and did this to me." *I'll hunt him down whether you help me or not*, he thought. *I'll hold his head in my hands.*

The Matriarch folded her thin arms across her chest. "*That is entirely a matter of opinion.*" She extended a skinny arm, her sleeve rippling. "*Now, go.*"

There was no point in staying. He couldn't fight the Hand, not even if he had the entire guild behind him.

He spun on his heel and limped away. Their words echoed down the marble halls after him.

"We have to help Karl, Mother. Or at least warn him."

"*Ahh. Your skills have improved, daughter. You read beyond Ahrmin's surface thoughts?*

"Yes—Karl must think he's dead. He doesn't know—"

"*Nor can we tell him. Our responsibilities lie elsewhere. And elsewhen. To interfere now, to involve the Hand further at this juncture . . . it would ruin everything. As well you know.*"

"I do know, but . . . Forgive me, Mother—I was lying. He just might be able to kill Karl, or have him killed. It's—"

"*You are forgiven. You are not the first of our order to tell a lie.*"

"He could kill Karl, if he took him by surprise—"

"*I think you perhaps underrate this Karl Cullinane of yours. In any case, my decision stands, daughter.*"

"But what can we *do?*"

"*For now, nothing. We must wait. Waiting is a difficult skill; I commend its practice to you, Doria. . . .*"

PART ONE:

The Forest of Wehnest

CHAPTER ONE:

The Hunter

Out of the darkness of the tent, a hand reached out and gently grasped his shoulder. "Karl, ta ly'veth ta ahd dalazhi." *Karl, it is time to wake up.*

Karl Cullinane came awake instantly. He clamped his left hand around the slim wrist and pulled, slamming the other into the tent pole, almost dislodging it. He brought his right hand around to block a possible knife thrust—

—and stopped himself when he realized who it was.

"Ta havath, Karl." *Easy, Karl.* Tennetty laughed, her breath warm in his ear. She switched from Erendra to her thickly accented English as she pushed away from him, rubbing at her shoulder. "I don't think Andrea would approve. Besides, if you move around much more, you'll bring the tent down around both our heads."

He released her and sighed. He would have preferred Tennetty to be a bit more nervous about waking him, a bit less trusting that he would recognize her before doing something sudden and fatal.

"What is it, Tennetty?" he asked in Erendra. "Is the dragon here?" *Ellegon?* he thought. *Can you hear me?*

No answer.

"Wake *up*, Karl—you're a full day off. He isn't due until tomorrow."

"Slovotsky, then?"

She nodded. "On his way up," Tennetty said, smiling faintly in the dim lanternlight as she untangled herself from his blankets. "Gerrin spotted him—and a small caravan, camped down by the fork."

"Slavers or merchants?"

"He couldn't tell, not from here." She shrugged. "But if they are slavers, it would explain Slovotsky's return." She rose to her knees and took up a piece of straw from his bedding, using it to carry fire from her lantern to his, idly pausing to straighten his tent pole in passing. Tennetty was a slim woman, but not a soft one; beneath her ragged cotton undershirt, strong muscles played.

"I've had my team's horses saddled and ordered a general weapons inspection." She flashed a smile at him, then dropped it. Tennetty seemed to have a permanent sneer, which somehow started with her narrow eyes and continued down her thin, broken nose, all the way to her cracked lips. A scar snaked around her right eye; a black patch covered the remains of the left.

"You take a lot on yourself, don't you?"

"Perhaps." Picking up her lantern, she rose smoothly from her half-crouch and held the tent flap open for him. "Let's go." She hitched first at the wide-bladed shortsword on the left side of her belt and then at the crude flintlock pistol on the right side.

"I'll be a minute," he said, his hand going to the spider amulet secured around his neck by a leather thong.

That was a long-standing reflex, its source back in his long-ago college days. Karl Cullinane had always had trouble keeping track of things; pens, pencils, books, lighters, change, and keys always seemed to vanish from his possession, as though they had turned to air. The amulet was too important; it couldn't become part of that pattern of lost valuables.

"If you see Slovotsky, tell him to get up here. In the meantime, give the order to break camp, then have your team wait by their horses—and tell Restius to keep the animals quiet this time, even if he has to slit the throat of that idiot mare of his."

"You want me to have your horse saddled?"

"Fine. But make sure the bellybands are tight—no, forget it." He shook his head. "No, I'd better take care of Stick." No reason to put someone else to the trouble when Karl would have to check the work himself.

"Anything else?"

"Mmm—tell Chak I want to see him when he gets a chance. That's all."

She nodded and left.

Tossing his blankets aside, Karl dressed quickly, first donning skintight knit-cotton pants and a thick under-shirt. He pulled on a pair of rough leather trousers before slipping on his socks and forcing his feet into his tight steel-toed boots.

Vibram, he thought, for the thousandth time. *How much would I pay for one pair of Vibram soles?* Certainly a hundred pieces of gold; definitely his third-best horse. But would he trade, say, Carrot or Stick for a good pair of soles? Probably not, but it would be a close call. Not that he'd ever get the chance; such synthetics were easily a hundred years away on This Side.

He uncorked a jug of water and drank a scant mouthful, then splashed some on his face, drying it with a dirty towel. He slipped his leather tunic over his head before belting his sword around his waist, reflexively checking to see that it was loose in its scabbard.

Forming his hands into fists, he stood and stretched broadly, trying to loosen the almost permanent knots in his neck and shoulders.

Dammit, he thought, *this doesn't get easier.*

He stooped to retrieve two unloaded pistols and a small pouch from his saddlebags, tucked the pistols crossways in his swordbelt, and tied the pouch to a small brass ring mounted on the right side of the belt. He gave his hair a quick fingercombing before blowing out the lantern and stepping out into the night.

Above, a million stars winked at him out of a coal-black sky. The faerie lights were active tonight. Sometimes, when they changed slowly, it was difficult to distinguish them from stars, but not tonight. Hovering halfway between forest and sky, they flickered on and off, pulsing through a chromatic scale. First a series of deep reds, then a quick flash of orange before they worked their way through the yellows, greens, and a chorus of blues, turning indigo and vanishing, only to reappear in a few moments in a flash of cerulean.

"Lights are bright tonight," Wellem said. He stood sharpening a dagger and staring up at the sky. His hands moved in

a smooth, practiced motion, stroking the stone lightly, evenly —
across the blade. "Awfully bright."

"That they are."

"Makes me feel like I'm back in Ehvenor, almost." He
sighed. "Not used to seeing them so far north."

"What do you think they are, really?" Karl asked idly.

"I haven't learned anything new, Karl Cullinane." Wellem
shrugged. "I can still only give you the faerie answer:
'Sometimes they are, and sometimes they are not.' Tonight
they are." He turned away, still whisking the stone against
the dagger.

There had been a time when a younger, less jaded Karl
Cullinane would have stood and admired the clear sky, the
many colors blinking in the night—

But that time, that youth, was gone. Now he simply saw a
sky clear enough, a night bright enough to provide little cover
for either the slavers or for Karl's people. Too bad—were it
cloudier, the darksight of his six dwarf warriors would have
given their side an extra edge. Karl always took any advantage
that came his way. He saw no sense pushing his luck further than
necessary; as it was, it was necessary to stretch it awfully far.

The encampment spread out around him on the mesa. His
hundred warriors were breaking camp. Some brought down
the tents and stowed the noncombat gear; some gave a final
cleaning to a crossbow or flintlock rifle; others took a few
moments to touch up the edge of a sword or a Nehera-made
bowie. The tiny cooking fires had long since been doused; a
few stray flinders might have betrayed their presence to slavers en route from Pandathaway to their hunting grounds in
the east.

All made their preparations quietly, with only an occasional grunt or muttered comment. Before a battle was always
a quiet time. By dawn, even if everything went well in the
forest below, some would surely be injured or dead.

The bushes behind him rustled. He reached for his sword.

" 'Yea, though I walk through the valley of death, I will
fear no evil . . .' " a familiar voice said.

Karl let his hand drop. " '. . . for I am the meanest son of
a bitch in the valley,' " he finished. "That's too long, Walter;
not a good password. Besides, I'm the one already in camp;
I'm supposed to give the challenge, not you. Cut the

crap and come on out. And be more careful next time—
Gerrin already spotted you.''

"Damn dwarf has good eyes," Slovotsky said, pushing his
way through the brush. As usual, he was dressed only in
sandals and a blousy pair of pantaloons, his throwing knives
strapped to his right hip, a shortsword belted to his left. His
chest, arms, and face had been blackened with a mixture
of grease and ashes, and his chest and belly were scraped
bare in spots, but his cocky, all-is-right-with-the-world-because-
Walter-Slovotsky-is-in-it smile was intact, although just barely
so.

"Welcome back," Karl said. "I've missed you. I've been
getting a bit nervous; it feels like it's been a long time."

"Sure does. It's good to be back." The corners of
Slovotsky's mouth lifted into a knowing smile. "You're not
the only one. But thanks, anyway." He fondled his own
spider amulet between thumb and forefinger. "You're not
going to like this, Karl," He said. "This thing started flashing red—the slavers have a wizard with them."

"Damn!" Karl spat. That was surprising, but not unpre-
cedented. Usually, only the largest Slavers' Guild raiding
parties would spend the money on the services of a wizard.
"Well, we can handle that—just have to take the wizard out
first." Wizards were just as subject to a surprise attack as
anyone else, after all.

"That was the *good* news. Karl, they have guns."

"*What?*"

"Guns. I spotted three, and there're probably others. Could
be rifles, maybe smoothbores—they look just like our flintlocks,
as far as I could see. I didn't want to get too close; I've
always thought I look better without bullet holes."

This was bad. And it shouldn't be happening. The secret of
making gunpowder was something that Karl, Walter, Ahira,
Andy-Andy, and Lou Riccetti guarded carefully. Riccetti had
yet to share the secret with any of his Engineers, though
undoubtedly most of them suspected what the ingredients
were. But Engineers didn't talk.

To the best of Karl's knowledge, no guns or powder had
fallen into unauthorized hands during the five years they'd
been using guns on This Side.

They'd known it wouldn't last forever, but Lou Riccetti's

guess was that it would take a minimum of ten years for the secret to get out, and Karl had thought Lou's estimate conservative, if anything. While there was room for error, the mixture had to be close to the traditional ratio of fifteen parts saltpeter to three parts sulfur to two parts powdered charcoal for it to be usable gunpowder. It would take a long time for others in this world to work out the ingredients and proportions, given only descriptions of the weapons that the Home raiders were using to supplement their bows and blades. The construction of rifles that didn't blow up in a user's face should have slowed the locals down, too.

It *should* have taken a long time. . . .

"Damn," he said. "You're sure? Never mind." He gestured an apology. If Slovotsky was willing to make the absurd claim that the slavers had guns, then the slavers had guns.

Karl beckoned to the nearest of his warriors, a gangling teenager whom he often used as a message runner.

"Yes, Karl?"

"Erek—message for Tennetty. No attack yet; tell her to have the horses hobbled. I want a staff meeting, right away. I'll need the squad leaders up here, and fast. And I'll want some fire for the lantern in my tent. Repeat."

Erek closed his eyes. "Attack postponed indefinitely; Tennetty to order the horses hobbled. Chak, Piell, Gwellin, and Tennetty to report to you, here, immediately. Your lantern to be lit."

He opened his eyes, looking questioningly at Karl. At Karl's nod, Erek smiled and ran off.

"Good kid," Slovotsky said. "Too bad he's such a lousy shot."

"Guns aren't everything." Karl snorted. "I wish you were as good with a sword. Little Erek can outscore Chak almost a quarter of the time." He beckoned Slovotsky into his tent as Wellem arrived with a lantern.

"You want it now?" Slovotsky asked, seating himself tailor-fashion on the rug.

"Save it. The others will be along in a minute."

Being in charge, Karl thought, all too often required listening to silly arguments. It wasn't enough to command obedience;

he had to earn it—not once, but over and over again. And one of the things that meant was giving his warriors room to be wrong, at least when being wrong wouldn't hurt anything.

"Why all the fuss?" Gwellin shrugged. "They might not move on in the morning—"

"They will," Slovotsky put in. "Why would they stay?"

"Come nightfall tomorrow, we'll have the dragon to help out. Bullets can't hurt it."

"Idiot!" Tennetty spat. "What if they have dragonbane? Besides, do you really think we can take them by surprise with a *dragon* in the sky?"

"So who says we have to surprise them? Ellegon should be able to roast all of them."

"*Fine* idea. I'd love to see that." She turned to Walter. "Roasted gunpowder is kind of noisy, isn't it?"

"Yup. Not a good idea, not if I'm going to be anywhere in the neighborhood—and most particularly not if we want a sample for analysis. Try again, Gwellin."

"Then," the dwarf said, pounding a fist on the ground, "I'd say we just let this group go." Gwellin and his six dwarves were serving with Karl's team only temporarily, saving their shares of the loot, building up their savings so that they could return to Endell well laden with both captured valuables and acquired knowledge. Karl liked having Gwellin around; it was good to have the advice of someone who could be more objective, more businesslike about the business of killing and robbing slavers.

"Go on," Karl said. "Why do you think we should let them go?"

The dwarf stroked at his craggy face. "They aren't pulling a chain of slaves, so all we could get out of this would be a bit of blood, whatever money they have on them, and maybe this powder of theirs. I don't think they'll be carrying a lot of gold, not a group this size. And I don't want to face guns, not if we don't have to." He hefted his oversized mace. "I can't move this faster than a bullet."

"Don't be stupid." Ch'akresarkandyn shook his head. He was short for a human, only a head taller than the dwarf. The movements of his head and hand were slow and lazy, but Chak was neither; the dark little man was a good swordsman and an energetic and effective teacher of both blade and gun. "Do you know how to make gunpowder?"

"No, do you? What's the point?"

"The point," Tennetty put in, her usual sneer firmly in place, "is that they shouldn't, either." She looked over at Karl, her forehead momentarily wrinkling, as though she was wondering why he let this discussion go on. Tennetty's squad was run without dissension; her warriors could either do exactly what she said, when and how she said it, or they could find someone else to lead them on the next raid. "And we have to find out how they got it, and—if possible—cut it off at the source."

Idly, she brought her right index finger up and slipped it underneath her eyepatch, scratching. Karl made a mental note to have Thellaren look at the socket, once they got back to Home. Or maybe he'd try to push her into getting the glass eye that the cleric had been trying to sell her on.

Gwellin shrugged. "That is your concern—the fire burns in your belly, not mine."

"You're right about that," Tennetty agreed grimly.

"But how did they get the powder?" Piell asked. The elf steepled his overlong fingers in front of his face, considering. "It must be that Riccetti. He must have sold out."

"Piell," Slovotsky said, with a loud snort, "there is an old saying, back on the Other Side—"

"Not again." Chak threw up his hands. "There's *always* an old saying back on the Other Side. And for some reason, they're always called Slovotsky's Laws. Which one is it now?"

"The one I was thinking of goes something like this: 'When you know not whereof you speak, your mouth is best used for chewing.' Forgetting the fact that Lou has never even had the opportunity to sell out, there's about as much chance of his betraying a friend as there is of your falling in love with a female dwarf." He pulled a piece of jerky out of his pouch and tossed it to the tall elf. "So try this."

Piell batted the jerky aside and glared at him. "Walter Slovotsky—"

"Enough." Karl raised a palm. Not that he had any objection to a little bickering among his squad leaders, as long as it was confined to a war council. A bit of argument helped to

blow off steam, helped to keep everyone's nerves from growing wire-tight before the battle. But enough was enough.
"You see the problem: If they do have guns—"

"I saw—"

"Shut *up*, Walter. If they do have guns, we have to find
out how and why. Most likely, the wards aren't as good as
Thellaren says they are."

And there was another possibility, and that one chilled his
insides: Home had paid the Spidersect a great deal of money
to install and maintain the wards that both served as a magical
burglar alarm and hid the valley from the view of Pandathaway
wizards' crystal balls. Both Thellaren and Andy-Andy had
said that it would have taken a wizard close to the level of
Grandmaster Lucius to pierce the spell.

What if they were up against someone like that?

He let the thought drop. No, there was no reason to worry
about that. If they were up against a wizard as powerful as
Lucius or Arta Myrdhyn, they would already be dead.

"In any case," Karl said, "we've got to rethink the attack."

Gwellin shook his head. "Even if what you say is true,
there isn't that much difference. If we can take them by
surprise, maybe—"

"—we can kill them all," Karl finished for the dwarf. He
shook his head. "And that's no good. We can't afford to
have just dead slavers on our hands. Not this time: Dead
bodies can't talk. I'll want at least one of them alive, preferably two."

"Make it three." Tennetty studied the edge of her knife.
"I am likely to use them up quickly." She raised an eyebrow.
"I do get to do the interrogation, don't I?"

"Maybe. We'll also need to capture one of their rifles—"

"That's no problem, not even if we—"

"—*and* at least a pouch of their powder for analysis. I'll
want to get as much as we can. So, the original plan is off.
We can't just have a horseback attack to draw them out so the
rifles can get at them. We're going to have to get a bit more
tricky."

Chak smiled. "I like it when you get tricky."

"Sorry, Chak. Not this time."

His face fell. "I have to stay with my squad?"

"Yup. Walter—"

"Now wait a minute, Karl. *I'm* not the one who likes it when you get tricky."

"You're going to like this even less than usual, Walter. How good are you with a crossbow these days?"

Slovotsky frowned. "Not very, as you know."

"Right." Karl could count on Slovotsky for a good recon. Slovotsky had made his way into and out of places that Karl would have sworn a stray leaf couldn't have invaded without notice. Walter was also a reliable knifeman and a passable swordsman; he was also one of Home's better rifle shots. But he wasn't good with a crossbow, and taking out at least one watchman without alerting the slavers might require a crossbow's range and silence.

He sighed regretfully, trying to decide if he was being hypocritical. *But I can't trust this to anyone else, dammit. It's my responsibility.* "You've just gotten yourself an assistant."

"Who?"

"Me."

Karl finished rubbing the greasepaint over his bare chest, then stood motionless while Walter tended to his face.

Slovotsky nodded. "That should do it. Remember to keep your mouth closed—don't want to flash those pearly whites at them. Also, if he starts to look your way, close your eyes as much as you can—the whites can stand out."

"Got it." Karl turned back to the others. It wasn't really necessary to give the final orders himself—Tennetty or Chak could have handled that—but Karl didn't allow himself to hold the others distant. They weren't just his warriors, they were his friends. This could easily be the last time he'd see some of them alive. He owed them at least the remembering.

Morality didn't prevent mortality. There was probably some sort of epigram in that, too depressing to be converted into one of Slovotsky's Laws.

But it wasn't just true, it was important. Good people could die fighting on the right side in a just war. It had happened at Gettysburg, and at the Somme, and at Anzio, Normandy, and Entebbe.

It had also happened in Ehvenor, when Fialt's death had bought Karl and the others a few seconds. And in Melawei, where Rahff Furnael's lifeblood had poured on to the sandy ground. And outside of Metreyll, and Wehnest, and . . .

"Chak?" He turned to the little man who stood quietly by his side.

"Yes, Kharl?" Chak was tense; his accent was slipping. "You were going to tell me about why you assigned Erek to my squad. It isn't because he's any good with a rifle or shotgun. Must be because you want me to keep an eye on the boy, eh?"

"Stop trying to read my mind. Ellegon's the only one who can do that."

"Sorry. What did you want?"

"Well . . ." Karl smiled. "As it happens, I was going to ask you to keep an eye on the boy. Eh?"

Chak returned the smile. "It's too bad that I can't read your mind."

Karl laughed.

Chak sobered. He opened his mouth, closed it, then shrugged. "He reminds me a bit of Rahff, too." He fastened a hard hand on Karl's shoulder. "But," he said in his thick English, "I want to turn the two-guns squad over to Wellem. He can handle this kind of slaughter as well as I can—and I've already told him to watch out for Erek."

"So—"

"So, I want to keep an eye on your back. It has a tendency to sprout holes when I'm not around." Chak raised a palm to forestall Karl's objection. "Think about it, please—Jason told me to watch out for you, and I don't like disobeying Cullinane orders."

Karl hesitated for a moment.

"One more thing to say, and then I'll be quiet: Three have a greater chance of getting a sample of this powder out than two do. Is that not so, Kharl?"

"It is so." Karl sighed. "Strip down—you won't need the paint." He picked Wellem out of the crowd and caught his eye. "Wellem, do you want it?" he asked.

At Wellem's nod, Karl gave him a thumbs-up sign. "Very well. Two-guns squad is yours for this one."

Wellem nodded again, then turned to the rest of his group and began whispering.

"Listen up, people," Karl said. "For those of you who

haven't heard, the slavers have guns. At least three, although we're going to assume that there are more. We also know that there's a wizard with them. Before all hell breaks loose down there, Walter and I are going to try to kill the wizard, then make a grab for a slaver or two, a gun, and some of their powder. It's our job to pick out the slaver and keep him alive—don't worry about killing the wrong one.

"There are two things I *do* want you to worry about. The first one is that Walter, Chak, and I are going to be out in front. Watch where you point your guns. I don't want a repeat of that Metreyll fiasco." He rubbed his back, just above the kidney. "It's not that I mind the pain, you understand, it's just that bullets and powder are too expensive to waste on my hide."

A rough laugh ran through the crowd. Good; that would loosen them up a bit.

"The second thing I want you to worry about is the fact that there are shortly going to be about thirty very scared slavers down there, all of whom will know that they're under attack, all of whom know that we're not interested in taking them prisoner. And they're not going to be too thrilled with Walter or with Chak or with me."

He nodded to Slovotsky. Better for Slovotsky to give them a firsthand description than for Karl to give them a second-hand one.

Walter Slovotsky knelt in the light of the shrouded lantern and smoothed the dirt. "Here's their campfire, right smack dab in the middle of the meadow, just east of the fork." He made an X on the ground. "Three wagons—here, here, and here. This one is the most ornate; I'm assuming it's the wizard's. The two—the three of us are going to make our move in from the southeast, parellel to the main road, here.

"That leaves two more watchmen. They were, umm, right about here and here. All of the watchmen have rifles. We have no way of knowing if there are other rifles located inside the circle of wagons, or in the wagons themselves." He shrugged. "Since they're coming out of Pandathaway, it's not surprising that they aren't carrying slaves; clearly, the wagons are all being used to hold their supplies. It could be just food—but, for all I know, they could be loaded with guns and powder. So watch out."

"Hear that, folks?" Karl said. "A barrel of powder can produce one nice explosion. So keep your eyes open. If you see any fire going into any wagon, yell 'Fire.' If you hear anyone yelling 'Fire,' try to get some cover between yourself and the wagons. Everyone got that? Fine. Gwellin—your turn."

The dwarf stood. "My squad stays as close behind you as we can, making sure we're far enough back enough so that we can't be seen or heard. If you come under attack, I light my rocket. Then we support you with a volley in the direction of the wizard or his wagon, and switch to crossbows for a second, third, and fourth volley. After that, we move in with axes, maces, and hammers. If you're not spotted, we wait for your signal, then do the same."

"Good. Piell?"

The elf nodded. "My group stays behind the dwarves, and becomes the second wave. Our objective will be to get the slavers to run away, into Chak—into Wellem's squad. If that is not possible, I will light off another rocket. Yes?"

"Yes. Tennetty?"

"I'm what you always call a free safety. My squad is the reserve; we wait with our horses on the road, making sure we're out of earshot until the attack is well under way. Then we mount up. If they're running, we help chase them into the two-guns squad, If they hold fast, we try to scatter them, then pick off the stragglers. We're also responsible for killing the two other watchmen, if Gwellin's or Chak's people don't get them first. It's simple stuff: If they run, we chase them. If they don't, we make them run, and *then* we chase them."

"And?"

She sighed. "And if everything goes bad, we rescue whoever we can, and pull out. We also pick up our wounded, carry them out of danger, and treat them with healing draughts, then haul ass back up here and wait for Ellegon. I'd rather—"

"—be in the thick of it." Karl repressed a sigh. Tennetty had spent ten long years as a slave; there was nothing she enjoyed more than bathing in a slaver's blood. *Lady, you're a psycho. But fortunately for the both of us you're one hell of an effective psycho.*

He looked from face to face. "Enough talk, people. Let's do it."

*   *   *

Down the road, the slavers' campfire burned an orange rift into the night. With Chak bringing up the rear, Karl kept himself two yards behind Walter, mimicking the other's half-stoop as he eased his way through the woods, parallel to the road, stepping carefully across the damp floor of the forest, a cocked but unloaded crossbow held in his left hand. Occasionally he patted the top of the quiver strapped to his right thigh.

A leather pouch slapped silently against his left thigh as he walked; his swordsheath pressed reassuringly against his back; a manriki-gusari, cloth strung through its links to prevent rattling, was slung across one shoulder. He let his hand rest against the two oilskin-wrapped flintlock pistols stuck crossways into his belt.

Goddam walking arsenal, that's what I am, he thought. *But there's always—*

"*Down,*" Slovotsky hissed, his voice pitched low enough to carry only a few feet, no more.

Karl stepped behind a tree and dropped to the ground. Half a dozen feet behind him, Chak dropped to the ground and froze in place, motionless as a statue.

The skin over his ears tightening, Karl strained to hear whatever had alarmed Slovotsky.

It didn't make any difference. The wind still whispered through the trees, and the flames of a campfire crackled somewhere off in the night, but that was all. Or were there distant voices? Maybe.

Slovotsky beckoned for Chak to move forward, then crabbed himself backward to join them, his mouth only inches from their ears. "Something's wrong. Hang on for a minute," he said. "I'm going to do a quick recon."

"Problem?"

"Maybe. Back in a jiffy. Watch my stuff." Slovotsky laid the oilskin containing his own pistols on the roots, set his scimitar down next to it, and crept off.

He was gone a long time; Karl stopped counting his own pulsebeats at three hundred, and lay quietly, waiting.

Dammit, hurry up, Slovotsky, he thought.

Chak patted his shoulder. "You worry too much, kemo sabe."

"It's my job, dammit," Karl whispered back. He couldn't wait forever; there were just too many people involved.

Eventually, Tennetty or Wellem or Gwellin would get too nervous to wait for a signal and trigger the attack. If Walter and Karl hadn't taken out the wizard by then, the odds would quickly switch from their favor to the slavers', despite the advantage of surprise, despite the fact that they had the slavers outmanned. "And don't call me 'kemo sabe.' "

"Whatever you say, kemo sabe."

The thing about Chak that Karl depended most on was the dark little man's rock-solid trustworthiness when it came to anything serious; one of the things about Chak that he liked best was his unwillingness to take anything seriously except when necessary. Chak always liked to joke around before a fight; he said it kept his mind calm and his wrist loose.

"Karl," Walter's voice whispered out of the darkness, "it's me."

"What—"

"Relax—we got a break, for once. The wizard was off away from the wagons and the fire. Seems there's a bit of a gang-bang in progress, and I guess it must have offended his delicate sensibilities. He'd walked at least a hundred yards into the woods to relieve himself, so . . ."

"What did you do?"

"I slit his throat. Stashed the body under the roots of an old oak. Getting a bit bloodthirsty in my old age, eh?"

"Never mind that—you said something about a gang-bang?"

"Yeah. They've got a couple of women. Taking turns. Strange, no?"

"Yes." That *was* bizarre. These slavers were coming from Pandathaway. Pandathaway was where guild slavers brought slaves to, not from. Bringing slaves out wouldn't mean just the extra expense of feeding them or the lost income of not selling them, it would also cut down on the available space for human cargo on the slavers' return trip.

"What do you make of that?" Slovotsky asked. "It just doesn't make sense."

Chak shook his head. "Yes, it could make sense—if they are not on a raiding mission but doing something else. If they're not planning on bringing slaves back, they might bring themselves some company. Or it could be some sort of purchase. If they're bringing back a big chain from somewhere, the added expense of bringing along a couple of women for pleasure wouldn't matter to them."

A buy? That meant that the slavers would have a lot of coin on them. Unless—

The guns. Maybe they were taking guns somewhere, planning to sell them. But where? Why? Now they needed a captive to question more than ever.

"Change of plans," Karl said. "we don't kill the guard—we snatch him."

Chak rolled his eyes heavenward. "You don't always have to complicate things, do you?"

Walter shook his head. "I don't like it. The guard's still where he was when I was here before—about a hundred yards ahead, but across the road from us."

"Which way is he facing?"

"Sort of sideways, looking down the road."

"Fine. You go back and tell Gwellin to bring his people up closer, just the other side of the bend in the road. Have him send Daherrin back with you."

"No good—you can't move that many people silently, Karl. The watchman would hear them from there."

"We'll have him tied down by then. After you bring Gwellin's people around, you and Daherrin hurry back to where the watchman is now. That's where we'll be. Daherrin hauls the watchman away, then the three of us work ourselves close to the fire, before the shit hits the fan. We've got to try to get the slaves out."

"I knew it." Chak looked knowingly at Walter. "That's what the change of plans is about." He shrugged. "I guess there's no need for me to get much older—how about you?"

"*Cut the crap*," Karl hissed. "Once the attack's fully under way, it might not be possible to get them out alive. How's all that sound to the two of you?"

Chak shrugged. "Not bad, not really."

"I don't like it, Karl. He's got kind of a thicket of brambles behind him; you'll have to come right across the road to get him. And I'm quieter than you are. I should take out the watchman while—"

"No." Walter might be quieter than Karl was, but Karl was stronger. That might be important. "Eventually, someone's going to check on the wizard. *Do it*."

Slovotsky clapped a hand to Karl's shoulder. "Good luck—"

"Thanks."

"—you'll need it."

Karl crouched behind a bush, peering through the dark at the watchman sitting across the road on a waist-high stone, staring blankly out into the night.

He would have to cross the road under the eyes of the watchman in order to get his hands on the other. And even then, he'd have to move quickly, in order to silence the watchman before the slaver could raise an alarm.

Not good odds. The deeply rutted dirt road was only about five yards wide at this point, but those would be a long five yards.

Maybe too long.

At times like these he could almost hear Andy-Andy's half-mocking voice. *Looks like your mouth has gotten you into trouble again. Okay, hero, how would Conan do it?*

Well . . . Conan would probably sneak up quietly behind the watchman and club him over the head, knocking him unconscious.

Then why don't you do it that way?

Because I'm Karl Cullinane, not Conan. Because things just didn't work that way. Even assuming that he could get within clubbing range, it was much more likely that such a blow would either draw a scream out of the watchman or simply crush his skull.

Better think of another way, then. He edged back into the woods, his fingers searching the ground until he found a small stone, one about the size of a grape. He worked his way back to the brush until he was beside Chak. Setting his crossbow, quiver, and pistol down carefully, Karl unslung his manriki-gusari and draped it carefully around his neck, then reached over his shoulder to loosen his sword in its sheath. He took a wad of cloth and several thongs from his pouch and held them in his left hand.

"Here," Karl whispered, handing Chak the stone. "Give me a slow count to fifty, then throw the stone over his head and past him."

Chak nodded. "One . . . two . . . three . . ."

Matching the count silently, Karl crept back to the road and waited. . . . *twenty-three . . . twenty-four . . .*

The watchman stood for a moment to stretch, then scratched at his crotch before seating himself again.

. . . *thirty-five . . . thirty-six . . .*

Karl braced himself, clenching his jaw to keep his teeth from rattling as he hefted his manriki-gusari.

. . . *forty-two . . . for—*

The stone whipped through the brambles; the watchman jerked to his feet and spun around, bringing his rifle to bear.

Karl eased himself up to the surface of the road, swinging and throwing the manriki-gusari in one smooth motion.

The meter-long chain whipped through the night air, wrapping itself around the watchman's neck, bowling the man over, his rifle falling into the bushes. Karl drew his sword and lunged at the other, slapping at the watchman's hands with the flat of his blade when the slaver reached for the knife at his belt.

Karl set the point of the blade under the other's chin. "If you cry out," he whispered, "you die. Be quiet, and you live. You have my word."

"Who—"

"Cullinane. Karl Cullinane."

The slaver's eyes widened. Karl toed him in the solar plexus, then stuffed the wad of cloth in the other's mouth while the slaver gasped for breath.

"I didn't say you wouldn't hurt—I just said you'd live."

CHAPTER TWO:

Battleground

First say to yourself what you would be; and then do what you have to do.

—Epictetus

As he had grown older, Karl had learned to deal with the fear. He'd had to.

Deal with it, yes, but not well. That would have been too much to ask of himself. Karl Cullinane had spent twenty-one of his twenty-nine years as a middle-class American, living safely in the last half of the twentieth century. Deep inside, he still wasn't used to having lost that safety, that comfort. The only way he could handle that was to push the fear away, if only for a time.

The quiet moments before a fight were always the worst. Too much time to think; too much opportunity to let himself be scared.

His heart pounding, Karl checked the slaver's knots and gag once more before turning him over to Daherrin.

"And take this, too," Karl said, handing the slaver's rifle and pouch to the dwarf. It was a strange-looking rifle: The lock, if any, was inside the stock; the trigger looked more like a miniature pump handle than anything else.

But there wasn't enough light or time to examine it fully; that would have to be saved for later. If there was a later.

Karl clenched his hands into fists. It wouldn't do for Walter, Chak, or Daherrin to see his fingers tremble.

Grasping the slaver by the front of his tunic, the dwarf swung him to his right shoulder, balancing the man easily, then accepted the slaver rifle and powder kit in his oversized left hand. Dwarves weren't just shorter and more heavily built than humans; their joints were thicker, their muscles denser, far more powerful.

"And remember," Slovotsky said, "if everything blows up in our faces here, this stuff has to get back—"

"—to Home," Daherrin finished. "Including this useless piece of meat," he said, bouncing the slaver up and down on his shoulder. "It will done."

The dwarf turned and walked away.

Karl finished unwrapping his pistols from their protecting oilcloth, then primed their pans. He tucked the vial of fine priming powder and oilcloth in his pouch before sticking the pistols back in his belt, making sure that the barrels pointed away from his feet.

Chak had done the same with his two pistols; he patted their curving butts and flashed Karl a quick smile.

"Gwellin had a couple of spares," Walter said, handing each of them one of the three shotguns he'd brought back, along with the dwarf. "Hope you don't mind my supplementing things a bit."

Chak hefted his shotgun easily. "I don't mind at all."

"Me neither." Karl propped the butt on the ground while he slipped a bolt into his crossbow and nocked it with a practiced motion of his thumb. "Is the gun loaded?"

"Standard shotgun load. Everything but the pan. Gwellin did it; I watched him myself."

"Good." Handing the crossbow to Chak, Karl picked up the shotgun. He took the vial of priming powder from his pouch and primed the pan, bringing the frizzen down and locking it into place with a quiet click. He handed the vial to Chak and waited while the dark little man primed his own shotgun.

Karl was a bit vain about the shotguns; they were his own innovation. Normally, when the lands inside a rifle barrel had worn down to uselessness, the weapon had to be rebored and rerifled, which changed the caliber, making standard rounds useless. Karl had come up with the notion of doing a more thorough reboring of the barrel, until the bore was a thumb's width, then cutting it down, turning the weapon into a smooth-bore shotgun.

Walter gave the crossbow back to Karl, then clapped a hand to his shoulder. "It doesn't get any easier, does it? You want me to do a quick recon?"

"No. Let's get this over with." He gave a quick glance down the road. Five dwarf warriors waited off in the distance, just on Karl's side of the bend.

He waved at them to follow, then started walking down the road, Walter on one side, Chak on the other, the campfire growing closer with every step.

"Here we go," Karl said.

Chak sucked air through his teeth; Walter brought his shotgun up.

Ahead, the road forked. In the dark, three boxy wagons stood around the campfire. While more than a dozen slept under their blankets, ten grizzled men sat around the fire, drinking and talking. Beyond them, several others stood over a huge blanket on which lay the moaning forms of the two women. The men called mocking words of encouragement to their friends while waiting their own turns.

Walter turned to beckon to the dwarves. With all the noise from the camp, they wouldn't be noticed for the next few seconds. "Ready when you are," he whispered, his voice faltering momentarily.

Chak brought his shotgun up to his shoulder.

Karl's hand grew tight around the crossbow's stock. He raised it to his shoulder, curled his fingers around the trigger as he took aim at the nearest of the slavers around the campfire, and squeezed.

Fffft! The slaver lunged forward, clutching at the feathers that just barely projected from his chest.

The crack of Chak's shotgun split the night. Three of the slavers screamed in pain as they caught some of the scattering pellets; a fourth clapped both hands to what had been a face.

As the other slavers leaped to their feet, Karl dropped the crossbow to one side, transferred the shotgun to his right hand, braced it against his hip, and fired.

Another man lunged for a rifle, but the blast from Slovotsky's shotgun opened his belly as though it were an overripe melon;

he fell to the grass, vomit pouring from his mouth in a bloody torrent.

Others dashed across the meadow, running for the road. Chak raised a pistol and sighted down his arm.

"No!" Karl shouted. "Leave them to the two-guns—follow me." He dropped the empty shotgun and sprinted for the blankets, snatching his pistols from his belt and cocking them.

The slavers were beginning to react to the attack. Several of them made a mad dash for the nearest of the boxy wagons, only to be cut down by two quick volleys of gunfire.

Piell's signal rocket screamed into the night.

"Down!" Karl threw an arm across his eyes and looked away as it exploded above the meadow, a white flash that momentarily dazzled his eyes.

The nine slavers around Karl, Chak, and Walter hadn't been prepared for it. They screamed, blinded, if only for a few moments.

One of the slavers, clad only in his leather tunic, was pawing around the ground for his sword. Karl kicked him in the face, bones crunching beneath his boot. He turned to shoot another who was trying to bring an unsteady rifle to bear on Chak. With his left-hand pistol, he quickly gutshot a third, then reached over his shoulder to draw his sword as a blocky man, his teeth bared in a snarl, lunged for him, a foot-long dagger clutched tightly in his white-knuckled fingers.

Karl's sword was barely out of its scabbard when a heavy mass slammed into his back, a hairy arm snaking around his throat.

There wasn't time to think about it. He could deal either with the enemy clinging to his back or with the one charging from the front.

Instinct took over. Ignoring the slaver on his back, he parried the other's knife with the flat of his blade, then thrust the point of his sword into the knife wielder's throat, twisting savagely as he pulled the blade back.

Crack! Impact shook the slaver on Karl's back as the pistol shot rang out. The slaver shuddered, and the arm around Karl's throat went limp. Karl grabbed the thick wrist, spun, and twisted, bringing his knee up into the man's chin, bone shattering like glass.

Two yards away, Chak favored him with a brief smile as he dropped his smoking pistol to the ground, then drew his falchion to parry the attack of another slaver.

Walter's scimitar clanged against the ninth slaver's steel. It looked as though Walter could handle the man, but it didn't occur to Karl to play fair: he skewered Walter's opponent through the kidney, then spun around into a crouch.

Chak's opponent was down, clutching at a wounded arm. The dark little man didn't waste any more time on the slaver; he drew his remaining pistol and shot him in the chest.

With a clatter of hooves, Tennetty's horsemen galloped through the meadow, sending the last of the uninjured slavers into flight. Therol detached himself from the rest of the group, leaping off his horse to dispense healing draughts to two injured dwarves, the only casualties on Karl's side. So far.

Karl breathed a sigh. It was over for him, at least for now. Piell's and Gwellin's squads had knocked down all of their targets, and the now combined squad was working its way through the scattered bodies, administering deathblows to the wounded.

Down the road, shots echoed, horses whinnied, and men screamed.

"Karl!" Gwellin called out, standing over the body of a slaver, a bloody battleaxe in his hands. "Do you want us to—"

"No. Not until the shots die down." Killing the rest was the job of the two-guns squad and Tennetty's horsemen, not Gwellin's dwarves or Piell's squad. For them, the fight was over. Unmounted men rushing the slavers from behind would risk being mistaken for slavers in the darkness. Karl had lost far too many of his warriors in his time, but not one had been killed by friendly fire, and he didn't intend that any ever should.

A low moan from the ground drew Karl's attention. The half-naked slaver that Karl had kicked in the face was starting to move, holding the shattered remnants of his jaw together.

Over his cupped, blood-dripping hands, the man's eyes grew wide as Karl approached him.

"*Karl*," Walter snapped. "We want another live one, remember?"

Karl kicked the man in the shoulder, bowling him over, then stooped to bring the slaver's hands behind his back and tie them tightly with a leather thong from his pouch.

"Therol, check the wagons for healing draughts, and treat this one. A few drops from every bottle, eh?" It was always necessary to test captured healing draughts on someone expendable; two years before, Karl had lost one of his warriors to what had looked to be a bottle of Healing Hand Society draughts, but had actually been poison.

"Done," Therol called back. "And how about you?"

"Me?"

"Don't talk about it, Therol," Chak shouted. "Just get your ass over here. Karl's hurt."

"Chak, I'm *fine*."

"Right." Slovotsky snorted. "Sure you are." Walter's hand slipped down Karl's back. When he brought it in front of Karl's face, blood dripped from the fingers.

"It's not too bad, Karl. Just a nick—but you'd better get it healed before your adrenaline level drops and it starts to hurt you."

What had been a dim, distant pain suddenly cut across his back like a whip. He gasped, then willed himself to ignore it. *There's no danger. Therol will have me healed up in a minute.* Pain was just a biologically programmed warning of danger. There wasn't any danger here, so the pain should go away. It was logical, but it didn't help.

It was best to keep busy, try to keep his mind off the pain. "Chak, you and Gwellin's people check out the wagons— except for the wizard's wagon. Just put a guard on that one and leave it alone."

"Do you think there's anyone in there?"

"I don't know, so assume that there is."

"I was just asking." Chak sniffed. "I *have* done this before."

"Sorry. Put it down to nerves."

"Yes, Karl." Chak ran off, calling for Gwellin.

Every motion making the wound on his back cry out in agony, he turned to face the two women huddling in the blankets. He took a step toward the nearest one, a blonde, her almond eyes and high cheekbones betraying a mixed heritage, with forebears from both the Kathard and the Middle Lands.

"No." Her eyes grew wide. "You're *Karl Cullinane*. Don't kill me, please. Please. I'll do anything you want. I'm very good, really I am. Please—"

"Ta havath." *Easy.* Karl tried to smile reassuringly. "T'rar ammalli." *I'm a friend.*

Therol arrived with the bottle of healing draughts and slopped some of the icy liquid on Karl's back. As always, the pain vanished as though it had never been. He worked his arms for a moment, relishing the comfort.

The blonde was still pleading with him. "Please don't hurt me. Please . . ."

Damn.

"Those *bastards*." Slovotsky shook his head. "Again?"

"Yeah."

Slovotsky held out a hand; Karl exchanged his saber for two of Slovotsky's knives.

The women edged away from him as he slowly approached, holding the knives out, offering them the hilts.

"Everything you've been told is a lie. I'm not going to kill you. I'm not going to hurt you—you're free, as of now." It was a calculated gamble, but one that hadn't yet failed, although he still had a scar on his right cheek from the time that it came close to failing.

The blonde took the proffered knife, holding it awkwardly at arm's length. The brunette mimicked her.

"Karl," Walter said in English, his voice pitched low, "either I've been away from Kirah too long, or both these ladies are gorgeous."

"Ta havath," he murmured. "So what if they are?" With the way they were huddled in their blankets, he couldn't see much of them, but what he could see looked good.

Awfully good, which was privately embarrassing. It wasn't just that he intended to remain faithful to Andy-Andy—he should have been feeling only sympathy for these two poor wretches, not noticing the swell of a full breast or the smoothness of a shapely thigh.

He switched back to Erendra. "Nobody's going to touch you. We'll get some clothes for you in a little while, just as soon as things settle down."

"*So*," Slovotsky continued in English, "we're looking at prime stuff, here. I could see the slavers taking some culls out of Pandathaway, but these two would go for a hell of a lot of money there. Or anywhere else.''

Slovotsky was right, of course. As usual. But what did it mean?

The pounding of a horse's hooves spun Karl around, his hand reaching for the hilt of a sword that wasn't there.

It was only Tennetty. She slipped from Pirat's back, her face creased in a broad smile. ''Everything's fine, Karl,'' she said. ''Three casualties on our side.''

''How bad?''

''I *said* that everything's fine. Wellem was the worst. He caught a round in the gut, but we got the draughts into him in plenty of time. Mm, I got a capture, too.'' She eyed the slaver that Therol was treating. ''That makes three, yes?''

''Yes.''

''Good. So—''

''Would you take care of the women, first? Later there'll be plenty of time to stick a knife in these bastards and get them to talk.''

''Agreed. But I'll take care of the women my way, since we have a spare slaver. Unless you're really set on stopping me?'' Tennetty carefully kept her hand away from her swordhilt. ''I'm asking nicely, aren't I?''

Karl shrugged. ''Go ahead.''

She took a shrouded lantern down from her saddle and slipped the baffles, then elbowed Therol out of the way and urged the slaver to follow her into the woods by the simple expedient of grabbing the man by his hair and pulling him to his feet.

''Follow me,'' she ordered the two women, smiling gently. ''And bring your knives. Relax—this is the best thing in the world for you.'' The slaver safely in hand, she led the two women into the woods, her voice trailing off in the distance. ''Now, you can take your time with him, but Karl doesn't like it, so it'd be better if you start with . . .''

Slovotsky started to object, but Karl quelled him with a sudden chopping gesture.

''She's been there, Walter. And we haven't.''

''I don't have to like it. I don't have to like any of it, and I don't, Karl. I've gotten used to killing, but—''

''*No*, you don't have to like it.'' Karl shrugged. ''What

you have to do is not let it get to you," he said, looking
Walter square in the face as he forced himself not to shudder
at the screams coming from the woods. "Let's check out the
wagons."

"Right."

"So?" Walter asked, squatting in front of the blanket Karl
had spread on the grass. "What do you make of all this?"

"Trouble." Karl stood and stretched, squinting at the noon
sun. He rubbed the back of his aching neck and sighed, then
held out his hand for the waterbag.

Walter tossed it to him. Karl drank deeply, then splashed
some on his face before recorking the bag and handing it
back.

Walter uncorked it and took a sip. "Speaking of trouble,
not only did I find three bottles of dragonbane extract in
one of the wagons, but Daherrin has been checking out their
crossbow bolts. A lot of them seem to be absolutely coated
with the stuff. Looks like the slavers are still interested in
offing Ellegon."

That wasn't surprising: Ellegon was awfully useful for the
Home forces to have around.

"Are you sure you burned it all?" Karl asked. Once thoroughly burned, dragonbane was every bit as harmless to Ellegon
as burned pollen would be to a pollen-sensitive human, no
matter how serious his allergy.

"Of course. Dumped the bottles in the hottest part of the
fire; threw in every suspicious bolt."

Karl looked over to the slaver's campfire, now barely
smoldering. "Have Daherrin build up the fire, just to be
sure."

"Right."

Karl looked around. The aftermath of the battle wasn't
pretty. It never was. But it had, in its own gruesome way,
become almost routine.

Just beyond the campfire, two piles of bodies lay, gathering flies. The smaller pile was a haphazard arrangement of
fully clothed slavers; it continued to shrink as Daherrin and
two assistants frisked the bodies, reclaiming both valuables
and whatever clothing was sufficiently unbloodied to be usable,
then stacking the corpses like cordwood.

By Karl's orders, the wizard's wagon had been left completely alone. There hadn't been any complaint; wizards had been known to leave hidden glyphs.

While the two remaining wagons had been left intact, their contents had been unpacked, sorted, inventoried, and repacked. Piell had removed the inlaid brass wave-and-chain insignia of the Pandathaway Slavers' Guild from the wagons' sides and propped up the plaques facing the road.

Standard operating procedure—slavers were always left for the vultures, along with some means for passersby to identify them as slavers. It was important that everyone know that only slavers had to worry about unprovoked attack by the Home forces; it took most of the steam out of pursuit by the locals.

"Well?" Walter raised an eyebrow. "What have we got?"

"A puzzle. I don't like puzzles." The guns weren't guns, and the powder wasn't gunpowder. What the slavers had been using was a fine-grained powder that looked more like ground glass than anything else. The gunlocks fired what appeared to be water through their breechholes and into the barrels. The water had to be loaded with something, but what?

Whatever it was, it worked. Loaded into one of the slaver's smoothbores, the powder could sink a lead ball a full two inches into a block of pine, only a quarter-inch less than a Home-made rifle firing Riccetti's best powder.

"Take a look." Karl unlooped his amulet from his neck and held it over the glass vial containing the slaver powder. The amber gem came alive: It pulsed with an inner light, first a dark red, then a greenish blue, then red, then blue again. "There's a charm involved."

"Well, your wife should be able to puzzle that out. What's bothering me is that it doesn't stink when it's lit off—however the hell their guns light it off. You try tasting it?"

"Tasting it?" Karl raised an eyebrow. "Do I look stupid?"

Slovotsky smiled. "Answer me first." His face grew grim; he shook his head. "We know that it works—somehow—and that it's charmed."

"Or the pouch is charmed, or something." Karl eased the cork out of the bottle and sniffed at it again. No scent at all. "Could it be cordite? Or just plain guncotton?"

"Not cordite. I've seen smokeless powder; it's darker, and

it stinks when it's lit off, not like this stuff. But I've never been around pure guncotton, although I think it *is* white like this." Slovotsky stood, stretching in the bright sunlight. "It can't be guncotton, though—you use fire to set off guncotton, not water." He jerked a thumb in the direction of the woods where Tennetty had gone off with the two surviving slavers in tow. "Maybe Ten'll have something more. She's taking her time with the prisoners."

"Maybe they've got a lot to say."

"Don't count on it. We killed the master in the fight, and master slavers don't tell their journeymen a whole lot."

"So? Where do we go from here?"

Slovotsky thought it over for a moment. He pursed his lips. "Go back to first principles. What would you have wanted Daherrin to do if he'd gotten out with that one pouch and gun, the rest of us left behind, dead?"

"Get it back to the valley; have Riccetti analyze it." Karl nodded. "Which is what we'll do—although we'd better include Andy-Andy and Thellaren in on the group."

Tennetty's slim form appeared through a break in the trees. Karl beckoned her over.

"How are they doing?"

"Just fine." She nodded. "Chak and I got them drunk; they're sleeping it off. I think Chak likes Jilla—the blonde."

"Really?"

"She could do worse," Tennetty said. "It's going to be a major adjustment for both of them. They were raised as room servants in the Velvet Inn in Pandathaway. Sternius picked them up at a foreclosure sale, for a bit of diversion during the trip." She jerked her thumb over her shoulder. "I gave them your tent; didn't figure you'd mind."

"Must have taken you quite a while to do all that."

She shook her head. "Not really. I spent most of the time interviewing the two slavers."

"What'd they tell you?"

She smiled thinly. "Everything they knew." The smile fell. "Which wasn't much. You were right; this wasn't a raiding party. It was some sort of a trade. They were on their way to the inn in Enkiar to deliver guns and powder to whoever the buyers are."

"Any idea how much they were going to be paid?"

"Sure. Each of them was to get—"

"Not that—how much were they going to get for the cargo?"

"They didn't know. I do know what they were going to be paid in: a chain of slaves. How many?" She shrugged. "Your guess is as good as mine."

"Or as bad." Thirty or so slavers could handle a chain of anywhere from about one hundred to well over a thousand slaves, perhaps as many as two thousand. It all depended on how closely chained and how well tamed their human merchandise was. "What else have you got?"

"Not much, and most of it negative. These two don't know where the guns and powder were supposed to go from Enkiar. They don't know who made the powder in the first place; Sternius had all the barrels loaded in his wagons before he put together his team."

"How about the guns?"

She shrugged. "They picked them up at a smith's in Pandathaway, just before they left. Arriken the Salke—he has a medium-big shop on the Street of Steel." She chewed on her lip for a moment. "You know, we could go into Pandathaway and look him up."

Karl nodded. "Not a bad idea. Although the idea of entering Pandathaway makes me a bit nervous." He fingered his beard. "I guess I could lose the beard, maybe dye my hair. Dressed as a sailor—"

"No way." Slovotsky shook his head. "Thousands of people in Pandathaway saw you win the swords competition; a lot of them must still be around."

"I wasn't suggesting that Karl do it. But me, well—"

"Right, Tennetty." Karl snorted. "And there are a whole *lot* of one-eyed women warriors wandering around."

"Well, there's that glass eye that Thellaren has been trying to sell me. Maybe it won't look natural, but . . ." She fingercombed her bangs to half-cover her eyepatch. "But if I wear my hair like this . . ."

"Hmmm." Slovotsky nodded. "It might work. But why not take it from the other end? Pandathaway is too risky—but we could try it from the Enkiar side. I'm more than a little curious about who the guns and powder were going to, and why. And particularly how much they were paying. There's a technical term for the kind of trouble we'll be in if this stuff is relatively cheap.''

"What's that?'' Karl asked.

"Deep shit.'' Slovotsky smiled.

"But how would we do it?'' Karl rose and stretched. "We don't know who we'd be looking for. The leader might have, but—''

"But what if he got himself killed? What if, say, the group was jumped by that evil, wicked Karl Cullinane and his raiders? And what if they lost, say, a quarter of their number before their guns drove that wicked Cullinane character off?''

Karl nodded. "Not bad.'' He turned to Tennetty. "How soon are they due in Enkiar?''

She shrugged. "Whenever they got there. Sternius wasn't rushing, but he wasn't lollygagging, either. I figure they're due in about three tendays, but I doubt that the buyer'd be worried if it took four. Only one problem.''

"Well?''

"We need the right . . . props. By the time we get to Enkiar, I'm sure we'll be able to handle these slaver rifles, but that's not going to do it, not all by itself.''

"So? What's the problem?''

"The first is the wizard. The buyers will be expecting one; apparently this stuff is too valuable to trust to such a small party without having a wizard around for the extra protection. Even if we put one of us into wizard's robes, that might not fool them.''

"That's easy.'' Walter said. "Ellegon's due tonight; we'll have him fly back Home, bring back Henrad. Time the kid earned his keep.''

"That's not enough.'' Tennetty shook her head. "What if the buyers are expecting the slavers to have a couple of slaves with them? I don't think we could expect Jilla and Danni to play along.''

"No,'' Walter said, "we couldn't. Besides, if everything blew up in our faces, they wouldn't be able to fight their way out. No, we'll do it this way: What happened is that one of the slaves got killed in the fight, and the other tried to escape. We flogged her seriously, then healed her up when infection set in and it looked like it was going to kill her. Left a few scars. . . .''

Tennetty finally got it; she gasped, her face paled. "I *can't*. No—nobody's putting a collar around my neck."

"Easy, Ten." Karl laid a hand on her arm. "You don't have to. Maybe it won't be necessary for the disguise to work. The thing is, though . . ." He let his voice trail off.

"Well?"

"Who else could do it? Who else could look the part—and fight her way out, if all hell breaks loose?"

Slovotsky nodded. "As it always seems to. The only other choice I can think of is Andy."

"No." Karl shook his head. "*No*. Not if I'm going to be around. And not if I'm not. Clear?" When Andy-Andy was endangered, it was hard for Karl to concentrate on anything but her safety. He owed the others better—he owed himself better.

Tennetty looked him straight in the eye. "So I'm expendable, but Andrea isn't. Is that the way of it?"

"If you want to think of it that way, then go ahead. It's your choice." He folded his hands over and cracked his knuckles. "But damned if I'm going to justify myself to you, or to anyone else. You got that?"

She grunted.

"*I asked if you got that*."

"Yes."

"I can't hear you."

"*Yes*, dammit."

"Fine." He closed his eyes for a moment. He was missing something.

Ahh—if they were going to impersonate the slavers, then this raid didn't happen. And if it didn't happen, then what were all these bodies doing littering the meadow?

He raised a hand and beckoned Erek over. "I want Stick saddled and brought to me; I'm going up to the mesa to wait for Ellegon."

"Messages?"

"Two. First is to Chak. Begins: You and Slovotsky are going to pick a thirty-man team to impersonate some slavers; report to Walter. I want the wagons cleaned up and the insignia remounted; they're to be ready to roll by morning—but keep everyone out of the wizard's wagon; it's to stay sealed up until we have Henrad check it out. Ends. To

Gwellin. Begins: Report to Tennetty, immediately. Ends. Go."

Erek nodded and ran off; Karl called Daherrin over. "Change of plans—I want the slavers buried in the woods."

"Buried? What for?"

"Practice."

Daherrin snorted, then broke into a deep-chested laugh. "I *will* get an explanation eventually, won't I?"

"If you live until dark. Bury them deep; I don't want any wolves digging them up. This raid didn't happen. Got it?"

"Yes, Karl Cullinane." The dwarf walked away, bellowing for his assistants.

Karl turned to Slovotsky. "Walter, I want you to pick the team carefully. No dwarves, and go light on elves."

"Of course."

"Compare notes with Tennetty and Chak. This could easily turn out to be messy; anybody who was even a bit off his game last night goes back Home."

"How about Donidge? I hear he was damn good last night."

"So?"

"So, his wife's due in a few tendays. I think it would be nice if he was around for it."

"Good point—count him out. Same for anybody else with pressing business back Home." He lowered his voice. "Exceptway orfay oinersjay; Ahiraway's avinghay enoughway oubletray, as it is. Kapish?" Pig latin wasn't exactly an elegant code, but no adults from This Side spoke English well enough to puzzle it out.

"Sí, señor. Gwellin's going to lead the overland group?"

"Right. Also, I want you to have the team work out with the slaver's guns, but make sure everyone's damn careful with that powder until we know more about it. Turn in your own guns to Gwellin; he's to have them broken down and loaded onto the flatbed."

"Can I keep a couple of pistols?"

"No—and none of our bullets or powder, either. We're going to play slaver until we get to Enkiar, and I don't want any slipups." Karl turned to Tennetty "You're to supervise the stowing of the slaver powder. I want a little taken out of each barrel and put in a flask. Carefully, now—this stuff might be poison; make sure you don't get any on you. Then seal the barrels back up tight and leave them alone."

"Fine." she nodded. "Who's going back Home with the powder?"

"You are. If Ellegon's brought the basket, you'll take Jilla and Danni with you. Otherwise they'll go back overland with Gwellin. Prepare them for both possibilities. Also, take three of the slavers' guns for analysis—put them with the powder. You're to take slaver rifles and powder to Riccetti and Andy-Andy; have them run an analysis. I'll want Ellegon to catch up with us somewhere this side of Enkiar; we'll set up a rendezvous when he gets here. He can bring Henrad along with him."

"And me?"

"Look—if you want in, you've got it. If you don't, you may as well take some time off at Home. If you do want in, you'll have to get yourself outfitted with that glass eye."

"Very well," Tennetty said. "You can count me out of this one, Karl. I don't want to wear a collar again. *Ever*."

That was too bad, but he wasn't going to try to push Tennetty into doing something that she really wasn't willing to do. "Fair enough. We'll have to do without."

Walter opened his mouth, then closed it. "Fine."

Erek arrived, leading Karl's horse. Karl pulled himself to Stick's broad back. "Anything else?"

"Yes." Tennetty jerked her thumb at the woods. "I've still got those two slavers."

Damn. Karl had forgotten about that for a moment— forgetting wasn't a luxury he could allow himself. "What kind of shape are they in?"

She shook her head. "Not too bad. Just a few cuts and bruises. I mean, I hamstrung them, of course—"

"Of course."

"—but they're not near dead. Should I fix that? Or do you want to?"

"The watchman lives. I promised him."

"Oh, *great*. 'Karl Cullinane's word is as good as gold'—is that it?"

"Yes."

"No!"

Stick took a prancing step backward; Karl reined in the

stallion with difficulty. "Easy, damn you. . . . Yes, Tennetty. My word counts for something."

"What do you want to do? If we're going to try to impersonate a slaver team, we can't afford to have him wandering around, working his mouth. Do you want me to turn him *loose?*" she shrilled, her hand resting on the hilt of her saber.

Walter moved behind Tennetty; Karl waved him away. "No, Ten. Take a bottle of healing draughts—one of theirs. Fix up his legs, and one arm. We'll take him back Home, keep him locked up. He won't see any more than traders already have. Once we come back from Enkiar, we'll turn him loose. I promised that he'd live."

Tennetty took a deep breath. "And the other? You didn't promise every bloody slaver his life, did you?"

"No, I didn't. Kill him. Walter, go with her; take charge of the prisoner. I won't want a *ley de fuga*, kapish?"

"Got it."

Karl gave a light tug on the reins; Stick broke into a canter.

CHAPTER THREE:

Ellegon

I am a brother to dragons, and a companion to owls.
—Job

The night passed slowly, filled with the chirping of crickets, the whisper of wind through the trees, the flickering of the stars, and the pulsing of the faerie lights overhead. The faerie lights were more subdued, tonight changing slowly, as though the bloodshedding of the preceding night had shocked them into sullen dimness.

Karl finished laying the fire, spread his blanket near the edge of the mesa, then sat down, watching the sky, leaving the wood unlit.

Be here tonight, he thought. *Please*.

Stretching out on the blanket, he pillowed the back of his head on his hands and let his eyes sag shut. It could easily be a long wait.

Karl wasn't on the watch list—rank hath its privileges; and he could have allowed himself to fall asleep in his own tent—but if he wasn't up on the mesa waiting for Ellegon, he would have to put up with the dragon's nagging complaints until Ellegon took off for the trip back Home.

Ellegon was reliable within his limitations, but he did have limitations. It usually took the dragon three days to make it from Home to this particular rendezvous, but any number of things could throw him off schedule. Sometimes, innocuous things—Riccetti might have delayed him to fire a load of

56

soft-pine charcoal, or Nehera might have been working on a batch of high-alloy steel.

Occasionally, Ellegon would be late because the dragon had been delayed at another resupplying stop, helping a hunter team out of trouble.

More than once, Ellegon's arrival had meant the difference between victory and death. A fire-breathing dragon was a nice hole card; standard doctrine, whenever possible, was to schedule a raid just before one of Ellegon's resupplying runs.

Karl smiled, remembering the expression on the face of the slavers who had trapped his team just outside of Lundeyll. Everything had gone wrong that time. A sudden rainsquall had come up, making it impossible for his team to reload their weapons, and it turned out that most of the supposed slaves chained behind the wagons had really been slavers. His back to the Cirric, Karl had resigned himself to a fight to the death, until a familiar voice sounded in his head.

So he had surrendered. Sort of.

Thermyn had been very pleased with his catch, until the moment Ellegon's massive head snaked out from behind a rock outcropping and bit off his legs, leaving an expression more of surprise than pain on his face. . . .

Usually, though, lateness was just a result of Ellegon's trying to avoid people. Dragons were close to extinct in the Eren regions; humans seemed to have an almost instinctive fear of the creatures.

Ellegon didn't fly over populated areas during the day. While the dragon was immune to almost any nonmagical threat, a dragonbaned crossbow bolt could cut through his scales like a hot knife through butter. And though he could fly far, far above the range of any bow, he did have to land eventually. It was best that nobody know when he was in the area, the dragon said.

That was true, but Karl had long suspected that fear of being attacked was only part of the reason the dragon avoided coming within range of strangers; Ellegon simply didn't like reading the hate and fear in their minds.

They had worked out a routine for Ellegon's resupplying trips. The dragon would leave the valley during the afternoon, flying throughout the night and reaching his first resting place just before dawn. He and his human assistant would rest during the day, taking to the air at night, flying as high as possible, crossing the land in night-long hops, finding another resting place before morning, then sleeping, eating, and talking during the day.

Karl had long ago noticed that the more Ellegon liked whoever had been assigned to assist him, the later the dragon tended to be. Extended conversation with adults was a rare pleasure for the dragon; the few Home citizens who really liked Ellegon and felt safe around him were usually too busy to spend much time with him.

Karl lay back, occasionslly nodding off, until a vague reassurance touched his mind, bringing him quickly out of his light sleep.

A familiar voice sounded in his head. *Well? I brought the fatted calf—where are the party hats?*

"Ellegon!" A smile spread across Karl's face; he jumped to his feet. *Where are you?*

*Just out of sight. I'll be there in a moment. Hang *on*, stupid.*

The flapping of leathery wings sounded from below. Ellegon's massive form rose above the edge of the mesa; the dragon folded his wings against his sides and landed on the flat surface like a sparrow rising to a perch on a rooftop.

A very massive sparrow—the shock of his landing knocked Karl off his feet.

Hello, clumsy, Ellegon said. He was a huge beast, fully the length of a Greyhound bus from the tip of his twitching tail to the end of his saurian snout. He loomed above Karl in the dark, gouts of smoke and steam issuing from nostrils the size of hubcaps.

Would you help Henrad down? The ride seems to have disagreed with him. He's been like this for the whole trip.

"I can't imagine why," Karl said. *Light the fire, if you can reach from here.*

No problem. Ellegon snaked his head out and carefully flamed the wood, while Karl walked around the dragon's side and climbed halfway up the rope ladder to help Henrad unbuckle his riding harness and dismount.

Even in the flickering firelight, the apprentice wizard was almost green. Karl brought Henrad over to his blankets and helped him sit down. The boy gratefully waved Karl away, then leaned forward, his head between his knees.

We ran into a bit of turbulence—rain clouds are moving in. I'll want to take off fairly quickly, if I'm going to outrun it.

Fine. But why Henrad?

Objection?

No, as a matter of fact, he should come in handy. In the morning, the boy could check out the wizard's wagon and disarm any magical glyphs, leaving any physical traps to Slovotsky. *But you didn't answer my question.*

Your wife's idea. His crush on her is getting a bit out of hand—stop that.

Stop what?

Stop reaching for your sword. Andrea can handle him; if she couldn't she would have let me know. She just thought she could use a break from his roving hands and from him "accidentally" bumping into her at every opportunity.

Karl glared at Andy-Andy's apprentice. *I'd better have a word with him, anyway.*

I don't remember you being tolerant of other people messing with your *apprentices. Leave it be, Karl, leave it be.*

As you did?

Me? The dragon's mental voice was all innocence. *What did I do?*

I suppose that you didn't make the ride as rough as possible. Karl snorted. *I guess I'm just overly suspicious.*

You should watch that tendency of yours. It's not one of your prettier failings.

Others had already arrived to help unload. They began by removing the saddlebag-slung leather sacks, then untied the huge wicker basket cupping the rear half of Ellegon's back and unloaded the burlap sacks underneath it.

Tennetty led the two former slaves up to the dragon, muttering reassuring words, while Daherrin carried the bound, blindfolded, gagged slaver over and unceremoniously dumped him in the basket.

"Daherrin," Karl called out, "sling the basket and rig the tarp. It might get a bit wet up there." *What did you bring?*

Lamp oil, salt, dried beef, mutton, vegetables, bread—the

usual. Open that wooden box first. Lou sent along a dozen bottles of the latest batch of Riccetti's Best.*

Oh? How good is it?

What does a dragon know about corn whiskey? I can tell you that Ahira swears by it, although I think he's been using a bit too much, of late.

Karl walked over to the dragon's head and reached up to scratch the fine scales under Ellegon's chin. It was like trying to pet a granite wall.

Mmm . . . nice. Harder. It was the thought that counted; Karl would have had to use a hoe for the dragon actually to feel it.

It's good to see you, he thought. *I'm sorry you can't stay long.*

Don't be too sorry. You'll be seeing a lot of me over the next few days. Chton and his Joiners have petitioned for a town meeting; Ahira said to tell you that he is—and I quote—"looking down the barrel of a vote of confidence" and that you are to—quoting again—"hie your ass Homeward, on the double." He's worried, Karl.

How about you?

I think it's going to be close. And with two hunter teams away, he could lose. Pity you didn't think to allow for proxy voting in the Constitution.

Well, if Thomas Jefferson didn't think of it, how would you expect me to?

I have higher expectations of you—

Thanks—

—despite the fact that you are a constant disappointment, and—

—a whole lot. Karl beckoned Chak over. "Which would you rather do: take a side trip Home with me, or run the team until Enkiar?"

"Run the team?" Chak opened his mouth, then closed it. "Why me? Why not Slovotsky?"

"I thought you don't like taking his orders."

He doesn't, but he didn't think you noticed that.

It's not polite to peek into somebody's mind without his permission.

True. Then again, dragons aren't particularly polite.

I've noticed.

Observant, aren't you?

"Well, Chak?"

The little man shrugged. "I'd just as soon go Home with you, all things being equal."

Why are you bringing him Home?

Peep better. Tennetty says that he likes one of the new women. I want to give him a good shot at her, so to speak. It's about time Chak settled down and started a family. Can you reach Slovotsky?

Mmm . . . got him. He's on his way up.

Good. Relay, please: Nothing to worry about, Walter, but I've been called Home.

Ellegon's mental interpretation of Walter's voice was even more animated than usual. *"Trouble? Please don't let there be trouble—"*

Honest. No real trouble. It's just politics. I've got to kick some tails—

Metaphorically, for once, Ellegon put in.

Right. How would you feel about running the team until Enkiar?

"No objection, other than the obvious one . . ."—he wants to go Home, is what he's saying, Karl—*". . . but why not Chak?"*

Relay: Because he's not married, and you are, and there are a couple of possible candidates that will be going home with Ellegon and me.

"Good idea. No problem; I'll keep things together."

Good. Hurry up and get up here. We're going to make this a quick turnaround.

Don't you want to know about your family?

There's nothing wrong with my family.

The reason Karl hadn't asked Ellegon about his family wasn't that he didn't care—it was just the opposite. The dragon knew that giving him news of anything wrong with Aeia, Jason, or Andy-Andy took precedence over everything else; since Ellegon hadn't said anything, there wasn't any problem.

True.

He turned back to the dragon. "Any chance of Walter's running into any of our teams between here and Enkiar?"

*None. The last of Daven's team have returned Home, and

Aveneer is working the edge of the Kathard. Hmmm, I'd
better play mailman. If you'll excuse me?*

"Sure."

Ellegon raised his head. *Personal messages,* he announced,
*for the following: Donidge, Ch'akresarkandyn, Erek, Jenree,
Walter . . .*

Karl always liked to watch people get their mail, although
Ellegon was scrupulous about tuning him out. As the dragon
relayed each message from home, the recipient's face would
light up like a beacon.

Chak's dark face broke into a wide smile as Ellegon gave
him the message. He nodded three times, then sighed, a far-
off look in his eyes.

Karl waited until Chak's eyes cleared. "What's the news?"

The little man shook his head, still smiling. "Your son
says that I should be real sure not to get my fool ass killed. I
think he's been spending too much time around U'len."

"Probably."

Walter arrived, almost breathless.

Karl stuck out a hand. "We're taking off. Run things as
you see best."

"I always do."

"But if you don't mind taking some advice . . . Ellegon
says that you can't get jumped by any of our teams, but don't
take chances. There may be some independents working the
road between here and Enkiar. I'd rather you avoid them. Use
roving point men, okay? Next, I want you to fill Henrad in,
and have him go over the wizard's wagon, for magical traps,
and—"

"Hey, if you're leaving me in charge, you'd better trust
me not to stab myself in the foot, eh?"

"Right." He clapped a hand to Walter's shoulder. "Take
care of things, okay?"

"Sure. Kiss my wife for me—and kiss yours for me, too."

Karl glared at him.

Walter spread his hands. "Face it: I'm irrepressible."

"Right." Karl helped Chak into the basket, then climbed
up the rope ladder to the saddle on Ellegon's back and
strapped himself in. "Everybody clear. Daherrin, are the
straps okay?"

"Tight and strong," the dwarf called back, as he finished

belting Chak, Tennetty, and the two women into the basket, then tied down the tarpaulin, leaving only their heads peeking out.

You ready?

Home, James.

My name is Ellegon. The dragon's wings blurred; he leaped skyward.

PART TWO:

Home

CHAPTER FOUR:

Karl's Day Off

If a man insisted always on being serious, and never allowed himself a bit of fun and relaxation, he would go mad or become unstable without knowing it.
—Herodotus

Almost Home. Close your eyes.

As they passed through the invisible barrier of the Spidersect wards, the air around the dragon shimmered and sparkled, reacting to Ellegon's partially magical metabolism.

Even through his tightly closed eyes, Karl was dazzled, although the momentary discomfort was reassuring. The ragged circle of wards enclosing the valley didn't only prevent outside wizards from peering in, it also prevented anyone from carrying anything magical inside. Soon after Thellaren had set up the wards, three different assassin teams had tried to slip through, but even when they had no other magical implements, their healing draughts had tripped them up.

Word had gotten out; there hadn't been an assassin team in the valley for more than three years.

The light faded; Karl opened his eyes as Ellegon banked and turned, circling in.

The valley spread out beneath them, the fields of corn and wheat a patchwork blanket, ragged toward the edges. Roads crisscrossed the valley like a spider's web, most of them crossing near the compound at the south end of the valley or just outside of Engineer Territory in the north.

Ellegon lost altitude as he swooped across the lake, circling in toward what once had been the original compound and now housed the grainmill, silo, Karl and Andy-Andy's first house, and the former smithy, now used for receiving and settling new arrivals.

The basket barely missing the sharp points of the compound's palisade, the dragon slowed, then hovered, lowering the basket to the ground with a gentle thump, then landing beside it.

Karl unstrapped himself from the saddle, then turned to untie the basket's straps. He quickly slid down the dragon's side to help Chak, Tennetty, and the two women out and onto the ground. They left the slaver inside. There was no rush about him.

"Solid ground," Tennetty breathed. She favored Karl with a smile. "I think solid ground is one of my favorite things in the world."

Chak stretched broadly. "I know what you mean."

"Hey," Karl said. "No complaints. Next time Ellegon'll let you walk."

"Karl's Day Off. I don't see you," Tennetty said, jerking her thumb toward the Old House. "I'll take Jilla and Danni through Receiving and see that the prisoner is properly guarded—my word."

"I can finish up—"

"Karl's Day Off," Chak said, nodding. "Go."

"But the powder. I've got to get that to—"

"The Engineers," Chak said. "And you want Riccetti briefed. Consider it done, kemo sabe. It's Karl's Day Off—begone!"

Chak and Tennetty turned and walked away as though Karl simply weren't there.

You seem to have difficulty winning arguments with people you care about. Ellegon chuckled mentally.

"Really? I never noticed," Karl said.

Sarcasm doesn't become you. School will be letting out shortly. I'm going swimming.

"But there's . . . I give up." Karl threw up his hands. "You win. I'll go change, then join you." He jogged over to the Old House, deliberately ignoring the three millworkers who were deliberately ignoring him.

Early on, Andy-Andy had insisted on a few luxuries for

Karl, for fear that if he didn't claim them firmly enough, he'd never get even a taste of them. One of the most important was Karl's Day Off.

The rule was this: Despite whatever was going on at Home, regardless of the fact that there were usually five to ten people who wanted to see him the instant he got back, Andy-Andy had made it clear that Karl was not to be bothered by anyone except members of his immediate family for a full day after returning Home.

It had become almost ritualistic; citizens would pretend not to see him, treating him as though he were invisible.

Shutting the door behind him, he unbuckled his swordbelt and hung it on a peg, then untied the amulet from his neck, stowing it safely behind the top door of a crude bureau. It wasn't necessary to keep the amulet on his person at Home; the entire valley was under the wards' protection.

Hopping on alternate legs he loosened his boots and kicked them toward a corner, then stripped, slipping on a pair of shorts and tucking a towel, shirt, a pair of drawstring jeans, and sandals under his arm before exiting the Old House and jogging the few hundred yards to the lake.

Down the beach, Ellegon had already set down in the water just beyond the end of the schoolhouse's dock. Only his huge head and a portion of his back rose above the clear, cold water, and both were almost concealed by the crowd of half-naked children swarming over him.

Relay, please: Andy?

She knows you're home, but she's busy. Leave her alone while you get clean.

Good idea. Karl dropped his bundle of clothing to the hot sands and dashed for the water.

As always, it was far colder than he'd remembered. The lake was fed by the icy streams that trickled down from the mountains; as he entered the water, he wondered for the thousandth time if it was possible that ice melted at minus forty on This Side.

He forced himself to run into the water until it reached his waist, then dove headfirst and set off with a clumsy but powerful breaststroke toward the dock and the dragon.

If God had ever set out to create the perfect swimming companion for adult or child, Ellegon would have been it.

With the dragon around, there was no need for a buddy system to ensure that any head going under the water surfaced with a live body attached. Ellegon would simply order any overtired child—or adult—out of the water, and *nobody* was interested in flouting his orders.

Well, almost nobody; Jason was a special case.

But Ellegon wasn't just a lifeguard.

Care for a dive?

As Karl reached the dragon, he set his feet against Ellegon's right forward knee and stood, rising half out of the water. He shook his head to clear the wet hair from his eyes, making a mental note that he'd better get another haircut, and soon.

I asked if you would care for a dive.

"Sure."

Ellegon carefully shook a pair of twelve-year-olds from his head, then craned his long neck so that Karl could step onto it.

Gently, this time. Wouldn't do for the kids to see me scream in terror.

The scales slippery beneath his feet, Karl stood gingerly and flexed his knees, balancing himself just behind the dragon's eye ridges. Ellegon quickly straightened his neck and tossed his head, sending Karl flipping head over heels forty feet into the air. Karl stretched out his arms, air-braking into a swan dive as he fell; he pulled himself into a tuck, then straightened as he slammed feet first into the water, slipping down into the dark iciness, rebounding gently off the sandy bottom of the lake.

As his head broke the surface, a slim arm snaked around his neck, a hand pressed hard against the back of his head, and a pair of firm young breasts pressed against his back, while powerful thighs scissored his waist.

"Hi!" Aeia said, kissing him on the back of the neck while firmly endeavoring to force his head underwater. "You're back."

"I noticed." *She's getting a bit too old for this,* he thought, far more conscious of her young body than was comfortable. He took a quick, deep breath, and dove.

Do you want to know what's really going on in her head?

No. Don't peep my family for me.

He'd caught her by surprise this time, diving before Aeia had the chance to grab a breath; she released her grip before he ran out of air.

He surfaced, blocked her next try, then grabbed her by the wrist and spun her around, pushing her toward the dock. "Go put on your halter."

"For *swimming?* Don't be such a—"

He forced a grim expression to his face. "Do it. Now."

She pouted and swam away, slipping seallike out of the water and onto the dock, then padding sullenly toward the schoolhouse, adjusting her shorts as she did.

What am I going to do about this?

*As I understand it, a bit of repressed sexuality between father and daughter is normal, whether the daughter is adopted or not."

Where did you get that *bit of bullshit?*

From the usual place: your head. Psych 101. Remember?

Oh.

One bit of advice, if you don't mind?

Yes?

It would be best for everyone if it's kept repressed. Adopted daughter or not, a husband really shouldn't cheat on a wife who can turn him into a toad.

Well, Andy-Andy couldn't really turn him into a toad, but the dragon had a point.

"Right." He looked around, then quickly submerged to avoid the outstretched hands of three boys and two girls who had apparently decided that it was time to drown Karl Cullinane. He swam underwater, ducking under Ellegon's broad belly, then surfaced on the other side. *Is she still busy? Where's Jason?*

She kept him after school. If you ask my opinion—

Which I didn't. But I have a hunch I'll receive the benefit of it anyway.

Good guess. I think she's too strict with him. Karl, he's only six years old. Just—

Ellegon was interrupted by the pounding of feet on the dock and a sudden splash.

Not again! The dragon ducked his head underwater and came up with the wriggling form of Jason Cullinane in his mouth, then carefully spat the coughing boy onto the pier.

Clearly forcing himself to stop coughing, Jason straightened.
He says that he's fine. I'm giving him a bit of hell.
Good for you.

With the sole exception of Jane Michele Slovotsky, Karl had never really been impressed with children. The so-called special things about them were clearly parents' illusions, born of parents' need to feel special.

Jason, on the other hand, was special. It wasn't just that he had Andy-Andy's knowing brown eyes and smooth olive skin, or that the boy's straight brown hair was somehow finer than hair had any right to be. Even at six, Jason Cullinane had developed his own skewed ideas about what was right and wrong, which tended to be resistant to anything short of *force majeure*, and were completely immune to a father's attempts at reason.

What was simultaneously convenient and completely infuriating was that Jason, who could give a donkey stubbornness lessons as far as Karl was concerned, was easily influenced by his peers, and would obey Ellegon almost readily.

*You're *not* old enough to keep the water out of your nose when you jump unless you hold your nose. Until I tell you otherwise, I want you to hold your nose when you jump into the water. I am not going to pull you out again,* the dragon threatened.

I am lying through my many teeth, he said to Karl in a mental aside.

I know.

Jason wiped his nose and sniffed; his brown eyes grew vague.

Talk with your mouth. I want your father to hear you promise.

"I'm sorry, Ellegon," he said. "I won't do it again."

Karl swam over to the dock and pulled himself onto the hot wood. "Hi there."

"Hi, Daddy." Jason walked over to where Karl stood and stuck out a tiny hand.

"What's this?"

"Wanna shake hands."

"What? Jase—"

"Too old to kiss. Only babies do that."

"Who says?"

"Mikyn says."

"He does, does he? Well, whoever Mikyn is, he's wrong. He—"

"Is *not*. Shake hands."

Karl shrugged and sadly accepted the boy's hand in his. "Well, if you're too old, you're too old. What's new?"

"Can I go play?"

Karl could almost have cried. Well, when he was six years old, a lake with a dragon in it would have been a lot more interesting than talking with a father. "Sure."

Before the word was halfway out of his mouth, Jason was already jumping into the water, this time holding his nose.

Karl sighed, then turned and walked down the dock to the schoolhouse. It was a single-roomed building, the classroom roughly the same size as those that had been used on the Other Side since the Sumerians invented schools. While the walls were of good pine, and the benches and desks solidly built, the windows were of smoky, barely translucent glass. Glassmaking was one of the crafts that Home was still deficient in.

At the far end of the room, Aeia and Andy-Andy were crouched in front of a young boy, perhaps two years older than Jason, who was seated on Andy-Andy's chair, shaking his head.

Seeing her always brought it back to him: A smile really could brighten a room. She fingered the bend in her ever so slightly too large nose as she listened to Aeia talking with the boy.

Andy-Andy's frown spoke volumes: She was unhappy, but not with either Aeia or the boy.

She tossed her head, sending her shoulder-length black hair whipping about her face as she turned to glance at him, rewarding him with that smile.

Lady, you still take my breath away.

Should I relay that?

Don't bother. If she doesn't know . . .

He cleared his throat. Aeia, now wearing a halter, turned to wave him to silence.

Karl raised an eyebrow. He'd never been shushed by Aeia before. He walked over and laid a gentle hand on Andy-

Andy's shoulder. She turned her face upward, giving him a quick peck.

"What is it?" he asked. "This all I get?"

Old saying: When you don't know what you're talking about, your mouth is best used for chewing.

"Mikyn?" Andy-Andy shook her head. "Please take off your shirt." She turned to Karl. "He's been holding his side all day; he almost couldn't get out of the chair."

"Can I help?" *Ellegon, please relay: Maybe he's a bit shy about taking off clothes in front of you two. Mikyn apparently has some funny ideas—it seems he told Jason that only babies can give their fathers a kiss.*

She says, "Karl, I think this is a bit more serious."

Ellegon, why don't you just peep him?

She already asked me to. There's a block—a lot of emotion going on under the surface, but I can't read it at all. I'm not perfect, you know. Sometimes, when you get too intense, I can't even read you.

Okay; back to basics. Relay: Let me give it a try. What's to lose?

She nodded, then rose, giving him a quick peck on the lips before taking Aeia out of the room.

Karl chuckled thinly. *Some welcome.* "Hi there," he said in English, then switched to Erendra when the boy didn't answer. "What's the problem?"

No answer.

"You know who I am?"

"J-Jason's father."

"Right. You can call me Karl. Andrea says that your side hurts. Can I take a look?"

Mikyn shook his head.

"You don't have to." Karl nodded. "We'll do it your way. Do you mind talking for a while?" Karl pulled over Andy's chair and seated himself ass-backward, folding his arms over the chair's back.

"No."

"I don't remember seeing you around. Are you new here?"

"Yes."

New here. Well, if Karl hadn't brought the boy in, then somebody else had; Jason was the oldest person to be born in Home, Jane Michele Slovotsky second by half a year.

Relay: Tell me about the boy.

She says, "Not much to tell. Sad story, but typical. Daven's team brought him and his father in, about tendays ago. They're cropping for the Engineers until they earn their grubstake. They're from Holtun—used to be owned by some baron or other who got burned out by the Biemish; apparently got scooped up early this year, after some battle or other. The mother got sold off. This isn't the first time he's been hurt; Mikyn bruises easily. I think one of the older boys may have been beating him up, But Ellegon can't peep out who—"

No need, dammit.

You know what it is?

I know what it sounds like. He dialed for his command voice. "Take the shirt off, *now*."

Wide-eyed, the boy started to comply, then remembered that he wasn't supposed to take his shirt off and pulled it back down.

But not before Karl saw the huge bruise across his ribs. "Aeia, get in here." His jaw clenched. *So much for my day off.*

He forced a smile to his face. "I'm going to have Aeia take you over to Thellaren. You won't have to take off your shirt for him to fix you up. And then you can go right home."

That last hit Mikyn like a slap. The boy's face whitened.

Karl smiled reassuringly. "No, not your home. Jason's and mine. You don't have to go back to your father, if you don't want to. But when you do, he's not going to hurt you anymore. I promise."

You want me to send for a sword?

No. Drop Ahira off at the Old House. Then find Mikyn's father and probe him. If I'm right, scoop him up and bring him, too.

He nodded to Aeia. "Take Mikyn to the cleric. When you're done there, find him a bed in the New House; he's staying with us tonight. I'll see you later."

He walked to the door and walked back to the Old House, his hands balling themselves into fists.

Leathery wings flapped outside the Old House, followed by a solid thump.

Limping slightly, Ahira swung the door open and walked into the room, his forehead creased in irritation.

The dwarf was barely half Karl's height, but fully as wide. That, combined with his heavy brows and overmuscled body, always made him look as though nature had intended Ahira to be a tall man, but his body had never gotten the hint.

Despite the situation, Karl had to repress a smile. He always had to, whenever he saw Ahira wearing a pair of Homemade jeans and a blue cotton workshirt. Somehow the dwarf looked more natural in chainmail and leather.

Karl gestured him toward a chair. "Good afternoon, Mr. Mayor."

The dwarf remained standing. "Cut the crap—I'm busy. I *was* busy, that is, until that damn dragon of yours swooped down out of the sky and scooped me up without so much as a by-your-leave."

"What's the problem?"

"Territory dispute. Riccetti's complaining that Keremin's encroaching on a field that belongs to the Engineers."

"Well? Is Lou lying?"

"Fat chance."

"So? What's the big deal?"

"Well, Keremin's a Joiner, but he's been a quiet one, lately. I'm trying to smooth it over, without getting him all that angry at me just before the town meeting."

"Any chance of giving Lou a substitute parcel?"

Ahira shrugged. "It's the lot just west of the cave." He sighed and sat down. "And it's his. Politics is thirsty work—hint, hint."

"Sure." Karl found two clay mugs in the near cabinet, then took a bottle down from the shelf, uncorked it, and poured each of them three fingers of Riccetti's Best. "You missed something kind of important."

"What is it now?" Ahira sipped his whiskey, then made a face. "This isn't too bad, but have you tasted the beer lately? I could swear that it's getting worse. I'd give my kingdom for a Miller, my empire for a Genee Cream."

"Ahira, we've got a case of childbeating, I think."

"Shit. Who?"

"New folks. The kid's name is Mikyn. I don't know the father's."

The dwarf's free hand clenched into a fist. "You want me to handle this? I don't like childbeaters any more than you do."

"Sure you do. You feel a lot of sympathy for the poor, misunderstood bastards. Matter of fact, you're the only thing that's standing between big, bad Karl Cullinane and this particular poor, misunderstood bastard."

"Really? You're sure about that?"

"Yup."

Leathery wings flapped overhead. *We are here. And you were correct about Alezyn. I'm sorry, Karl.*

Why?

Dammit, this is the sort of thing I'm supposed to spot, and prevent. It's just that I hate probing people I don't know, and it's really—

Shh. We're not required to be perfect. We're just required to do our damnedest.

But what do we do when that isn't enough?

There wasn't an easy answer to that. Karl lifted his head. "Alezyn, get in here. *Now.*"

The door swung tentatively open, and Ellegon nudged Alezyn into the room. Alezyn sprawled face-first on the floor, then picked himself up.

The trouble was, Alezyn didn't look like a childbeater. He was a short, balding little man, with a round face and wide eyes; his expression was half hostile, half frightened; he looked far more like someone beaten on than the sort of brute who would take his frustrations out on a child.

"What is this all about?"

"We want to talk with you," Ahira said.

"Yes, Mr. Mayor." Alezyn started to tug on his forelock, then caught himself.

"And," the dwarf went on, "either we're going to have a very productive talk, or . . ." He let his voice trail off.

"Or?"

Ahira turned to Karl. "Show him."

Karl stood. He grabbed the smaller man by the front of his tunic and easily lifted him off the ground.

"We haven't met before. My name is Karl Cullinane. And what I want is for you to understand why I'm going to start with *this*." He bounced Alezyn off the nearest wall, then took a step forward as the other lay on the bare wood floor, gasping for breath.

Ahira caught his arm. "No, don't kill him."

Ellegon poked his head through the door. *No, I have a better idea. Let me eat him. I've always wondered how a man who beats children would taste.*

Karl wouldn't have thought it possible for the little man's eyes to grow wider. He was wrong.

"Never mind, Ellegon," Karl said. "It'd probably poison you."

From Ahira: "You're planning to put the fear of God into him, right?"

No, the fear of me. *Sometimes God doesn't follow through.*

"Too risky. He might take his frustrations out on the kid, then panic and kill him."

So?

"So follow my lead." "Put him down, Karl."

"But—"

"Put. Him. Down." As Karl complied, the dwarf helped Alezyn off the floor, and threw an arm around the man's shoulder. "Let's talk, just you and me."

Alezyn made an abortive attempt to shake the arm off, but he might as well have been trying to pry away a steel bar.

"I understand what you've been going through," Ahira said gently. "Captured, enslaved, your wife sold off. And now, you're in a new country, and we don't do things the way you did them at home. Frustrating, eh?" He helped Alezyn to a chair, then offered him a sip of whiskey. "Go ahead. It'll be good for you."

The little man took a shallow sip. "Yes, b-but—can I talk freely? Without *him* hitting me again?"

"Of course. You're under my protection while you're in this room." The dwarf turned to glare at Karl. "You hear that?"

"Yes."

"Yes, *what?*"

"Yes, Mr. Mayor."

"Better." Ahira turned back to Alezyn. "You were saying?"

"Mikyn is my son. When he disobeys, I have the right to punish him. He's *my* son. *Mine.*"

"That's right. And what you're going to have to learn is

that here, 'my son' or 'my wife' or even 'my horse' means something different than 'my shovel.' Or . . .''

"Or?"

"*Or I'll kick your ass out that door and let Karl slice you into breakfast for Ellegon,*'' the dwarf bellowed, his face a mask of rage. "As I was saying," he said in a calm voice, "you've got a lot to learn. And I don't think you're going to learn it cropping for the Engineers. I've got just the school-room in mind. Karl.''

"Yes, Mr. Mayor?"

"Escort Alezyn over to the parade ground. Daven's team is running some maneuvers." He switched to English. "The other day, I was telling him some stories my father used to tell me about Marine boot camp. He'll understand when you tell him that Alezyn is to be treated as a boot." He turned to Alezyn and spoke in Erendra. "Karl will take care of your son until you're done training."

"Training?"

"Yes. We're going to make a warrior out of you."

"A warrior?" Alezyn's face whitened.

"Yes. It's either that, or banishment. You can start running right now, if that's what you want. Or . . .''

"Or?"

The dwarf chuckled. "Whenever I end a sentence with an *or*, you really should hold on to your curiosity. We're going to make a warrior out of you, or we're going to kill you trying. You can either get your stupid butt out the door and wait for Karl, or . . .'' His voice trailed off.

Alezyn didn't ask; he bolted for the door.

Karl chuckled. "Ahira, I like your style." He sobered. "We've got lots to talk about. Why don't you bring Kirah and Janie over to the New House for dinner?''

Ahira picked up his cup and drained it, then looked inside. "I seem to be out of whiskey." Karl passed him the bottle; ignoring the cup, the dwarf uncorked it and tilted it back. "Mmm . . . dinner sounds good—want to include Riccetti?''

"Sure. Can you put him up for the night, though? I'm putting Mikyn in our guesting room, and I wouldn't want to slight Lou.''

"Damn well better not. And sure, he can have my room. I don't get much use of it, lately.''

"Really? I didn't know that your social life had picked up."

"Very funny. Janie's been having nightmares again. I have to sleep with her most nights." The dwarf snorted. "At least, she says she has bad dreams; I think maybe she just wants some more attention."

"You're spoiling that kid."

"You think so, eh?" Ahira cracked his knuckles. "You want to try to stop me?"

"Me?" Karl raised his hands in mock surrender. "I wouldn't dare—but I'd better get over to the house; U'len will have my hide if I don't give her a bit of warning. And we'll add Thellaren, too. Get some work done tonight."

"How about Karl's Day Off?"

"Screw Karl's Day Off." He walked out into the square, where Alezyn stood waiting.

CHAPTER FIVE:

Dinner Party

No medicine can be found for a life which has fled.
          —Ibycus

Karl considered the last thick wedge of blueberry pie on the earthenware serving tray, then decided that the remaining shards of Karl's Day Off entitled him to it.

He slipped it onto his plate and brought a spoonful to his mouth. Damn, but it was sweet. Fresh-baked goods were what he missed most when he was on the road.

At the other end of the table, Andy-Andy smiled a promise at him.

Well, maybe fresh-baked goods weren't exactly what he missed most.

Sometimes, life is almost worth living. He folded his hands over his belly and sat back, letting his eyes sag half-shut.

Reaching for a piece of cornbread, Ahira accidentally elbowed a knife from the table; it clattered on the floor.

Karl leaped out of his chair, his hand going to his waist for the hilt of the sword that wasn't there.

"Karl!"

He stopped himself in midmotion, feeling more silly than anything else. Gesturing an apology, he took his seat, feeling every eye in the room on him. "Sorry, everybody. It's . . . just that it takes a while, after you've been out. I kind of need to . . . decompress."

"You're not the only one," Chak said from the doorway,

chuckling as he sheathed his falchion. The little man walked over to the table and took a piece of cornbread from the breadboard. "When I heard the clatter, I rolled, drew my sword, and was halfway down the stairs before I realized that it was probably just some eating ware."

"How are the children?" Andy-Andy asked.

"Wonderful." Chak smiled. "Jason and Janie are snoring, and I was finally able to get Mikyn to fall asleep."

Karl snorted. "You didn't have to play baby-sitter, you know. You're allowed to come up and eat with the rest of us."

"I never see enough of Jason and Janie," Chak shrugged. "I've seen you eat more than often enough, Karl. It's no thrill."

"Thanks." Karl gestured to a chair. "Do you want to join us, or would you rather go watch the children sleep?"

The dark little man pitched his sheathed falchion into the swordstand in the corner and sat, pulling himself up to the table next to Aeia. "U'len, I'll have some beef," he called toward the kitchen.

The answer came back immediately: "Then go bite a cow!"

A chorus of quiet chuckles sounded. Karl looked around the long table. Except for Chak, everyone seemed satisfied, although Aeia's plate was closer to full than he liked to see. Was she eating so lightly because of some teenage pickiness, or because she was afraid to appear less than grown-up in the way she handled a knife and fork?

Well, either way, she could always snack later, he decided. U'len wheedled easily.

In the seat of honor at Karl's left, Lou Riccetti had pushed his chair away from the edge of the table and loosened his trousers' drawstrings, accepting the offer of a damp cloth from the teenage junior apprentice Engineer who waited attentively behind his chair, one hand always resting on a holstered pistol.

More than once, Riccetti had privately offered to waive the bodyguard when he was visiting, but Karl had vetoed that. For the next few years, Lou Riccetti would be the most valuable person in the valley, and the rituals that Riccetti and Ahira had developed for the Engineers were too useful to allow for weakening exceptions. Karl wasn't necessarily going to remain the only target of guild-inspired assassination attempts.

He frowned; Riccetti's weight bothered him. Karl had always secretly suspected that Riccetti, pudgy before they'd been transferred to This Side, would run to fat, but he'd been dead wrong. Lou was almost skeletal these days; he claimed he was just too busy to eat, and while his junior Engineers cooked for him, none was ever presumptuous enough to tell the Engineer to slow down or eat more.

"I should send U'len over to cook for you," Karl said. "Got to get some meat on your bones."

"I'm doing fine."

"I'll tell you when you're doing fine, asshole. Eat regularly, put on some weight, or I'll tell U'len to keep the stew coming while I hold you down and force-feed it to you."

The apprentice—Ranella, that was her name—kept her pimpled face calm only with visible effort. In Engineer Territory at the north end of the valley, nobody spoke to the Engineer that way. Ever.

"And I get no say in the matter?" U'len said with a sniff, as she bustled through the curtains covering the arched doorway that led from the kitchen to the dining room, two fresh pies balanced on a wooden slab next to a platterful of roast beef that overflowed, dripping red juices. She was a profoundly fat woman of about fifty, her face perpetually red from the heat of the stove.

"You think I have little enough work to do here, that you can make me cook for those filthy Engineers as well? You should lay off your sword practice for a few tendays, and exercise your mind. If you have one." She handed Chak the platter of beef, then set one pie down gently on Andy-Andy's end of the table and slammed the other down on Karl's. "Always making problems for me, for your wife, for everyone and everything . . ."

"Easily solved—at least as far as you're concerned," Karl said. "You're fired."

"I am *not*. You wouldn't dare, you brainless son of a —"

"*Enough.*"

"*I* will tell *you* when I've said enough," she called over her shoulder as she vanished back into the kitchen. "Damn fool swordsman. I'd say he had droppings for brains, except that'd be unfair—to droppings. . . ."

Well, U'len was the best cook in the valley, although her tongue was just as sharp as her kitchen knives. Karl was secretly pleased with her irritability; U'len had come a long way from the cringing wretch in the slave markets of Metreyll.

Sitting on Riccetti's left, Thellaren brushed a few stray crumbs from his black robes and smiled as he reached for a piece of pie, his hands seemingly immune to the hot drops of bubbling blueberry filling.

"You seem to collect irritating people around you, Karl Cullinane." The fat Spidersect priest shook his head. "One would think that you like it that way." Thellaren broke off a crumb and blew on it before feeding the tarantula-sized spider on his shoulder. The creature grabbed the morsel in its mandibles, then scurried away, hiding itself somewhere inside the priest's ample robes.

"True enough." Ahira grinned slyly. "After all, look who he married."

The dwarf had timed that just right, just as Andy-Andy had lifted her goblet and begun to drink. Water spurted out of her mouth and onto her plate.

Riccetti flashed a brief smile. "Two points, Ahira."

Andy-Andy glared at both the Engineer and the dwarf, then broke into a fit of giggles.

Karl sighed happily. He hadn't heard her actually giggle for years.

After a brief glance at Ahira for permission, Kirah joined in the general laughter. Walter's wife was still, even after all this time, reserved, almost silent, around Karl. The dwarf was a different case; since Ahira lived with her, Janie, and Walter, she had come to take him for granted.

Karl pushed his chair back from the table and folded his hands over his navel. "So? Where do we stand?"

"Which?" Riccetti downed the last of his water. "Politics or powder?"

"Dealer's choice."

Ahira bit his lip. "It's the politics that worries me. Even if the locals—"

"The slavers."

"—even if the slavers have figured out how to make

powder, we have quite a few tricks in reserve. Nitrocellulose,"
Ahira said with a sigh. "If necessary."

Riccetti snorted. "Fine. *You* figure out how to keep it
stable."

Karl raised an eyebrow. "How's the research going?"

"Not well. It's still averaging around ninety, ninety-five
days before the damn stuff self-detonates." He threw up his
hands. "It could be that I've got to figure out a better
wash—or maybe just bite the bullet and admit that I can't do
it with the kinds of impurities we're getting in the sulfuric. Or
maybe I should just tell you to find yourself another jackleg
chemical engineer."

"Hey, Lou—"

"Don't heylou me, dammit. If I had *wanted* to major in
chemical engineering instead of civil engineering, I would
have. You know how I was taught to procure explosives?"

"Well—"

"I was taught to *order* them. Out of a *catalog.* You get a
license, you fill out the *forms*, you write a *check* . . ." He
chewed his thumbnail. "And really pure chemicals—"

"Wait." Ahira held up a hand. "Lou, with all due respect,
do we have to go through this again? We all know that you're
going to keep working on guncotton, and everybody in this
room believes that you'll lick the self-detonating problem,
eventually."

"*Sure* I will. Ever read that Verne book about a trip to the
moon?"

"The one where they shot them out of a cannon? No.
Why?"

Riccetti spread his hands on the table. "Observe—at no
time do the fingers leave the hand. I like it that way." He
drummed his fingers on the table. "Most of the book was
nonsense. But ol' Julie had one thing right. Most of his
characters—people who spent a lot of time dealing with
explosives—were missing a few body parts. If I had to start
making explosives in quantity, God knows what'll happen."

"So don't make any quantities until you're ready to."

"I guess I should have studied chemical engineering. Or
brought along a few pounds of PYX, maybe."

"There is a . . . nastier alternative." Andy-Andy's face
grew grim. "I could put in the work to learn transmutation of

metals, instead of just doing this agricultural kid stuff. How many pounds of uranium would it take to—''

"Forget it." Riccetti shook his head. "Three problems. First, without good explosives for the lenses, setting off a fission bomb isn't easy. Second, it isn't only uranium you need, you need uranium that's ninety-seven plus percent U-two-thirty-five. Third, you won't live to get good enough to do any kind of transmutation. It's not like rainmaking. Aristobulus wasn't far enough along for transmutation, and you're still not half the wizard . . . he was."

"Delicately put." Ahira raised his eyes to heaven. "But Lou's right, although for the wrong reasons. We're not taking that route."

Thellaren raised an eyebrow, but didn't ask. "Mr. Mayor, what do you think we ought to do about the political situation? You are not willing to consider Lord Khoral's new offer?"

"New offer?" Karl asked. "Something I don't know about?"

"Yeah." The dwarf shook his head. "We've got another emissary from Khoral due between now and the town meeting, and I expect he's going to go up the ante. More serfs; titles enough to go around—how would you like to be Karl, Baron Cullinane?"

Karl snorted.

"All he wants is your fealty, Karl. And, just maybe, he wants Lou to give him the secret of gunpowder."

"What he wants, Ahira, is both Lou and a bargaining chip to bludgeon the Slavers' Guild with."

"It's not the bludgeoning that bothers you. It's the possibility of *not* bludgeoning. C'mon, now, there's never been a human baron in Therranj," the dwarf teased. "Wouldn't you like to be the first?"

"No, thanks." It was partly a matter of ego, partly a matter of dignity. But mainly it was a matter of independence.

Karl didn't like the idea of being told what to do by anyone, and he most particularly didn't like the idea of becoming a second-class Therranji. Elves had ruled in Therranj forever; the present Lord Khoral claimed to trace his ancestry back for thousands of years. Humans were second-class citizens in Therranj, and though most of them were as native-born as the elves, descendants of immigrants from the Eren regions, humans were forbidden to own land, ride horses, or practice half a score of professions.

And despite the fact that Khoral had already offered full Therranji citizenship to everyone in the valley—humans, elves, and dwarves alike—Karl was more than sure that that wouldn't quite take. Racial prejudice was different here, but still every bit as firmly entrenched on This Side as back on the Other Side.

Maybe worse, in a way; here, there was a sound basis for at least some of it. While Karl didn't have anything against dwarves or elves, he wouldn't want Aeia to marry either; any children would be sterile, mules.

And then there was the matter of the Slavers' Guild. Western Therranj was a prime raiding ground for the slavers, and certainly that was a common interest between Home and Therranj for now—but that could change. There was no doubt that Khoral wanted to hold the threat of Karl Cullinane over the slavers' heads, promising to restrain him if the guild would lay off the raids on Therranj.

What bothered Karl was that Khoral just might persuade the guild. The spreading war in the Middle Lands increased the supplies of slaves in its wake; it was becoming increasingly easy for the guild to trade in Bieme and Holtun rather than raiding into Therranj.

There was an even darker side to it. What if Khoral was sincere? What if he really would make Karl some sort of baron?

That was a trap for both ruler and ruled. Karl's authority over his warriors flowed from respect and choice—both theirs and his. There might come a time when he could give up that authority and what went with it, when he'd be able to say that he'd never again have to see friends' intestines spill onto the grass.

But that could only happen as long as he remained free. Not trapped by a title.

"The town meeting is the problem," Karl said. "At least for now. It might get a bit dirty—"

"Karl—" Andy-Andy started.

"—*politically*," he went on. "No bloodshed. I'll handle it. Just make sure that the envoy's kept busy until the meeting. Give him a full, in-depth tour, excluding Reserved caverns.

Hell, you can have Nehera discourse for a couple of hours on alloys. Hmmm . . . I don't see any need for the envoy to be muttering with the Joiners—so be careful." He turned to Lou. "Anything outside of the caverns that shouldn't be seen?"

"Well, nothing critical, but yes," Riccetti said, frowning. "There's a charcoal heap still smoldering—that's no problem. But we've got a few pots boiling over wood fires. I'll draft Ellegon to hurry the job, but getting them inside before they cool would be a problem. Andrea, would you levitate them for me?"

"After that crack about how easy rainmaking is, I shouldn't—but I will." She wrinkled her brow. "I hope they're covered, though. You did know I'm rainmaking tonight?"

"I knew," Riccetti said. "The pots are under flies. As for getting it out of sight . . . I can have everything inside by tomorrow night if you'll come over after school and give us a hand."

"Sure."

He didn't say what was in the pots, but Karl assumed it was dirt from the cave floors, saltpeter being crystallized out of the bat guano as an ingredient for gunpowder. There was no need to be overly secretive. Everyone in the valley either knew or suspected that the making of gunpowder involved boiling something. Exactly what would be hard to guess, but there was no need to take extra chances.

Karl nodded. "Sounds good. As far as the emissary goes, he can say what he wants to; I just want the last word. Both with the elf and before the voting."

"Karl, you're treating this too lightly," the dwarf said, shaking his head. "I really think you ought to go around and talk to people."

"Too obvious. The Joiners will be expecting me to do some politicking for you."

"Hell, I'm expecting you to go around politicking for me."

"Guess again." Karl shook his head. "You're thinking like a politician."

"Which you're not."

"Precisely. We living legends do things differently." Karl blew on his fingernails and buffed them on his chest. "By now, it's common knowledge from here to the caverns that I'm back because you sent for me. And since I've always hated to do the expected, I'm going to do nothing political, say nothing political, until the town meeting.''

"And then?"

"And then I . . . transcend the political."

Ahira chuckled. "The last time I was around when you 'transcended the political,' you beat the hell out of Seigar Wohtansen. Hope you don't end up as unpopular around here as you are in Melawei."

"*Don't mention Melawei.*" Karl slammed his fist down on the table, sending plates and silverware clattering. "*Ever.*" It wasn't just that Melawei was where Rahff had died; Melawei was also where the sword of Arta Myrdhyn lay waiting in a cavern beneath an offshore island, clutched in fingers of light.

It's not waiting for my son, you bastard. You keep your bloody hands off Jason. He rubbed his fingers against his eyes until sparks leaped behind his eyelids. "I'm sorry, Ahira—everybody." He opened his eyes to see Lou Riccetti standing, his fingers clutching the apprentice's wrist. Chak stood behind her, one hand gripping her hair, his eating knife barely touching the wide-eyed girl's throat.

"Easy, Chak," Karl said. "Let her go."

Eying the apprentice suspiciously, Chak let go of her hair and took his seat again, carefully examining the knife's edge.

"Ranella," Riccetti said quietly, releasing the girl's arm. "We have discussed this. You may pull a weapon on *me* before you threaten Karl. Understood?"

"But I was just—"

"An excuse? Did I hear an *excuse?*"

"No, Engineer."

"Am I understood?"

"Yes, Engineer."

Riccetti held out his right hand; the apprentice laid the pistol gently in it. "Report to the officer of the watch as quickly as possible, and ask him to send me a pair of *decent* bodyguards; I'll remain here until they arrive. You won't need to use your horse; the run will be good for you. Begin now. Dismissed."

"Yes, Engineer." Her face a grim mask, the girl spun on her heel and sprinted from the room.

Riccetti turned to Karl. "I . . . understand about some things making you angry, but I really don't want you to ever force me to do that again. Ranella's a good kid; I don't like having to punish her."

Riccetti was right. At Karl's original insistence, Engineers were trained always to be careful of Riccetti's safety, and anything that might dull that training was wrong.

Karl raised a hand in apology. "Sorry, Lou—you, too, Ahira. My fault, again. I've been out too much lately; I really should spend more time at Home."

Thellaren cleared his throat. "I believe we were discussing the political issues?"

"Right." Karl smiled a quick thank-you at the cleric. "There's two sides to the problem: the Joiners and Khoral's emissary. We've got to pry enough votes away from the former to make sure you stay in office, while letting the latter know that Therranj is better off with us as a friendly neighbor than they would be if they decide to get nasty. So . . ."

"So?"

"So, trust me."

The dwarf sat silently for a moment. "Done."

Karl picked up the handbell from the table and rang it. Footsteps sounded on the stairs; Ihryk stepped into the room.

"Hell, Ihryk. I didn't know you were working." Ihryk worked part-time for Karl and Andy-Andy as a houseman, using the income to supplement his work on his own fields. He could have expanded his fields and supported himself and his family entirely by farming, but he seemed to like the variety almost as much as the pay.

"We finished planting my wheat two days ago; I start my tenday tonight."

"It's good to see you. How are things upstairs?"

"The children are fast asleep."

"Good. Aeia, why don't you say goodnight to everybody and let Ihryk tuck you in."

She frowned. "But Karl—"

"Enough of that," Karl said. "If you don't get enough sleep, the kids'll run you ragged tomorrow."

"Uh, Karl?" Andy-Andy raised a finger. "With all due

respect, buzz off. While you were on the road, Aeia and I decided that she's old enough to pick her own bedtime.''

"Right. Sorry, Aeia." Karl added another entry to his ever-lengthening list of things to do. He'd have to get Aeia married off. Not that he could force her into anything. God knew where she'd picked up that stubborn streak, but she had.

One way to do it might be to pick someone appropriate and forbid Aeia to see him. But who? Karl couldn't see turning her over to some ex-slave farmer who didn't know one end of a sword from another, but the idea of Aeia ending up as a warrior's widow didn't thrill him, either. Besides, Andy-Andy wouldn't stand for that.

Maybe an engineer. He'd have to talk to Riccetti, have Lou keep an eye out for someone who might be right for Aeia.

Well, I'm not going to solve that one tonight. Karl turned to Kirah. "It would be a shame to wake Janie. Why don't you let her spend the night here?"

It wasn't just that he liked having Janie around, although he did. Mainly, he was thinking of the morning; Jason thought of Jane Michele as a sort of younger sister who required a good example in order to stay out of trouble, and that tended to suppress Jason's natural inclinations to get himself into trouble.

She nodded.

"Good," he said, standing and stretching. "Sorry to interrupt the party, people, but I've had a long day, and I've got to turn in."

Andy-Andy rose. "Ahira, Lou, Thellaren, I'll give you enough time to get home before I start the rain."

Riccetti frowned. "Do you have to do it tonight?"

"I promised. Ihryk isn't the only one who's planted in the past few days; a good rain will give those fields a nice start." She smiled at Karl. "I'll help them all on their way. Why don't you go up and stretch out?"

He opened the door slowly. Karl stepped into Jason's room, moving quietly, softly, like a thief in the night.

Barely visible in the dim starlight that streamed in through the open window, the three children slept together, Mikyn's and Janie's bedding rumpled, but empty.

Janie was snoring, as usual. How a cute little girl like Jane Michele had developed such a snuffling snore was something that escaped Karl.

Mikyn huddled on his left side, curled into a fetal position, his breathing shallow, ragged, as though he didn't dare relax, not even in his sleep.

Maybe I let Alezyn off too lightly, Karl thought. Well, if so, that would be easy to fix. Then again, killing somebody just because he was a bastard was probably not the best way to handle things—the world was so damn full of bastards.

He had to chuckle at the way Jason slept between the other two children, stretched out flat on his back, one little arm thrown protectively around each of the other's shoulders.

Karl seated himself tailor-fashion next to the bed as the rain began, falling softly, a gentle benediction on the ground outside. He reached out and gently cupped the back of Jason's head with his hand. Jason's hair was fine, silky . . . and clean, for once.

Little one, he thought, *I don't see nearly enough of you.* That was one of the troubles with this damn business. It took Karl away from home too much, and left his nerves frazzled too much of the time that he was home. Normally, it wasn't as bad as it had been tonight; usually, the trip back gave him a chance to decompress. But riding Ellegon back had cut that time short. Too short.

Slowly, gently, Karl bent over and carefully kissed Jason on the top of his head. *Arta Myrdhyn,* he thought, *you're not going to get your hands on Jason. Not my son.*

He heard Andy-Andy's footsteps on the stairs, and waited to hear her walk to their room, and then, seeing that he wasn't there, turn around and look for him with the children.

She surprised him; she came directly to Jason's room. She stood in the doorway, the light of the hall lantern casting her face into shadow. A stray breeze touched the hem of her robes, swirling it around her ankles.

"Everything okay in here?" she whispered.

"Fine," he answered, rising. "Come take a look."

"No." She touched a finger to his lips. "You come with me." She blew out the hall lamp and led him down the hall to their room.

Wind whipped at the curtains, sending their hems fluttering over the bed. Andy-Andy pulled the covers aside.

"Well, well." He raised an eyebrow. "Andy, what do—"

"Shh." She shook her head slowly. "Don't say anything." She pulled her robes over her head, tossed them aside, and stood naked in front of him. "Your turn."

He returned her smile, pulled off his shirt, and stooped to unlace his sandals.

Ellegon's roar cut through the night. *. . . assassins,* his distant voice said. *With crossbows, dragonbane . . .*

Karl could barely hear the dragon. *Where?* he thought, trying to shout with his mind.

The mental voice cleared. *Better. Werthan's farm. They have taken the house, but they aren't planning on staying inside. I'll have to get closer to read them better.*

"You said they had dragonbane. Get the hell up in the sky. I want you on high sentry. Do not get within range of the bows. How many of them are there?" And what the hell was wrong with the wards? They should have picked up the assassins' healing draughts, even if they weren't carrying anything else magical.

They don't have any healing draughts—and dragonbane isn't magical. It just interferes with the magical parts of my metabolism.

Never mind that. How many of them are there?

Three. I couldn't get much out of their minds, but they're headed this way.

"*Ihryk!*" he shouted. "Unlock the guncase and get me two pistols. Move." He saw that Andy-Andy was already struggling back ino her clothes. "Chak! To me!"

He turned to his wife. "We'll play it just like a drill, beautiful," he said, forcing a calm voice to come out of his throat. "You get the children into the cellar."

Andy-Andy was capable of giving him a hard time, but not in this sort of situation; she dashed for Jason's room.

Karl ran to the top of the stairs. "U'len, bring the maids; I'll send the stableboy and Pendrill."

Until and unless he knew better, Karl was going to assume that the assassins were after him; the first thing to do was to see to the safety of his family and servants.

At the bottom of the stairs, Chak had already retrieved Karl's saber as well as his own falchion. He tossed the scabbarded sword up to Karl, then gave a quick salute with his falchion. "You have a better second in mind?"

Karl was about to answer, but a shout from outside interrupted him.

"Karl! It's Ahira. I have Lou and Kirah with me."

Karl ran down the stairs and swung the door open. The three of them were half naked, although Ahira had his battleaxe clutched firmly in his hands.

"Get in here—*move it*. Kirah, help Andy get the kids to the cellar. Ahira and Lou, get down there. Chak, you go with them. I'm going to take Tennetty, if she's available, or go it alone."

"But—"

"My family comes first. I'm counting on you and Ahira to keep them safe for me. I need to worry about my own neck."

Chak opened his mouth to protest, then shrugged. "Yes, Karl. Nobody will get past me."

The dwarf nodded grimly. "Understood." Handing his battleaxe to Chak, he helped Andy and Kirah usher the three sleepy-eyed children down the stairs to the basement.

Karl paused to think. Reinforcements, that was the first order of business, but the New House was between where Ellegon reported the assassins were and where Daven's encampment was. Not good.

Ellegon—where's Tennetty?

She'll be outside in a moment. She plans on having Carrot saddled for you.

"Good. I want Daven's team surrounding this house. Light bonfires. Nothing and *nobody* gets inside until you sound the all-clear."

On my way. The dragon's mental voice began to fade in the distance.

"*Wait*—this all could be a feint. After you alert Daven, I want you to fly a spiral search pattern."

Over the whole valley? That will take—

"Just do it. Then back to high sentry over the assassins, but not until you're sure that we're clear."

I believe that the three of them are alone—

Ellegon—

But I hear and obey. Luck.

Ihryk arrived with two pistols from the downstairs weapons case, plus a beltpack containing powder, bullets, and swatches for bullet patches.

Karl nodded his thanks as he belted on his saber, tucking the pistols in his belt. He'd better get outside immediately and let his eyes begin to adjust to the dark. He glanced down at his naked chest, drawstring jeans, and open-toed sandals. Not a good idea. His scabbarded sword in his hand, he ran for the door and up the stairs to his bedroom.

He stripped quickly in the dim light of the overhead glowsteel, then dressed himself in black suede trousers and a black wool shirt, drew a black wool half-hood over his head, pulled on his steel-toed boots, belted on his sword, and ran down the stairs.

The barn was less than a hundred yards from the New House; Pirate, Tennetty's usual mount, stood properly ground-hitched in the light drizzle.

Despite everything, he almost laughed. Pirate was a snow-white mare, her sole marking a black patch over right eye—sort of a horsy equivalent of Tennetty, although Pirate's patch was only a marking.

He stepped inside the barn. Assisted by sleepy-eyed Pendrill and the stableboy, Tennetty had already bridled Carrot and slipped a horse blanket onto the chestnut mare's back.

Karl jerked his thumb toward the house. "Both of you, get into the cellar, and tell Ahira I said to bar the door. *Run.*"

As Pendrill and the stableboy exited the barn at a trot, Karl took his western-style saddle down from the rail and saddled Carrot, matching his strength against the mare's as he pulled the cinch tight, then tucked the pistols into the top of his pants before he slipped his scabbarded sword into the boot and lashed it into place.

He felt very much alone. There were three of the others, and unless he wanted to wait for reinforcements, it would be only him and Tennetty facing them. Not that he despised Tennetty's or his own skills, but three against two was not good odds, not when the three could be waiting in the bushes for the two. Too bad Slovotsky wasn't here; this was definitely Walter's sort of party.

"Chak?" she asked.

"With the family."

"Good." Tennetty nodded. "I wish Slovotsky were here," she said, as though she were reading Karl's mind. "Do we wait and pick up some of Daven's crew?"

HIs first inclination was to say no, but he caught himself. "What do you think?"

She shook her head as he led Carrot out of the barn and onto the dirt of the yard. "I don't like working with new people. Daven's may be good, but we're not used to them. And in the dark? They'd just as likely shoot us as them. Besides," she said, patting her saddlebags, "if any of Werthan's family are still alive, they might need some healing draughts, and soon. I say go."

He pulled himself to Carrot's back and settled the reins in his left fist. "We go." He dug in his heels; Carrot cantered over to the back porch, where Ihryk stood, waving at him.

"Karl, you said to get into the cellar, but—"

"Your family." Karl nodded. "If Ahira can't handle things here, you won't matter much. Take one of the horses."

Tennetty kicked Pirate into a full gallop; Karl spurred Carrot to follow.

The east road led directly toward Werthan's farm; they galloped side by side down the muddy road, the drizzle soaking them down to the skin, rain and wind whispering through the cornfields.

No, he thought. This didn't make sense. An ambush wasn't a strategy Karl and his people had a patent on. If he was going to set up an ambush for someone moving between Werthan's farm and the New House, he'd set it up along the road. No guarantee that the assassins weren't at least that minimally clever.

"Wait," he called out, pulling Carrot to a halt. He wiped the rain from his face and shook his head to clear the water from his hair.

Tennetty braked Pirate fifteen yards ahead, then waited for him to catch up.

"We can't stay on the road—we're too vulnerable. This way." He urged Carrot off the road and into the fields, Tennetty following. It would slow them down; the horses couldn't move as quickly between the rows of corn and

across the wheat fields as they could on the road. But galloping full-speed into a hail of crossbow bolts would slow them
down even more.

Less than fifteen minutes later, they were within sight of
Werthan's one-room farmhouse.

Light still burned through the greased-parchment windows,
but everything was deathly still. Even the normal night sounds
were gone; all Karl could hear was the panting of the two
horses and the thudding of his own heart.

He vaulted from Carrot's back, landing clumsily on the
soft, wet ground.

Tennetty dismounted next to him. "Do you think they're
still inside?" she asked in a low whisper. "Damn silly way to
run an assassination."

"It won't be so damn silly if you and I are stupid enough
to knock on the door and walk in. No chances; we'll assume
they're inside, maybe with one hidden outside, on guard."

"And if that's not the way it is?"

"If they're not, we'll work out what to do next. Right now
I want your cooperation, not your temperament."

He untied his scabbard and slipped it out of the saddle
boot. "Keep your blade sheathed—got to watch out for light
flashes." He'd hold his scabbarded sword in his left hand, a
pistol in his right. If necessary, he could fire the pistol, drop
it, then draw his sword in little more than a second, tossing
the scabbard aside. Much faster than the time it would take to
draw a sword by reaching across his waist.

Tennetty went to Pirate and took saddlebags down. She
slung them over her shoulder, lashing them tightly against her
chest with leather thongs.

Karl dropped Carrot's reins carefully to the ground and
stepped on them. "Stay, girl," he said, then beckoned at
Tennetty to follow as he walked away in a half-stoop, dropping to his belly and crawling when he reached the edge of
the fields.

They worked their way around to the back of the house,
and waited there, crouched silently on the hard dirt, listening.

Werthan didn't have a proper barn, just a smaller shack
that served as a toolshed and chicken coop. Whatever had
happened in the house hadn't left the chickens awake.

Tennetty pressed her lips against his ear. "Do you know the layout inside?"

"No. Do you?"

She shook her head. "Sorry."

"Then I'll take it." He handed her both of his pistols and slipped his saber from his scabbard, laying the scabbard gently on the ground. In the cramped quarters of the shack, a sword would be a better weapon than a pistol. The pistols would be more useful in Tennetty's hands.

"Work your way around to the front, then make some noise—nothing too obvious. I'll move when you do. If I need your help, I'll call out—otherwise, stay outside. But if I kick anyone out the front door or window, he's yours."

She nodded and started to rise.

He grasped her shoulder. "Watch your back—they may not be inside."

Tennetty shook his hand off. "You do your job, I'll do mine."

Karl stood next to the rear window, waiting. The shack could easily be a trap, but so what? Let it; let the trappers become the trapped.

Tennetty was taking her own sweet time. She should be making some—

Crack!

The snap of a twig sent him into action; he kicked open the rear door and then moved to one side and dove through the greased-parchment window.

He landed on his shoulder on the dirt floor and bounced to his feet, his sword at the ready.

All his precautions were unnecessary. Nobody was in the shack.

Nobody living. The room stank of death.

Karl forced himself to look at the three bodies clinically. Werthan lay on his back, staring blindly at the ceiling, the fletching of a crossbow bolt projecting from the left side of his chest. His wife and daughter lay on their sides, their limbs and clothing in disarray, the pools of blood from their slit throats already congealing on the floor.

It wasn't hard to reconstruct what had happened. Werthan must have heard a noise outside and gone to investigate, expecting that perhaps a weasel had gotten in with the chickens. The assassins had killed him, then murdered his wife and daughter to prevent them from raising an alarm. Scratches on Werthan's heels showed that they had dragged him inside the shack.

He couldn't bear to look closely at the little girl. She was only about three.

I won't let myself get angry, he thought, willing his pulse to stop pounding in his ears, failing thoroughly. *Anger leads to reaction, not thought. My anger is their ally, not mine. I won't be angry.*

"Tennetty," he said quietly. "I'm coming out." He walked to the front door, opened it, and stepped through, closing it gently behind him. The rain had stopped; the damp night air clung to him.

"Well?"

"Dead. Werthan, his wife, and his daughter."

I have them pinpointed, Karl.

He tilted his head back. High in the sky, Ellegon's dark form slid across the stars. "Where are the bastards?"

Alongside the road, a quarter-mile from here, just beyond that old oak.

Karl nodded. He could barely see the tree in the dark.

They've spotted the glow from the bonfires around the New House and are trying to decide what to do next. The leader suspects that somebody may have raised an alarm, but he isn't sure. And they are *after you, in case you were curious. You ought—*

"Weapons?"

Two crossbows, plus swords, knives. Karl, I can get one of Daven's squads, and—

"No." He stuck two fingers in his mouth and whistled. "They're mine."

"What are you whistling for?" Her eyes wide, Tennetty snatched his hand away from his mouth. "They're not that far away; they'll hear you."

"That's the idea." He pulled off his shirt. "And they'll see me, too." He raised his voice. "*Did you hear that? Can you hear me?*"

No answer.

"You're crazy, Karl, we can't—"

"*No.*" He stopped the back of his hand a scant inch from her face. "They're all mine," he said quietly. "Each and every one."

"At least take your pistols—"

"No." He shook his head slowly. "I want to feel them die. I want—" He stopped himself. *Save the feeling for later. When they're dead.*

He raised his sword over his head and waved it as he ran down the road toward the old oak.

"My name is Karl Cullinane," he shouted. "I've heard you're looking for me, you bastards. I'm waiting for you. If you want me, come and get me."

As he neared the tree, a dark shape rose between two rows of cornstalks; Karl hit the ground and rolled as a bolt whizzed overhead.

Karl sprinted for the man. But the assassin didn't simply wait for him; he ducked back down in the corn and ran. He was in too much of a hurry. Karl could plot his progress by the rustling of the stalks. He leaped through a row of corn and crashed into the assassin, both his sword and the assassin's crossbow tumbling away somewhere into the night.

It didn't matter; he was half Karl's size. As they rolled around on the ground, Karl kneed the other in the crotch, then slammed the edge of his hand down on the assassin's throat, crumpling his windpipe.

The assassin lurched away, gagging with a liquid awfulness as he died.

One down.

Karl rolled a few feet away before rising to a crouch and looking around, the skin over his ears tightening.

Nothing. No sound. The other two weren't stupid enough to flail around in the cornfield in a panic.

And Karl was unarmed, his sword lost somewhere in the darkness.

Not good. He regretted his stupidity in charging blindly into the field and ordering Tennetty to stay away, but there was nothing he could do about it now. If he raised a voice to call for help, all that would do would be to pinpoint his position for the two remaining assassins, one of them still armed with a crossbow.

Then again, you might want to use me, no?

Right. I'm missing two—where's the nearest one?

For a moment, Karl felt as though distant fingers stroked his brain.

I can't go deep enough, not without getting closer. I can't tell which way you're facing. Where is the bonfire in relation to you?

Karl raised his head momentarily above the cornstalks. Down the road, a distant glow proclaimed that the bonfires surrounding the New House were still going.

Got it. The one with the crossbow is two rows behind you, just about halfway between you and the road. But he's looking in your direction, and you're not going to be able sneak up on him.

And the other one?

You're not going to like this. He's running alongside the road, about halfway between here and the New House. No crossbow, but he's carrying more throwing knives than Walter does, and I think one or two of them may be dragonbane-tipped.

He's Tennetty's—you spot for her. I'll take care of things here.

The dragon swooped low over the cornfields toward the house.

Karl cursed himself silently. His temper could yet be the death of him. Kill the slavers—hell, yes—but letting his anger instead of his intellect control the means was something that he should have outgrown.

The first thing to do was to find his sword.

He searched around the soft ground, finding nothing but weeds and dirt. Come daylight, finding it would be no problem, but daylight was hours away.

Let's test his nerve a bit. Karl lifted a dirtclod and pitched it off into the night, aiming roughly where Ellegon had said the assassin was.

It whipped through the cornstalks, and then . . .

Silence. Nothing, dammit. This one knew his business; if he'd fired blindly, Karl would have been able to attack before he reloaded his crossbow.

On the other hand . . .

Karl walked back to the dead assassin and relieved the man of his beltknife. Not a bad weapon; it was a full-sized dagger, with almost the heft of a Homemade bowie.

He hoisted the corpse to his shoulder, then walked opposite to where Ellegon had said the remaining assassin was and crashed through one row of cornstalks, propelling the body ahead of him through the next row.

The bowstring twanged.

Karl stepped through the stalks, the knife held out in front of him.

Kneeling on the ground, the slaver was using a beltclaw to pull back his bowstring.

"Greetings," Karl said.

CHAPTER SIX:

Mindprobe

He who has a thousand friends has not a friend to spare,
And he who has one enemy will meet him everywhere
      —Ali ibn-Abi-Talib

At the sound of a gunshot down the road, Karl spurred Carrot into a gallop.

Everything is under control, Ellegon said, momentarily probing deeply. *As I see it is for you.*

Sure. Fine. Three more innocents dead, their throats slit. Just fine.

He eased back on the reins; the horse settled into a gentle canter.

You take a lot on yourself, Karl Cullinane.

There was no answer to that; he didn't try to find one.

He rounded the bend. In the vague glow of the distant faerie lights, Ellegon stood over Tennetty and the prostrate corpse of the last assassin.

No—not a corpse. While Tennetty's shot had opened the assassin's belly nicely, the bastard's chest was still slowly moving up and down.

The dragon lowered his head.

"What's going on?"

"Shut up—Ellegon's busy." Tennetty turned to glare at Karl, her fingers fastened on the assassin's wrists. "It might be a good idea to find out what this one knows, if anything."

Too much pain. I can't get through.

"Damn." Tennetty spat as she pulled the bottle of healing draughts from her pouch and sprinkled a bit of the liquid on the assassin's wounds, then dribbled some more in his mouth. "I hate wasting this stuff." She raised her head. "How about a hand here?"

Tennetty had already frisked the assassin and relieved him of his knives and pouch. Karl gripped the assassin's right wrist and pressed it firmly against the ground while Tennetty did the same with his left.

Better. Shh—no. He's blocked too thoroughly. I can't go beyond his conscious mind.

She shrugged. "No problem." She picked up his knife and flicked the scabbard away.

The assassin's head started to stir; his eyes opened.

"Who sent you?" she asked. "Tell us, and you'll live."

The round-faced man clenched his jaw. "I tell you *nothing*." He struggled, uselessly.

"Thank you." She smiled as she set the knifepoint against the side of his face, just over the trigeminal nerve, barely breaking the skin.

Stop that, Tennetty. It was not necessary. Try another question, but don't distract him this time. He has to think of the answer for me to read it.

Karl shrugged. There was always the obvious question. "What do you know that you don't want us to? What are you hiding?"

"Ahrmin. He wants to know about Ahrmin."

Ahrmin? Karl almost lost his grip.

Ahrmin was dead in Melawei, burned in the *Warthog*.

Guess again. He hired these three in Enkiar less than a hundred days ago. They're not slavers, they're mercenaries . . . I've broken through, Karl. Give me another moment, and . . . I have it all. Ahrmin, Enkiar, the Healing Hand, everything.

The Hand?

It seems Ahrmin requires major reconstruction. I'll give you his face later. For now . . . stand back from him, and move away.

"No!" Tennetty drew her beltknife with her free hand. "He's my kill."

You will stand aside, Tennetty.

"Why?"

Ellegon's mental voice was calm, matter-of-fact. *You will stand aside, Tennetty, because the little girl's name was Anna. They called her Anna Minor, as Werthan's wife was Anna Major.

*You will stand aside because I had promised to teach her how to swim. And you will stand aside because she always called me Ehgon, because she couldn't manage the l-sound.

*And you will stand aside because this is the one that smiled down at her to quiet her as he opened her throat with his knife.

And if you don't understand any of that, you will stand aside, Tennetty, and you will do so now, because if you do not stand aside I will surely burn you down where you stand.

Tennetty moved away.

Gently, Ellegon picked up the struggling assassin in his mouth and leaped skyward, his mindvoice diminishing as he gained altitude and flew away. *There are balances in this world, Afbee. And while there is no justice, some of us do our best. I see you have a strong fear of falling. . . .*

"Karl? You want me to finish up here?"

"Can't. I lost my sword somewhere, and then there's—"

"I'll find it. You go home." Tennetty's face was wet. "Go."

Karl lay back in the huge bed, his head pillowed on his hands. Homecoming was supposed to be a joyous time, a passionate time for him and Andy-Andy. No matter what happened on the road, this was separate, different. Home.

But not tonight. He just couldn't—

"You're not sleeping," Andy-Andy whispered.

"I can't." His eyes were dry and aching. *You'd think, after all I've seen, after all I've done, it would get easier.* He patted her shoulder and slipped out of bed. "You've got school and some crops to deal with tomorrow—better get some sleep. Don't wait up."

"Karl—"

"Please."

*   *   *

Ahira was waiting in the hall. The dwarf was in full combat gear, his battleaxe unsheathed, his chair propped up against the door of Jason's room, his feet not reaching the floor.

Karl raised an eyebrow. "Trouble?" he asked in a whisper.

"Not at all," the dwarf answered him quietly, shaking his head. He cradled a clay bottle in the crook of his arm. "Everything's quiet. Chak and Ellegon are doing a search out over the plain, although I'm sure it won't turn up anything. It's just that . . ." He rubbed his hand down the front of his chainmail vest, then tinged his thumbnail against the axeblade. "Sometimes I forget what we're all about. I get caught up in the politics so much, sometimes . . ." He let his voice trail off, then smiled sadly. "Tomorrow, I've got to raise a burying party, to go out to Werthan's place and put him and his two Annas in the ground, and that hurts.

"But that's tomorrow." Ahira uncorked the bottle and took a sip, then offered Karl the bottle. "Tonight I'm going to drink a swallow or two of Riccetti's Best.

"But mainly, I'm going to sit here in my armor, with my axe at hand, and keep in my mind the simple fact that there are three children sleeping safely in that room there—two of whom I couldn't love more if they were blood of my blood and flesh of my flesh—and that nothing and nobody is getting past me to hurt them."

"Damn silly thing to do," Karl said, his eyes misting over.

"Isn't it, though? Mmm . . . you want me to find you a chair?"

"I can find my own chair."

CHAPTER SEVEN:

The Bat Cave

It is always good
When a man has two irons in the fire.
                —Francis Beaumont and John Fletcher

The best way, maybe the only way, to deal with the pain was to get to work, whether or not the work was pleasant. Riding into Engineer Territory at the north end of the valley was a mixture of the two; it was something Karl always enjoyed, the pleasure dimmed only by the awkward necessity of stopping to see Nehera when he did.

The weathered Erendra sign on the split-rail fence was unchanged; it translated to "Proceed further only with permission"; it was amply decorated with the glyph for danger.

Karl laughed. Riccetti had changed the English part of the sign again, or at least had had it changed.

> ### ENGINEER TERRITORY
> Louis Riccetti, Prop.
>
> Screw the rest—we work REAL magic here.

The smithy interrupted the miles of fence; huge doors like those of a barn stood on both sides of the line, although the eight half-sheds containing wood, charcoal, and iron stock were on the Engineers' side of the fence.

Nehera was a quasi-Engineer; his services and those of the

107

apprentice Engineers learning smithing from him were needed by everyone in the valley: There were always horses and oxen to be reshod, plow blades to be sharpened and straightened, nails to be drawn from thin nail stock, tools to be made and repaired, horsecollars forged, and so on.

Not all of his work was secret, nor did he do all of the secret work. While Nehera did virtually all of the barrel-making, the rest of the gunsmithing was done deeper in Engineer territory, in the two other smithies.

Better get it over with, Karl thought, as he dismounted from Carrot's broad back, then stepped on her reins for a moment, ignoring the hitching post in front of the smithy. *If Nehera hears that I had someone else do the work, I'll have to put up with more sniveling than usual.*

But dammit, why couldn't the dwarf be more like U'len? Just once, couldn't he snap at Karl, or tell him to go to hell?—anything that showed a bit of spine.

The civilian-side door was closed, indicating that something secret was going on inside. Karl walked toward the apprentice Engineer outside the guardhouse at the gate.

The boy was well trained. "Vhas!" he called out, bringing his rifle almost in line with Karl's chest. *Halt.* "Who goes there?"

Karl obediently halted, keeping his hands well away from his sides. "I am Karl Cullinane. Journeyman Engineer," he added, with a smile.

The boy nodded and smiled. "You are recognized, Journeyman Engineer Karl Cullinane, and welcome to Engineer Territory. I have a message for you from the Engineer: You are to join in the cave at your convenience."

"Thank you." *Might as well have some fun*, Karl thought. "Your name and orders, apprentice?"

"Journeyman!" The boy drew himself into a stiff brace. "I am Junior Apprentice Bast. My general orders are as follows:

"My first general order is: I am to remain at my post until properly relieved.

"My second general order is: I am to challenge anyone who approaches the fence or the gate, calling for them to halt as they do so.

"My third general order is: I am to allow no person to

cross through the gate or over the fence into Engineer Territory within my sight unless and until he has halted for my challenge, and I am satisfied that he is authorized to do so.

"My fourth general order is: Should any situation not covered by the first three general orders arise, I am to send my second for the senior apprentice of the guard."

"And what would you have done if I had advanced after your call to halt?"

The boy sobered. "I would have sent my second for the senior apprentice of the guard, Journeyman," he said, pointing his chin toward the guardhouse.

"What for, Bast?"

There were only two answers; the boy picked the right one.

"To haul away your dead body, Journeyman," he said with utter seriouness.

"Good." Fortunately, there had never been a case in which an innocent citizen had tried to cross the fence after being hailed. It was just as well; many Home citizens resented the Engineers' patent arrogance.

Karl vaulted the fence and walked into the smithy.

Nehera was busy at work at the forge, two apprentices working the bellows while the smith held the long-handled tongs, occasionally pulling them back to check the color of the work.

From where he stood, Karl couldn't be sure, but it looked as if Nehera might be working on another sword. Homemade blades weren't popular only with Home warriors; they were slowly becoming a major trade item. Nehera had taken Lou's and Karl's scant knowledge of how Japanese swords were made and added his own considerable knowledge of steelworking; the result was finer blades—lighter, stronger, better able to hold an edge without chipping—than could be found elsewhere.

As the dwarf pulled the bright-red iron out of the fire and spun on his peg, bringing it over to the blocky anvil, Karl's guess was verified: Nehera sprinkled a scant spoonful of carbon dust over the steel, then hammered the iron bar over double, the anvil ringing like a bell.

He stuck the dull-red bar back in the fire, then turned to splash water on his face.

As he shook his head to clear his eyes, he spotted Karl for the first time.

Here we go again.

"I crave pardon, master." Nehera dropped to his knee, his peg skittering out sideways at an awkward angle. "I did not see you."

Karl didn't bother to tell Nehera that he didn't have to go through this every damn time; the dwarf still didn't get it, couldn't get it. Somewhere, somehow, Nehera's spirit had been broken, beyond Karl's ability to repair it.

That was the pity of it all: Nehera couldn't understand that he wasn't property anymore. The deep scars that crisscrossed his face, back, arms, and chest showed that he had been hard to break; the peg that served as his right leg confirmed that he had once too often tried to run for his freedom.

"Rise, Nehera," Karl said. "You're forgiven, of course."

"I thank you, master." The dwarf's puppy-dog smile almost made Karl vomit.

Dammit, you don't have to kneel in front of me, you don't have to beg me for forgiveness for not kneeling immediately, and you sure as hell don't have to look at me like that for forgiving you for not cringing quickly enough.

But what was the use? He could, once again, explain to Nehera that he didn't have to do that—he could even make it a command—but neither explanations nor commands of that kind had any effect. Whether Karl liked it or not, Nehera felt that he belonged to Karl, and that this was the way a slave was supposed to act; he simply refused to comprehend orders to the contrary.

The strange thing was, there were actually people in the world who liked this sort of thing, who felt that some other person cringing in front of them was their right, and their pleasure.

At that thought, Karl's fists clenched.

Nehera's face blanched.

"No, no," Karl said, forcing a smile to his face, "it's not you. I was thinking about something else. How goes the work?"

"I work hard, master. I swear it." The dwarf snuck a sideways glance at the forge, caught himself, then gave the slightest shrug Karl had ever seen.

Karl raised a hand. "Please, don't let me interrupt. We can talk while you work. I wouldn't want you to ruin something."

"I obey." Nehera momentarily drew the steel out of the fire, then replaced it, gesturing at the apprentices to pump the bellows harder. He treated them with a distant sort of superiority. After all, though they were free men, Nehera's owner had put him in charge. "It will take some time, master. Is there something I can do for you?"

"Three things, actually." Karl unbelted his scabbard. "First, this edge needs a bit of touching up. Do you think you might be able to do that for me sometime today?"

"Immediately."

"No rush, Nehera. I have to visit the Engineer, and I'll hardly need a sword here."

"May I speak?"

"Of course."

"I humbly crave your pardon, master, but you should always carry a sword." He limped quickly to the wall and brought down a scabbarded saber, pulling it a few inches from the scabbard, then offering it to Karl. "If you would care to test the edge?" Nehera extended his arm.

"No. I'm sure that it's fine."

"But, master—"

"*No*, Nehera," Karl said, cursing himself immediately for raising his voice as the dwarf dropped to his knee again.

"I have offended you again, master. I am sorry."

Karl sighed. "Forgiven, Nehera. Rise."

The dwarf got back up with irritating speed. "You said that there were three things, master?"

You make my teeth itch, Nehera. "Yes. Number two: I know you'd rather work in steel, but I need a golden collar made—human size. You can melt down some Metreyll coin."

The dwarf bowed his head. "Yes, master. That will be done before the next time I sleep."

"No, it won't—take your time. But I do want it before the town meeting. There is one other thing, Nehera. I've been hearing stories about how you've been working yourself too hard. That is to stop. When you are too tired to work, you must rest."

"As you command, master."

Damn. Enough of this; I'm going to go see Riccetti.

*   *   *

Karl accepted the clay bottle and took a light swig, then washed down the fiery liquor with a long drink of water. "Thanks, Lou. I needed that."

Still, the whiskey didn't wash the bad taste out of Karl's mouth. Which was perhaps just as well. Life was full of bad tastes.

He sat back in his chair, enjoying the coolness of the cave.

Well, this section of the warrens wasn't a proper cave, but a relic of the long-ago dwarven inhabitants, driven away, so legend had it, by Therranji elves. But it looked like a cave, and that was what they called it.

Caves were supposed to be damp and musty places—and most of the caverns were—but Riccetti's quarters were different, almost homey.

Riccetti's apprentices had cleared out the dirt, all the way down to the bare rock. Then they had installed four wooden walls and built a massive oak door to block Riccetti's quarters off from the rest of the tunnel, chiseled the floor smooth, and then finally bored openings through the rock to the outside to allow both for airflow and for the pipe venting Riccetti's Franklin stove.

Glowsteels hung from pulleys set into the arching ceiling above, fitted with ropes and winches so that they could easily be lowered and removed for Andy-Andy to recharm.

It was very much a Lou Riccetti type of place: rows of wooden worktables stood along two of the four walls, well laden with bottles and vats of various and sundry preparations, steel pens, bottles of ink, and stacks of notes awaiting copying and filing by apprentices.

But it was Riccetti-type homey: the sleeping and socializing part of the room consisted only of a pile of bedding in a corner and two armchairs, now occupied by Karl and Lou.

"Try the beer," Riccetti said. "I think it's the best batch yet."

Karl set down the whiskey bottle, lifted his mug, and sipped at his beer, forcing himself not to make a face. Ahira was right: While Riccetti's corn whiskey was usually good, his beer was a crime.

"Drink up," Riccetti said, chuckling. "You're being awfully patient. It isn't like you."

"I'm not like me. Not today." There were things that a human being just couldn't get used to, not if he wanted to remain a human being.

Riccetti *tsk*ed. "I should give you hell, for once. You're the one who's always saying that instead of getting worked up over something you don't like, you should do something about it." He snickered. "Not that I've always been a fan of how you've handled things. But you usually do well enough."

Yeah, Lou? And how am I supposed to bring a murdered baby back to life? But he didn't say that. "Any progress on the slavers' powder? I know you'll need help from Andy and Thellaren, but—"

"Guess again." Riccetti smiled. "Nope. It's all done. I stayed up part of the night, doing a few simple experiments. I finally figured out how they were doing it this morning. I'm going to have Andrea check my results, but—"

"What? And we've been sitting here making idle chatter for—"

"Take it easy, Karl. I'm sorry. It's just that . . ." Riccetti's voice trailed off.

Karl nodded his understanding. It was lonely, constantly dealing with people who were subordinate to you, even when some of those people were friends. Riccetti rarely could make the time to visit Ahira or Andy-Andy at the south end of the valley; last night had been an exception. "Sorry. So, what is it? Some sort of explosive?"

"Nope." Riccetti set down his own beer mug and rose from his chair. "Just let me show off for a minute."

He walked to the worktable and took down a small glass vial and a stone bowl. "This is slaver powder." He uncorked the vial and tipped about a quarter-teaspoon into the bottom of the bowl. "And this," he said, taking down another vial, "is distilled water—about the only really pure substance I can make. Stand back a second." Riccetti tilted the bowl to point against the naked wall, then dribbled a careful drop of water onto the bowl's lip. "It'll take a moment for it to work its way down to—"

Whoosh! The backblast of heat beat against Karl's face.

"Just plain water did that? What the hell kind of compound—"

"No, idiot, it's not a compound, it's a mixture." Riccetti

poured more powder on a marble slab, then beckoned Karl to come closer. "Take a good look at this—and don't breathe on it; it's already sucked up some water from the air."

Karl looked closely. Mixed among the white powder were tiny blue flecks. "Copper sulfate?"

"Yup. Heat it up, and it becomes cupric sulfate—plain white. Add water—even let it pick up some from the air; it deliquesces nicely—and it sucks it right up; turns blue. Which is what it's in there for."

"Now, wait a minute. Copper sulfate isn't an explosive. You use it for—"

"—blueing rifles. Right. But in this, it's a stabilizer. It's there to absorb the water, and prevent the real stuff from being exposed to too much. Visualize this," Riccetti said, cupping his hands together. "You've got a hollow iron sphere, filled with water. Got that?"

"Yeah."

"Okay, now, heat it over a fire, a damn hot one. What happens?"

"The water starts to boil."

"Right. But since it can't escape?"

Karl shrugged. "If it gets too hot, it blows up, just like a pressure cooker does if it isn't vented right."

"Right." Riccetti frowned. "But what if you're cheating? What do you get if you're using some sort of spell to hold the iron sphere together?"

"Huh?"

Riccetti snorted. "Pretend that the sphere is absolutely, unconditionally unbreakable—doesn't break, doesn't bend, doesn't stretch, doesn't warp. Nothing. What does the water become?"

"Superheated steam?"

"Right—maybe even a plasma. Now, imagine that someone puts some sort of preservation spell on the contents of the sphere, forcing what's inside to remain as is. Let the sphere cool, remove the protection spell so you can cut it open, and what do you find inside?"

"Something that's very hot, but isn't." Karl's brow furrowed. "That doesn't make any sense. What would it be like?"

"This." Riccetti pursed his lips. "That's what they did, I think. Some sort of preservation spell, with a built-in hole: If the stuff gets in contact with too much water, the spell fails, and what do you have? You've got superheated steam—lightly salted with copper sulfate—which wants to expand, and fast.''

"And if the only direction to expand in is along the barrel of a gun—''

"—pushing a bullet ahead of it . . . you've got it. There's nothing special about the water that their guns use—doesn't have to be.''

Karl buried his face in his hands. "Then we're in for it. If they can do it—''

"Hang *on* for a second, Karl. You're not thinking it through. Look at the brighter side. These aren't easy spells. They're a hell of a lot more advanced than anything your wife can do—and she's not bad. They're even beyond what I used to do, way back when.''

"All of which means what?''

"I just build things.'' Riccetti shrugged. "That's your department. I can tell you that it takes a very heavy-duty wizard to do this, and that there aren't all that many of them, and that they won't work cheap. My guess is that this powder cost your slavers one hell of a lot of coin.

"Take it a step further. Even in Pandathaway, there aren't more than a handful of wizards capable of something this difficult.''

"So? Even, say, five or six of them, working full-time—''

"Never happen. I can tell you that from personal experience.'' Riccetti shook his head. "Magic is like cocaine, Karl, assuming you have the genes that let you work it in the first place. Anyone who does can handle a bit now and then, but everybody has his limits. Once you get beyond those limits, you're hooked. All you're interested in is learning more, getting more spells in your head. Drives you a bit crazy.''

That sounded familiar. That was the way Riccetti had been, back when he was Aristobulus, back when the seven of them were first transferred over to This Side. The only things that had mattered to Aristobolus were his spell books and his magic.

Come to think of it, it was reminiscent of the crazies who hung around the Ehvenor docks. *Being around Faerie too long drives some crazy,* Avair Ganness had said. Maybe it wasn't just Faerie—maybe it was magic itself.

"Now,'' Riccetti went on, "look at it from the point of

view of whoever got the Pandathaway wizards to make this stuff. It's going to be hard to pull the wizards away from their studies to do it, and it won't be possible to do that very often. This slaver powder is going to stay rare—unless they start producing it in Faerie.''

Karl nodded. ''That'd do it.''

''Damn straight. If the Faerie were to line up against us . . .'' He shrugged. ''You may as well worry about Grandmaster Lucius deciding to take us on, or somebody bringing an H-bomb over from the Other Side.'' He waved at the door. ''In any case, compare their production of this with our production of real gunpowder. You notice any shortages?''

''No.''

''Exactly.''

There was something Lou was missing about all of this; it hovered on the edge of Karl's mind.

Andy-Andy! ''But Andy—she's a wizard. She could—''

Riccetti threw his hands up in the air. ''Of course. Idiot. Do you want more beer or would you like a whiskey?''

''But—''

''Shh.'' Riccetti poured each of them more whiskey. ''Drink up. And for God's sake have a little faith in your wife.''

Karl sipped the whiskey. ''You've got a lot of respect for her, don't you?''

''Damn straight. You lucked out, Cullinane.'' Riccetti nodded. ''But, if you'll notice, she spends most of her time teaching school, and almost all the magic she does is agricultural, bug-killing, glowing steel, the occasional levitation when somebody runs across a boulder when trying to clear a new field. It's all baby stuff; she has almost no time to learn more.

''Hell, she only picked up the lightning spell this year. She hasn't had the chance to push herself as far along as Aristobulus did. And in my opinion, deep down she's even more strong-minded than . . . he was.'' He shook his head. ''Relax. In order for her to push her skills to the addiction point, she'll have to have years of leisure time—just as Pandathaway wizards do.''

Or as Arta Myrdhyn must have had, at some point. He was a wizard powerful enough to turn the forests of Elrood into the Waste, to charm a sword to protect its bearer against magic, then set up a watch-charm to hold it for its proper user.

Not my son, bastard. Karl shook his head to clear it. No more time to waste, not with Riccetti having figured out what the slaver powder was. The question was, what was going to happen in Enkiar? And how were Ahrmin and the Slavers' Guild connected with the powder?

Riccetti cleared his throat. "If you don't mind, I have to get back to work. I've got a few things going, and I'd better go chew out that idiot apprentice who tried a quarter-charge of powder in a new rifle. *Quarter*-charge—I told him to use a quadruple charge, but his English isn't as good as it's supposed to be."

Karl shrugged. "Quarter charge? What's the problem?"

"He hung the bullet, that's what the goddamn problem is. He has to take the lock off the gun and the barrel off the stock, then clamp down the barrel and unscrew the breech plug—and then shove the damn thing out with a rod—" Riccetti caught himself. "But I was forgetting!" he said, brightening. "Got a present for you."

He walked to one of the shelves and pulled down a plain wooden box, holding it carefully but proudly as he opened it.

Inside were six iron eggs, a seam running across their equators, each with a small fuse protruding from the top.

"Grenades?"

"Yup. They break up nice—jagged pieces, about the size of a dime. Cast iron does that." Riccetti took one out of the box and held it up, flicking a bitten fingernail against the three-inch fuse. "Slow fuse, burns for just about five seconds. Then, *whoom*. Use them a bit sparingly, eh? They each contain enough powder for a signal rocket." Riccetti closed the box and fastened the lid.

There was a rap on the door.

"Enter," Riccetti said.

A teenage apprentice opened the door and stepped inside. "Message from the Mayor, Engineer: The emissary from Lord Khoral has arrived, and seeks an audience with Journeyman Karl Cullinane. The Therranji are camped just outside the customs station."

Karl sighed. "Back to work. Both of us."

"See you before the town meeting tomorrow?"

"Probably not. Can I count on you, anyway?"

"Always, Karl. Always."

CHAPTER EIGHT:

An Acquaintance Renewed

Slaves cannot breathe in England; if their lungs
Receive our air, that moment they are free!
They touch our country, and their shackles fall.
— William Cowper

"I don't like it. Don't like it at all." Daven shook his head, his hairless scalp shining in the sunlight. He was probably the most battered human being Karl had ever seen. His left eye was covered by a patch; half of that ear and three fingers of his right hand were missing. Long scars ran down his face and neck, vanishing into his tunic.

"Your opinion wasn't asked, Daven," Chak said.

"Be still, Chak." Karl shook his head and switched to English. "Don't irritate him, understood?"

"Yes, Karl." Sitting astride his gray gelding, Chak glared down at Daven. It was possible that he naturally had little liking for Daven, but more likely Karl's own distaste was infectious.

Karl didn't particularly like the former Nyph mercenary, not the way he enjoyed the company of Aveneer, the third raiding-team leader.

Still, Karl had to admit that Daven had a certain something. A year or so back, after a raid on a slaver caravan, one of Daven's men had gotten the bright idea of selling some slaves instead of freeing them. Daven hadn't returned Home for advice or instructions; he had hunted the bastard down himself and brought the charred bones back.

"The Mayor agreed to allow an emissary," Daven went on as though Chak weren't there, "but they've sent more than two hundred—and I wouldn't swear on my life that the only soldiers among them are the fifty wearing armor."

"Can't blame them," Karl said, fitting his boot into Carrot's stirrup and pulling himself up to the saddle. "There've been enough slaving raids into Therranj; traveling without military escort would be asking for trouble."

Daven smiled. "So why are we here?" He gestured at the log cabin that was officially Home's customs station, and the grassy slope below the cabin, where fifty warriors from his team waited, guns loaded and horses saddled.

"Because I don't like to take chances."

"No, not you." A snort. "I believe that. How many of my men do you want to take with you?"

"None. You're here for show. Period. I'm just going over to chat. I don't care what you hear, all of you stay here until and unless I send for you." Karl jerked his thumb skyward. "Ellegon covers me on this." He pulled on the reins and turned Carrot away, Chak following on his gelding.

Daven shrugged. "You have all the fun." His laugh followed Karl and Chak over the rise.

The Therranji had camped on the plain, almost a mile from the ridge that overlooked the valley. Khoral's emissary traveled in style; the encampment reminded Karl of an old-time circus, the several dozen tents ranging in size from three barely larger than a typical Boy Scout Voyageur to a mammoth red-and-white silk one that could almost have served P.T. Barnum as a big top.

Near the entrance to the main tent, a team of cooks attended to a side of beef, turning it slowly over a low fire. The wind brought the scent to him; it smelled absolutely wonderful.

Mounted elven soldiers in chainmail and iron helmets patrolled the perimeter. Three of them approached Karl and Chak as they rode toward the camp.

Don't make any unnecessary enemies.

Karl looked up. High overhead, Ellegon circled.

"Since when do I go around making enemies unnecessarily?"

Chak laughed. "How about the time you drew on Baron

Furnael? That could have turned bloody. Or when you beat Ohlmin—''

"Enough. It was necessary, or I wouldn't have done it."

That's what they all say.

Karl ignored the jibe. *Tell me, Kreskin, what are the elves up to?*

My name is Ellegon. And they're all shielded. Sorry. But you might want to get on with this; your wife is already inside—

What?

—with Tennetty to keep her company. Not my idea, Karl; I told her you wouldn't like it.

Karl quelled the urge to spur Carrot past the horsemen, then forced himself to pull her gently to a halt. This was a time for negotiation, not violence.

Just keep it that way. I can recall a time or two that you've turned—

Enough. Don't you ever forget anything?

Nope. Just think of me as a many-tonned conscience. A gout of fire roared through the sky.

Chak shook his head. "I don't like it."

"Neither do I." Karl bit his lower lip for a moment. "When we dismount, hand the nearest elf your falchion—don't wait for him to ask—then go inside, quietly. When I call for you, I want you and Tennetty to bring Andy out. Move slowly, but get her on a horse and over the hill."

"And what will you be doing?"

"That all depends on them. But I don't want any potential hostages clogging the negotiations." Karl wound his reins around his saddle horn and folded his arms over his chest. He didn't even have a pistol with him; SOP was to avoid letting any foreigner see guns, although he had made several exceptions to that rule in his time.

"Greetings," the foremost of the soldiers said, in an airy voice. In full armor and padding, he looked almost fully fleshed, if exceedingly tall; elves always looked like regular people, stretched lengthwise in a funhouse mirror. But the appearance of fragility was deceptive; pound for pound, elves were stronger than humans. "You are the human called Karl Cullinane?"

I'm called Karl Cullinane because that's my name—and what do I look like, a dwarf?

Temper, temper.

"Yes, I am Karl Cullinane."

"You are expected. You and your servant will follow me."

I just might have to teach you how to say please, but this isn't the time—not quite yet. Karl unwound his reins and nudged Carrot into a walk. The speaker took the lead, while the other two rode beside Karl and Chak.

Can I trust you to keep out of trouble for a while? I have a patrol to fly, and I've got to see that Aveneer's supplies are packed.

Go ahead.

I'll be back. The dragon wheeled across the sky and flew away.

The soldiers led them toward the large tent, then stopped their own horses, waiting for Karl and Chak to dismount first.

Nodding at Chak to copy him, Karl levered himself out of the saddle.

While Chak surrendered his sword to the elven armsman and was ushered inside, Karl dug into his saddlebag and removed a carrot for Carrot. He slipped her bit, dropped the reins to the ground, then stepped on them before feeding it to her, running his hand down her neck. "Good girl."

The soldier cleared his throat. "They are this way."

Karl turned and started to follow him into the tent; one of the other soldiers reached out a hand and grasped Karl's arm.

"I'll have your sword, human."

Karl didn't answer. *On the other hand, maybe this* is *the time to teach you some manners.*

He looked down at his arm, then up into the elf's eyes, and smiled. He had put a lot of practice into that smile over the years; it was intended to frighten, to suggest that the bared teeth were going to be sunk into a throat.

The elf dropped his hand. "I will need to take your sword before you enter," he said, his voice a touch less arrogant.

"Guess again." Moving slowly, Karl walked back to Carrot and tied her reins around the saddle horn, then let her nuzzle his face for a moment before turning her around and slapping her rump. "Go home, Carrot. Git!"

He turned back. The three soldiers had been joined by six others; mounted troops were gathering around.

Good.

"Why did you do that?"

"I don't want my horse to get hurt." He raised his voice. "Chak!"

"Yes, Karl," came the distant answer.

"Get Andrea out of there."

"Understood."

I'd damn well better be doing this right, he thought. He turned back to the elf who had demanded his sword. "Now, you were going to try to take my sword away from me?" He stuck his fingers in his mouth and whistled, beckoning to all the elven soldiers in the area.

He drew himself up straight, resting his right hand on the hilt of his sword. "Listen carefully, all of you. This . . . person—what's your name?"

No answer.

"I asked your name!"

"Jherant ip Therranj, personal armsman to—"

"I didn't ask your rank." Karl sneered. "I'm not interested. Now," he said, addressing the rest, "Jherant here wants my sword. He didn't ask politely; he demanded it.

"I don't think he's good enough to take it." Karl smiled again. "Little Jherant here doesn't look quite sturdy enough." He looked from face to face as he gripped the sharkskin hilt. "Which of you wants to help him?"

An elf dismounted and tossed his helmet aside. "I will, human," he said, pronouncing the word like a curse. The elf nodded to another, who began to circle around behind Karl. Karl heard a distant whisk of steel on leather as the elf drew a dagger.

"Good," Karl said. He pointed to another. "You, too. And you, and you, and you. We're going to play a little game now. What we're going to do is to see how many of you have to die because Jherant hasn't learned a little bit of elementary politeness. I'm willing to bet my life that it's all of you." He looked Jherant straight in the eye. "But don't go away. You're going to be first. Even if your friend at my back closes—"

Karl kicked back, catching the elf in the solar plexus. As

the air whooshed from the elf's lungs, Karl reached up and twisted, relieving him of the dagger, then dropping it point-first into the ground.

Karl lifted the gasping elf in his arms and handed him to the nearest of his companions. "Next?"

Jherant paled. This was ridiculous—one human against more than a dozen elven soldiers?

Slowly, Karl drew his sword, then raised it in a salute. Three of the elves copied him, while others moved away, also drawing their weapons.

He stood, waiting.

Tension hung in the air like taut wires. His sword in his right hand, Karl crooked his fingers and beckoned to Jherant. "Come here. You wanted my sword—here it is."

Another elf snickered and nudged Jherant from behind. White-faced, he drew his sword—

"What goes on here?" a firm contralto demanded. The tent flap was pushed aside and a woman walked out, blinking against the bright sunlight.

She was something from a dream: tall, slim, and fine-boned, her long hair so blond it was almost transparent. Her features were delicate; most beautiful human women would have looked gross and crude standing beside her.

She looked down at the nearest of the soldiers and frowned. "What goes on here?" she asked again.

The elf ducked his head. "Your pardon, Lady. This . . . human wants to fight with us."

She looked over at Karl, one eyebrow raised. "Is this so?"

"Not necessarily. I just want to kill the ones without any manners. Improve the breed a bit for you. I might have given this idiot my sword if he'd asked politely, but he demanded it."

"You're Karl Cullinane, I take it." Her lips twitched. "I see that the stories are true. You'd take on all of my soldiers, hoping to hold out until your reinforcements arrived?"

"You don't know my husband, Lady Dhara," Andy-Andy said, as she pushed through the tent flaps and stood beside the elf woman, Tennetty and Chak to either side of her. "I don't think he's waiting for reinforcements."

"Now," Karl said quietly, "get Andy out of here. No reinforcements. Tell Daven."

Tennetty nodded and pulled at Andy-Andy's arm.

One of the soldiers reached out a hesitant arm as though to bar them; Chak grabbed, twisted the elf's arm up and behind his back, then booted him away, snatching the sword out of his scabbard as he fell on his face.

A thin smile crossing her face, Tennetty's hand snaked out and seized another elf by the trachea. Not daring to move for fear that she would rip his throat out, the elf stood there as she quickly unbuckled his swordbelt and let it drop to the ground. Looking him straight in the eye, Tennetty suddenly snapped her knee into his groin, then stooped to retrieve the scabbard. She turned around, her newly acquired sword held easily in her hand.

Nobody else moved.

"Sorry, Karl," Tennetty said. "I gave them my sword. Andrea said there was to be no trouble."

Dhara eyed Karl. "I take it that you have other ideas."

"Perhaps, Lady. It all depends on you. I've been told that you've come here to negotiate. Would you rather do it with words, or with swords?"

"Words," she said. "Definitely words." She gestured at Jherant. "You are dismissed from my service," she said, before turning to another elf. "Captain, have that fool stripped of his weapons and driven away. Karl Cullinane may keep his sword. Anyone who is discourteous to him will answer to me. If he survives." She gestured toward the tent flap. "Karl Cullinane. If you, your wife, and your two friends would be kind enough to join me?"

Karl sheathed his sword. "Delighted, Lady. After you."

You were taking a big chance.

Karl sipped at his wine. *It would have been more of a chance not to.*

You can explain that later.

"Your eyes look . . . distant, Karl Cullinane," Dhara said, reclining on the opposite couch. She held out her own wineglass for a refill.

"Just talking to the dragon." He jerked his thumb skyward. "No offense intended."

Dhara chuckled. "In your world, politeness must be much more important than it is thought to be here." She wetted a slim finger and ran it around the rim of her glass, enjoying the clear, ringing tone. "Although I must confess that I wonder how serious you were. Mmmm . . . 'No offense intended'—is that the correct phrase?"

Andy-Andy shook her head gravely. "Lady, I wish you wouldn't do that. You weren't around when he declared war on the Slavers' Guild single-handedly. I was."

From Andrea: "I could back your play better if I knew what it was." She's not thrilled with you, Karl.

Tell her I'll thrill her later. "If you'd care to find out just how serious I was, Lady, it could be arranged."

Chak sighed and got slowly, painfully to his feet. "Here we go again."

"Hold on for a moment." Tennetty drained her glass. "Can I get in on this? You always get all the fun." She tested the blade of her newly acquired sword with her thumb. "I've heard dull blades are good for cutting cheese—how's yours?"

"Another cheese cutter." Chak shook his head. "Maybe Nehera can put a decent edge on it."

From Tennetty: "You're absolutely insane, you know."

"Don't bet against Karl Cullinane, Lady Dhara," Tennetty said. "The odds are too long."

"You think he could take on my fifty soldiers? Even with your help?"

"I didn't think that was the issue. You're an emissary from Lord Khoral, and one of your men challenged Karl—doesn't that make the question whether or not Karl is going to declare war on Therranj itself?"

Dhara paled. "Are you—" She caught herself. "I find myself in an awkward position. Lord Khoral sent me to negotiate your incorporation into Therranj. I seem to find myself having to negotiate a peace treaty instead."

From Andy-Andy: "I see a method in your madness, but there's still too damn much madness in your method."

Thanks. "Sit down, Chak. Frankly, I'd rather not get involved in a war with Therranj," he said to Dhara, trying to sound as though he were considering the subject casually.

I get it. I don't like it, but I get it. If you can create the slightest doubt in her mind that Therranj couldn't take on you alone, then she's not going to have any trouble swallowing the idea that leaving Home alone is the best move—assuming that she can't get you to join up.

Right. And we've made that point. The threat is patent nonsense—

Which only makes it better.

Exactly. 'Legend' is another word for 'nonsense.' She's not sure that she believes any of this, but there have been too many stories about me being passed around, growing in the telling. Last time I heard about how I took on Ohlmin, Slovotsky wasn't in on it, and Ohlmin had a hundred men, not eight. The rest of this is just pro forma; I've made the point.

And if she had called your bluff?

Karl didn't answer. There wasn't a real answer. Years ago, it had become clear that he wasn't likely to die of old age. His situation wasn't like that of an Other Side soldier in a normal sort of war; Karl had enlisted for the duration, and the duration was sure to be longer than even his natural lifespan.

If this was where he was going to die, that was the way it would have to be. Chak and Tennetty would have been able to get Andy-Andy out in the confusion, and that would have had to be enough.

Well, as long as you don't believe your own bullshit . . .

You so sure it's bullshit?

Yup. And you are, too. Now, stop sweating and start negotiating.

The elf woman beckoned another servitor to refill their glasses. "Now, where were we?"

Karl smiled back at her. "We were discussing peace between Therranj and Home. Sounds like a good idea to me—as it should to you."

"I thought the issue was to be the incorporation of the Valley of Varnath into Therranj proper. That is its proper name, you know."

"Not anymore." Karl shrugged. "Look. We're going to have a town meeting on the question of joining Therranj. The majority will decide—"

Tennetty interrupted him with a loud snicker. "Karl's always thought that counting noses means something "

Dhara raised an eyebrow. "And you don't?"

She laughed. "Of course not. But my opinion doesn't matter—it's my loyalty that does."

"Enough," Karl said. "As I was saying, I'm voting against. I think Ahira is going to stay in office, and Home is going to stay independent. But that doesn't mean that we can't continue to trade with you. We have things you want: Riccetti's horsecollars, better plows than you're used to, finer blades—"

"Guns. And gunpowder. We want your Lou Riccetti to produce them for us."

"—and we also produce a food surplus, each and every year. That doesn't amount to much yet, but we're still growing. And as far as the guns go," he said with a shrug, "those are our secret, and are going to stay that way for the foreseeable future."

"Really?" She raised an eyebrow. "I've heard otherwise."

I don't like this, Karl.

Neither do I. Has anyone been talking about the slaver powder and guns?

Negative. Ellegon made it a blanket statement of fact.

"As a matter of fact," Dhara went on, "there have been guns operating in the war between Bieme and Holtun. I have it on good authority that the Biemish reverses have been due to the Holts' having some."

I haven't heard anything about this. Pry for more information.

"I'd have to doubt that, Lady. Your sources must be mistaken. We haven't taken sides in the war—"

"Nevertheless, there have been guns. You would like witnesses?"

At Karl's nod, Dhara snapped her fingers. "Bring them in."

Elven soldiers brought three humans into the tent, guarding them closely.

"Thinking that you might demand reliable witnesses, I couldn't resist buying these, when I ran across them in a Metreyll market. Which is somewhat ironic; it seems that they were originally headed to Metreyll, although not to become slaves. They were captured by mercenaries employed by Holtun—mercenaries who used guns to kill their bodyguards."

Karl started to speak, but as the three were led in, his

words caught in his throat. He didn't recognize the adult man, but both the woman and the boy were familiar.

"*Rahff!*" Karl leaped to his feet. "How? I saw you die—"

"Karl!" Chak caught his arm. "It's not him."

No, it wasn't Rahff. Rahff had died in Melawei, protecting Aeia. If Rahff had lived, he would have been older than this boy. If Rahff had lived . . . but he hadn't.

And then there was the woman. White streaks had invaded the black of her hair, but the high cheekbones and eyes were a feminine version of Rahff's.

They were Thomen Furnael and his mother Beralyn, the baroness.

Years ago, Karl had suspected that Zherr Furnael had a plan to get the rest of his family away from the oncoming war. Just as he had apprenticed Rahff to Karl, hoping that Karl could teach the boy enough to lead the barony through the war.

But it hadn't worked. Rahff had been killed in Melawei, and now it seemed that Furnael's plan to safeguard the rest of his family had failed.

Until now. *Ellegon, get the dwarf. I want him to take over Daven's team. Just in case.* "Thomen, Baroness," he said, inclining his head. "It has been a long time."

Dhara snapped her fingers. "Beralyn, you will tell him about the guns. Now."

"You don't understand, Lady Dhara," Karl said, his hand on the hilt of his sword. "The baroness and the boy—all three of them are here now, they're under my protection now. They're free. They're beholden to nobody, owned by nobody."

"Another bluff, Karl Cullinane?"

Tennetty was the first to move; she kicked a table toward the nearest guard, then leaped at Dhara, wrestling the elf woman from the couch, bringing one arm up behind Dhara's back in a hammerlock, setting her blade against the elf woman's throat.

One of the soldiers drew his sword and lunged toward her from behind. Chak parried, then kicked at the elf's elbow; the blade fell from nerveless fingers. He stood, smiling at Dhara's guards.

In the distance, three gunshots rang out.

*Nobody's hurt, yet. I've sent for the dwarf instead of

fetching him; Daven needed a bit of persuading to stay put. We compromised on a few warning shots.*

"Nobody's seriously hurt yet, Dhara. Those shots were just a warning."

Andy-Andy raised her hands and wet her lips. "These are the mother and brother of Karl's first apprentice, Lady Dhara. I wouldn't push the matter."

Even with Tennetty's blade at her throat, Dhara managed a smile. "Lord Khoral intended to give the three of them to you, as tokens of our sincerity. If you wish to free them, well, that is your concern. Not mine."

Gently, she tried to push Tennetty's blade away; at Karl's nod, Tennetty let her.

"We'll have to continue this discussion later," Karl said. "Baroness, Thomen, and you, whoever you are, if you will follow me, we'll see to your needs."

The three didn't say anything; they just followed sullenly.

CHAPTER NINE:

A Matter of Obligation

A sense of duty pursues us ever. . . . If we take to ourselves the wings of the morning, and dwell in the uttermost parts of the sea, duty performed or duty violated is still with us, for our happiness or our misery. If we say the darkness shall cover us, in the darkness as in the light our obligations are yet with us.

—Daniel Webster

"You expect me to be grateful, Karl Cullinane?" Beralyn sneered. "You, who might as well have murdered my son." She sat back in her chair. "Go ahead, kill me. That won't change anything."

The shack was small, but neat; originally, it had been Ahira's house, but now it was one of the three small log cabins that were used for receiving new arrivals, giving them a place to sleep and take their meals until they could adjust to Home life.

Karl bit his lip, opened his mouth, closed it. He turned to the boy.

"Thomen, I need to know something." Karl tapped at the two rifles on the table in front of them. "One of these is a Home rifle; the other is one we seized from slavers just about a tenday ago. The men who killed your guards and took you—which kind did they have?"

Karl was sure what the answer would be—but what if he was wrong? What if someone on his or Daven's or Aveneer's squad had taken up slaving?

Hesitantly, the boy started to point toward the slaver's gun, but his mother's voice brought him up short.

"Don't answer," the boy's mother snapped. "We will give your brother's killer no help."

Anything I can do?

No. Just go away. Karl couldn't even work up the strength to blame Beralyn. She had been against apprenticing Rahff to Karl from the first, knowing that it would endanger the boy.

It hadn't just endangered him. It had killed him.

There was a knock on the door, and Aeia walked in without waiting for an answer. "Greetings," she said, her face grave. "Andrea says that Rahff's mother is here. Are you her?"

Beralyn didn't answer.

"We didn't meet when I was in Bieme. But I did get to know Rahff well. You should know something about how your son died."

"I know how my son died."

Aeia shook her head. "You weren't there. I was. If it hadn't been for Rahff . . ." She let her voice trail off

Thomen looked up. "What if it hadn't been for Rahff?"

Aeia smiled gently. "I would have been killed instead. The slavers had gone crazy; they were killing everyone they could reach. Rahff stood between me and one of them."

Karl pounded his fist against the table. *If only I'd been a little smarter, a little faster.* If he had been only a few seconds faster he would have gotten to the slaver before the bastard opened Rahff's belly. If only Karl had worked out that Seigar Wohtansen would treat his own people first, he would have been able to get the healing draughts to Rahff in time.

Aeia sat down next to Thomen. "Rahff hit me once, did you know that?"

"What for?"

She shrugged. "I doubted Karl—out loud. Rahff sort of elbowed me in the side. What did you tell him, Karl?"

"Aeia . . ." Karl shook his head. "I don't remember."

"I bet Rahff did. You said, 'A man whose profession is violence must not commit violence on his own family, or his friends. You and I are supposed to watch over Aeia, protect her, not bully her.' "

Just as I was supposed to protect Rahff. Teach him, protect him, not watch him die.

It has been more than five years, Karl. Isn't it time you stopped flogging yourself over Rahff?

"Don't you ask me that." Karl jumped to his feet. "Ask her, dammit, ask Beralyn. Tell her that it's okay now."

He pounded his clenched fists in front of his face. "There hasn't been a day gone by when I haven't remembered. He trusted me. The boy practically worshipped me." He turned to Beralyn, trying to think of the words that would soften her stony expression. "Baroness . . ." But there weren't any words.

It was too much; Karl pushed away from the table and walked out into the courtyard. He leaned against the wall of the old smithy.

High above, Ellegon's dark form passed across the stars. *Anything I can do?*

"No. Just leave me alone." Karl buried his face in his hands. "I've just got to be alone for a while."

Time lost its meaning. He never knew how long he stood there.

A finger tapped against his shoulder. He turned to see Beralyn standing next to him, her face wet. "You loved him, too, didn't you?"

Karl didn't answer.

"I've spent years hating you, you know. Ever since a trader brought us your letter, telling us that he was dead."

"I . . . understand."

"I thank you for the understanding. What do we do now, Karl Cullinane? Do we go on hating each other?"

"I don't hate you, Baroness. You've never given me any reason to hate you."

"But you don't like me much, either. You feel that I should be grateful because you freed Thomen, Rhuss, and me."

"Just tell me what you want, Lady. Don't play games with me."

She nodded slowly. "My husband sent Thomen and me away, once the Holts started using these guns and the tide of the war turned against us. He thought we would be safe. But it seems that guns are flowing out of Enkiar these days—flowing toward Holtun.''

Enkiar, again. That was where the slaver caravan had been heading. That was where Ahrmin had hired the assassins. What did it all mean?

Well, he'd find out soon enough.

"Aeia told me that you're going to Enkiar. She didn't say where you would be going after that.''

He shrugged. "I guess that depends on what happens there. Maybe back here, maybe on another raid.'' And maybe to the source of the slavers' guns. Not only was there a score to be settled there, but even light trading in slaver guns and powder had to be stopped.

"You owe me, Karl Cullinane. You owe me for my son. I wish to collect on that debt.''

He looked her full in the face. "How?''

"You know my husband. Zherr isn't going to survive this war. I'm likely never to see him again. Unless . . .''

"Unless what?'' Dammit, couldn't anyone speak plainly?

"Unless you take me back to Bieme. I want to go home, Karl Cullinane. And I want your word.'' She gripped his hand. "I want your word that if it's humanly possible, you'll take me home, after Enkiar. That's little enough payment for my son's life.''

"Baroness—''

"Isn't it?''

"Yes, but—''

"Do I have your word? This . . . word of Karl Cullinane that you prize so much?''

"You have it.''

"There is one more thing.''

"Yes?''

"Thomen. He is to stay here, to be sent with another party. I won't have him around you.''

CHAPTER TEN:

Practice Session

Even if you persuade me, you won't persuade me.
—Aristophanes

Karl gobbled down the scrambled eggs, then took a last bite of the half-eaten ham steak before pushing his chair away from the table.

"And just where do you think you're taking your brainless body off to, Karl Cullinane?" U'len asked, her fists on her more than ample hips.

Suddenly he felt about eight years old, and was surprised to find that he liked the feeling.

"Gotta rush, U'len. I've got a workout with Tennetty and a couple of Daven's men, and then I've got to get ready for the town meeting."

"First things first. Eat."

"No—"

"Yes." Andy-Andy shook her head. "U'len's right. Sit down and finish your breakfast."

Jason hid a broad smile behind his tiny hand. "Daddy's in trou-ble," he announced in a stage whisper, addressing nobody in particular.

"Damn straight," Aeia said, the English words still incongruous coming from her. "He acts as if he's in charge here or something."

He glared at her.

"Siddown, hero," Andy-Andy said. "Out *there* you may be the legendary Karl Cullinane, but in *here* you're an all too often absent husband and father who thinks he can wolf down his food and run.''

Relay, please: You didn't think I was so damn absent last night.

There was no answer: He snorted. *Question: Why is a dragon like a cop? Answer: You never can find one when you need one.*

''Give me a break, please.'' *Keep it light,* he thought. There were too few opportunities to have an argument that could be treated lightly, where winning or losing didn't really matter; he decided to enjoy this one. ''I've got things to do.''

''Exactly right. And the first heroic thing you're going to do today is to finish your ham. All of it.''

''Yeah,'' Jason piped in. ''Children of Salket are starving, and you wanna throw away good food?'' he went on, in a fine imitation of his mother's voice when she got angry.

''Name two.''

''Karl—''

''I'm eating, I'm eating.'' He pushed his chair back to the table. Somehow, it seemed that the remaining ham had grown larger in the past seconds.

Karl's workouts tended to draw crowds. Even on a morning when most people were doing their best to finish whatever they were working on so that they would be free for the late-afternoon town meeting, more than fifty had gathered around the corral to watch.

Pendrill and the stableboy chased the three horses out of the corral, while Wraveth and Taren cleared out the fresh dung, then stripped to the waist before donning padded shirts and trousers and slipping the wire-mesh masks over their heads.

Karl settled for just a mask. The practice swords' edges had been dulled, and the points had had steel balls welded to them; with the mask precluding the possibility of losing an eye, there was little chance of much more than a bruise or two, and Karl wasn't likely to get bruised. Besides, the padded practice garments tended to interfere with his freedom of movement. His overfilled belly was going to do enough of that; no need to aggravate the problem.

Tennetty was late. After a few minutes that Karl spent

chatting with Wraveth and Taren, she rode up, then hurriedly slipped from Pirate's back, waving away Taren's offer of a mask and practice sword.

Her wrists were bandaged. Karl walked over to her.

"Problem?"

She shook her head. "You still want me in the Enkiar operation? I'll need some fresh scars on my wrist, and I'd rather get them from Thellaren's scalpels than by wearing cuffs a moment longer than I have to." She tapped at her patch, her lips pursed in irritation. "Thellaren's working on the glass eye, and I asked Chak to ride out and get Nehera started on trick chains—you happy?"

"It's necessary, Tennetty." But why the sudden change of mind? Karl shrugged mentally. It wasn't any of his business.

She broke into a smile. "I have a surprise for you. Remember Jilla and Danni?"

"Yes?"

"They want to join our team. Seems that they've decided to become warriors, get a bit of revenge."

Wonderful. Once Karl had let a woman join up just because she had a thing for seeing slavers' blood. That someone had been Tennetty; he had lucked out.

But he didn't want to push his luck. He'd been fortunate enough to find in Tennetty someone with a natural bent for combat, plus a personality skewed enough to be able to handle it. "How did you talk them out of it?"

"Well . . ."

"You *did* talk them out of it, didn't you?"

"No." She snorted. "They don't think it's all that hard." She set a hand on her hip and bent her other wrist. " 'It looks *soooo* easy. You pull a trigger, slice with a sword—' "

"You're joking. Tell me you're joking."

"Nope. They'll be here in a while. I made them a deal: Whoever scores on you we'll sign up. Whoever you beat has to find herself a man and settle down—and we get to pick the man."

"We?" He raised an eyebrow. "You got anyone in particular in mind?"

"Obvious: Chak for the blonde, Riccetti for the brunette. By the way, they're both good cooks, although I can't vouch

for their . . . other talents. You might want to try them
out—''

"Tennetty . . ."

"Think about it, Karl. Might give Chak something to come
Home to, put a little weight on Lou, and maybe smiles on
both of their faces."

That might not be a bad idea, provided Chak and Lou
agreed to it. Not bad at all. As far as Karl could tell, none of
the female apprentice Engineers were sleeping with Lou;
Riccetti had always been shy around women. And while Karl
trusted Chak with his life, discussing Chak's relationships
with women—or, rather, the lack of them—wasn't something
he was comfortable doing.

Karl raised an eyebrow. "They went for it?"

Tennetty nodded. "That they did. Remember, for most of
their lives, they were owned by a Pandathaway inn. Their only
real talents are over a stove and in a bed, unless you consider
arranging flowers to be a major skill. I don't think that either
of them would have a hard time getting Riccetti to agree. If you
want, we could rig it so that Lou thinks it's his own idea. I
don't vouch for Chak; he can be clever, in his own little way."

"That wasn't what I was asking. They really agreed to
sparring with me?"

"Well, I had to throw in a few conditions for them to be
willing to face the great Karl Cullinane."

"Such as?"

"First, they get to use real swords."

"Great. Thanks a lot." That was pushing things a bit far.
Even an absolute tyro could get in a lucky slash. "I'd better
send for some armor." Normally, Karl didn't like wearing a
lot of armor; in combat, speed was more important, particularly if you had a bottle of healing draughts handy to take
care of the occasional nick.

"Umm, that was the second condition. You don't get to
wear armor. No mask. Nothing but your pants—''

"Thank heavens for small favors."

"Really?" Tennetty snickered. "I never noticed. The third
handicap is that you use only a practice sword."

Karl snorted. "Anything else? Do I have to fight with one
hand tied behind my back?"

Tennetty produced a leather thong. "Number four."

*   *   *

Look, Karl wanted to say, *this isn't a pleasant business. Don't get into it if you don't have to.*

But he didn't. It wouldn't have done any good. For some people, blood was a drug. Tennetty was that way; the killing never really bothered her.

Then again, how do I know that? Karl hid his own feelings as much as he could, even from Andy-Andy.

There were things he had to do; horrible, awful things. The only justification was that not doing them was worse. Remonstrating with himself was a luxury for late at night; he couldn't spend precious moments in combat remembering that an enemy had once been a cute little baby, bouncing on a mother's knee.

But he didn't have to like it. He didn't have to force himself to feel the pleasure that Tennetty got from the killing, and that Jilla and Danni seemed to have learned at her hands.

He worked his left hand in the leather thongs that bound it behind his back. It wouldn't be hard to work it out of the thongs, but that would take time. And it would be seen as cheating.

Not that he had anything against cheating, not if it made the difference between bleeding and not bleeding, but . . .

Damn. One of the watchers in the crowd was an unfamiliar elf, not a Home resident. One of Dhara's people, no doubt. Which upped the stakes: Karl wouldn't only have to win; he would have to win in such a way as to impress the elf. The Therranji had already been shocked by the scene Karl had pulled the day before; best to keep them impressed.

How the hell do I get myself into things like this?

Do you really want an answer? With a rustling of leathery wings, Ellegon landed next to the corral. *It's because you're egotistical, smug, stupid, foolish—*

Ellegon—

—and those are your good points.

"Thanks."

Jilla and Danni walked out through the gate from the Receiving complex, naked swords held clumsily in their hands, whispering conspiratorially to each other. Each wore a deeply cut halter and a sarong slit well up the thigh. Rather nice thighs, at that.

Naughty, naughty. And if you're thinking that's accidental, guess again. Jilla decided that if you're watching other parts of their anatomy, you won't be concentrating on the hands with the swords. By the way, the halters are loosely tied; they'll slip off with just a bit of exertion. Sort of a second line of defense.

Well, at least Andy-Andy isn't—

"Hey, hero," Andy-Andy said, tapping him on the shoulder. "What goes on here?"

"Great. Just great." He put his free hand on the corral railing and vaulted over, accepting a practice sword from Tennetty. "Let's get to it."

Naked blades didn't always make Karl nervous, but they did always make him serious. He eyed both of the women professionally as they circled him, waiting for him to make the first move.

If this had been for real, he would have tried for a quick injury to either—preferably a leg wound, some sort of disabler—and then taken out the other, finishing off the injured opponent at his leisure.

But that wouldn't work here. There was prestige at stake, as well as injury.

Why you're worrying about prestige when you're facing two swords is something I fail to understand.

He made a tentative lunge toward Danni, allowing her to retreat, the sword held awkwardly in front of her face. *Because I can't afford to lose face before the town meeting.*

In either sense. Think about it. You're not all that pretty to begin with—

Shh. He forced a casual smile to his face.

Mr. Katsuwahara had had it right, way back when.

The way to think of *kumite*, of practice, he had said, is to treat it as real, except for the last inch of your own blows. Block as though the punches really would crush your trachea, the kicks would truly rupture your diaphragm. Your strikes should be aimed just outside the kill points—the navel instead of the solar plexus, the upper thigh instead of the groin, the orbital ridge instead of the eye—and then focused just an inch away from the flesh.

That wouldn't quite do it here, but it was the right idea. Treat the swords as real—because they were, dammit—and then work out how to come up with an offense that wasn't really an offense.

Danni slashed at his leg; he parried easily, putting enough force into the move to make the steel sing.

He spun to block Jilla's stab at his left shoulder. Dammit, they had him between them, and both of them had moved in too close.

But why was that bad? In a fight, you wanted your opponents' blades to endanger each other; they had to avoid cutting into an ally's flesh, while any meat your sword met was an enemy's.

And what of someone who was foolish enough to move in too close? Why wasn't that a problem? That was supposed to be an opportunity to bring feet and elbows into play.

Because this isn't a real fight, dammit. It isn't supposed to be.

Danni poked her sword at his shoulder—

Where thought would have failed him, reflex took over.

He didn't stop to think that ducking aside brought Danni's sword into line with Jilla's face; there just wasn't time to think about it.

It wasn't thought that opened his right hand, letting the practice sword drop, while his left arm clenched, snapping the leather thongs that bound it.

And it wasn't thought that brought his two palms together, clapping his hands against the flat of Danni's blade, stopping it a scant half-inch from Jilla's left eye.

"*No.*" Danni gasped. "I almost—"

"Right." He twisted the sword from Danni's hand, then turned and snatched Jilla's blade from her nerveless fingers.

Jilla rubbed at her left eye, although it hadn't been touched. Her breath came in short gasps; her face was ashen.

Karl forced a chuckle. "You've just had a taste of what it's really like. Just a little taste, mind." He tossed one of the swords end over end into the air, letting the hilt *thunk* into his palm. "You know what we really do? We're merchants, in the business of selling pieces of ourselves. Tennetty's eye,

Chak's toes—take a look at Slovotsky's scars sometimes, or Daven's.

"Look at my chest," he said. "I picked up this scar outside of Lundescarne. A slaver had a chance to whittle on me with a broken sword while I was busy choking the life out of him. And then there's—" He stopped himself. "And we're the lucky ones."

Anger welled up and choked him. "Idiots. You don't have to see a friend's intestines spread across the grass because he wasn't quick enough with his sword. You can let yourselves sleep soundly at night, because a little sound or a light touch doesn't have to mean anything to you. You don't have to jump through a window and find three people dead, their throats cut because someone was after your blood and they happened to be in the way.

"And you don't have to keep going, death after death, killing after killing, year after year.

"But you want in on it?" He offered them each a sword, hilt first. "Congratulations. You've got it."

Eyeing the sword with horror, Danni staggered away.

"*Yes*, Karl Cullinane." Jilla gripped the other one tightly. "I want in. I understand what you're saying; I've spent the past tenday listening to Tennetty. And I know I'll need training, but—"

"You want in." He shrugged. "Tennetty, she's in your charge. You get to train her. I want you to start by running her until she drops." He turned and walked away.

CHAPTER ELEVEN:

Town Meeting

The deadliest enemies of nations are not their foreign foes; they always dwell within their borders. And from these internal enemies civilization is always in need of being saved. The nation blessed above all nations is she in whom the civic genius of the people does the saving day by day, by acts without external picturesqueness; by speaking, writing, voting reasonably; by smiting corruption swiftly, by good temper between parties; by the people knowing true men when they see them, and preferring them as leaders to rabid partisans or empty quacks.
—William James

Ahira snickered "Ever wish you hadn't freed Chton? Just sort of let him slide by that time?"

"No." Karl pursed his lips. "Just 'cause he has clay feet like everybody else?" *Including me, for that matter.*

He bit into his sandwich, refusing the offer of a wineskin from a passing carouser.

Town meetings were half a political event, half a valley-wide party. Since everyone in the valley took at least the afternoon off from work, the meetings would have been called far more often if they didn't require a petition by twenty-five percent of the voters.

Behind the speaking platform and its chest-high ballot box, six whole sheep were slowly turning over cooking fires. A team of volunteer cooks took turns cranking the spits and basting the carcasses with wine and oil, slicing off sizzling pieces of meat, wrapping them in fresh-baked flatbread, handing out the sandwiches as they were ready.

Someone had broached the whiskey bottles and beer barrels early. Karl noted with satisfaction that none of the Engineers or the warriors joined in the throng milling around the booze, filling their mugs with the trickling liquid fire.

Good. Let the Joiners get drunk. Anyone who was passed out couldn't vote.

Like most things democratic, Home town meetings were a zoo. There were many things to be said in favor of democracy, but neatness wasn't one of them. With the exception of the absent warriors and a few outlying landowners who were too busy with their own fields, all of the voters and most of the other citizens had elected to attend.

He turned back to the dwarf. "Any landowners playing games?" Karl patted at the large leather pouch dangling from the right side of his belt. Still there; good.

Ahira shook his head. "Not that I can tell. I'll keep my ear to the ground for complaints, though—assuming I'm still Mayor by nightfall."

The law involving town meetings was explicit: Nobody was ever to be pressured not to attend, under penalty of fine, confiscation of property, or banishment, at the pleasure of the Mayor, depending on the nature of the pressure.

That applied to nonvoting citizens as well as voters; it was important that nonvoter citizens get a taste of democracy. Get someone hooked on deciding his or her own fate, and the security of cropping quickly lost its appeal. The trouble with sharecropping back on the Other Side hadn't been the basic idea of trading labor on someone else's fields for a portion of the harvest and a place to live; the flaw was that it could easily become a form of debt slavery.

In the short run, the cure for that was easy: Just make sure that there were more proven fields than there was labor to farm them. Let the landowners bid for labor, rather than letting laborers bid against each other.

"Should be straightforward, assuming things go right." Ahira nibbled at his sandwich. "Although we're likely to run into at least one challenge."

"Oh?"

"See that kid over by the barbecue?"

Karl followed Ahira's pointing finger. The subject was a

boy of about twelve, dressed in dirt and rags. He was busily feeding himself, wolfing down sandwich after sandwich.

"New arrival? What the hell is going on with supply?"

"Not new; he's a voter, believe it or not. He's been here for the last quarter. Aveneer brought him in while you were gone. Umm, Peters? No, Petros—Petros is his name. Stubborn kid. He didn't want to crop and build up his grubstake, so he managed to sweet-talk Stanish out of the use of some rusty old tools, then proved a field halfway up the mountain, just above and beyond Engineer Territory. It's barely inside the wards. I don't know what he's been living on, or how he managed to clear the ground without the woodknife, but he did. Then—

"Then, he trailed a flatbed carrying seed corn out to your fields, and picked up the spillings from the road—at least, that's what he says. More likely, he stole a few pounds of seed, but just try to prove it."

"I don't think so." The theft of a few pounds of seed didn't bother Karl. But a twelve-year-old child looking like a famine victim did. "He's working a full-sized field all by himself?"

"Yup. Scraggliest-looking field I've ever seen; I doubt that there's as much as one cornstalk per square meter. The rest is weeds. He sleeps under a brush lean-to. Last time I was inspecting, I saw what he had, and it's not much: crummy handmade bow and arrows, fire-hardened spear—probably lives off weeds and rabbit. There's at least one mountain lion working that area; likely he'll wake up in its belly some morning. Pitiful."

"Damn." Karl shook his head. "You really think anyone's going to challenge his vote?"

Ahira nodded. "He says he's fifteen, but nobody believes it. I think he should be in school, but you want to argue it with him?"

"Not at all. You'll have to excuse me; this is someone I've got to meet. Go do some politicking."

Karl worked his way through the crowd around the barbecue until he was next to the boy. It wasn't much of a problem; nobody wanted to be downwind of Petros.

"Greetings," he said.

The boy's eyes widened. "Are you who I think you are?"

Karl stuck out a hand. "Karl Cullinane."

Petros' eyes shot from side to side.

"T'rar ammalli." Karl smiled. "I just want to shake your hand; no harm."

The boy extended his own hand. Karl took it briefly, then released it, forcing himself not to wipe his own hand on his tunic. "I have a proposition for you."

Petros shook his head. "I will not crop for anyone. My field is mine, and so is my vote. I don't need help."

Then why do you look more like a Biafran refugee than anything else, kid? And has anybody ever told you what a bath is? But Karl didn't say that. A twelve-year-old former slave with this kind of pride, this kind of stubbornness, was a treasure. The trick was to make sure that this particular treasure survived, its pride intact. "Maybe not, but I could use yours—and not with cropping, either. You know Nehera?"

"The smith? Of course. What of it?"

"Take a walk with me," Karl said, taking a couple of sandwiches, then urging the boy away from the rest of the crowd.

Petros shrugged and followed him.

"I have a problem with Nehera," Karl said, handing the boy a sandwich and taking a bite out of the other one. "He hasn't gotten the idea that he's free. Thinks he has to belong to someone, and he figures that someone is me."

"Poor you."

Karl let a bit of steel creep into his voice. "You think I own people, boy? Ever?"

"Well, no. I've heard about you."

"Better, then. As I was saying, I can't break him of the notion."

"Damn dwarves are supposed to make lousy slaves. That's what my mas—what someone who used to own me said."

Karl shrugged. "That's the theory. His spirit's broken, though. And I don't know how to go about fixing it. That's your job, if you want it."

"Broke spirit?" Petros snorted. "How am I supposed to fix that?"

"If I knew how, I wouldn't need you—that's your problem. I want you to play apprentice one day out of three. I'll clear it with the Engineers. While he's busy teaching you about smithing, I want you to teach him how to be free. Interested?''

''What's the pay?''

''Not much. You get to work on your own tools, and while you're playing apprentice, you eat out of Nehera's pot. Might even pick up a few skills while you're at it.''

Petros shook his head. ''My fields take too much time—''

''Nonsense. All you're doing between now and harvest is a bit of weeding. If you didn't have to spend so much time gathering food, you'd have plenty of spare time on your hands.''

The boy considered it. ''Maybe. That your best offer?''

''What else do you want?''

''Next planting, I want the use of a horse and plow.''

Was that an honest counteroffer, or was the boy pushing, testing him?

Karl shook his head. ''Just the horse. I've got plenty of horses You'll have to rent a plow yourself.''

''Deal.'' The boy stuck out his hand. ''Shakeonit ''

''One more thing.''

''Well?'' Petros eyed him suspiciously.

''You smell like an outhouse.'' Karl jerked his thumb toward the lake. ''Take a bath. Now. You can pick up a cake of soap at the schoolhouse. Tell Aeia I said so.''

''Done. But I'll be back in time to vote. Nobody taking my vote from me.''

The boy walked off toward the lake, trying his best to hold back a smile.

Karl didn't bother trying; he just turned his head away. *Go ahead, Petros, think of me as a sucker.*

Standing on the speaking platform, Ahira pounded his fist against the metal gong. ''Your attention please,'' he called out, his voice even louder than the gong. ''The twenty-third Home town meeting is hereby called to order. Get the food off the fire and plug the kegs,'' he called out to the cooks. ''There is a decision to be made.''

''. . . and the offer is a *good* one,'' Chton said, for the eighteenth time. Karl was sure it was eighteen. As he lay back on the grass, propped up on his elbow next to Andy-Andy, he hadn't had anything better to do than count.

Oh. Before I forget. Ahira says that there's a mountain lion around Petros' farm—

Such as it is.

Right. It would be kind of convenient if that lion got itself eaten.

Consider it munched.

". . . what are we here? Just a few thousand, barely eking out a living from the soil and what we have to trade our blood and dying for."

That did it. *Enough of that crap. Point of fact, please*

Who? Moi?

Chak, please. And cut out the Miss Piggy imitation; you don't have the right intonation down.

Then you don't remember it clearly; I stole it from Andy-Andy's head, and she's got a better aural memory than you.

"Point of fact," Chak said, leaping to his feet.

Chton tried to go on, but Ahira interrupted him. "Point of fact has been called. Your claim?"

"I don't remember Chton shedding any blood. I don't know him all that well, but I thought he was just a farmer."

Correct that, and quick.

Chak's eyes momentarily glazed over. "Pardon me, I didn't mean to say something bad about farmers. What I was objecting to was Chton's taking credit for the blood that the warriors and the Engineers shed—not him."

Ahira nodded judiciously. "You may continue, Chton, but omit taking credit for prices you haven't paid."

For a moment, Karl thought that Chton was going to burst a blood vessel. "*Haven't paid?* How about Werthan, and his woman and child? Were they not farmers? Is a farmer's blood any less red than a warrior's? Would they not be alive today instead of lying in cold graves if we were under the protection of Lord Khoral?"

Karl kept his face blank, but he couldn't help how his fists clenched. A child, body sprawled on a rough wood floor, her lifeblood a pool that would stain forever . . .

A murmur ran through the crowd.

You'd better answer that, Karl. If that wasn't addressed to you, I don't know what is.

No. There wasn't an answer; there wasn't an excuse.

Ihryk rose to his feet. "I'll answer him, Mr. Mayor."

"You?" Chton sneered. "One of Karl Cullinane's hirelings?"

"I don't remember that sneer in your voice when Karl pulled you and me out of the slave wagon, Chton. I don't even remember you at Werthan's houseraising." Ihryk raised his fist. "But I'll tell you this—Werthan and Anna would have spent their lives with collars around their necks if it weren't for the likes of Karl Cullinane. And so would you and I."

"Yes," Chton shot back, "the *noble* Karl Cullinane, the *great* man. Who just happens to be the richest man in the valley. If we join with Therranj, we'll all be as rich as he is, have as many servants as he does. Is that what bothers you, Karl Cullinane? Is that why you oppose Lord Khoral's offer?"

Karl, I think it's about time. If he calls for the vote now—

I know. Karl rose to his feet. "Point of personal privilege, Mr. Mayor."

Ahria nodded. "You may address the point."

Karl walked to the platform, forcing himself to move slowly, knowing that a hurried step might make it look as though Chton's taunts had scored.

He stepped up onto the rough wood and turned to face the crowd.

"About damn time, Karl," Ahira whispered. "This better be good."

"It will be." He raised his voice. "Chton has made a point, and a good one. I . . . guess I should be ashamed. Yes, of course, the reason that I don't want Home to become part of Therranj is that I'm afraid for my status. It's only logical, isn't it? If everyone is better off, then it only follows that I would be worse off. . . ."

He wrinkled his brow. "Wait. That doesn't make sense. Wouldn't I be better off, as well?" He nodded. "I know what Chton means, though." He picked a familiar face out of the crowd. "Harwen, I was just talking about it to you the other day, remember? I was complaining about your being out riding. I figured I'd be more comfortable riding both Carrot and your horse," he said, taking an absurdly wide stance.

A quiet chuckle ran through the crowd.

"And Ternius, you noticed me over by the cooking fire? I was glaring at everyone who was eating. After all, I can eat more than will fill my belly. can't I?" He glanced at the remaining roasts near the fire. "Well, I'll try, but I don't think I'd enjoy it.

"You know something, Chton? I just can't do it. I just can't ride more than one horse at a time, or sleep in more than one bed at once, or eat more than my belly will hold. Or lie with more than one woman at a time—"

Now.

"You had damn well better not, Karl Cullinane." Andy-Andy leaped to her feet. "Point of information, Mr. Mayor."

"Recognized. What information do you want?"

"None. It's information I'd better give. You cheat on me, Karl Cullinane, and you'll be missing something I have reason to know you're fond of." She produced a knife from the folds of her robes and considered the edge.

The quiet chuckle became a full-throated laugh.

Now that you've got them laughing, what are you going to do?

That was just the warm-up. Watch me.

Karl raised his hands in mock surrender. "You see my point, Chton."

"Listen—"

"You've had your say; I'll have mine now." He hitched at the leather pouch at his waist. "Khoral doesn't want much from us, and that's a fact. All he wants is our fealty, and he'll give us much in return." Karl untied the pouch from his belt and held it in both hands. "Very much. He'll make me a baron, and give me the whole valley as my barony. Maybe, if I turn it down—and make no mistake, I would turn it down— he'll give it to Chton.

"He'll send us serfs. All of you who have farms will have people around who will have to work your fields for you, or starve. Doesn't that sound good? Doesn't that sound familiar? Khoral will divide up the land for us, and then we can make them farm it. We won't even have to clap collars around their necks—they'll either work for us or starve.

"And what does he want for this? Stand up, Lady Dhara, and tell us what he wants for this."

She stood, but Karl didn't give her a chance to answer. "All he wants is our fealty; each and every one of us. That's all. He will give us gold, he says, and promise that our taxes will be low. All he wants is our fealty. All he wants is for us to say that he, Lord Khoral, is better able to decide how we should live than we are. You like that idea, Tivar?" He beckoned to a farmer who he knew was undecided. "You like the idea of turning your destiny over to that elf?"

"N-no."

"Wait!" Chton spun on Karl. "What's the difference between having Khoral rule and letting you and Ahira run the valley as though it were your fief? Tell me that."

Karl walked to the ballot box and slammed his hand down on it. "This is the difference, fool. The difference is *choice*. Khoral wants you to trade this in—you know what he'll give you instead of this?"

"Yes, gold—"

Now.

Don't teach your grandfather— "Gold. That's what it comes down to, isn't it, Chton? You and the rest of your Joiners want gold, and Khoral offers gold." Karl dug his hand into his pouch. "I have some of that gold right here." He pulled his hand out.

The buttery golden collar shone in the bright daylight. "Is this what you want clamped around your neck?"

"No," several voices cried out, most of them Engineers.

"I can't hear you. Do you want this?"

"No!" The voices were stronger, although the warrior and Engineer factions were still the most vocal.

"Now," Karl said, deliberately lowering his voice, forcing them all to listen carefully, "you have a choice. You can vote your confidence in the Mayor, or you can throw him out. Even if Ahira stays in as Mayor, you can still change your minds later. But this?" He raised the golden collar over his head. "Once you clamp this around your throat, do you think you can decide to take it off later? What if it doesn't fit you, Chton?" He tossed the collar to the platform. "What if it chokes you?"

"Wait, that's not fair—"

"Fair? I'll show you fair. Lady Dhara—catch this." He kicked the collar at Dhara; she caught it automatically, then dropped it as though it were on fire. "You can take that back to Lord Khoral and tell him that Home might make a good ally for Therranj, but if he tries to swallow us, he'll choke."

He strode to the ballot box and stopped in front of the two barrels next to it. "You all can vote in privacy, if you wish," he said, selecting a single stone from the barrel of white ones, "but here's how I vote; I don't mind any of you seeing." He held it up for all to see. "I vote my confidence in Ahira—and for independence." He slammed the stone down into the ballot box, then walked off the platform.

Daven, Andy-Andy, Tennetty, and half a dozen others want to know if they're supposed to join you.

No, not yet. Let someone else go first.

Petros vaulted to the platform. "I vote with Karl Cullinane," he said, taking up a white stone. Somewhere or other, the boy had managed to procure a knife; now he brandished it. "Does anybody value his life little enough to try stopping me?" He dropped the white stone in the ballot box, then leaped from the platform, standing beside Karl.

Before Chton had his mouth half open, Ranella, the apprentice Engineer, had jumped to her feet. "The Engineers stand with Ahira," she said. "All of us."

"I do, too," Ternius said. "And I don't see any need to wait."

"And I—"

"I will—"

The trickle became a torrent, and then a flood

"Transcending the political, eh, Karl?" Ahira smiled up at him as they walked down the road in the starlight. "Sounded to me like you were being very political, in your own way. Including lying."

"Lying? Me?" Karl stooped to pick a pebble from the road, then threw it off into the night.

"That golden collar was inspired."

Karl breathed on his fingernails and buffed them against his chest. "Thank you. I thought it made a nice metaphor. Didn't you?"

"Right. But I don't recall that as being one of Khoral's gifts."

"I never said it was, did I?"

"No. You didn't." Ahira was silent for a few minutes as they walked along the road toward the house that the dwarf shared with Walter and his family. "We make a good team, you and I. I can handle the day-to-day stuff, but I can't . . . inspire people, not the way you do." He shrugged. "Just not in me."

"Don't put yourself down."

"I'm not. It's just that if you hadn't been here, we might have lost. You might have found yourself faced with Chton as Mayor the next time you came Home."

"Stop talking around whatever it is that you want to talk about, Ahira. Just say it."

"You've got to settle down, Karl. Spend more time here, not on the road. If you'd been here, you might have been able to shame Chton into not pushing for a town meeting in the first place."

"Can't. Too much work to do. There's the Enkiar operation coming up, and I've promised to take Beralyn home."

The dwarf nodded grimly. "It might be best, in the long run. I've been talking to Gwellin; he's always thinking about going back to Endell."

"I knew that—but why you?"

"You notice a lot of dwarf women around?"

Karl nodded. "Well, it was always understood Gwellin and his people are only temporarily with us. But their word is as good as—"

"The word of Karl Cullinane." Ahira chuckled. "Quite right; no word will be said about guns. But, Karl . . ."

"Well?"

"Well, if they ever throw me out of office, I'm thinking that it might be a good idea if I went with him. I'm still not sure what I am, Karl. I've spent seven years now as a cross between a human and a dwarf, and I'm beginning to wonder . . ."

Karl stopped. "Ahira. Look me in the face. You wanted to lose today, didn't you?"

The dwarf didn't answer.

"Didn't you?"

"Karl, I . . . just don't know." Ahira pounded his fist against the flat of his hand. "I really don't know, not anymore.

It's different for me than it is for you. You subordinated
Barak to your own needs years ago. I'm . . . still betwixt and
between. And I know that I owe my life to Walter, and
Riccetti, and Andy—and most particularly to you, but . . .''
He looked up. "Dammit, Karl, why can't things be clearer to
me? You always seem to know what you're doing."

"Not you. Please." Karl threw up his hands. "Don't you
start to buy into the legend. I'm still me, Ahira, just plain old
Karl Cullinane who staggers through life, improvising as he
goes." *And some of those improvisations have cost lives,
Jimmy.* "I just do the best I can." He clapped a hand to
Ahira's shoulder. "But once I finish with this Enkiar opera-
tion and get Beralyn back to Bieme, what say I hang around
Home for a while? Would that do for the time being?"

"Let's try it." The dwarf nodded. "I think so. It wouldn't
be all bad, you know. You could teach some school, spend
more time with your wife and son."

"Okay. Just give me time, Ahira. It'll take a while to
finish up what I've started. One favor, though."

"Yes?"

"When it's just the two of us alone, could I call you James
Michael? It'd be sort of a taste of home."

"And it might remind me who I really am supposed to be,
eh?"

"No. That you've got to decide for yourself."

They walked along in silence for a long time. In front of
them, the lamp still burned on the porch. The dwarf climbed
the steps and turned to him. "You do what you have to, Karl.
And I'll hold out here just as long as I can. Who knows? This
whole Joiner nonsense may subside."

But your own problem won't. "Maybe it will."

"About that favor . . ."

"Yes?"

"I think you'd better call me Ahira. It's who I am, after
all. Goodnight."

CHAPTER TWELVE:

Parting

The voice of the turtledove speaks out. It says:
Day breaks, which way are you going?
Lay off, little bird, must you scold me so?
                    —Love Songs of the New Kingdom

Karl checked the third packhorse's cinch for the twentieth
time as he eyed the house in the predawn light, wondering if
he'd ever see it again. *I've always got to make my goodbyes
count*, he thought. *They may end up being all too real.*

*You're stalling. Which is probably the most sensible thing
you've ever done. You should let me—*

No. Case closed.

Beralyn and Tennetty sat astride their horses, waiting with
patently false patience. Chak, sitting comfortably in the saddle on his gray gelding, was more phlegmatic. It didn't
matter to him whether they left now or in a few minutes.

Karl shook his head. *I'd better go.*

Andy-Andy stood on the porch, watching him silently.
There was nothing more to say; all of it had been said last
night.

I'll miss you terribly, he mouthed. As always.

One more thing to do. He walked up the steps and into the
foyer, then climbed the stairs to Jason's room.

Mikyn and Jason lay sleeping under their blankets.

Karl knelt on the floor and gently kissed Jason on the
forehead. No need to wake him. *Watch over him, will you?*
He tore himself away from the room, and the boy.

As always, Karl.

U'len caught up with him on the steps. "Look, you—be careful," she said, her voice a harsh whisper. "I have a bad feeling about this." She shook her head, her hands behind her back.

"You always have a bad feeling."

She snorted. "True enough. Here," she said, producing a muslin sack, then turning away. "For the road."

"But we've got plenty of food—" He stopped himself. "Thank you, U'len," he said. "See you soon."

She nodded gravely. "Maybe. Maybe this time. But one time you won't come back, Karl Cullinane. Get your fool ass killed, you will, sooner or later."

"Maybe." He forced a smile. "How about double or nothing on your salary? If I'm not back in, say, two hundred days, you get double your pay for that time—otherwise, you work for free for however long I'm out."

"I don't bet against you." She cocked her head to one side. "Although, if you'd care to give me odds?" She put her hands on his shoulder and turned him about, then pushed him toward the door. "If you're going, get out of here."

Andy-Andy was still waiting on the porch. "I still think you should let Ellegon fly you."

He shook his head. "I don't want him away from Home. Not until Gwellin and the rest are back on guard. They should be back in a couple of weeks at the outside; then he can go back to resupplying runs. But until then, I'd just as soon not have to worry about whether or not you're safe when I go to sleep at night."

"And I'm not supposed to—" She stopped and shook her head in apology. Arguing over a settled issue wasn't a luxury that Andy allowed herself. "Did you mean what you told Ahira the other night? About spending some more time around here, after this one?"

He nodded. "I think a couple of years of semiretirement would do me a bit of good—let or Chak run the team for a while. Besides, if the guild keeps raiding into Therranj, I might just take a small group out for a tenday every now and then, keep them on their toes."

The whole world didn't rest on Karl's shoulders, not anymore. With Aveneer's and Daven's teams working, with rumors of others attacking and robbing slavers, the guild was on the run.

Even if he knew that he couldn't possibly live to see the end of the work, it was fairly begun. A phrase from Edmund Burke popped into his mind: "Slavery they can have everywhere. It is a weed that grows in every soil."

Not any soil around me, Eddie. Just think of me as a weedkiller.

No. Lou Riccetti was the weedkiller, although eventually, the secret of gunpowder would get out. And that might not be a bad thing. Like them or not, guns were a leveling phenomenon, a democratizing one, in the long run. "All men are created equal," people would say. "Lou Riccetti made them that way."

He hitched at his swordbelt, then threw his arms around her, burying his face in her hair. "Be well," he whispered.

"You'd damn well better take care of yourself, hero." She pressed her lips to his and kissed him thoroughly.

He released her and walked down the steps, then over to the roan he had picked for the trip. Carrot was getting a bit too old to be taken into battle; this mare would have to serve until he was able to reclaim Stick from Slovotsky.

He levered himself into the saddle.

Tennetty tossed him a square of cloth. "Wipe your eyes, Karl."

He tossed it back. "Shut up. Let's get out of here."

PART THREE:

Enkiar

CHAPTER THIRTEEN:

To Enkiar

Cease to ask what the morrow will bring forth, and set down as gain each day that Fortune grants.
— Quintus Horatius Flaccus

The watchman picked them up less than a mile outside of camp.

"Two all-beef patties," a harsh voice whispered from somewhere in the trees, "special sauce, pickles, cheese . . ."

The voice fell silent.

". . . lettuce, onions on a sesame-seed bun," Karl called back, deciding that he was going to have to have a serious talk with Walter about the passwords Slovotsky was selecting.

It was a sound idea, in principle, and Karl had approved of it when Walter had suggested it several years before: The password phrases were culled out of Other Side popular culture, guaranteeing that Karl, Walter, or Ahira could answer a challenge without having been given the response ahead of time.

But this was just too much. It was too damn much. Karl had been dreaming of Big Macs and similar delicacies for years.

His mouth watering, he dropped his reins and turned to Beralyn. "Baroness, raise your hands."

"What?"

"There is someone pointing a gun at you who doesn't know you, and doesn't know that you don't have a pistol trained on my back. He will know it if you get your hands high in the air. *Now.*"

Slowly, she complied.

Piell stepped out onto the road, his slaver smoothbore carefully just out of line with the baroness' chest. "Greetings, Karl." The weapon didn't waver. "I don't recognize your . . . companion."

"Ta havath, Piell. Beralyn, Baroness Furnael, I'd like to introduce Piell ip Yratha."

"May I lower my hands now?"

"Certainly," Tennetty said. "If you really want a hole through your chest. Piell isn't going to take either Karl's or my word that you're harmless, not until he's sure that we're not under some sort of threat. You still could have a pistol up your sleeve; if you were fast enough, you'd be able to get it out before we could do anything about it. We've got to prove that you don't."

Chak snorted. "You could have warned her *before* you said 'certainly,' instead of after."

"It's more fun my way."

"Shut up, both of you." Karl slowly edged his horse over to the baroness, drew his saber, and held the point a scant few inches from her throat. "Satisfied, Piell?" He resheathed his sword.

The elf lowered his rifle. "Yes." He turned and gestured to someone hidden in the woods; leaves rustled momentarily.

Piell bowed deeply as he turned back. "Please lower your arms and accept my apologies, Baroness—*Furnael?*" He raised an eyebrow. "Rahff's mother?"

"Right." Karl nodded. "Now, I don't want to get shot on the way in. How much of a lead should we give your second?"

"He is quick on his feet, Karl Cullinane. I suggest you take a few moments to water your horses, then ride directly in." Piell eyed the late-afternoon sun. "We are camped in a clearing—you'll be met. I'd better move up and find another watch station. If you'll excuse me?" He bowed deeply toward Beralyn, then vanished into the bushes.

Karl dismounted, took a waterbag and a wooden bowl down from a packhorse's bags, and began to water the horses. "Sorry about the discourtesy," he said. "But it can save a bit of trouble. If you *did* have us covered, all we'd have to do is go along with whatever you wanted, and count on Piell to take care of things from the other end."

"There seem to be many . . . strange rituals involved in this business of yours."

Tennetty snickered.

The interior of the late wizard's wagon was elegant: The floor was deeply carpeted, the wooden walls covered with tapestries. Karl, Chak, Walter, and Henrad, Andy-Andy's apprentice, sat around a common bowl of stew, eating a late supper. Piell was busy settling the baroness in for the night, while Tennetty was off by herself, working on her disguise.

Setting down his spoon, Karl reached over to what had been the wizard's study desk, took down a leather-bound book, and idly flipped through the pages, ignoring Henrad's wince. He hadn't brought up the Henrad problem with Andy, but there was no sense in taking it any easier on the boy than necessary.

The pages of spells were just a blur to him, although anyone with the genes that allowed him to work magic would have found the letters sharp and black.

There was no sense in staining the pages; Karl tossed the book to the boy, then picked up his spoon.

"You cut it kind of close, Karl," Slovotsky said, folding his hands behind his head and lying back on a floor pillow. "I was beginning to worry. Piell, Henrad, and I have been talking about doing Enkiar without you. Why didn't you just have Ellegon fly you over? Come to think of it, why haven't you lost the beard, like we were talking about?"

Karl swallowed another mouthful of stew before answering. "I didn't have Ellegon fly me over because I'm nervous about leaving the family alone, after that last attempt. I want him guarding them until Gwellin, Daherrin, and the rest are Home, and on watch. Besides, there's another reason that I'm nervous about leaving the valley alone right now. . . ."

"Well?" Slovotsky raised an eyebrow. "Don't you trust me anymore?"

Karl forced a chuckle. It wouldn't do to go public about Ahira, and about Karl's own doubts that Ahira would want to stay on as Mayor forever. That was for Walter's ears only.

"No, not at all. It's just that . . . don't you think that this business with the baroness smells kind of funny? Supposedly, she, Thomen, and Rhuss were just witnesses that guns have been used in the Bieme-Holtun war. But why *them* in particular? Why did Khoral go to the trouble to find someone that he must have known I'd feel beholden to?"

"To get you out of the valley for as long as possible." Slovotsky nodded. "To let them push for another town meeting while you're gone. Why did you play along?"

Karl shrugged. "I think that Khoral is underestimating our people—the Engineers, in particular. I think I persuaded Dhara that they won't go along with any sort of fealty to Khoral. It's Riccetti's Engineers that Khoral really wants, not the land."

Henrad spoke up. "But what if you're wrong?"

"If we don't solve this powder problem, it doesn't matter," Chak said, talking around a mouthful of stew. "I think this slaver powder is more dangerous than all the elves in Therranj put together."

Slovotsky raised an eyebrow. "Why?"

"*Ow!* This is *hot*," Chak said, his eyes tearing.

"You probably just bit into a pepper."

"Pass the water." Chak accepted the jug, tilted it back, and drank deeply. "You know, this isn't bad stew, but someone has to teach your cook that pepper's a spice, not a vegetable."

"You didn't answer my question."

Chak snorted. "I was busy being peppered to death. . . . It's a matter of status, of legend. We are . . . the feared Home raiders; we carry thunder and lightning with us. And as long as we're the only ones who can do that, local lords and princes are going to be nervous about interfering with us, no matter what the reward; as long as we don't make a habit of taking on local lords and princes, they won't feel obliged to.

"But what if they can come up with their own guns? Couldn't that change the whole balance?"

"Maybe." Karl wasn't sure that Chak had a solid point, but he didn't like contradicting him in public.

"In any case," Walter said, "you're probably right that Ellegon's the best person to keep an eye on things—including politics. Even if the elves are shielded, Chton and the rest of the joiners aren't, eh?"

"Right. But the person that they're really underestimating is Ahira, I think. He can keep a lid on Home for years." *As long as his heart is in his work,* Karl added to himself. "And then . . ."

"And then?"

He sat back in his chair and closed his eyes. "We had a huge victory; I don't know if anyone else saw it. There's this twelve-year-old kid, name of Petros. He lives in a lean-to next to what Ahira says is the scraggliest field that he's ever seen. Doesn't crop for anyone, because he wants his own land, his own vote, and he wants it *now.*"

Karl opened his eyes and smiled. "You give me another hundred like Petros, and I won't ever have to worry that Home might be bought out by anyone. Ever." He waved it away. "But forget about that for now. We've got Enkiar to deal with. And Ahrmin."

"Ahrmin." Walter shook his head. "I hope Ellegon's wrong about him. His father scared me shitless. The son is probably going to be worse."

"He's badly burned and scarred, but he's still alive—and he hired the assassins. In Enkiar."

Slovotsky pursed his mouth. "If I remember right, he's the one who killed Fialt. Tennetty'll be all over him like ugly on an ape—which explains her being here. I've got to admit that her being with you surprised me."

"*Dammit.*" Karl threw up his hands. Of course. That was why Tennetty had changed her mind, decided that she was willing to play slave. *Sometimes I think U'len's right about my lack of brains.*

Slovotsky smiled. "You missed one, eh? Happens to the best of us. You think we'll have a shot at Ahrmin?"

"Maybe. *If* he's still in Enkiar. *If* he show his face. *If* this whole thing isn't a trap for yours truly." Karl bit his lip. "Which is why we're going to do things a bit differently than we'd planned. I don't think that Lord—what's the name of the Lord of Enkiar?"

"Gyren," Chak said. "Otherwise known as Gyren the Neutral. Trying to make Enkiar the trading center of the Middle Lands—he never gets involved in anything."

"Exactly. I don't think we have to worry about the locals being involved in some sort of guild plot, but we do have to face the possibility that the other end of this gunrunning operation is going to put us face to face with Ahrmin.''

Karl rubbed a hand against his face. "Which is why I haven't shaved. He's seen Tennetty and Chak, although only for a few minutes and in the dark. He probably won't recognize them. I'm the problem. No matter what I do, if Ahrmin sees me, he's going to recognize me.''

"So? What are you going to do? Sit this one out?''

"No, Walter. I want you to keep an eye on Beralyn.''

"You're going to stay behind?''

"No, I'm going ahead. I'm going to be the bait. Well, half of the bait, anyway.''

Chak smiled. "If I'm reading your mind correctly, I'm the other half.''

"Any objections?''

"Well . . . I've always liked it when you get tricky.'' Chak eyed the edge of his eating knife. "I liked Fialt a lot, Karl. And Rahff.'' He nodded grimly. "And if you'll recall, I was the one who chiseled through Anna Major's chains.''

"Well?''

"Promise to save a piece of him for me. If you can.''

"If I can. I won't try too hard, though.''

Chak laughed. "At least you're honest.''

"Someone has to be.'' He turned to Walter. "We brought only half a dozen rifles and four pistols. I can't exactly hide the rifles under my cloak—so I'll take whatever pistols you have.''

"Hey, you had me send all of our weapons back Home with Gwellin. Don't blame me if—''

Karl held out a hand. "I love you like a brother, Walter, but that doesn't mean I don't know you. You held out a few pistols and rifles as insurance, didn't you?''

"Well . . .'' Slovotsky spread his hands. "Can't blame a guy for trying.''

"Not this time, anyway.''

CHAPTER FOURTEEN:

Valeran

What we anticipate seldom occurs; what we least expected generally happens.

—Benjamin Disraeli

"I'm getting a bit irritated," Karl said, keeping his voice pitched low as they rode side by side down the street toward Enkiar's inn. "Nobody seems to have recognized me."

"What a pity!" Chak laughed. "So—Karl Cullinane is supposed to be the center of the world, eh? Have you been taking lessons from Walter Slovotsky on the sly? We don't have . . . teebee on This Side, remember?"

"Teevee."

"Eh?"

"Tee*vee*, not tee*bee*. Teebee is something else."

"In any case, we don't have it. As I was saying, your visage isn't all that well known. Which is just as well."

"Right." But if Ahrmin was still in the Enkiar area, he would certainly have somebody out watching, just on the off chance of spotting Karl Cullinane. The ill-feeling was mutual; Karl had killed Ahrmin's father, Ohlmin.

One of the few times I really enjoyed killing, he thought, remembering.

Whatever had happened to Ohlmin's head? They had left it behind in the wagon outside of Bremon, and the Gate Between Worlds; likely the skull was still there.

A sextet of foot soldiers approached them as they neared the inn.

"Greetings," their leader said. He was a tall and rangy man, perhaps in his mid-forties, though his hair and short beard were still coal-black. His stern blue eyes considered them carefully. "Your names and purpose in Enkiar?"

Chak spoke up first. "I am Ch'akresarkandyn ip Kath-arhdn—"

"I can see that you are a Katharhd, fellow." His pursed lips made it clear that seeing a Katharhd wasn't his idea of a great treat. "Your business?"

"I watch his back." Chak jerked a thumb toward Karl. "To see that it doesn't sprout knives."

"I see. And you are?"

"My name is Karl Cullinane." Karl smiled genially, raising his right hand, keeping his left hand near where the two pistols tucked into his belt were hidden by the folds of his cloak. "And I am just passing through. Have you any objection to that?"

"None. As long as you don't bring your . . . feud into Enkiar." The leader turned to the man next to him. "Though I don't believe that there are any Pandathaway guildsmen in Enkiar at the moment, are there?"

"No, Captain. There have not been for several tendays, at the least. Just the—"

"Good." He turned back to Karl. "Keep your war out of Enkiar, and you and your gold are welcome. Unless you intend to free our slaves?"

"Not today." Under special circumstances, Karl made exceptions, but a general policy of slicing up all slaveowners was a general policy of suicide. *Give us a generation, and we'll change that.*

The man next to him tugged at the captain's sleeve, then whispered in his ear for a moment.

Karl shook his head. "I wouldn't."

"You wouldn't what?"

"I wouldn't think too seriously about trying to collect the bounty that the Slavers' Guild has placed on my head, no matter what it's risen to. Not that you couldn't take me, but I do have friends; the final cost is likely to be far too high, all things considered. Best to check with your lord before taking the matter any further."

The captain smiled back at him, almost affectionately. "I

will. Assuming that he doesn't want you poisoned, would you join me for dinner?"

"And if he does want me poisoned?"

"Would you join me for dinner anyway?" He smiled with patently genuine friendliness.

"My pleasure, Captain." Karl laughed. "My pleasure."

"Ta herat va ky 'the last run' ky, ka Haptoe Valeran," Karl said. *It is called the last run, Captain Valeran.* "The notion is that none of our lives are taken cheaply. Ever."

A servant brought another bottle of wine. Valeran pulled his sleeves back before uncorking it, then splashed some wine first in his own glass, then in Karl's, then in Chak's.

Valeran drank first. "Not bad. I think you'll like it. And as for this 'last run' of yours, I have heard about it. Reminds you of the old days, Halvin, eh?" He smiled at the silent soldier standing next to the door. "It tends to take all the fun out of treating you and your people as outlaws, I suspect." Valeran nodded sagely, then sighed. "Not my sort of life, not anymore, but an . . . interesting one, I take it."

Karl chuckled. "There's an old curse, back in my homeland: 'May you live in interesting times.' " Well, that wasn't much of a lie; from here, China was as close as America. Or as far. "Not something I'd suggest, given an alternate. And it looks like you have a good one, here. You're from Nyphien, originally?"

"All my men are; we were first blooded against the Katharhds, in the Mountain Wars." He considered Chak carefully. There was a trace of hostility in Valeran's voice, although the Mountain Wars between the Nyphs and the Katharhds had fizzled out more than fifteen years before. "I've always preferred being a barracks commander to being a field soldier, even being a field soldier against the Katharhds."

The little man shrugged. "My family was in the north during the Mountain Wars, Captain Valeran. My father died fighting against the Therranji and their dwarf hirelings. Bloody work, Captain Valeran, just as bloody as the Mountain Wars."

"Yes," Valeran conceded. "It was bloody. But . . . I must confess I miss it, from time to time. There was a certain something to it, no?"

Karl shook his head. "All things considered, I'd rather be in Phil—I'd rather be bored."

"Then I beg to suggest that you could find boring employment as a soldier anywhere in the Eren regions. Although . . . perhaps Lord Mehlên of Metreyll wouldn't be interested, or Lund of Lundeyll, come to think of it—and perhaps Enkiar's neutrality would make it difficult for my lord to employ you. But, if you'd like, I could broach the subject to Lord Gyren?"

"I'm not much for giving fealty."

Chak snickered. Karl silenced him with a glance, then turned back to Valeran. "Meaning no offense, in my native land your present function wouldn't be considered a soldierly one."

"No?" Valeran raised an eyebrow as he sipped his wine. "What would they call me, a doxy?"

Karl had found himself liking the guard captain. There was an undefinable something in the captain's manner that made Karl certain he was a man to whom honor wasn't just a word, but a valued possession.

"No, not at all," Karl said. "We would call you a 'policeman'— your primary task is to maintain internal order, not protect Enkiar from invading forces."

"True, true, but it must be a strange country you come from, Karl Cullinane, where such subtle distinctions are considered important."

Karl laughed. "We had many strange distinctions. There's the color of one's skin, for example. In my land, my friendship with Ch'akresarkandyn would be thought strange—"

"—as it is here; I've no fondness for Katharhds. Meaning no offense," he said, ducking his head momentarily in Chak's direction. "Are you certain you'd care for nothing?"

"I can't eat the local food," Chak said, glaring at Karl. *Just once,* his look said, *could you be the one with the delicate digestion?*

"You were telling me why those in your land would think your friendship strange, I believe?"

"Because of Chak's skin color. Or mine, for that matter. Depending on which point of view you took, he would be considered too dark, or I too light. It was our version of racial prejudice."

"Racial? But he's every bit as human as you and I. It's not as though he were a dwarf or an elf."

"In my world there are no elves or dwarves. We have to make do with . . . peripheral distinctions."

"Skin color. *Skin* color. Skin *color*." Valeran tried the words as though tasting them. "*Skin color*." He shook his head. "And were you and I friends, my own coloring would cause comment?" Valeran extended a deeply tanned arm.

"No, because it's acquired, not natural. You tan more thoroughly than I do, that's all. It wouldn't be a matter of import."

"And I suppose that, say, a Mel's eyefolds would be considered significant."

"Of course."

Valeran laughed. "A strange land, indeed. You were telling me in which direction it lies?"

"No, I wasn't. Although if you're interested, there is a way to get there, if you'd like to try it. You just have to tiptoe past the father of dragons, that's all."

"No, though I thank you for the kind suggestion."

They drank in silence for a few minutes.

"It must be interesting work, though," Karl said. "Few people meet many outlanders; you must encounter them all the time."

"True, true. And a strange lot many of them are." He snorted. "We have had a lot of Biemish and Holts coming through, of late—some deserters, more slaves. Vicious war—and over what?"

Valeran meant it as a rhetorical question, but Karl decided not to take it that way. "Depends on how you look at it. Last I heard, the war was started by some raiders coming down from Aershtyn into Holtun. The Holts decided that Bieme was responsible, and there you have it."

"War, and a dirty one. You can tell by the scavengers, coming through with chains of slaves. We had another one here, just a couple of tendays ago."

"Really? The guild operates regularly out of Enkiar?"

"Not a guild man, no—we haven't had one since Ahrmin was here."

Karl's wineglass snapped in his hands.

Valeran laughed again. "So. That is what this is all about.

You have been prying for information on Ahrmin, eh?'' He shook his head. ''You won't find him here; he left . . . some time ago, to pick up another chain of slaves . . . somewhere or other. Nice fellow, actually, although it's pitiful the way he looks. Did you have something to do with that?''

''Why do you ask?''

''He was just as eager for news of you as you are for word of him.''

''Understandable.'' Karl nodded. ''I . . . burned him a little.''

''I wouldn't have thought you so foolish. You should have killed him, or let him be.''

Chak snorted. ''He has a point there, Karl.''

''I *thought* I had killed him; I'd intended to. He was bound for Bieme, you said?''

''I didn't say. And won't. He will be back here eventually, although you will be long gone by that time.''

''I will?''

''I'm afraid I'd have to insist.'' Valeran looked him straight in the eye. ''I'm really afraid I would.''

At the door, a soldier thumped his hand against his breastplate. ''Message, Captain,'' he said, entering the room at the captain's nod of permission and handing Valeran a scrap of paper.

Valeran read the message twice before cocking his head to one side and looking Karl over. ''I am not one to believe in coincidences, Karl Cullinane. It seems that a group of guild slavers have just entered the town and taken rooms at the inn. I'm curious as to your intentions.''

Karl sat back, pretending to consider the matter. ''How many of them are there?''

''Thirty or so. And they are armed with guns, as you may have gathered. I wouldn't suggest that you attack them, not in Enkiar.''

''I agree.''

Valeran raised an eyebrow. ''I'm surprised. You agree not to attack them?''

''No, all I agreed was that you would suggest that I not attack them.''

''Thirty to two?'' Chak put in. ''Long odds—''

''Then you will agree to leave them alone while in Enkiar?''

"—but I guess they'll just have to take their chances."

Karl raised a hand. "I'll give you my word, Captain. This group of slavers . . . as long as they do not attack either Chak or me, we will not attack them, for as long as they remain in Enkiar." He wrinkled his brow. "Or let us say for up to a tenday. I wouldn't want them to think that they can safely set up shop permanently here, or anywhere else."

"I have your word on this?"

"You do. I'll swear it on my sword, if you'd like." Slowly, Karl drew his saber and balanced it on the flat of his palms. "As I have agreed, so will I do." He polished the blade with a soft cloth before resheathing it.

"Very well. You won't object to my posting a guard outside of your rooms, will you?"

"Do I have a choice?"

"Certainly. You may object, or you may not object." Valeran shrugged. "I'll post guards, either way."

The Enkiar inn was seven two-storied buildings of varying sizes, grouped around a common courtyard. Karl and Chak's suite was on the second floor of one of the smaller buildings. Its balcony and windows faced outward, away from the courtyard. The inn was at the edge of the town; beyond the road, a sea of wheat beckoned in the starlight.

Below, Karl could see three soldiers on watch, although there were others nearby; he knew of another three on guard outside the single entrance to the suite.

That could be trouble. Karl couldn't see a way out of the suite that wouldn't involve fighting past the guards. He drew the curtains.

"I can't think of anything useful to do," Chak said. "We're fairly neatly hemmed in for the night. Best to leave things to Slovotsky, eh? Come morning, he should have some idea of who's buying the guns and powder, and maybe what Ahrmin's connection is. We might as well get some sleep, eh?"

"Might as well."

Bare feet thudded quietly on the balcony outside. The curtains were momentarily whisked aside, and a dark shape moved into the darkness of the sleeping room. It stepped toward the nearest of the two beds and leaned over it.

Karl silently rose from the pile of blankets in the corner and tackled the intruder, grasping the other's right wrist and bringing the arm up behind the other's back, to the hammer-lock point.

"It's just *me*, dammit," Walter Slovotsky said. "Leggo."

Karl released him. "Sorry. Announce yourself next time, okay?"

"Definitely. I'd have done it this time except there's a guard patrolling below, and I was sure he'd hear." Slovotsky seated himself on the bed, rubbing his right shoulder. "Do me a favor and put that down, Chak." He gestured a greeting at the little man, who sat in his pile of blankets, a cocked pistol pointed at Walter's midsection.

Chak uncocked the pistol and set it on the floor. "We weren't supposed to see you until tomorrow. And how did you get past the guards?"

"I came over the roof—that sort of thing's my specialty, remember?" He eyed the ripped hem of his pantaloons with distaste. "Got my pants caught between two shingles; had to rip them loose.

"We've got trouble. They made contact too quickly. The deal's been concluded."

"Dammit, why—"

"Because I didn't have any choice!" Slovotsky's whisper was harsh. "Because there wasn't any way to stall without making things look funny. The Holts have taken their powder and guns and left town, leaving me with the claim token to the slaves in the pens." He spread his hands. "Nothing I could do."

"Holts?"

Slovotsky nodded. "They're the buyers. Prince Uldren sent High Baron Keranahan, his nephew. We got more than three hundred slaves, all Biemish. They're apparently most of what's left of barony Krathael; the fighting there has been bloody. I tried to stall, honest, telling him about the raid by you, but that only made him more eager to finish things up and get out of here. He's a lot more interested in getting the guns and powder to Holtun and passing along word of your location than he is in trying for the bounty himself."

"Did he say who he was going to pass word along to?"

"No, but I've got a good guess. Ahrmin. I don't know exactly what's going on, but that little bastard seems to be working hand in hand with Holtun—and with the Aershtyn raiders—"

"Shut up for a second." Karl waved Slovotsky to silence.

It was finally starting to make sense. Bieme and Holtun had been at peace for two generations, until the raiders from Aershtyn had reawakened old hostilities. It was possible, perhaps even likely, that the Aershtyn raiders who had triggered the war had been encouraged by the Slavers' Guild, if they were not actually part of the guild itself.

Cui bono? Who benefits? That was the question.

The answer was simple: The war left the guild and its allies easy pickings in its wake.

Karl nodded. Guild backing also explained why the Holts were able to keep the war going, despite the incompetent generalship of Prince Uldren: With the guild supplying Holtun with guns and powder, it was possible that the Holts could win, or that the war would go on forever.

The only beneficiaries would be the guild. And the buzzards.

"There's more," Walter said. "And you're not going to like it. Tennetty went with them."

"What?"

"Her idea—she doesn't want to see the powder get to Holtun, and she had this crazy idea that she can do something about it. And Keranahan seemed sort of interested in her, so I . . . kind of gave her to him. But she was still wearing those trick chains. She should be able to—"

"She'll get her fool ass killed is what she'll do. You spotted the reason she decided to play slave, to come along. How could you be such an *idiot?*" Tennetty wasn't going to do anything about the powder, not until she got within range of Ahrmin. She hated Ahrmin as much as Karl did; the little bastard had killed Fialt, speared him through the chest.

No. Not Tennetty, too.

Karl sat down on the bed and rubbed his hands against his eyes.

"Karl," Chak said, "we can't do anything about it tonight. We have to trust her to know what she was doing."

"Like hell we do." He stood. "Walter, get going, over the roof. You're pulling up stakes and heading out tonight. Your story is that you're nervous after hearing that I'm in town. Leave one of your knives stuck in the roof, right near the peak.''

''Why—''

''Shut up. Have Piell split off and work his way around; I'll meet him east of town—tonight if I can manage it, tomorrow if not. He's to have two extra horses, healing draughts, his longbow, and all the guns and powder that you can scrape together.''

''What do I do?''

Karl closed his eyes, concentrating. ''One: Play slaver—take the Biemish slaves down the road to the rendezvous; wait for Ellegon. Explain to the Biemish who you are and that they have a choice of going back to Bieme or going to Home. We're going to have to split the team more, dammit.

''Two: Those who want to go to Home, send them back with the smallest group you think safe.

''Three: Drop the masquerade—''

''All *right!*'' Slovotsky slapped his hands together. ''You mean I can stop playing slaver?''

''Shut up and listen. I want you to wait at the rendezvous for Ellegon's supply drop. He should be there any day now, and he'll probably have some guns and powder. Tell him I'll want a massive drop outside of Biemestren—we'll use barony Furnael as a backup—every gun Home can spare, powder, grenades, the bloody works. Tell him to add Nehera and a couple of apprentice Engineers to the drop.

''Four: Once you've rendezvoused with the dragon, I want you to ride after us. With a bit of luck, you'll catch up with us this side of Bieme. Make sure you keep Beralyn safe—she's our passport.'' Karl opened his eyes. ''Am I missing anything?''

''I don't like this.'' Chak shook his head. ''I thought you didn't want to choose sides in this stupid war.''

''I didn't; it seems that Ahrmin's chosen them for me. The way I read it, the guild is backing the Holts. We're siding with Bieme, at least long enough to break up the guild-Holt alliance.''

''And what are we going to do about Tennetty?''

Karl bit his lip. ''Walter, how many of them are there?''

''Fifty or so. All armed to the teeth, now.'' Slovotsky

spread his hands. "I'm sorry, Karl, but you know Tennetty. When she's got her mind set on something . . ."

"Just get out of here."

White-faced, Slovotsky turned to go, but Karl caught his arm. "Walter . . ."

"Yeah?"

"I'm sorry. I should have anticipated this." Tennetty hadn't had any enthusiasm for this, not until she had heard that Ahrmin was still alive, and had been in Enkiar. This was what she had been planning all along. Damn—if Karl had thought it through, or had Ellegon probe her, this could have been avoided.

It isn't Slovotsky's fault; it's mine.

"Right." Slovotsky shook his head. "I'll be telling myself that for years." He clasped Karl's hand. "You getting her out of it?"

"I'm going to try. Now get lost."

Chak looked at Karl and raised an eyebrow. "You, me, and Piell against fifty?"

"Don't forget Tennetty."

"I wasn't. But I don't know how useful she's going to be, not in this."

"You don't like the odds?"

"No. Not one little bit." Chak shrugged. "Do you see another choice?"

"Maybe." Karl pounded on the door, then swung it open. "*Hey!* I want to talk to Captain Valeran, and I want to talk to him now."

"I thought Enkiar claimed to be neutral in the war between Holtun and Bieme, Captain." Karl gestured Valeran to a chair and poured each of them a mug of water.

"Yes, Enkiar is neutral, Karl Cullinane. Anyone may trade for anything here." Valeran rubbed a knuckle against sleepy eyes, then sipped at his water. "Am I to assume that you had me waked at this hour to discuss our neutrality?" he asked acidly.

"No. I had you waked to discuss Enkiar's siding with Holtun in the war—a fact that is shortly to become *very* public knowledge, from Sciforth to Ehvenor."

"Nonsense. Lord Gyren does *not* take sides; both Holtun and Bieme are free to trade in Enkiar."

"Including for *gunpowder?* You consider allowing the Holts and the Slavers' Guild to trade here in guns and gunpowder to be neutral?"

"What is this nonsense?"

"High Baron Keranahan brought in a chain of slaves to trade with the guild—"

"Yes, yes, for gold. To pay—"

"No. For this." Karl took a small vial of slaver powder from his pouch. "A form of gunpowder, made in Pandathaway. Enkiar has been where the trade has taken place." He tipped a spoonful onto the floor—"Stand back, please"—then picked up a water pitcher, stepped away, scooped up a handful of water, and threw it.

Whoom!

"Think about this long and hard, Captain. Bieme will soon know that the Holts were able to trade for guns and powder in Enkiar, while the Biemish weren't. Do you think that they will consider that neutral?" Karl cocked his head to one side. "If you were they, would you? Do you think that *anyone* will think of Enkiar as neutral?"

"N-no. Not if . . . what you say is true," Valeran said slowly, eyeing Karl with suspicion. "How do you know all this?"

Karl smiled. "That's the first good question you've asked, Captain. Sit back and relax; this is going to take a while. Now . . . we were on a sweep through the forests near Wehnest, when I received a report that there were slavers in the meadow below with guns. . . ."

". . . and I can tell you that if you were to search Keranahan's wagons, you'd find almost one hundred guns, and eight large barrels full of this," Karl finished.

"Which *your* man sold to him, Karl Cullinane. Not the Slavers' Guild—"

"Captain. You are trying to avoid facing the simple truth that the Holts have used Enkiar as an unintentional partner in their . . . arrangement with the guild. Do you really think that tonight was the first time Enkiar has been used to trade slaves for powder?'' Karl said. ''Tell me, Captain, how do you think that would reflect on Enkiar's supposed neutrality?''

''Not well.'' Valeran shook his head slowly. ''But what do you expect me to do?''

''That all depends on whether you are only Lord Gyren's puppet, or can think for yourself. You and your men are sworn to uphold Enkiar's neutrality?''

''My oath is to Enkiar; my men are fealty-sworn to me.'' Valeran pounded his fist on his open palm. ''But I *can't* remain faithful to that oath, not and challenge Baron Keranahan at the same time. That would kill the neutrality, just as surely as if Enkiar was seen as taking sides with Holtun. It's the principle, Karl Cullinane: Once Enkiar's neutrality is shattered, it can't be restored.'' He pursed his lips for a moment. ''Unless . . . unless nobody ever hears of how Enkiar's neutrality has been violated. The Holts could be quietly persuaded to conduct their gunpowder trade elsewhere. . . .''

''It's too late for that,'' Karl said. ''My friend Walter Slovotsky has already been in and out of here tonight.''

''So you told me.'' The accent on the second-to-last word was definite. Valeran eyed him levelly, as though to say, *I may well not be your match, Karl Cullinane, but that will not stop me from trying to do my duty*.

Karl nodded his understanding. ''Unless I tell him otherwise, the story will soon be spread wide and far of how Enkiar has been the place where Holtun got guns and powder. And to tell him otherwise, I'll have to live.''

''That would go well with some proof.''

''Check the roof. You'll find a knife at its peak. Slovotsky left that as a bit of evidence that he was here. Or do you want to believe that I walked out on the balcony and climbed up the sheer face to the roof without being spotted?'' Karl rose to his full height and stretched. ''I don't think I can climb that quietly—do you?''

''No. I'll have it checked immediately.'' Valeran beckoned to the guard at the door and whispered briefly in his ear. The man ran out of the room.

''But I ask again,'' Valeran went on. ''Assuming that you're telling the truth, what do you suggest that I do?''

''It all depends on you, Captain Valeran, you and your twenty men. *I* ask again: How loyal are you to Lord Gyren?''

"What do you mean, sir?" Valeran drew himself up straight. "Are you questioning—"

"No, I'm not questioning your honor, Captain. I'm asking if you're loyal enough to Gyren to have him put a price on your head, if it comes to that. Well?"

Valeran sat silently for a moment. "I see what you mean. And the answer is yes, Karl Cullinane. But if you've lied to me . . ."

"I know. But I haven't."

Valeran sighed. "Then I must see Lord Gyren, explain the situation, and . . . resign from his service. He will understand, Karl Cullinane. I assume you wish to employ my men and me in hunting down the Holts?"

"Obviously. You and your men have families?"

"Not I, but most do, yes."

"Chak, how are we fixed for money?"

The little man nodded. "Well enough. I've got about six pieces of Pandathaway gold on me, five sil—"

"Fine. Give." Karl accepted the pouch from Chak and tossed it to Valeran. "That is for their women and children, to maintain them until a group from Home comes to guide them. Leave one of your men; they will remain in his charge until then."

Valeran bounced the leather pouch up and down on his palm. "I may regret doing this, but . . ." He nodded, a vague smile playing across his lips. "Damn *me*, but it's good to be alive again. *Halvin!*"

The guard at the door turned about. "Yes, Captain."

"I thought I would never say this, but . . . we ride tonight."

Halvin gave him a gap-toothed smile. "Yes, Captain. It has been a while, sir."

"Put that smile away, fool. Your memory fails you." Valeran turned to Karl. "I repeat: Should I find that you have lied to me, Karl Cullinane, one of us will die."

"Understood. And until then?"

"Until then . . ." Valeran got to his feet and drew himself into a rigid brace. "What are your orders, sir?"

CHAPTER FIFTEEN:

Firefight

Take calculated risks. That is quite different from being rash. . . . The most vital quality a soldier can possess is self-confidence, utter, complete and bumptious.
—George Patton

Ahead, the well-rutted road twisted and turned in the predawn light. As Stick cantered down the road, Karl reached down and patted at the stallion's neck. "Faster, Stick, faster," he said, digging in his heels and settling himself more firmly in the saddle, his hand automatically checking to see that the rifle was still secure in its boot.

Valeran spurred his large black gelding, barely matching Stick's pace. "I would like to hear your plan, Karl Cullinane, if that's permitted," he called out above the clattering of hooves. "You *do* have a plan, don't you?"

"Of sorts. Be still for now—and hang back, if you don't want to risk getting shot."

Piell was waiting around the next bend. Karl pulled on Stick's reins, swinging his leg over the saddle and dismounting as the stallion halted.

The elf was not pleased. "Ch'akresarkandyn told me what you're going to do—what you're going to *try* to do. I don't like it at all."

"I don't remember asking your opinion."

He snorted. "You're going to hear it anyway—"

"Shut *up*." Karl reached up and gripped the front of the

179

elf's tunic. "If you want out, you've got it. Just leave the bow and guns and get the hell out of my way."

"Ta havath." Piell raised both palms. "Ta havath, Karl."

As the others rounded the bend and cantered into sight, Karl released the elf. "How many rifles do you have?"

"Five—and I have two shotguns left; I gave one to Chak. I also have my bow and just over twoscore arrows."

"Can you rig a few of the arrows for fire?" Karl asked, beckoning to Valeran and his men to dismount.

"Yes. You intend to fire the wagons?"

Karl nodded. "Think about what happens if they try to put out the one with the slaver powder in it."

"I have." The elf smiled. "Do you think we can actually get Tennetty out?"

"Oh? So you're in on this?"

"I always was."

Karl took his shrouded lantern down from his saddle, pulled back the baffles, and hung it from a knot in a tree. He turned to Valeran. "It normally takes anywhere from two to ten days to teach someone how to use a gun correctly. We don't have the time to teach reloading and safety, but I'm going to teach you and four of your men to use guns right now." He extended his hand. "Unloaded?" he asked, flicking open the pan and feeling inside.

"Yes."

"Good. Valeran, pick four of your people."

Valeran pointed at four of his men. "Over here, if you please."

Karl called out to the other fifteen. "You can listen to this, too, but those of you with crossbows, get them cocked and loaded.

"Now . . . using a rifle is simplicity itself. There are five steps. First, you pull back the hammer—that's this thing— until it locks." He thumbed the hammer back until it clicked. "Hear that sound? Second, you raise the rifle to your shoulder, selecting a target."

He aimed the empty rifle at a nearby tree. "Third, you line up your front and back sights right on the center of whoever you're going to shoot. At the range we're going to be, do not allow for drop as you would with a crossbow. Four, hold your breath and squeeze the trigger—"

Snap! Sparks flew from the lock.

Halvin spoke up. "You said that there were five steps?"

"Yes. Five: Drop the damn rifle and get your sword into your hand as quickly as you can, because there are going to be one hell of a lot of very angry Holts around you, even if you've killed your target."

He tossed the rifle to Halvin. "Practice."

Hoofbeats sounded from down the road; Karl beckoned Valeran and his soldiers over to one side, drawing a pistol and cocking it.

It was only Chak. His horse was panting, the cloths wrapped around its hooves cut to ribbons.

The little man dismounted, almost out of breath. "They're not moving too quickly; we should be able to get around in front of them by taking the north road."

"Did they see you?"

Chak snorted. "Screw you, kemo sabe," he said in his halting English. "Your nerves are making your mouth say stupid things."

"True. Sorry." Karl jerked his head toward the road. "Grab another shotgun, and a crossbow. I want you and Piell to take the north road, and set up some sort of roadblock; the rest of us will lag behind until we hear shots. Piell, listen up: When they near your roadblock, I want you to drop the lead horse of the lead wagon, then fire that wagon. Got it?"

Piell nodded.

"Go."

Valeran opened his mouth as though to say something, then changed his mind.

God, but I wish Ellegon were here. Was Valeran as trustworthy as he seemed? The dragon could have found out with a moment's effort.

Karl shrugged. No point in worrying about it; he was already committed to trusting Valeran. He lowered the pistol's hammer, flipped the pistol, and caught it by the barrel. He held it out to Valeran. "This works just like a rifle; you hold it at arm's length, pull the hammer back, then sight down your arm. Squeeze the trigger gently; don't pull at it. Or you can just press the gun against my back."

"Your back?"

"You're wondering if I've been leading you on—if I have, you can get even very quickly. In the meantime, mount up."

A single shot sounded from down the road. Karl kicked Stick into a gallop; behind him, Valeran urged the others along.

Ahead of them, the Holts had dismounted from their horses and the three wagons. The lead wagon was skewed sideways across the road, its lead horse lying on its side on the road, whinnying in pain, an arrow projecting from its chest.

Damn. "Take cover, everyone. Valeran, assign somebody to handle the horses. Make sure he keeps a good grip on their reins."

So much for Karl's original idea. Piell could have picked a worse place for the ambush, but not much worse. The Holts had already set up a line of defense behind their wagons and in the irrigation ditch along the side of the road. Rushing them would just be suicide. The worst of it was that dawn was already breaking; in the light, Karl's people, already outnumbered and outgunned, would be even more vulnerable.

Another shot sounded; a bullet whizzed overhead, snapping through the leaves.

"Don't shoot yet," Karl shouted, untying his own rifle from the saddleboot, slinging his saddlebags over his shoulder.

"Go!" He slapped Stick on the rump, sending the stallion back down the road, out of the line of fire. He ducked into the ditch on the right side of the road, tossing the saddlebags to one side.

"Piell, can you hear me?" he called out in English, knowing that Tennetty would also recognize his voice. "Fire the wagons, now. Then move; I don't want them fixing on your position." He cocked the rifle, then looked out onto the road. There were plenty of targets; the Holts weren't used to facing guns. Karl took aim at a head, took a quick breath and held it, then squeezed slowly on the trigger.

The rifle kicked against his shoulder as the Holt's head exploded in a bloody shower; Karl ducked back behind into the ditch, fumbling in his pouch for a rag and his powder horn, leaving the tallow box—here, a spit patch would serve just as well.

Coughing in the acrid smoke, he blew down the barrel to clear it, then poured a measure of powder from the horn into the rifle, spat on a patch and slipped it over the hole, then thumbed a ball into place. He drew his ramrod and shoved the ball and patch down the barrel, seating them firmly.

"Karl Cullinane," Valeran called out. "There are a group of them, moving toward us."

"On my command," he called back. "You with the rifles will rise, raise your weapon to your shoulder, pick a target, and fire—and then duck back down, quickly." He pulled back the hammer to half-cock, quickly cleared the vent with his vent pick, then took out his vial of priming powder.

"They're moving, again."

"Now!"

Gunshots thundered. Karl charged the pan, then snapped the frizzen securely into place.

He raised his head above the ditch. All of the Holts had taken cover, except for one wounded man lying on the road, cradling his belly in his hands. One out of four shots reaching a target wasn't too bad, not under the circumstances.

Another of the Holts rose, only to drop his rifle and scream as a longbow's arrow sprouted from his side.

Thanks, Piell.

But this wouldn't do. The Holts would gather themselves for a charge in a few minutes, once they realized that they had their enemy outgunned and outmanned.

"Bows, covering fire. Valeran, get that lamp to me." He untied the straps from his saddlebags, then pulled out the box of grenades, opened it, and extracted one from its padded compartment.

Valeran arrived with the lantern. "I don't like this. They have all used rifles before, and we haven't. And my men aren't used to facing these . . . guns."

"I know." Karl slid the lamp's baffle open just a crack, then stuck the end of the fuse into the flame.

It caught immediately. He raised his head above the boulder and threw the grenade high and far, directly for the spot in the ditch where he hoped the remaining nine rushing Holtish soldiers were.

"Down!" he called, following his own advice.

The grenade dropped behind the road and into the ditch,

then exploded with a loud *crump!* followed by a chorus of screams.

Karl looked out. The lead wagon was burning nicely; Piell's fire arrow must have gone inside and caught something flammable. Tennetty's slim form was outlined against the fire as she worked her way behind one of the Holtish soldiers, then slipped an improvised garrote around his neck, pulling him back, out of sight.

Good. She'd worked her way free. The Holts didn't know it, but they had more to worry about than some outsiders attacking; they had a tiger among them.

More gunshots sounded. One of Valeran's men pitched forward, clutching at his throat; another stooped, uncorking a bottle of healing draughts, then shaking his head and recorking it.

This just wasn't going to make it. *There're too many of them, and Valeran's people aren't used to this kind of fighting.*

Karl didn't like it, but he would have to settle for getting Tennetty out and forget about the slaver powder.

"Withdraw," he called out. "Everybody—and I mean *everybody!*" he shouted, hoping that Tennetty could hear him over the crackling of the fire. He sneaked another glance. One of the Holts had spotted her and was bringing his gun to bear.

Karl raised his rifle to his shoulder and took aim, ignoring the *whipcrack* of bullets around him, then squeezed the trigger. The bullet caught the Holt on his chestplate; it knocked him down, his own weapon discharging toward the sky. Tennetty dove for cover, disappearing into the ditch.

"Withdraw," Karl repeated. "Piell and Chak, acknowledge, dammit."

A distant shout marked Piell's position, but where was Chak? Perhaps it was just as well. If Karl couldn't spot him, likely the Holts couldn't, either.

Chak sprang up next to the second wagon, fired his shotgun into an intervening soldier, then disappeared into the wagon's interior, a waterbag clutched in his hands.

What the hell does he think he's doing? Karl had given the order to withdraw. The main objective had been accomplished; they would just have to let the powder go by.

Three of the Holtish soldiers followed Chak into the wagon. That was probably their mistake. In the close quarters of the wagon, they would probably get in each other's way more than Chak's. *But what's he doing with a waterbag—*
  "No!"

The wagon exploded in a cloud of steam and dust, sending pieces of horses and soldiers tumbling into the still air.

That was enough for the few uninjured Holts. Some mounted their horses and galloped away; others just ran.

Valeran grabbed at Karl's arm. "What happened?"

"Chak. He . . . took out their powder. Lord Gyren will be satisfied," he said, his voice sounding curiously flat and emotionless even to his own ears. "We have preserved Enkiar's neutrality."

"There are still some of them alive."

Karl tossed his rifle to one side, bringing his sword into his right hand and drawing his remaining pistol with his left. "Not for long. Follow me."

There is nothing quite as ugly as sunrise over a battlefield. In the dark, it is possible to ignore the spilled contents of the bags of skin, the flesh, blood, and bones that once were human beings.

During a battle, it's necessary to look beyond the carnage, in order to avoid becoming part of it.

But in the light of day, it's a different matter entirely. This battlefield had once been a wheat field. It would again be just a wheat field, someday.

But not this day. Now, it was the blood-drenched floor of a slaughtering ground, corpses already attracting scavengers.

Using his saber like a flail, Karl shooed two crows away from the body of a Holtish soldier and forced himself to look at the man's face.

No, not a man, a boy, perhaps seventeen, maybe eighteen years old, beardless. Under a shock of brown hair, his ashen face was pale, still; a casual glance would have made Karl think he was only sleeping.

Valeran cleared his throat. Karl turned to see Tennetty standing next to the captain.

"Karl—" she started, then caught herself. "We . . . haven't found any sign of Chak. Could he—"

"No." Karl shook his head. "There was only one door to the wagon. He must have set the waterbag on top of one of the powder barrels, then put his pistol right up against the bag."

He could almost see it in his mind's eye: the three Holts satisfied that they had Chak cornered; Chak quirking a smile at them as he fired, the bullet crashing through the bag and wood, driving the water into the slaver powder, then . . .

He looked Tennetty square in the face, at first not trusting himself to speak. If only she had followed orders, none of this would have happened; Karl would have let this shipment get by, rather than attack at such unfavorable odds.

And Tennetty knew that. Let her live with the guilt.

Why, dammit, Chak—why?

What happens when you decide that some objective is more important than your own life is?

But it wasn't as important as Chak's life, not this. The Holtish had gotten powder before, and would again. Not in Enkiar, though. Enkiar would now be closed to them for the trade in slaver powder, but Enkiar would have been closed to them in any case.

It wasn't worth Chak's life. But it had been, to Ch'ak-resarkandyn.

That wasn't enough. "Tennetty."

"Yes, Karl." She stood in front of him, her hands well away from the sword at her waist, making no movement to protect herself.

"We're moving out." He kept his voice low, little more than a whisper. He knew that if he started shouting, he would lose control completely. "I want you to start Valeran and his men on marksmanship tonight, when we camp. By the time we reach Bieme, they are to be as competent as possible. When Slovotsky and his people catch up with us, you turn the training over to him. Bieme is going to be tough; I want us up to strength."

"Yes, Karl. Although I don't know what you think a few tens of us can do in that sort of—"

He reached out and gripped her throat, the tips of his fingers resting against her trachea. He could bring his fingers together—

—but that wouldn't bring Chak back. "Shut your mouth,"

he said, dropping his hand. "If I want your opinion, I'll ask for it."

She started to turn away.

"One more thing, Tennetty," he said, grabbing her by the arm, spinning her back to face him. "I don't want you to get yourself killed. You're to live a long, long life—hear me? And every day, you're to remember that it was you who killed Chak, just as surely as if you'd slipped a knife between his ribs. If you hadn't gone independent, if you had just played things out as I told you to, this wouldn't have happened."

"If *you* had let me try for Ahrmin—"

He backhanded her to the ground, then booted her in the shoulder as she started to rise, sending her sprawling on the dirt. "Don't speak to me, not anymore. Not unless I speak to you first. Understood?"

Her hand slipped to the hilt of her sword.

"Go ahead, Tennetty, *please*."

She shook her head slowly, her hand falling away from her sword. It wasn't fear that saved her life at that moment, it was guilt.

And what do I do about my own guilt? he thought.

There wasn't any answer.

"Just get out of my sight," Karl Cullinane said, as he turned to Valeran. "Have you buried your man?"

Valeran shook his head. "Not yet."

There was no real point in hurrying. *I should probably wait here for Walter, Beralyn, and the rest, instead of letting them catch up farther down the road.*

That would be the logical thing.

"Bury him, Valeran. We're getting the hell out of here."

That evening, they made camp beside a brook to wait for Walter Slovotsky and the rest.

In the morning, Tennetty and two of the horses were gone.

PART FOUR:

Bieme

CHAPTER SIXTEEN:

Prince Pirondael

Our fathers and ourselves sowed the dragon's teeth.
Our children know and suffer the armed men.
                              —Stephen Vincent Benét

Biemestren, the capital city of Bieme, reeked of a long peace, now shattered.

The castle itself was surrounded by two zigzagging stone walls, each barely shy of ten meters in height, the inner one with eight guard towers scattered around its circumference. The residence tower rose from inside the inner wall, resting on the flat top of a twenty-yard-high, almost perfectly circular hill.

But the castle itself was only a handful of buildings that housed the prince, his court, and the House Guard; the vast majority of the population of Biemestren seemed to live in the newer buildings outside the wall, clinging to it as they fanned out like a tree ear on an old oak. Beyond them were the rude encampments housing several thousand refugees from the west.

A breeze brought a foul reek to Karl's nostrils. If the local clerics weren't on the ball, vermin-spread diseases would likely do as much damage as the war.

"Nice location for a castle," Walter Slovotsky said. "That hill is the highest spot for twenty miles around."

"It's too round to be a real hill; it's a motte," Karl said. "This was probably a basic motte-and-bailey castle, originally."

"I know what a bailey is, but what's a motte?" Slovotsky raised an eyebrow.

"The hill that the castle's on." Karl searched his memory for an Erendra equivalent, but there wasn't one. "Basically just a pile of dirt. If we dug down, we'd find timbers of the original castle's foundation buried in it.

"It's an old trick. Goes back to before Charlemagne; it was how the Norman nobles held out, carved out their own fiefs in both France and Britain. Siege engines can break the walls, but the motte itself is practically indestructible. Even if invaders breach the outer wall, they have to fight their way up a steeper hill than nature would probably provide, and *then* have the inner defenses to contend with."

"And meanwhile the defenders don't have to sit on their hands. Nice bit of defense." Slovotsky nodded. "Back Home, when we were building the original palisade, why didn't you suggest a motte?"

"If you'll remember, Riccetti was running that show. Besides, we didn't have the manpower to move a whole lot of earth, not even if you include Ellegon. He's got his limitations, just like the rest of us."

"Besides, you didn't think of it."

"True."

"This is pretty damn near impregnable, though," Walter said. "Even if the Holts get this deep into Bieme, there's no law that says the Biemish have to sit tight and not shoot back, while they're working on breaking the walls. One wizard shooting out a flame spell or two a day—"

"Wouldn't do it. Not if I was running the siege, and I'm sure that the Holts know a lot more about siege warfare than I do." Karl shrugged. "Bring up ten, twelve onagers at once, and it's watch-the-walls-go-down, even if they have a garden-variety wizard and you don't."

"But you said that they wouldn't be able to break through."

"Not immediately, no. Ever hear of a siege? Breach the walls in a few places, keep the defenders too busy to plug the holes, and you can still starve them out if they don't drop their guard enough for you to take the castle any other way. If the defenders are really good, it could take years, but who's going to come to Bieme's rescue? The Nyphs? They're more likely to try to lop off a piece of the country, if they can be sure that Khar or some Katharhd bands won't move on them while they're distracted."

"Motte, eh?" Slovotsky said, clearly preferring a lighter subject. "I'll remember that. They probably just call it a mound."

"So we'll teach them the right word."

Slovotsky laughed. "Your mind is a junkpile, Karl. I know for a fact that you know squat about world history—"

"Give me a break. I never got around to majoring in any kind of history. Too much work. Always liked the soft sciences; if you had anything on the ball, they'd practically give the school to you."

"So where did engineering come in? You were going to be an electronics engineer when I first met you."

"Just that one semester; I was young and ambitious. Too much work. I switched to poli sci right after that; electoral behavior is a hell of a lot easier than electrical behavior."

The outer wall's portcullis was raised, announced by a squeal of metal on metal that could be heard for miles.

A troop of fifty armored, mounted soldiers rode through, cantering down the road toward Karl and his people.

"Pay attention, folks, we've got company," Karl said in English, repeating it in Erendra for Beralyn, Valeran, and his people. "Let's hope that Baron Tyrnael's runners got the message through. I'd rather not get mistaken for an enemy."

Once again, he found himself pausing, waiting for a cynical bit of bravado from Chak. Chak would have said something, maybe "Too bad for them if they do, kemo sabe."

Damn you, Chak, he thought. *Who said you could up and die on me?*

"Pay attention, Karl. Shall I go back for Beralyn?"

"No. Stay with her; bring her forward when I call. I want to make sure that these folks are ready to talk, not fight. Her face is our passport; I wouldn't want to get it slashed."

"Right. One suggestion, though: Your temper gets out of hand every now and then. This might be a good time to keep hold of it. Beralyn says that temper is one thing that Prince Pirondael doesn't put up with."

"Don't end a sentence with a preposition."

"Fine," Slovotsky said. He broke into a broad smile.

"Temper is one thing that Prince Pirondael doesn't put up with—asshole."

Karl disliked Prince Harffen Pirondael at first sight, although he wasn't quite sure why.

It wasn't because the prince had kept him waiting for more than an hour for no apparent reason, or that his men-at-arms politely but firmly insisted on relieving Karl and Walter of their swords before they were ushered into the Presence.

The first was an irrelevant, if petty, perquisite of office; the second was an understandable precaution, under the circumstances. This wasn't the same sort of situation as he had faced with Dhara; there was no need to step on Pirondael's toes until he apologized.

So that wasn't it. Karl wrinkled his brow. Then what was it? He didn't dislike the prince simply because he had chosen to meet with them in a large, bare room in the dwelling tower that had only one chair, now fully occupied by Pirondael's sizable bulk—that was just another princely perk.

Karl didn't dislike the prince because of the way that his two guards stood just beyond springing distance, their crossbows loaded, eyeing Karl with professional caution. Quite the contrary: Karl had a profound respect for Pirondael's guards. Back home, back on the Other Side, there were people who sneered at the notion of honor. But that was clearly the only thing that kept Pirondael's House Guard faithful. They weren't surrounded, not yet; those who wanted to desert could have escaped to the west.

Those who remained with Pirondael couldn't have been expecting that Bieme would win the war, not against an army armed with Slavers' Guild guns.

Why were they waiting for the coming of the Holt army?

Because they had sworn their loyalty to Prince Pirondael, and they meant it.

Maybe that was it. Pirondael didn't look like the kind who deserved that kind of loyalty, this fat prince lolling back on his throne, wearing his purple-and-gold finery, his silver crown of office resting on his oily black curls, not a hair out of place.

And perhaps Karl resented the unnecessary formality of

Pirondael's wearing his jewel-inlaid crown instead of a simple cap of maintenance.

He knew that he resented the way that Beralyn had gravitated to her prince's side, occasionally interrupting him to whisper in his ear. No, that wasn't a betrayal, even if it felt like one. Beralyn didn't owe Karl anything. It wasn't like Tennetty running out on him.

He shrugged to himself. It didn't matter why he disliked the prince, or even that he disliked the prince. This wasn't about personalities.

"There's an old saying where I come from, your majesty," Walter said in Erendra, then switched to English. " 'The first hit's free, kid.' "

"Which means?"

"Utshay upway, Walter." Karl elbowed Slovotsky in the side, then turned back to the prince. "It tranlates to 'A wise man accepts a gift in the spirit in which it is intended.' It's a simple proposition, your majesty," he said. "We're willing to get rid of the slavers and their powder—and we'll start by lifting the Furnael siege."

He crossed his arms over his chest. "We'll have to capture two or three slavers or Holtish officers for one of my people to interrogate; she can find out where their center of operations is. All I need is a few mercenaries, provisions, and the temporary use of enough land for our training and staging grounds. The rest is up to us."

"But as an independent force, not under my barons' command." Pirondael stroked his salt-and-pepper beard. He looked vaguely like Baron Furnael, which was understandable: apparently, all of the Biemish nobility were more or less related. "You see the problems that would cause?"

"No. I don't. And, honestly, I don't care. Before the slavers brought guns and powder into the war, you took how many baronies away from Holtun? Two?"

"Three." Pirondael smiled, remembering. "The Holtish should not have started the war. Prince Uldren isn't much of a general. Then again, neither am I. The difference is that he insists on being one, while I do not; I leave the planning to those who know war."

"And how many of those baronies do you still hold?"

The smile vanished. "None. Since they brought those

accursed weapons into the war, we've lost those, plus barony Arondael, Krathael, and most of Furnael—most of them almost emptied of their people, hauled away by slavers. As we speak, Furnael Keep is under siege.'' Pirondael shrugged. ''It may already have fallen, for all I know—''

''Your majesty,'' Beralyn put in, only to be quieted by a quick chopping motion.

''—and while I wish I could, I can't spare the troops holding the line in Hivael to try to break the siege. You say that you can do that, with how many men?''

''One hundred—forty of mine, sixty of your mercenaries to be released into my service. Plus a few . . . surprises that I have in mind.''

''I'm told that there are more than a thousand Holts maintaining the siege.''

Karl smiled. ''Their misfortune.''

''Or mine, if you are not sincere.'' Pirondael shook his head. ''My men tell me that you are . . . not oversupplied with these guns of yours.'' He raised a palm. ''No, Karl Cullinane, none of my soldiers have tried to capture any. I'm told that would not be wise. But I was asking what else you require.''

''To break the siege and take the slavers out of the war? Nothing. Except . . .''

''Except? I *thought* that there would be more.''

''I'll need you to get rid of any dragonbane in Biemestren and its environs. I want it all burned—by the end of tomorrow.''

The prince spread his hands. ''That is hardly a problem. We have not cultivated dragonbane for hundreds of years. I wouldn't know where to find any. Why is this important to you?''

''Within the tenday or so, a friend of mine is arriving. He doesn't like dragonbane.''

''A friend?'' The prince whitened. He started to turn toward Beralyn, but Karl stopped him with a nod.

''Yes. And if you're still thinking about trying to torture the secret of gunpowder from Walter and me, I'd caution against it. For one thing, neither of us knows how to make it,'' he lied. ''And for another, my . . . friend wouldn't like it. Don't get Ellegon angry, your majesty. Dragonbane or not, you wouldn't like him when he's angry. Now, have we an agreement, or not?''

"Possibly, possibly. If you manage to break the siege of Furnael Keep, what then? You will require additional forces in order to attack the main guild camp on Aershtyn, no?"

"Possibly. We'll talk about it then, your majesty. Have we an agreement?"

The prince nodded.

Karl turned to Walter. "Walter—"

"I know, I know." Slovotsky raised his hands. "You want a recon of the siege of Furnael Keep, and you want the report yesterday. It'll take me a bit more than a week; you think you can live without me for that long?"

"Yup." Karl turned back to Pirondael. "Your majesty, if you'll have your soldiers lead us to our staging grounds, we have many preparations to get under way."

The prince nodded. Karl and Walter turned and walked out of the room, reclaiming their weapons at the door. Accompanied by three guards, they walked down the stone staircase of the tower and out into the bright daylight.

"I don't like it, Karl. I don't like it at all. Assume we succeed at barony Furnael and in knocking out the slavers on Aershtyn. What if Pirondael decides that's enough, once we've taken guns and powder out of the war? It could be Holtun that gets chopped up and shipped off by the slavers— after all, the guild has been free to deal in Bieme before. Would that be any better?"

"No. But I don't think he'll push for that."

"And if he does?"

Karl looked him full in the face. "Three guesses. The first two don't count." They emerged from the arched doorway, squinting in the bright sunlight.

"That's what I thought. Who've you got in mind to replace him? The line of succession passes to his sons—"

"Both of whom are dead." Maybe that was it. The death of his sons should have been bothering Pirondael. What kind of man shrugged that sort of thing off?

"And then probably to a near relative, no?"

"As I understand it, right now the legitimate succession would be pretty much up for grabs among the barons—at least one of whom is a man of honor, one who will keep any agreement we make with him. And he's under siege. For now."

"Which is why you want to break the siege of the keep, instead of going directly to Aershtyn. I don't like it when you get tricky." Slovotsky caught himself. "Sorry."

"Better get going."

"Right."

"One more thing, Walter?"

"What?"

"Don't get yourself killed."

Slovotsky smiled. "My pleasure."

CHAPTER SEVENTEEN:

"One Thing at a Time"

Do not peer too far.

—Pindar

Karl spread his blankets on the ground and lay back, staring up at the night sky.

There were no faerie lights dancing in the overcast sky tonight; only a dozen of the brightest stars were visible through the haze. Across the field, the five equally spaced signal fires sparked their message up into the night. Either Slovotsky or Ellegon would recognize the signal; both of them should be showing up soon.

He closed his eyes, but he couldn't sleep.

This time I may have bitten off more than I can chew, he thought. Even if Ellegon brought enough guns and powder, the odds were just too much on the other side. The sixty mercenaries that Pirondael had released to him would have to be watched carefully; it was unlikely that they'd be worth much in a firefight. Valeran's men were coming along quickly, granted, but riflery wasn't something that they could learn enough of in only a few tendays, not when it was such a new skill. While their marksmanship was adequate, their reloading speed was pitiful even during practice; in combat, it could only be worse.

That left Karl, Walter, Piell, and their ten remaining warriors, plus Henrad. Maybe Ellegon would bring along a couple of warriors, in addition to Nehera and the Engineers.

That still wasn't enough, not even with Ellegon. The dragon

couldn't be risked in close combat; the slavers would surely have some dragonbaned bolts.

Reflexively, he started to curse Tennetty for deserting, but one more person wouldn't really have made any difference.

Dammit, I can't do it all by myself, he thought.

But this war had to be stopped, no matter what. The guild couldn't be allowed to trigger a war with impunity. This was even more dangerous than slaving raids: Human spoils of war could easily and cheaply supply Pandathaway and most of the Eren regions with slaves for years to come.

This wasn't how Karl and the others had planned it. Their plan to interfere with the slave trade was three-pronged: first, to make the business deadly to the slavers; second, to drive the price of slaves up, forcing the locals to invent and adopt better ways of getting things done; third, to turn Riccetti and his Engineers loose, seeing that new technology was a medium for freedom, not repression.

That last was always a real fear. The invention of the cotton gin had brought new life to slavery in the United States.

So . . . the slavers had to be stopped, and stopped here; war was too efficient a way for them to procure human merchandise.

But how?

We just don't have enough manpower, just don't have enough time.

It was conceivable that they could break the siege of Furnael Keep; possibly they could surprise and savage a slaver encampment; but ending the war was just too much to ask. Old hatreds, old angers had been awakened. How could they be stilled?

That's what it came down to: If the war couldn't be ended, the guild would profit. The Holtish and the Biemish were willing to sell each other off. It had to be stopped.

But I just don't know how to shut a war down.

He shook his head. It would have been nice to have Chak to talk to. Chak had long ago come to terms with the notion that he was going to die in battle, and had accepted it almost eagerly. Or maybe not almost.

How do you stop a war?

I don't know. But since when is not knowing an excuse?

"Hail, Caeser: We who are about to die . . ." Walter Slovotsky's voice sounded in the distance.

Karl stood. ". . . are going to take one hell of a lot of the bastards with us," he called back.

"That's not the response."

"It'll have to do, for now. When did you get back?"

"Just a few minutes ago. Valeran said you left orders I was to report to you the instant I arrived. I'm reporting."

"How does it look?"

Slovotsky rubbed at his tired eyes. "Look, Karl, I had a hard four days' ride to Furnael, a tough all-night recon, and a harder ride back. Can we let it wait until morning? I've got to get some sleep. One thing at a time, eh?"

"What did you say?"

"I asked if we can wait until morning."

"No, not that—what did you say after that?"

Slovotsky's forehead wrinkled. "One thing at a time?"

"One thing at a time." Karl nodded. "Sometimes, Walter, you're a genius."

"Huh? I don't follow."

"Never mind." Karl shook his head. "Don't worry about it." *One thing at a time. First we save Furnael Keep, then kill Ahrmin and his group, and then stop the war—somehow, dammit, somehow.* "That's my department. You get some sleep; we'll talk in the morning."

"Fine by me."

As Slovotsky stumbled off, Karl lay back down.

"One thing at a time," he said to himself.

And then he was asleep.

CHAPTER EIGHTEEN:

Aveneer

*One finds many companions for food and drink, but in a
serious business a man's companions are very few.*

—Theognis

"Karl," Walter called out from the top of the low rise, "I
think you'd better get up here."

"Trouble?"

"No, but move it, anyway."

Karl handed the rifle over to Henrad. "Keep them working
at it—dry firing only."

The boy nodded, his face a sullen mask. Henrad was
supposed to be Andy-Andy's apprentice, learning magic, not
teaching basic riflery.

Too bad for him. Karl started up the slope, pausing for a
moment to speak to Erek, who was busy conducting a class in
speed reloading for the benefit of Valeran and his men.

"How's it going?"

The boy smiled. "Good. Valeran is almost as fast as I am;
Halvin's a touch faster."

"Great. Keep at it." Karl broke into a jog.

Slovotsky was beaming as he stood atop the rise. "Things
just started to look up," he said, as Karl trotted over. "Check
this out."

Off in the distance, a line of more than two hundred
mounted soldiers rode toward them. But not Biemish soldiers;
even at this distance, Karl could see that they were armed with
rifles. He squinted; the man at the head was a barly redhead.

"Aveneer!" He turned to look at Slovotsky. "How—"

"I don't know." Slovotsky shrugged. "It sure wasn't me."

"Maybe Ellegon? When you met up with him west of Enkiar—"

"I just relayed your orders, Karl. As far as I know, the dragon was planning to head home and pick up the supplies and crew you ordered, then rendezvous here. If he had anything else in mind, he kept it a secret."

"I guess we'll know in a minute."

Aveneer spotted Karl and waved, then gestured to Frandred, his second-in-command, to have the men dismount. Aveneer spurred his roan into a full gallop, braking the horse to a panting halt as he neared Karl.

He dismounted heavily, then stood for a moment, over-sized hands on his hips. Nature had intended Aveneer to be a towering giant of a man, but something had gone wrong; although his hands, feet, and facial features were larger than Karl's, the Nyph stood more than a head shorter.

"You look well, Karl Cullinane," he said, turning for a moment to check the leather thongs that bound his battleaxe to the side of his fore-and-aft-peaked saddle. Aveneer was the only human Karl knew who preferred a battleaxe to a sword; an axe was typically a dwarf's weapon.

"I heard," Aveneer said, his voice a slow basso rumble, "that you could use some help." He ran blunt fingers through his dirty red hair. "I hope you don't mind the presumption. But it was . . . convenient for us to ride this way."

His appearance and that of his men made his words a lie. They were all road-dirty, with the deeply ingrained filth that only a long forced ride could cause.

"No, I don't mind." Karl took Aveneer's outstretched hand in his. Aveneer's grasp was firm, although he wasn't trying for a bone-crushing grip; Aveneer wasn't much for childish games. "I don't mind at all. But—how?"

Aveneer nodded slowly. "I told her that would be the first thing you would want to know." He raised an arm; a lone rider broke off from the rest of the group. "She caught up with us in Khar."

It was Tennetty, the glass eye gone, now replaced by a ragged eyepatch that somehow looked much more fitting.

Karl didn't know whether he wanted to hug her or shoot her down as she stopped her horse in front of him and waited, her face impassive.

"Tennetty . . ." What could he say? Karl had been sure that she had deserted; it now was clear that she had decided to hunt up some reinforcements. Did that make up for her indirectly causing Chak's death? No, but . . .

Dammit, why couldn't she have stayed a deserter? That had made things so much simpler.

"Greetings, Tennetty," he said, the words sounding warmer than he had intended.

She nodded grimly, not saying anything.

"We have plenty of powder left, and a few spare guns," Aveneer said. "The pickings have been slim. We were hunting for a slave-raiding party in the Kathard, but . . . nothing."

"Well, you won't be able to say that in a while. How tired are you?"

Aveneer rubbed at his bloodshot eyes. "Bone-weary, Karl. As is obvious. And our horses—"

"Walter, have their animals seen to."

"Right." Slovotsky trotted away.

Karl turned back to Aveneer. "What I meant was, can you and your people ride with only a day and a half of rest?"

"Of course. What will we be facing at the end of the ride?"

"Slovotsky says that there are a thousand men holding Furnael Keep under siege. He guesses that there's anything from one hundred to four hundred warriors inside."

"Can we count on them? Do they know we are coming?"

"No. If Walter could have snuck inside, then—"

"—the Holts could have done so, too. Hmm. . . . The Holtish have these slaver guns I've been hearing about recently?"

"Yes. Not many, though—Walter guesses less than two hundred, about one gun for every five men."

"Most of their weapons are up north, where most of the fighting is going on, eh?" Aveneer pursed his lips and nodded. "Let me see if I understand this: You want to take less than three hundred of us against a thousand Holtish line troops—

perhaps with some slavers mixed in—relying on Baron Furnael to support us, although there won't be any way for us to coordinate our movements with him. Correct?''

"Correct."

"Well." Aveneer brightened. "Then it looks like I won't die in bed after all. Now, is there someplace where an old man can sleep?"

Karl started to open his mouth, then closed it. Karl wouldn't have gone to sleep unless he was sure that his people were settled in, but there were sound arguments for doing it the other way.

It's Aveneer's team, not mine; criticizing would only be asking for trouble. "Use my tent," he said. "See you in the morning." He called for Erek, then had the boy lead Aveneer away.

Behind Karl, Walter Slovotsky cleared his throat.

"I thought you were going to see to the horses," Karl said.

"I delegated it. Just as well I did, Karl—I heard that last." Slovotsky shook his head slowly. "I don't like the idea of riding out. I thought we were going to wait for Ellegon."

"And *I* thought he'd be here by now. We can't wait forever; we move out day after tomorrow, regardless. He'll probably catch up with us en route."

I hope, he completed the thought. Though Aveneer's people had plenty of rounds and powder, that could be eaten up quickly in battle. Besides, since Chak had died, there had been nobody around who Karl could talk freely and comfortably with. Being around Slovotsky wasn't the same as being around Chak or Ellegon.

"He'd better." Slovotsky nodded grimly. "And Aveneer's team? How are you going to split them up?"

"I'm not. He and Frandred know their people better than I do, and they're all used to the way he splits them into three equal-sized teams. We're better off adapting to him, rather than the other way around. I'm going to stay in overall command—"

"Surprise, surprise."

"—and keep Valeran and his squad with me. We'll scatter Pirondael's mercenaries among Aveneer's squads."

"Sounds okay."

"One more thing: I want to get as close as possible to the

keep before we're spotted. I guess that means we'll have to travel at night.''

"That won't do it, not all by itself. You'll need somebody extremely talented—ahem!—riding ahead, doing recon and watcher removal.''

"Can we do it?''

"Maybe.'' Slovotsky considered it for a moment. "They've set out watchers along the Prince's Road, so the obvious route is out. I'm sure that they've also got some in the forest, but not as many. Besides, the visibility is poor; we'll be able to slip by a lot. If you're willing to go the forest route, I'll try to clear the way, about half a day ahead. But I can't do it by myself. Not and have a half-decent chance of getting all the watchmen.''

"That's the problem. If one reports back we're in trouble.''

"It's worse than that. Think it through, Karl: If one of them *doesn't* report back on time, that's a warning. But that kind of warning should move slowly; we can probably outrun it.'' He paused, closing his eyes. "Ten. Give me Piell and nine others who can move quietly, all of us with the fastest horses available. Crossbows and longbows—if we need to use guns, then we've already blown it.''

"Any chance of pulling it off?''

"Fifty-fifty. *If* Aveneer's people are any good. Do I get my choice of backup?''

"Talk to Frandred, but he'll want to clear any selections with Aveneer.''

"Fine. How about Tennetty?''

"No.'' Karl shook his head. "She's my second.''

"You'll trust her with your back?''

"Looks like it, no?''

CHAPTER NINETEEN:

The Siege

He either fears his fate too much,
or his deserts are small,
That puts it not unto the touch
To win or lose it all.
　　　　　—James Graham, Marquess of Montrose

During peacetime, a trip from Biemestren to Furnael Keep would have been a slow, pleasant five-day ride along the Prince's Road, their nights spent in the inns scattered along the road, each inn an easy day's ride from the next. They would have slept on fluffy down mattresses in dry, airy sleeping rooms, taking their meals at the common table along with merchants and and other travelers.

But this wasn't a normal time. None of the inns were open; trade along the Prince's Road was suspended for the duration of the war.

They had to try to avoid being spotted. So they traveled at night, eating cold meals when they camped at daybreak. Daytime was for sleeping, the night for traveling, carefully, quietly, trusting to Walter Slovotsky and his scouts to kill or capture any watchers, to ride back to warn of any concentration of troops, or to tie white cloths at eye level on the proper side of forks in the paths, blazing the trail in the only way that they could follow at night.

It took a full ten days to get from the outskirts of Biemestren to where the forest broke on cleared farmland in barony

Furnael. Ten days of interrupted sleep during the day, uninterrupted hours of plodding on horseback at night.

In the distance, the battered keep rose above the morning fog. From his hiding place just within the tree line, Karl could see the charred remnants of a siege tower against the south wall, the stone near it blackened, some merlons cracked, others broken and tumbled to the ground below.

The keep was battered, yes, but not broken. Several of Furnael's soldiers stood watch on the battlements, occasionally peering out an embrasure to try a chancy crossbow shot at one of the Holts below.

Slovotsky had been right: The Holts were tunneling, and that meant trouble.

Karl swore softly, then stopped himself. It could have been worse. There were basically four ways for the Holtish to lay siege to the castle. First, they could just try to starve the defenders out. That would be a long and drawn-out process, one that the Holts had undoubtedly discarded immediately.

Thank goodness for small blessings. That would have been most dangerous for Karl and his people; if the Holts were taking a passive view about attacking the keep, they would likely be ready to repel a relieving force.

The Holts' second option was to try getting over the walls, either by siege towers, ladders, climbing ropes, or some combination. The charred remnants of one siege tower showed that they had tried that, and it had failed; the lack of further tower or ladder construction suggested that the Holts had abandoned that idea.

The third possibility was for the Holts to try to break the walls of the castle or force the gate. They could do it with rams, or with siege engines like catapults and onagers.

Karl had been hoping that the Holts had switched to that. It would be the easiest technique for Karl to counter; a quick attack on the siege engines would leave them in flames.

But the Holts had chosen the fourth method: They were mining, attempting either to break into the keep at a point which they hoped would be a surprise, or simply to undermine the walls and collapse them.

The chained workers were likely captured Furnael slaves or freefarmers, now forced to work for the Holtish, which explained why the watchmen on the walls didn't simply fire their bows at the workers bringing wheelbarrows loaded with rocks and dirt from the tunnels.

Doesn't look good, and that's a fact.

Karl worked himself back from the tree line and made his way into the woods to the clearing where Walter, his outriders, and Tennetty stood waiting with their horses.

The problem was one of coordination. Between Karl's people and Furnael's warriors, they probably had force enough to disperse the Holts, despite the fact that the Holts probably had them outmanned. Home guns were more accurate than slaver blunderbusses, and a score of sharpshooters on the keep's ramparts would quickly make the notion of an active siege unattractive. Combined with a couple hundred mounted troops that could strike anytime, anywhere, the Furnael/Home forces should present a strong enough threat to scare the Holts off, or kill them all, if necessary. But in order for it to work, the keep's defenders would have to know that they had allies out here, and Furnael—or whoever was commanding the defenders, if he was dead—would have to agree to cooperate, to coordinate.

And even so, it would be bloody. "I read something once, something that concluded two armies of roughly equal strength meeting is a recipe for disaster," Karl said. "You know where that comes from?"

"Sorry," Walter Slovotsky said. "Sounds familiar, though." He raised an eyebrow. "You've got something better in mind?"

"Yup. Two things. First, we have to do some damage to the Holts, to demonstrate our credibility. Second, we've got to get someone close to the wall with a voice and a note—and that calls for a major diversion."

"So? You're going to try something tricky. Maybe a combination ambush and bluff?"

Karl smiled. "Almost right. A combination feint, decoy, ambush, and double bluff." He turned to Tennetty. "You willing to take a few chances?"

She nodded. "As many as you are, Karl Cullinane."

Good, he thought, *here's where you can die to settle your score for Chak. You deserve—*

He caught himself. No, that wasn't right. There was enough

evil in the world, more than enough. There was no need to
add to it by betraying one of his own people.

"Tennetty," he said, "ride back and tell Aveneer to set
out guards with crossbows, then bed everybody down until
dusk. I'll want him to bring his people forward then. Dig up
eight volunteers who don't mind trying something a bit risky,
and bring them back with you at dusk—oh, and bring Erek,
too."

"Make that seven volunteers, Tennetty," Slovotsky said.
"I haven't volunteered for a long time; I want to make sure I
remember how."

"No." Karl shook his head. "Before this is over, you're
going to remember why it's been so long. Besides, I've
got something else for you. Get moving, Tennetty. Remember,
it's eight volunteers, with their horses."

Slovotsky stared into his face. "What are you up to, Karl?
Am I supposed to sneak through the Holts' camp while the
fight is going on, or is it something even more idiotic?"

"How did you guess?" He jerked his thumb over his
shoulder. "Go back into the woods and get some sleep.
You're going to need it."

A cool night breeze whispered through the branches, ca-
ressed his face.

The night was clear and almost cloudless. Which was just
as well, for once; rain would make that it anywhere from
difficult to impossible for Karl's people to reload.

He patted at Stick's neck, then reached across to check the
short horn bow lashed to his saddle horn, and the quiver,
crammed full of short arrows, that was stuck tightly in his
rifle boot. There would be no guns, not for the first rush.
Guns would announce who they were, and that had to be
avoided.

He swore, uncomfortable in the cold steel breastplate and
helmet, but there wasn't a remedy for that, not this time. This
was one time that putting up with his armor's weight was
going to be a necessity, even if the damn breastplate and its
underlying padding did seem to weigh half a ton. It would
deflect anything but an unlucky point-blank shot, and it was
more than likely that he'd need that luck and that breastplate
before too long.

He looked over at Tennetty. "Think we've given Slovotsky enough time?" It would take Walter a while to work his way close enough to the keep to take advantage of the diversion.

She nodded.

"Then let's do it." He hoisted himself to the saddle, then leaned forward and reached down to hitch at his greaves. The damn armor kept slipping.

He made sure that his sword was firmly seated in its scabbard, although he hoped that he wouldn't actually have to use it on this run. If Karl ended up in sword range of any of the Holts, that would mean that everything had fallen apart. Still, he'd rather have it and not use it than the other way around.

At his right, Tennetty and the eight others were already mounted, their horses snorting and pawing the ground in impatience. No guns for them, either; they carried only cross-bows and bolts, except for Bonard, who had a horn bow like Karl's.

Aveneer signaled for Erek and Frandred to raise their lamps; the two mounted them on the trees on either side of the path, the baffles barely letting traces of light peep through.

"Let's go," Karl whispered, digging in his heels and ducking his head as Stick stepped over the stone fence and into the fallow field, the others following.

He spurred the horse into a canter, and then a trot.

There were things about This Side that still amazed Karl, even after all this time. The number of soldiers around the keep, for one. Back at school, there had been dorms with more people than the thousand or so laying siege to Furnael's keep.

It seemed strange that something as impressive-sounding as a siege was capable of being carried out by only a thousand or so soldiers. Maybe it really shouldn't have; hell, Richard Lion-heart's Crusade expedition hadn't numbered more than eight thousand, and that was a force that had been raised throughout all of England. Maybe it was reasonable that the whole Holtun-Bieme war was being fought by just a few tens of thousands of soldiers on both sides.

But it still looked funny.

The Holtish commander had divided his force of a thousand men into four groups, each one camped just out of bowshot of one of the four walls of the keep.

They hadn't been divided equally, of course. That would have been foolish. The largest group, slightly more than a third of the Holtish force, was camped opposite the keep's main gate. Another two hundred and fifty were planted across from the minor gate, the two remaining groups of about a hundred and fifty each camped opposite the remaining two walls.

It was an intelligent arrangement, one that prevented the keep's defenders from safely attempting any sort of horseback smash-and-retreat sortie; in the time that it would have taken Furnael's forces to raise even the small portcullis, both of the smaller Holtish forces could have joined the attackers at the rear gate and used the opportunity to force an entry.

Furnael and his people were sealed in, tight.

Karl rode slowly across the fallow field toward the main force of the Holts, the others strung out to his left.

Off in the distance, he could barely see the main gate of the keep, its iron portcullis visible against the flickering flames of a watchfire inside the keep. Karl had ridden through that gate years before; now, he hoped that Slovotsky had worked close enough to it to alert those inside when the time was right.

He transferred the reins to his teeth and unlashed his bow, nocking an arrow.

The Holts clearly weren't ready for an attack from outside; Karl had closed to within two hundred yards of the guards' fire when a soldier leaped to his feet and shouted a warning into the night.

"Do it," Karl said, drawing back the arrow to its steel head, then sending it whistling off into the night. Karl was an indifferent shot with a shortbow or longbow; no sense in trying for an accuracy that he didn't have, not from Stick's pitching back.

He drew another arrow and fired it at a forty-five-degree angle, aiming as best he could for the center of the encampment.

Tennetty steadied her crossbow and pulled the trigger. A Holtish soldier screamed and grabbed at the bolt in his thigh, then fell forward.

"Aim higher, dammit!" Karl yelled. "This isn't the time

to play sharpshooter.'' A low shot would just plow into the ground; a high one might find flesh deeper in the camp.

''No closer, anyone,'' he said. The nearest of the Holts were at just about maximum effective range for the slaver rifles.

He let another shaft fly, noting with surprise and pleasure that as the arrow fell it caught a Holtish soldier in the throat.

Screams and shouts echoed through the camp. Karl unstrapped his lantern from his saddle and dashed it to the ground. Stick danced away from the flaring fire that marked his position, just in case any of the Holts had missed the point.

As gunshots sounded from the camp, Karl quelled an urge to dive from the saddle. At this range, the enemy's guns were next to useless. They would have to mount up and give chase. Which was just fine.

''Ready another volley.'' He nocked an arrow and waited for the crossbowmen to load their weapons. ''Aim high, now, and . . . fire!''

Nine bows went off in a volley, immediately rewarded by more cries and screams from the Holts.

It had been only a few moments since the fight had started, but already a troop of a hundred, perhaps a hundred and twenty, soldiers were mounting up, preparing to repel the attack. Good. Both the size and the speed of the troop spoke well for the abilities of the Holtish commander, and Karl was counting on him to be good at his job.

''Secure weapons and prepare to run,'' he called out, already tying down his own bow.

One of Karl's horsemen started to bring his horse around.

''Hold your position!'' Karl snapped. ''Run before I tell you to and I'll shoot you down myself.''

It was going to be tricky. They would have to draw the Holtish along with them, not letting them get close enough to do any damage, not outdistancing them altogether. *About ten seconds*, he thought. Nine. Eight. Seven.

To hell with it. ''Run for it!'' He wheeled Stick about and galloped for the trees, the others following him.

Their baffles now fully aside, the lanterns at the tree line beckoned to him; the path broke through the forest exactly halfway between the two. Stick galloped for the path, hooves throwing soft earth into the air as the stallion leaped over the low stone wall.

It was fortunate that the path back into the forest was straight: Stick's hooves had trouble finding it; branches and brambles beat against Karl's helmet and face until he had to close his eyes tightly for fear of losing them. Behind him, the others crashed through into the forest.

A signal rocket screamed into the sky; Karl opened his eyes to see it explode high above the trees in a shower of white-and-blue fire.

Aveneer's basso cut through the night: "Fire!"

Seventy rifles went off in a volley, their almost simultaneous *whip-cracks* sounding more like a sudden flurry of popcorn popping than anything else.

Horses and men screamed.

The path widened. Karl pulled Stick to a stop and dismounted from the horse's back, while Tennetty and the others galloped beyond him.

"Second section," Aveneer's basso boomed, somewhere off in the distance, "*fire!*"

Again, the crack of seventy rifles firing in a volley sounded; Karl dashed back down the path.

Aveneer's first section, the one that had fired the initial volley, advanced over the dark and bloody ground, their rifles now slung, using their swords and knives to administer the *coup de grace* to wounded animals and humans alike. Of the hundred cavalrymen who had pursued Karl and his nine warriors, barely a dozen had survived unscathed, and those few were riding hell-for-leather back toward the main Holtish camp.

Karl began stripping off his armor as Erek ran up with Karl's rifle, pistols, and a large leather pouch; he accepted Karl's breastplate, helmet, and greaves in return.

"Message to Aveneer—deliver, wait for a response," Karl said. "Begins: No casualties on my team; Tennetty and others moving into position. Orders: Advance by section, volley fire and leapfrog. Send another runner back with Erek. Query: Any casualties? Ends. Go."

The boy ran off.

Karl primed his rifle's pan. *Now we'll see if the third part works*. The first part of his plan had worked like a a charm: A hundred Holts lay dead on the ground, and the Holtish were buzzing like bees. The second part had either succeeded or failed by now; either Slovotsky had or hadn't been able to take advantage of the distraction to get within throwing and shouting range of one of Furnael's warriors manning the ramparts of the keep.

But the third part depended on just how good the Holtish commander was. When what had appeared to be a small Biemish raiding party had approached, his first response had been the conservative one of sending out an apparently overlarge troop of cavalry.

But then, when the guns had gone off, his whole picture of what was going on would have, and should have, changed. As far as the commander had known, his side was the only one in this war that had guns—the only other force in the world with guns and powder was Karl Cullinane and his warriors—so he would identify Karl as his opponent. Or, perhaps, he would consider the possibility that his slaver allies had turned on him.

Either way, it would be a whole new development. And what would a good commander do when confronted with an attacking force of indeterminate size?

In another tactical situation the right response would be different, but here the commander knew he was already up against the keep's defenders, and had arrayed his forces for a siege; the conservative response, the safe reaction, would be to withdraw his entire force along the Prince's Road toward Holtun and barony Adahan, probably sending a cavalry detachment through to make sure that the way was clear.

His command should be more important to him than his mission. If he was good enough.

Karl stepped out through the trees and into the starlight. While the cavalrymen mounted up, a large contingent of Holtish soldiers were setting up a quick line defense, bringing guns and bows around to face Aveneer's slowly advancing sections.

"First section, fire!" Aveneer called out.

Karl crossed his fingers. It didn't look good; the Holts were setting up for defense, not withdrawal.

"You've got guts," he whispered to his unseen adversary.

"Too damn much guts." Hadn't the bastard decided that he was outnumbered? Was he about to try a last run, himself?

Erek ran up, one of Aveneer's younger warriors beside him.

"He says," Erek said, panting, " 'Understood; firing by your order. Casualties low: seven wounded, none dead.' " Erek shook his head. "I don't think he's seen everything, Karl. Some of those horsemen broke through the line."

Easily a mile away, two more signal rockets momentarily brightened the night, as if to say, *We're on our way.*

Karl let himself ignore the report on casualties for the time being. *I'll worry about it later, when I know how many lives my being clever cost this time.* "It looks like Tennetty and the rest of the horseborne squad got to their signal rockets," he said. "And made it into position."

"Yes, Karl." The boy smiled."Will the Holts run?"

"Count on it," he said.

I hope so, his thought echoed. *Okay, General Patton. How about now?*

"Second section, *fire!*"

That started a rout. The small detachment camped opposite the gateless northern wall broke and ran, some soldiers fighting each other for possession of a horse, others dropping their weapons and running down the road.

Karl couldn't see the other small detachment, but he was willing to bet that they'd be the next to break.

The group camped opposite the keep's rear gate began to move out, but in an orderly fashion: foot soldiers double-timing toward the road, cavalrymen with crossbows riding ahead to clear the way. Apparently their commander had decided that discretion was the better part of valor.

Good. But the main force wasn't moving, and with the one remaining small force, those almost three hundred men were enough to hold off Karl's people indefinitely, unless Karl was willing to shed a lot of Aveneer's men's blood.

"Erek—message to Valeran, return. Begins: Do it. Ends."

Again, the boy dashed off, this time in a different direction.

This was the last trick Karl had up his sleeve. If it didn't work, things were going to get very messy. If the hundred men now under Valeran's command weren't enough to persuade the Holtish commander that there was a huge force opposing him, Karl would have to count on Slovotsky's being able to get more than his note through to Furnael, on Furnael's believing him, *and* on Furnael's being able to take effective action.

All of which wasn't too likely, not in combination.

Well off on the right flank, Valeran's group stepped out of the forest, firing in volley.

But the Holts held, firing and reloading their guns and bows.

And then it happened: The main gate to the keep began to creak open, accompanied by battle cries from within the keep's walls.

The Holts had had enough; their line broke.

Karl beckoned at Aveneer's runner. "To Aveneer, and return. Begins: Belay volley fire. All reload, advance. Targets only by eye and ear. Ends. Go." The runner ran off.

At a brightening on the horizon, Karl's head jerked around. A gout of flame scoured the eastern sky.

Flame? What the hell was going on?

What . . . think . . . on?

"Ellegon!"

He could barely hear the mental voice as the dragon roared across the sky, well above the range of the most powerful crossbows as he vented fire and steam, hastening the Holts in their headlong flight.

The air cavalry is here. I see I'm a bit late. Hope I didn't inconvenience you too much.

No, not at all. It gave me the chance to figure out how about two hundred and fifty could send four times that number running, Karl thought, letting his mental voice drip with sarcasm. *Thanks for the experience, Ellegon.*

No problem.

Karl felt the dragon probe more deeply.

I'm sorry about Chak. We'll have to talk about him.

Later. Business first. "Erek, get over here—*move* it, boy. Message for Aveneer, return. Begins: Belay attack. Nobody takes a step forward of your first section until further orders."

With the Holts on the run, and with Ellegon in the skies to make sure they kept running, there was no reason to take any chance on getting someone killed by friendly fire. Furnael's people had been under siege for a while; it was likely that they were more than a little trigger-happy. "Healing draughts to be dispensed as needed," he went on. "Ends. Message for Valeran. Begins: Acquire three prisoners for interrogation. Keep your distance from Biemish until further orders. Ends. Go."

His neck muscles were already starting to unkink. It was as though a huge weight had been lifted from his shoulders; Ellegon's presence in his mind buoyed him like a lifejacket.

Lightning crackled from the dragon's back, the white ribbons descending into the midst of the fleeing Holts, now more mob than army.

Lightning? *Ellegon must have picked up Henrad and*—no, not lightning. Henrad wasn't up to anything that difficult.

Ellegon, tell me Andrea isn't with you.

There was no answer.

Please.

It was her idea, Karl, not mine. The same for Ahira. I told them you wouldn't like it, he said petulantly.

Ahira? What the hell is going on at Home? Are the children—

The children are fine. Kirah and all of them are staying with the Engineers for the time being. Ellegon banked, wheeling across the sky. *Let me bring her to you*—*

"No!" *Stay the hell up in the sky until everything settles down.*

He would have to talk to Furnael, and—

No, better—*tell Aveneer to move one of his companies back to the campsite, and then you can land there.* First things first. He had intended to go down and talk to the baron, but this had to take priority. *Can you reach Slovotsky?*

Yes.

Tell him I'll be a while. Then get your scaly self over to the LZ, on the double.

Yes, Karl. It's good to see you again, too.

Despite everything, he smiled. "Right. . . . Hey, you— yes, *you.* Get me my horse."

CHAPTER TWENTY:

Several Acquaintances Renewed

Only the brave know how to forgive. . . .
—Laurence Sterne

Karl pulled the stallion to a halt, then swung his leg over and lowered himself slowly to the ground. He reached up and tied Stick's reins around a branch of a tree; unlike Carrot, Stick wouldn't stay ground-hitched, although the stallion usually respected a light hitching.

Are you sure enough of that that if your horse tries to run, I can eat it?

Ellegon sprawled on the grass, his massive saurian head cradled on his crossed forelegs.

No. And why is it that you always want to snack on my *horses?*

Everyone always says that when it comes to horseflesh, you've got great taste.

Apparently, the dragon had included Andy-Andy in on the conversation. She groaned as she stooped to pick up a fist-sized stone and bounced it off his thick hide, before turning back to her work.

Ahira and Thomen Furnael sat on the grass, resting against one of the dragon's treetrunk forelegs, while Andy-Andy and Ranella directed ten of Aveneer's warriors in the unpacking of the dragon's harnesses and the huge wicker basket.

"Leave that keg alone," Ranella said, indicating a small one that was tied tightly into a padded nook of the basket.

"Do not try to move it, do not drop anything on it, do not even look cross-eyed at it."

"Okay, what the hell's going on?" Karl said, glaring at Ahira and Andy-Andy. "I sent for—"

"Shh." Andy-Andy smiled as she threw her arms around his neck and gave him a quick kiss. "Mendicants can't be choosicants. Hey, *you*—easy with that box." She pushed away from him and walked over to where Ranella was directing the unloading.

"Help is what you sent for, and you got it," the dwarf snapped. "As I remember it, nobody elected you God, Karl."

"Just what are you doing here, Mr. Mayor?"

"Call me Ahira." The dwarf shrugged. "I'm not mayor anymore. I lost a vote of confidence four tendays ago. Which is why I'm here—"

It hit Karl like a slap. "You *what?*"

"I lost. Chton called another vote of confidence, and a lot of the farmers who would have voted the way you wanted them to didn't vote for me." He shrugged again.

"You left Home with Chton as mayor? You—"

"Do I look stupid? I didn't have enough votes to hold on to the job, but the Joiners couldn't get enough support to win a clear majority, either."

"So who—"

"Riccetti, of course."

"Now, wait a minute. How did you get him past Chton's faction?"

Ahira turned to look at Andy-Andy. "Should I tell him? Or did you really want to try that experiment?"

"Experiment?"

She ignored him for a moment, talking quietly to Ranella. "You can handle the rest of it, yes?"

"Yes, Andrea."

Andy-Andy turned and walked over to Karl. "The experiment is to see if someone can actually die of curiosity."

Enough. How safe are we?

Not an unfriendly thought as far as my mind can reach. Why?—oh. The dragon snorted, parboiling a stretch of grass.

"Ahira, I don't want anybody going down toward Furnael Keep until the mopping-up is done. When that happens, you can take Thomen to his father, but not until then."

The boy spoke up. "But, Karl Cullinane, this is my home. I know—"

"You may know every rock, tree, and bramble, boy, but we're on the fringes of a war. I'm *not* going to have to tell your father that I got his other son killed, understood?" He turned back to Ahira and switched to English. "Slovotsky is down there; coordinate things through him. Keep the kid alive, kapish?"

"Yes, Karl." The dwarf hefted his battleaxe. "It's good to be back in business."

Karl snorted. "A hell of a lot you remember." He walked over to the carrying basket and pulled out three blankets, throwing them over his shoulder. Without a word, he scooped up Andy-Andy in his arms.

If I remember right, there's a tiny clearing about a quarter mile this way. Tune us out, and make sure we're left alone.

Yes, Karl. Have fun.

"Karl!" She struggled against his grip. "What do you think you're doing—"

"It's pretty damn obvious what I'm doing, Andrea. The question is, do you intend to stop me?"

"And if I do?"

He shrugged. "Then you will."

"That's fine, then." She leaned her head against his chest. "Just so I have a choice. I missed you too, you know."

"Don't tell me, show me."

Andy-Andy peered over his shoulder. "We're out of sight, Karl. You can put me down now," she said. Her voice was flat, businesslike.

He lowered her legs to the ground, then released her. "You didn't buy the act?"

She shook her head. "I know you too well. That pseudo-macho act probably fooled everyone except maybe Ahira. I still don't know why you bother with it, though."

"Got to keep up the image, beautiful." He sighed. Getting the job done depended on whether others would follow him, and that depended in large part on his image. There was another side to it, too: Sending his friends out to die was bad enough; public breastbeating wouldn't make it one whit better. But this wasn't public.

He swallowed. "Let me give it to you straight: Chak was killed outside of Enkiar."

A brief intake of breath, and then: "How?"

He shook his head. "He . . . decided that stopping the slaver powder from getting through was more important than his own life." He pounded his fist against a tree, sending chips of bark flying away. "The little *bastard* . . ."

He dropped to his knees. As she crouched beside him and wrapped her arms around his neck, he closed his eyes, buried his face against her breasts, and finally let the tears flow.

After a while, she reached into her robes and rummaged through an inside pocket for a cloth, then handed it to him. "Better wipe your nose, and give your eyes a chance to clear up, hero," she said, her voice infinitely gentle, despite her words. "You'll blow your image to hell otherwise."

"Thanks." He forced a calm tone. "Now, tell me: What the hell is going on back Home? Did Ahira blow the vote, or was Chton too good for him?"

She shook her head. "I think he blew it, maybe even deliberately. Gwellin's finally decided to go back to Endell—" She raised an eyebrow. "That isn't a surprise to you?"

"No," Karl said. "He mentioned it a while back."

"In any case, he invited Ahira to go along with him. Ahira said no, but . . . after that, it seemed like he was . . . deliberately going out of his way to annoy people. You remember the dispute between Lou and Keremin?"

"Something about some farmland?"

"Right. Keremin was in the wrong, but it's an honest disagreement. When Ahira manhandled him—in front of a dozen farmers, Karl—and told him to stop trying to steal the fields . . ." She shook her head. "He earned himself another enemy. And then he insisted on working out with Daven. Ahira beat him badly in front of his own men."

Was it conscious or not? Had the dwarf deliberately been trying to get himself thrown out of office, or had it been an unconscious unwillingness to hold on to the responsibility?

He didn't ask. If anyone would know, Ellegon would—best to save it for later.

"I tried to smooth it over," she went on, "but I didn't get

far. When the town meeting came up, Ahira just didn't have the votes, not without you there to back him up."

"So how did you get enough of the Joiners to agree to Riccetti as mayor? Magic?"

"Better than that." She grinned. "Sneakiness. I had Riccetti explain to one of Chton's Joiners that the Engineers weren't interested in *any* trade with Therranj, not if Chton became mayor. Apparently, Chton figured out that Khoral wouldn't take that at all well, so he decided to outsmart us: Chton *nominated* Riccetti. Clever move, really: It satisfies Khoral by letting him try to negotiate with Riccetti directly, and lets Chton drive a wedge between us and Lou."

"But Chton ought to know that won't work. Lou's loyalty isn't in question." *Is it?*

"Well, it wasn't." She breathed on her fingernails and buffed them against her chest. "Uhh . . . it seems that Riccetti has long had a *horrible* crush on me, and that he made some moves on me in your absence. And when I was overheard telling him to keep his filthy hands off me . . ."

Cute. A phony division for Chton to try to exploit. But just a bit *too* tricky. "I think you've been hanging around Walter Slovotsky for too long."

"Oh?"

"That's his style, not yours."

"And where is it written that I can't learn?"

He didn't answer that. Obviously she could learn the sneaky side of Home politics. *Matter of fact, there's a lot she could teach me. My natural inclination would have been to stick my thumb in Chton's eye.* "Last question: Why did Ahira come along with you?"

She didn't answer for a moment. "I don't know; he just volunteered. Gwellin agreed to hold off going back to Endell until he returns. Tell me, if you had to guess what one thing he'd miss most about Home, what would it be?"

"Close call—it'd be either Janie or Walter." Karl sucked air in through his teeth. "He's going to ask Walter to come along with him, and bring Kirah and Janie."

She nodded. "That's my guess."

Damn. Well, there wasn't anything that could be done about it now. But maybe, later on, either Ahira could be talked out of asking, or Slovotsky could be talked out of saying yes. "Do me a favor. Keep your head down and your eyes open, okay?"

"Okay." She smiled thinly up at him. "But tell me: What would you say if I told you to do the same thing?"

"I'd say that I already do." He helped her to her feet. "C'mon, let's join the others."

A smile creeping over her face, she shook her head. "No. I've got a better idea." Extending a tanned forefinger, she ran a fingernail up his arm. "Since we're trying to maintain an image and all . . ."

Fingercombing the dirt and leaves from his hair, Karl led the way back to the clearing.

Ranella had most of the gear unpacked, and spread out on tarpaulins on the ground. There seemed to be about two hundred guns, plus several kegs that undoubtedly contained powder and shot, as well as some lead ingots, no doubt for bullets. He nodded silent approval; running bullets was easy enough, and ingots took up less space than premade rounds.

"Karl Cullinane," Ranella said, nodding. "It is good to see you, Karl."

He raised an eyebrow, and opened his mouth to ask why an apprentice Engineer didn't treat a journeyman with a bit more formality, but caught himself. Riccetti must have promoted her during Karl's absence.

"Journeyman Ranella," he said, returning her nod. "It's good to see you, as well."

Her face fell. She had expected him to snap at her, and had been looking forward to flaunting her new status at him.

"What have we here?" he asked.

"Quite a lot, Karl. Fifty-two pistols, one hundred and sixty shotguns, thirty-three rifles—"

"Where did you get all these?"

"You said to bring every weapon we could, so we . . . requisitioned Daven's team's old rifles and most of your squads' weapons. Nehera is working full-time on barrels until they are replaced. Apprentices are taking care of the stocks, locks, rifling, and boring."

That still would be one hell of a lot of work for the dwarf. Turning a flat bar of iron into a rifle barrel took hundreds of welding heats, and even though Nehera could work on several barrels in rotation, he would have to sleep sometime.

Well, Karl would send word to Riccetti not to work Nehera too hard.

Don't be silly. Ellegon snorted, sending Aveneer's men reaching reflexively for their swordhilts. *Lou Riccetti is not as old and wise as some people, but he is no fool, either. He will see to Nehera's health.*

Karl nodded. *Good point.* "What else do we have?"

"Three thousand rounds in that sack, Karl—lead ingots, a bullet-running kit. Those two barrels contain gunpowder—and the Engineer sent along a surprise."

"Yes?" Karl raised an eyebrow.

"Do you see those two small kegs, Karl?"

"Yes."

"One of them contains a gross of the Engineer's new grenades. They're loaded with . . . guncotton." She raised a palm. "The Engineer said to inform you that he has not solved the instability problem—but we have kept it cold." She shrugged. "He won't swear how long it'll go without self-detonating, but he said he would be surprised if any of them go before another six tendays. Now, Karl, the other hogshead contains very carefully packaged detonators—"

"Detonators?"

"Fulminate of mercury, Karl. Silver fulminate goes off if you blink at it. This is stable. Relatively."

He repressed a shudder. Fulminate of mercury was touchy stuff. Almost anything could set it off—heat, friction, a sudden blow. "Any special instructions for the detonators?"

"No, Karl." She shook her head. "Other than not to insert the detonators into the grenades—or keep them near the grenades—until you're ready to strike them."

"Strike them?"

She smiled. "He said that would impress you. He's rigged a sulfur-tipped fuse. You rub the fuse tip against a rough surface until it catches fire, and then throw." She held up a cautionary finger. "There is no guarantee that it won't explode on impact, though."

Surprise, surprise. Still, that sounded good. "Assuming that things go well down there, I'll requisition some space in Furnael Keep for a magazine—mmm, make that several magazines." It would be best to keep the grenades spread out; if one self-detonated, it would send the others sky-high.

"You'll take charge of that—talk to Frandred and Aveneer about guards."

"Understood, Karl."

Ranella had been giving his first name a thorough workout. He let a chuckle escape, then dismissed her questioning look with a shake of his head. "Very well. Later, I'd like to—"

The pounding of a horse's hooves sounded from down the path. Erek rode up, then descended from the saddle of his mottled pony in what was more of a barely controlled fall than a voluntary dismount. "Aveneer . . . reports," he said, gasping for breath.

"Trouble?"

Erek shook his head. "No. He says . . ." He paused, panting, then tried to start again.

Karl held up a hand. "Ta havath, Erek," he said. *Sometimes,* he thought, *it feels like I spend half my life telling people to take it easy.* "If there's no problem, then take a moment and catch your breath."

Erek nodded, then waited while his breathing settled down. "Aveneer reports . . . that all is clear. Walter . . . Slovotsky reports that the baron will . . . see you."

"Andy? Could you get Erek some water?" He clapped a hand to the boy's shoulder. "I want you to rest, Erek. I won't need a runner for a while."

"Yes . . . Karl."

Karl beckoned to Thomen. "Let's get you to your father, boy."

Baron Zherr Furnael was waiting for them just inside Furnael Keep's main gate, fifty of his warriors keeping him company while the rest manned the ramparts.

Karl almost didn't recognize the baron; the years hadn't treated Zherr Furnael well. Before, he had been a solidly built man, sporting a slight potbelly; now, his leather tunic hung on him loosely, as though it had been made for a larger man, a younger one, less skeletal.

Deep lines matted the baron's face; the whites of his eyes had developed a definite yellow tinge. Worse, Furnael had developed a nervous twitch around his left eye; he constantly seemed to be winking.

But there was still an echo of his old inner strength. He

threw an arm around Thomen's shoulders for only a moment, then stood with his shoulders back, his spine ramrod-straight, his face somber as he faced Karl.

"Greetings, Karl Cullinane. It has been a long time." Furnael's voice was more fragile than it had been, but a trace of its old power was still there.

Karl dismounted, handing the reins to one of Furnael's men. He wasn't sure how Furnael would feel about him. Would the baron blame Karl for Rahff?

Right now, he needed Furnael's cooperation as much as the baron had needed Karl's help in breaking the siege; it took a great deal of effort not to break into an idiot smile when Furnael extended a hand.

The baron's grip was astonishingly weak. Karl tried to keep an acknowledgment of that from his face, then regretted his success when he saw the implied pity mirrored in Furnael's eyes.

Releasing Karl's hand, Furnael turned to one of his men and called for his horse. "We have much to discuss, Karl Cullinane. Will you ride with me?"

"Of course, Baron. I am at your service."

An echo of a smile pierced through the gloom that hung over Furnael like a shroud. "That, Karl Cullinane, remains to be seen."

Six years before, on the night that Furnael had indentured Rahff to Karl, the two of them had ridden down the road from Furnael Keep to the row of clean shacks that served as Furnael's agricultural slaves' quarters.

Although the question of whether or not that night was going to end with spilled blood had hovered over them like a crimson specter, it had been a pleasant ride: lush fields of corn and wheat had whispered gently in the night wind; they had talked idly, while Furnael had dismounted from Pirate's back to remove a stray stone from the smooth dirt road.

There had been changes. Now, ruined fields sprawled on either side of the deeply rutted road, the cornstalks trampled by booted feet and shod hooves. The Holts hadn't wanted head-high cornstalks obscuring their view, possibly hiding an enemy; what they hadn't harvested for their own use they had trampled or burned, like a jackal covering the remnants of a too-large meal with its own vomit.

Furnael pulled on the reins of the brown gelding, then dismounted, beckoning at Karl to do likewise.

"Not quite like last time, eh, Karl Cullinane?" The baron stared at him unblinkingly. "You look older."

"I feel older. About a million years, if not one whit wiser."

"Yes." Furnael sighed. "Yes, that's a feeling I can sympathize with. Remember when you offered to take on the Aershtyn raiders if I would free all the slaves in my barony?"

Karl nodded. "Maybe I should have tried harder to persuade you. I've often wondered about that."

"No." Furnael shook his head. "I wasn't . . . equipped to believe that you were serious. Not then. Not until word of you and your Home raiders trickled back. Many good men have died because I didn't believe you. Rahff, for one. . . ." The baron stood silently for a moment. "Did you know that I had my best friend killed half a year ago?"

"No, I didn't." Karl shook his head. "Baron . . . Adahan of Holtun?"

"Yes. Vertum was one of Uldren's better strategists; it was necessary to order him assassinated." Furnael clenched his fists momentarily. "I am grateful that Bren is up north; perhaps at least Vertum's son will survive."

Karl breathed a sigh of relief. With Bren up north, at least he wouldn't have to kill Rahff's best friend.

Furnael chuckled hollowly, as though reading Karl's mind. "And what if someone else kills Bren? Will that make him any less dead?" He clapped a hand to Karl's shoulder. "We think alike, Karl Cullinane. Tell me: How did my son die?" the baron asked, his voice infinitely weary.

"I sent a letter with a trader, years ago," Karl said, toying with Stick's reins.

"Your letter only said that he died honorably, protecting another. *How* did he die, Karl Cullinane? You must tell me. I . . . need to know."

"Understood." Karl sucked air through his teeth. "Do you remember Aeia, Baron?"

Again, Furnael's face momentarily became an echo instead of a ghost of what it had been. "Call me Zherr, Karl. And yes, I remember her. The Mel child that you were returning to Melawei.''

"She didn't stay in Melawei; she's my adopted daughter, now. A slaver was trying to kill her. Rahff stopped him. I don't know . . . maybe I hadn't trained him well enough; perhaps he just wasn't fast enough. Before I could intervene, the slaver . . . ran him through.''

"He died quickly?''

"It must have been almost painless," Karl lied reflexively. Didn't Furnael have the right to know that his son had died in agony, his belly slit open by a slaver's sword?

Probably. *But I'm not going to be the one to tell him.*

"The man who killed him . . ." Furnael's eyes burned with an inner fire. "Did you . . . ?''

"I broke the bastard's neck." Karl spread his hands. "With these hands, Zherr.''

"Good. Now . . . it seems that what is left of my barony is in your debt. How can we repay it?''

"For one thing, all my people need food and rest. Aveneer's soldiers have been on a forced march for more days than they care to count. I'd like your people to see that they're fed, and given a chance to rest.''

"Done. You plan is to move on the Holts' slaver allies, I take it.''

"Yes." *And then to—somehow—shut this war down, deny the buzzards and the slavers their profits.* "Have you heard of a burn-scarred slaver working with the Holts?''

"That I have." Furnael nodded. "Name of Ahrmin?''

"Right. He led the slaving raid in Melawei when we were there, and he's backing the Holts, providing them with their slaver gunpowder." Karl reached up and stroked Stick's muzzle. "I'll have one of my people interrogate the prisoners, and we'll see if we can find out exactly where on Mount Aershtyn the raiders are camped, precisely what resources they have there. I'm willing to bet that somewhere on Aershtyn is the guild's headquarters in the Middle Lands.''

"But even so . . ." Furnael shrugged. "What good will that do? No matter where they're camped, there's no way you could approach them without being spotted at least a day in advance. With a chance to prepare for an attack—''

"You're forgetting Ellegon. While the main force is work-

ing its way up and hanging on to their attention, I'll have the
dragon drop me and a few others in from behind." Karl
hitched at his sword, forcing a smile. "If we can do it, if we
can break the back of the Holt-slaver alliance, maybe the
Holts will sue for peace."

That was the best shot, if it all could be done quickly. It
would require Prince Pirondael and his barons to accept an
unsatisfactory truce, in place of a war they were losing, while
Holtish Prince Uldren and his barons would end the war
knowing that the tide of battle was about to turn against them.

Winning a cease-fire instead of losing a war would make
both sides feel very clever . . . for a while; within ten years,
both sides would probably claim that they would have won if
the peace hadn't been forced on them.

Karl repressed a sigh. He could spot at least three major
weaknesses in his plan, but at least it had a chance.

Furnael held out a hand. "It is good to see you, my
friend."

Karl accepted the baron's hand, and was pleased to find
that the grip was stronger now. "Zherr . . ." He closed his
eyes and forced himself to say it. "I'm sorry about Rahff. If
only . . ."

"No." The baron shook his head. "We both have to go
on." He easily pulled himself to his horse's back. "There's a
war to be won." He slapped himself on the leg and laughed
as he spurred his horse. "Damn me, but there's a war to be
won!"

Karl smiled. Furnael had been given just the barest taste of
possible victory, of possible life for his barony and his people;
and the baron had shed about twenty years.

So Karl kept quiet as he spurred Stick, all the while
thinking: *No, Zherr. There isn't. There's a war to be stopped.*

CHAPTER TWENTY-ONE:

Ahrmin

Whom they fear they hate.

—Quintus Ennius

"Master Ahrmin?" Fenrius' basso boomed from outside his tent. "It is time to go."

Painfully, slowly, Ahrmin got to his feet and limped out of his tent, squinting in the early-morning sunlight. His carriage was waiting for him; he let Fenrius help him through the door and onto the padded seat.

The slaver camp at the base of Aershtyn was different from its cousin halfway up the slopes. Up there were the pens and corrals holding the well-chained cream of the captured Biemish population, guarded only by the few guildsmen necessary to keep them safely confined.

But this camp was a military operation, a place where Pandathaway-made powder was stored, guns made and repaired. Until today—now, the camp was breaking up, as Ahrmin's guildsmen prepared to move out.

It would be difficult to move three hundred men silently, and when they joined up with Prince Uldren's Holtish troops it would be impossible. Fortunately, the element of surprise wasn't always necessary.

The problem with you, Karl Cullinane, isn't that you challenge me. Were that all, I would still have you killed, but you wouldn't haunt my dreams so. If you were only the murderer of my father, I would have you killed slowly.

But I was wrong about you: You are not only my enemy;

*you challenge the fabric of what is. I can't allow myself
the luxury of killing you slowly; it is vastly more important
that I kill you surely.*

"You're sure of the assassins?" he asked Fenrius.

"Nothing is certain," the big man said, choosing his words
carefully, "but they are said to be competent. I am . . .
confident that he will be dead, or at least out of action, by the
time we get there."

"Good." No, surprise wasn't necessary. Not when your
enemy was trapped like a bug in a well-corked bottle. Then,
all that was necessary was to heat the bottle. . . . "Very
good. Make sure the barrels are tied down." Ahrmin leaned
out the window, his good left hand pointing to the wagon that
contained the huge barrels of powder; the massive, well-oiled
oaken barrels were sealed so tightly that neither air nor water
could have penetrated their sides.

"Yes, Master Ahrmin." Fenrius snapped his fingers and
pointed toward the wagon; a dozen journeyman slavers ran to
it, giving tie ropes another examination.

"You have had word from the Holts?"

"Nothing new." Fenrius shrugged. "Prince Uldren has
pulled out most of his army from the battle in Arondael, as
promised—although I'm not sure he believed the message—"

"*I* believed the message. And that is more than sufficient.
As Uldren knows." If Uldren hadn't been willing to cooper-
ate fully, well, the Biemish would have made adequate allies.
Perhaps better ones—it was unlikely that Pirondael would
stupidly fail to press home a tactical advantage, the way
Uldren had in the north. It was clear to Ahrmin that Prince
Pirondael was determined to benefit from every possible
advantage.

Still, switching alliances hadn't been necessary; Uldren
knew that his own survival depended on slaver powder and
slaver guns.

"There should be more than enough for the task—once we
join them." Fenrius gestured toward the tarpaulin-covered
cylinder, twice the length of a tall man, that was mounted on
the largest of the flatbed wagons.

Ahrmin nodded. "True. Have you seen the latest shipment
from Hivael?"

"Yes." Fenrius nodded happily. "A hundred slaves came through this morning."

"I take it they aren't like that last batch?"

"No, not at all. Baron Drahan seems to have understood your message."

Ahrmin smiled. "A simple matter of withholding powder until their commitments were met. And with the shipment to Keranahan destroyed, the shortage was acute."

"Perhaps, Master Ahrmin, but it was effective." Fenrius smiled his approval. "I held back a dozen women. Definitely not culls." He smiled thinly. "Prime stock, although perhaps a bit spiritless."

"Fine. Send two of the best to me as a diversion for the trip."

"Yes, Master Ahrmin. At once."

That was a pleasant prospect. The trip was likely to be agonizingly long; best to have a distraction. "When they are delivered to me, move us out."

"Yes, Master Ahrmin."

Ahrmin leaned back against his cushions. Soon. It would be soon.

You and I have a score to settle, Karl Cullinane. It is only proper that a . . . version of one of your own devices will kill you.

CHAPTER TWENTY-TWO:

Betrayal

If you pick up a starving dog and make him prosperous, he will not bite you. This is the principal difference between a dog and a man.

—Mark Twain

The aftermath of the siege and the battle was, in more ways than one, a bloody mess.

Karl happily left the beginnings of reconstruction to Furnael and his people. War could ruin in weeks what had been built up over many years; it would be a long time before the barony was back to anything near its former prosperity. The lack of people to work the fields was compensated for only by the lack of mouths for the keep's siege stores to feed.

Furnael now had an excess of land in what would have been a buyer's market—if there had been any buyers. Of course, there were none: The populations of the neighboring baronies had been decimated, slaves and freefarmers alike clapped into chains and shipped off to be sold along the Cirric coast, to work in the mines of Port Orduin and Sciforth, plow fields in Lundescarne, or serve in fine houses in Pandathaway and Aeryk.

There was a chance that some could be freed, up on the slopes of Aershtyn, where a few escapees reported that the slavers had their camp, a staging ground for what the captured Holtish prisoners said was to be a vast human cattle drive to Pandathaway.

Maybe they could be freed. But there were preparations to

be made. The most important ones were the ones that Karl found most pleasant: resting and eating. Aveneer's team was road-weary almost to the point of exhaustion; Valeran's people and the mercenaries who had signed on in Biemestren weren't in much better shape. Even Karl had to admit that regular meals and regular sleeping hours had their attractions.

Well, the regular sleeping hours *would* have been nice. There was just too much work to do. The foremost priority was maintenance on the firearms. There were flints to be cut, frizzens to be rewelded, bent triggers to be straightened, barrels to be freshed out, split stocks to be glued or replaced. That had to be left to Ranella and Slovotsky, who spent their days closeted in the keep's smithy, the doors always heavily guarded.

The gunsmithing, though, interfered with another high priority—reshoeing of the horses. Most of the animals were long overdue, and the necessity that they be reshod created a logistics problem: All gunsmithing procedures were secret, and had to be conducted in the privacy of Furnael Keep's sole smithy, but shoeing required some of the same facilities.

The solution was more work for Karl. While he wasn't enough of a smith to turn bar stock into horseshoes, he could take shoes that Ranella made in the smithy and then fit them to the horses.

Of course, the shoes did have to be adjusted, and that required an anvil—and a forge. Or a reasonable facsimile.

Stop that, Ellegon—you're scaring the—would you please try to broadcast calm? Karl thought as he ducked aside, trying to avoid the brown mare's kick.

He was almost successful: The hoof just barely caught him on the right thigh, knocking his leg out from underneath him. It felt as if he had been hit by a hammer; he fell to the ground and rolled to safety.

Rubbing at his thigh, he glared at Theren and Migdal while they struggled with the horse. "I thought you were supposed to be helping me shoe this fleabag," he said, keeping his voice calm and friendly for the mare's benefit, not theirs.

"Sorry, Karl," Migdal said, pulling down on the reins.

Erek ran over and helped him to his feet. He stood on his

good leg for a moment, debating whether or not to just pack it in for the day and let this idiot mare go only three-quarters reshod. It was always the last horse that could break a bone, just as it was that one last run down the ski slope that had once broken his leg.

Distant fingers touched his mind.

That's true. But remember: There was a very simple reason that it was the last run in which you broke your leg.

Oh? What was it?

After you broke your leg, you weren't interested in skiing anymore.

Always got to keep me honest, eh?

It's a tough job, but somebody's got to do it. Ellegon closed both eyes.

"Okay, people, let's give it another try. Just one more shoe and we finish this one off—then I'm calling it quits for the day." And a rather productive day at that, he thought, eyeing the late-afternoon sun with satisfaction.

There wasn't a whole lot of thrill in this stint as a farrier, but there was a certain something to it. Karl had always found a certain magic in metalworking, and while shoeing was something that a real smith would have found almost agonizingly routine, Karl liked it. Working with horses and working with metal, both at the same time—what could be better?

"Retirement," he muttered to himself. He set his nippers down next to the anvil and reached for the right rear hoof, turning around and pinning the hoof between his thighs.

Now, keep the animal calm, okay?

Ellegon gave out a mental sniff as he lay on the ground on the other side of the low brick wall that had a one-foot-square hole in it. *Go to sleep,* he began to sing, his mental voice low, but intense, *go to sleep, go to sleep, little horsie . . .*

Karl felt his own eyelids start to sag shut. "Stop that!" *All right, you made your point. Now cut that out. Just don't scare the horse, okay?*

The dragon didn't answer; Karl decided to take that for an assent.

He picked up his nippers and began to loosen the old nails. Sometimes the hardest part was getting the old shoe off, particularly if the foot had had time to overgrow it too much.

As this one had. He grunted as he pulled out the last nail, then pried the shoe off, throwing it on the all-too-large pile of used shoes. Accepting the wood-handled trimming knife from Erek, Karl quickly trimmed the sole, the frog, and the hoof wall, then tossed the knife back to Erek, who handed him the rasp in exchange.

Rasp gripped tightly, Karl gave the bottom of the hoof wall two dozen quick strokes, then eyed the hoof.

Not quite right, but almost. He tried an additional half-dozen quick passes with the rasp, then looked again. Better, nice and level. The toe length looked about right, too. He rasped away the splinters around the old nail holes, then held out his hand for a shoe.

Damn. "Anything less round? These feet are about as pointed as I've seen today."

Erek handed him another. Close, but not quite.

That is what I'm here for, isn't it?

Straightening, Karl let the foot drop and walked over to the brick wall.

Well, it really wasn't much of a wall, just a six-foot-long, four-foot-high stack of bricks with a hole in the middle, right next to where the small anvil stood on its stump. Karl gripped the shoe with a yard-long pair of pincers and stuck it through the hole in the wall.

Ellegon breathed fire, the backwash of heat almost sending Karl stumbling away. Instead, he closed his eyes and forced himself to hold on.

That should do it.

Karl pulled the red-hot shoe back through the hole and brought it over to the anvil. A few quick taps with the hammer, then he dipped it into a pail of water, ducking his head aside to avoid the hissing steam. He brought the shoe over to the mare and picked up the horse's foot, comparing.

Not a bad fit, not bad at all, he decided as he brought the shoe back for Ellegon to heat. It took only a few seconds before he was able to bring the hot shoe back to the horse, lift the hoof, and set the shoe against it, watching the hoof smoke as the shoe burned itself into place.

Quickly, he nailed the shoe in, bent the excess length of nails down, clipped them off, and clinched the nails.

His thigh was still throbbing where the horse had kicked him.

Enough. He let the foot drop. "I'll let you rasp off the edges," he said to Migdal. "I'm done for the day."

He eyed the setting sun, then waved up at one of Furnael's guards on the ramparts. No need to ask if the watchman had spotted anything unusual; that would have resulted in an immediate alarm.

Where's Andy? he thought, as he exchanged his tools and apron for his sword, pistols, and pouch.

Up in your rooms, Ellegon answered. *Doing some work with Henrad.*

Anything you can interrupt?

A pause. *Nothing dangerous.*

Good. Relay: I'm done for the day—any chance we can get some time to ourselves?

She says: "Give me about an hour—Henrad's almost got this cantrip down, and I don't want to break quite yet."

Fine. It'll give me a chance to take a bath.

Thank goodness for small favors, the dragon said, sniffing in distaste.

Karl laughed. "Come heat the water for me," he said, rubbing at his thigh as he limped across the broken-ground courtyard toward the bathhouse, the dragon lumbering along beside him like a four-legged bus.

Over by the east wall, Valeran was teaching a class in Lundish swordsmanship, both of his blades flashing in the light of the sun that hung just over the wall of the keep. Karl didn't dare interrupt him; what if, up on the slopes of Aershtyn, one of the warriors Valeran was teaching missed a parry?

Not everything that goes wrong is your fault, Karl.

Maybe not. But why does it always feel that way?

Egotism.

Thanks.

You're welcome.

Karl passed by the low stone smithy. Wisps of smoke floated up from its brick chimney, only to be shattered in the breeze. Two guards stood with their backs to the door, while the clattering of metal on metal came from inside.

Karl nodded to them as he walked by and into the low bathhouse next door.

The room was dark and dank. Karl set his weapons and his amulet on a dry spot on the rude shelf before stripping off his clothes and pumping water into the huge oaken tub. Ellegon snaked his head inside and dipped his mouth into the tub. Almost immediately the water started hissing and bubbling.

Touch—carefully, now.

Karl dipped a hand into the water. It was nicely warm.

Then I'll be on my way.

"What's up?"

Ahira wants some help with the timbers he's clearing out of the Holts' tunnels, and I have to get my patrol out of the way if I'm going to help him.

"Fine."

About his leaving . . . do you want me to—

"No. I don't want you peeping my fam—my friends for me."

Without another word, the dragon ducked his head back through the door. Momentarily, wind whipped dust in through the open door . . .

. . . and then silence.

After rinsing the dirt from his body with the icy water from the pump, Karl went to the tub and lowered himself slowly, gingerly, into the steaming water. As always, what had been comfortably warm to his hand felt as if it would parboil his calves and thighs, as well as more delicate parts of his anatomy.

But he forced himself to sit back against the oak sides of the tub and relax in the heat. Gradually, the tension in his neck and shoulders eased. He rubbed his hands against his face, then shook his head to clear the water from his eyes before leaning back.

Aershtyn was going to be bad, there was no doubt about it. If the slavers had as large a collection of slaves there as Karl suspected, they would guard them well.

And that probably meant guns. Karl didn't like the idea of sending his people up against guns. That was how Chak—

No. His hands clenched into fists. No, he couldn't keep thinking about Chak. That was the way of it: Good people had died, were going to die before this was all over.

There wasn't any cheap way out. There never was.

A round cake of scented soap lay on the rough table next to

the tub. Karl picked it up and began to work up a violet-
smelling lather.

Smell like a goddam flower, I will.

His face washed and rinsed, he lay back and tried to relax.
But the water cooled all too quickly. He could either get out
now, lie in a tepid bath—

Or do something else. "Guard," he called out, careful to
make his voice both loud and calm.

Almost immediately, Restius stuck his grizzled face through
the door. "You called, Karl?"

"Yes. Knock on the smithy door and see if Slovotsky
would be willing to join me for a moment. Wait," he said as
Restius started to leave. "Not so quick. Ask him to bring a
red-hot bit of bar stock," he said, splashing the water. "A
large bit."

Restius smiled. "I see." He disappeared, returning in a
few minutes with Walter Slovotsky.

Walter held a large iron bar in his massive pincers. Even in
the light coming through the open door, it glowed redly,
although it was only a dull red.

"My, but we're getting fancy," Slovotsky said as he
dipped one end in the tub, the water quickly burbling, boiling.
"How's this?"

' Better," Karl said, working his hands underwater and
kicking his feet to spread the hot water around. "Much
better. I owe you one. If you want the next bath, I'll heat it
for you. Deal?"

"Deal." Slovotsky made no motion to leave. He lowered
the pincers to the ground and threw a hip over the edge of the
tub. "Got something to talk to you about." He pursed his
lips, opened his mouth, closed it.

"Well? You getting shy in your old age?"

"Me? No, it's just that . . . How long do you think it'll be
before we finish up here?"

Karl shrugged. "Well, I figure we'll move on Aershtyn in
about three weeks. That should be over quickly. It's shutting
down the damn war after that that bothers me—that could
take anywhere from a few tendays to . . ." He let his voice
trail off.

"To however long you'll put into it before you give up."
Slovotsky nodded. "Which is probably the way it's going to

be. Listen to Furnael's people, Karl, *listen* to them. They don't just want peace, they want revenge." He shrugged. "Can't say as I blame them, but that's not the point."

"And is how long this war is going to go on. Is it?"

Slovotsky didn't meet his eyes.

Karl reached out and gripped his hand. "Walter, be a bit bolder. Remember how it used to be? You weren't ashamed to look me in the eye after the time you made it with my wife—"

"Hey!" Slovotsky's head jerked up. "Andy wasn't your wife, not then."

"True enough."

"But I wasn't all that eager to discuss it with you, even then."

"True again. But that wasn't because you were ashamed, was it?"

"No." Walter chuckled. "That was because I didn't want my head bashed in."

"I won't bash your head in. Not even if you take Kirah and Janie and go to Endell with Ahira."

Slovotsky's jaw dropped. "You knew?"

"Andy worked it out."

They sat in silence for a moment until Karl snorted and tossed the soap away. Somehow, even warm, the bath wasn't comfortable, not anymore.

"Hand me that towel, will you?" he asked as he pushed himself to his feet and stepped out of the tub.

He dried himself quickly, then slipped his amulet over his head and began to dress. "What do you want from me, Walter? My permission? You don't need that." He buckled his swordbelt around his waist, his hand going to its hilt for a moment.

Slovotsky looked him straight in the eye. "Maybe . . . maybe sometimes it feels as if I do, Karl. It's just that all of this . . ." His awkward gesture seemed to include the entire universe. "It's starting to get to me. I can remember a time when the most violent thing I'd ever done was sacking a quarterback, Karl. It's . . . I don't know how to say it."

He started to turn away. Karl caught his arm.

"Listen to me," Karl said. "You don't need my permission,

but if you want my blessing, you've got it. We've . . . been through a lot together, Walter, and I love you like a brother. If you really need to spend a few years away from the action, then you do it. That's an order—understood?"

"Understood." Slovotsky smiled weakly. "Besides, it may not come to that. Who knows? I could get myself killed on this Aershtyn thing."

"Always looking at the bright side, eh?"

"Always."

They emerged into a golden, dusky light.

Slovotsky held out a hand. "Thanks, Karl. I appreciate it." He seemed to be about to say something else.

Karl took his hand. "Walter—"

Alert! Danger! Warning! came the distant voice.

Karl's head jerked around. Nobody else was reacting.

"What is it, Karl?"

"Ellegon—can't you hear him?"

Slovotsky shook his head.

Ellegon, what is it?

He felt that Ellegon was trying to answer, but he couldn't hear him. The dragon must have been at his extreme range, and only Karl's mindlink was tight enough to pick up Ellegon's broadcast, and that only irregularly, unpredictably.

"There's trouble." Karl cupped his hands around his mouth and called up to the watchman. "Sound the alert!"

The warrior began beating rhythmically on the alarm gong.

"Walter," Karl snapped, "get your squad armed and up on the ramparts. Take charge there. Erek! Where the hell's that—" He stopped himself as the boy ran up. "Message to Piell, Chak—" He clenched his fists. "Belay that last. Add Aveneer. Begins: Ellegon has sounded an alert. Nature unknown. I'll be at the main gate. Arm your people, report via message runner to me there. Ends. Message to Valeran. Mount up and bring your men and my horse to main gate. Ends. Message to Baron Furnael: Begins: Trouble. Am at main gate. If it pleases you, meet me there with your chief man-at-arms. Ends. Go."

Karl? The distant voice was clearer, firmer. *Can you hear me?*

Yes, dammit. I've sounded the alert. What's going on?

The dragon swooped over the ramparts and dropped into

the courtyard, sending up puffs of dust as he landed heavily on the sunbaked dirt. *I'm not sure. Did we want a troop of about five hundred Holtish cavalry to be about half a day's ride east of us on the Prince's Road?*

"No—did you say *east*?" That didn't make any sense. Biemestren lay in that direction. How had the Holtish worked their way that deeply into Bieme, and why? It didn't make any tactical sense, not after the way that Karl had broken the siege.

They could have been sent before the breaking of the siege, but any force sent to reinforce the Holtish siegers would surely have been sent in via the west, through Holtun.

It just didn't make any sense, none at all, unless—

"Ellegon, check the west road. Now."

The west road?

"Yes, the west road, dammit." It was the only explanation. A cavalry force of that size wouldn't be sent to reinforce a siege. It had to be intended to block an escape.

An escape from what? From whatever was moving in on them from the west. "Get airborne, do a nice, high recon until you see something interesting, and then get back here. Move it, dammit."

You're welcome. His leathery wings a blur, the dragon leaped into the air and flew over the ramparts. *I will keep you in—*

Ellegon screamed; his mind opened.

Pain tore through Karl's chest as three oily-headed cross-bow bolts sank into his massive chest, passing through his thick hide as though it weren't there. He tried to flap his wings, struggled to pull upward with his inner strength, but he crashed to the ground and—

"Karl!" Furnael slapped his face again.

He shook his head as he lurched to his feet. "No! Ellegon—"

On the ramparts, a dozen guns fired in volley. Slovotsky turned to call down to Karl. "The dragon is *down*. We've fired on four crossbowmen, driving them back into the woods."

Hooves clattered as Valeran, leading Stick, arrived with his twenty mounted men.

"Four bowmen—watch for them." Karl leaped to the horse's back and spurred him through the gate, Valeran and his men galloping along behind.

Ellegon lay writhing on the ground by the side of the road, half in, half out of the ditch, his grunts and screams strangely animalistic, his flailing treetrunk legs sending huge volleys of dirt into the air.

Three crossbow bolts projected from his chest, their fletchings barely visible.

Karl dismounted from Stick's back. "Go," he shouted to Valeran. "Find them. I want them dead."

There was nothing to do as the huge dragon lay there, dying. Dragonbane was a poison to Ellegon, and every second it was working its way deeper into the dragon's body.

No. I won't give up. Ellegon had been able to survive his only other contact with the stuff, more than three centuries before. There was a chance that he could survive this. The poison would have to be gotten out—but how? Karl couldn't even break through the wall of pain around the dragon's mind.

I have to. Ellegon, he thought, *can you hear me?*

Yes. But the word was accompanied by nauseating waves of pain. Clutching at his chest, Karl crumpled to the ground.

No, *don't,* he thought, as the mindlink faded. *Don't answer. Just hear me. I have to get those bolts out of you. Try not to move.*

He worked his way in between the writhing forelegs, only to be batted aside by a fluttering wingtip that knocked him off his feet.

"No, Ellegon. Don't move." The three bolts were spread out across the dragon's chest, all but one above Karl's reach.

He quickly pulled that one out and tossed it away, then tried to climb up the dragon's side to get at another.

But his toes couldn't find purchase among Ellegon's hard scales. There was just no way to reach them.

"Karl!" A hand slammed down on his shoulder. "Lift me!" Andy screamed at him, a long-bladed knife in her hands.

Karl stooped, clamped his hands around her ankles, and lifted her up, holding her tightly as high as he could.

The dragon screamed again—

Don't move, Ellegon. Please don't move. If you knock us away, you'll die.

Karl . . . The mental voice was distant. *My friend . . . I'm afraid that this is goodbye—*

"No, dammit, don't you *dare* die on me, you scaly bastard. Not you, Ellegon. Andy—"

"Shut up," she hissed. "I've almost gotten the second one."

The dragon's mental presence was fading quickly, and his struggles were slowing, not from control, but from weakness.

"*Got* it," she exclaimed. "Take five big steps to your right so I can get at the last one."

While it felt like hours, Karl knew that it was only a few seconds later that she cried out, "Got it. Let me down."

He lowered her, shaking the tears from his eyes. "No, that's not enough. We've got to do something about the poison in the wounds."

Think, dammit, think. He looked up the dragon's side to the red holes in Ellegon's gray hide, and at the slow ooze of thick blood dripping down Ellegon's scales. The trouble was that dragonbane was poison, a chemical poison that dragons, virtually immune to most forms of physical attack, were subject to.

Andy-Andy buried her head against his chest, the bloody bolts falling from her hands. "He's not going to make it, Karl." The dragon's breathing was almost imperceptible.

"Shut up. Let me think." There had to be something to do, some way to clear the poison out of—

Got it!

He opened his pouch and pulled out his powder horn. "We'll burn it away," he shouted. "With gunpowder." Drawing his beltknife, he snatched at the hem of her robes and cut a swatch off, then used the rag to dry the most accessible of Ellegon's wounds as best he could.

He handed her the knife. "Give me another swatch," he said. He packed the wound with the fresh cloth, then opened his powder horn and tipped a third of the powder into the cloth. "Valeran!" he shouted, "get me a torch, some fire—now!"

Her face brightened. "Lift me."

He braced his back against the dragon's chest, caught her

by the waist, and lifted her. As she planted her feet on his shoulders, he passed up the horn. "Do the same thing I did. Then get as much powder as you can into the swatches."

In moments the remaining wounds were packed with gunpowder. Lowering Andy-Andy to the ground, Karl accepted the torch from Valeran and touched it to the nearest of the wounds.

It puffed into flame and acrid smoke. He touched the torch to the other two rents in Ellegon's hide, and again they burned.

Andy gripped his arm. "Do you think—?"

The dragon was still breathing, but that was all. *Ellegon? Can you hear me? Dammit,* say *something.*

He shook his head. "I don't know. And I don't know what the hell else to do. We'll just have to wait." He bent over and kissed Andy-Andy gently on the forehead. "Make that 'I'll just have to wait.' This area isn't secure, yet." He turned to Valeran. "Put a guard around him—borrow men from Aveneer. I want a full circle, twice as wide as a bowshot, well lit with watchfires. There may be other assassins around. They're not to get within crossbow range—*nobody* is to get within crossbow range—understood?"

"Understood." Valeran nodded. "But—"

Karl turned. "*Erek!* Gather all team leaders and seconds for a full staff meeting, main dining hall; ask the baron's permission. Invite him and Thomen to join us—particularly Thomen. Go."

The boy nodded and ran off.

Valeran looked as though he was about to ask why, then shrugged. "Yes, Karl. But I was trying to tell you that we captured one." He led Karl around to the other side of the dragon and pointed to a greasy little man who lay on the ground, tightly bound, next to Norfan's horse. "Do you want me to hand him over to Tennetty?"

"Yeah." He nodded.

"Instructions?"

"She's to make him talk, and then she's to make him die."

Karl stood at the head of the long table, gathering his thoughts, trying to forget about Ellegon for the moment.

There was nothing that could be done about the dragon now, but this meeting was critical.

Gathered around the table, the others sat quietly, waiting for the storm to break.

Sitting together at the far end of the table, Valeran, Frandred, and Aveneer talked calmly, in soft tones, as though nothing at all bothered them.

Karl had never truly understood that mentality. He understood the necessity of generating the image, of course, but the calm resolution that one was going to die in battle, and that this coming battle might easily be *the* battle, well, that was something Karl could simulate, but never quite understand. That was something he had given up when he had deliberately subsumed his Barak persona.

Sitting next to him, Andy-Andy reached over and squeezed his hand momentarily, then dropped it. *Relay, please*—he caught himself. *Damn.* "I'm glad you're here," he whispered, smiling back at her.

"Hate sleeping alone that much, do you?" She smiled back.

"Right." ·

Next to her, Tennetty and Ahira sat quietly, their faces more impassive than calm. But the dwarf's brow was furrowed. His stubby fingers steepled in front of his aquiline nose, he occasionally glanced over at Karl, then resumed his own thoughts.

Karl let a chuckle escape his lips. Ahira was trying to anticipate him. There had been a time when the dwarf was a better military tactician than Karl, but practice and study had honed Karl's skills. Still, Ahira's ability to think well under pressure was something to reckon with . . . or to rely on, depending.

On the dwarf's right, Piell sat back on his high-backed chair, feigning calm, while opposite Ahira, Walter Slovotsky waited patiently, his all-is-well-with-any-universe-clever-enough-to-contain-Walter-Slovotsky smile intact, as always.

Next to Slovotsky, Zherr Furnael sat stiffly, looking like a compromise between the way he had been six years before and the way Karl had found him. Well, a compromise it would have to be. Furnael was the key to everything, and if the baron could just hold himself together for a few more years, maybe . . .

Thomen sat quietly next to his father, his eyes watching everyone, missing nothing. Thomen was different from his brother: Rahff had been much more of a talker, less of a watcher.

"It's going to be tough, people," Karl said. "The first item of business is getting Ellegon in through the gates. Andy, can you levitate him?"

"I've been expecting that. And I . . . think so." She nodded, biting her lip uncertainly. "I may be able to lift him, but that doesn't mean I can float him in here—and with his mass . . ."

"That's easily solved. We tie some ropes to his legs and everyone helps pull him in through the main gate." He looked over at Furnael. "If he does survive, he's going to need to eat a *lot* of food. You can start with your scrawniest animals—he won't care."

"It will be done." The baron nodded. "We have some smoked beef in the cellars that has turned. If that wouldn't do Ellegon harm—"

"Turned?" Slovotsky raised an eyebrow. "Why haven't you disposed of it?"

Furnael answered slowly. "Because, Walter Slovotsky, when you are under siege you would rather your people have moldly beef to eat than see them starve in front of your eyes. That is . . ." He pinched the bridge of his nose between thumb and forefinger. "My apologies. I was asking—would the meat be bad for the dragon?"

"Not at all," Karl said. "He doesn't poison easily."

Aveneer raised his head. "I don't understand all this hurry. It can't be because of five hundred cavalrymen a day's ride away to the east, so I—"

"Wait," Ahira interrupted. "How do you know it's not?"

Aveneer threw his head back and laughed. "You may have observed that Karl Cullinane does not panic easily. Five hundred cavalrymen would not panic him, not when we've that many effectives here, most armed with guns."

"No, it's not the horsemen." Karl shook his head. "They're only there to cut off our remaining avenue of escape. The reason that I'm worried is that I'm all but certain there are at least two thousand heavily armed soldiers only a few days to the west. I've been sold out, people, and Ahrmin is about to arrive and try to collect."

"Surely," Valeran said, studying the fingernails he was cleaning with the point of a dagger that he hadn't been holding moments before, "you aren't accusing anyone here? I realize that I am new to your service, but I've never been fond of being the target of a false accusation."

Tennetty pushed back her chair and rose slowly, her hand on the hilt of her sword. "If it is you—"

"*No*, Tennetty," Karl snapped. "It's not Valeran. Think it through.

"Holtish cavalry moving in from the east on the Prince's Road is an obvious suggestion that there's more trouble brewing in from the west. They can't be here to reinforce the siege—they wouldn't chance swinging in through Bieme if that were the case. Doesn't look like a normal military procedure, does it?

"The attack on Ellegon cinched it." He looked at Tennetty. "You interrogated the surviving assassin. Who were they after?"

"Ellegon. At least, that's what he said."

"Right. Think about it. Assassins armed with dragonbane, sent to kill Ellegon. That has to mean that whoever is behind this is after me—and who has known that I'm here long enough to prepare and send out assassins?"

The words hung in the air for a moment.

"Not the Holts," Furnael said, tenting his fingers in front of his chin. "If they had known about you and your people, they would have been prepared for your lifting of the siege, and reinforced their positions, not sacrificed the horsemen who chased after you, then retreated. You're saying that your betrayer is Biemish, some traitor in Biemestren?"

Karl nodded. "In a sense. Assume that I'm right, assume that a large part of the Holtish army is headed this way—who would benefit?"

Furnael shrugged. "The Holts, of course, if they can take the keep."

"Nonsense. The Holts already had the keep under control; they could have cracked it like an egg anytime they wanted to divert the manpower from the north. But they didn't do that, did they?''

Furnael wrinkled his brow. "No, but . . ."

"But who else stood to benefit? Who had already written off barony Furnael as a lost cause? Who would love to divert a few thousand Holts and their slaver allies south—''

"Wait—''

"—and who would gain by weakening the Holtish advance in the north, possibly taking advantage of the situation to order a counterattack? Tell me, Baron, *who?*''

"Son of a *bitch!*'' Slovotsky nodded. "Pirondael.'' He threw up his hands. "Look at it from his point of view. It'd be a gorgeous bit of betrayal. It was common knowledge in Enkiar that Ahrmin's as irrational on the subject of you as you are on the subject of him—why wouldn't Pirondael know? He's counting on the little bastard's taking off after you with every gun and soldier he can muster.''

He pushed his chair back from the table and began pacing up and down. "Shit, Karl, that changes *everything*. We don't have any line of retreat at all. Even if we could somehow punch through the Holtish cavalry at our back door, we can't sneak hundreds of warriors through Bieme.''

Furnael sat up straight. "Bieme is not your enemy, not even if—''

"Nonsense, Baron,'' Andy-Andy snapped. "If your prince has betrayed Karl, he'll know it, and he'll be deathly afraid of my husband. As he has a right to be.'' She looked up at Karl. "Assuming that I don't get to him first.''

Furnael shook his head. "I find this difficult to believe. My prince would not dishonor his crown this way.''

"You're confusing the myth with the reality, Zherr. Wearing a crown doesn't make a man honorable.'' Karl turned to Slovotsky. "Walter, how many men do you think you could sneak past the Holts?''

"Depends. You thinking about sending me back to Biemestren?''

Karl nodded.

"Damn.'' Slovotsky shrugged. "Then you'd better tell me what you want me to do.''

"I want you to find out if I'm right or not about Pirondael's betraying us. If I'm wrong, you've got it easy: Talk him into sending some reinforcements.''

''If you think that's easy, would you please tell me what you consider hard?''

''If I'm right, then I think it's time we put a new prince under that crown of Pirondael's, and make sure that the new prince sends out reinforce—''

''*Who?*'' Furnael snarled. ''Both of my prince's sons have died in this cursed war; Evalyn is long past child-bearing. The succession is in doubt. The best claim is probably Baron Tyrnael—''

''Not if we seat the crown firmly on *your* head, Zherr.'' Karl looked the baron straight in the eye. ''Not if we . . . persuade Pirondael to abdicate in your favor.''

Furnael looked him straight in the eye. ''You are asking me to commit treason, Karl Cullinane.''

''But what if I'm right? What if he's betrayed you, your barony, and your son?'' Karl pointed toward Thomen. ''He'll die here, as surely as the rest of us.''

Furnael sat back in his chair. ''It does come to that, doesn't it?'' For a long moment he sat motionless, his eyes fixed on Karl's.

Then he shook his head. ''No. There's no way it can be done. I can't be in two places at once. How can I defend my barony and decide whether or not Pirondael is guilty?''

''You can't, Baron. You're going to have to go along with Slovotsky, and decide for yourself.'' Slowly, Karl drew his sword and balanced the flat of the blade on the palms of his hands. ''We'll button up here; I can't go anywhere until Ellegon's well enough to travel, anyway. I'll do my best to safeguard Furnael Keep for you. You have the word of Karl Cullinane on that.''

Furnael hesitated. Karl wanted to take that for assent, but he sensed that if he pushed the baron at this moment, it would only push him away from what had to be done.

Finally, Furnael nodded. ''We shall do it.''

''Fine.'' Karl slipped the sword back into its sheath. ''Walter, I want you out of here before sunup. How many do you want to take with you? Twenty, thirty?''

Slovotsky spat. ''Don't be silly. That'd be suicide. It's got to be a tiny group, to have any chance of getting through, and into the castle.'' He leaned back in his chair and closed his eyes, sitting silently for so long that Karl was beginning to wonder if there was something wrong.

Slovotsky's eyes snapped open; he shrugged. ''Okay. The group is me, the baron, either Henrad or Andrea—''

''Not Andy. I need her here.''

''Make it Henrad, then—I'm going to need some magic. And I'll need someone to handle the horses—Restius should do for that—and one other. Ahira?''

The dwarf nodded. ''I was hoping you'd ask.'' He pushed his chair back away from the table. ''We'd better decide on equipment and get packed.'' Ahira looked up at Karl. ''Are you sure you can hold out here until we can relieve you?''

Karl shrugged. ''No. But I'd better. You see another way?''

''No. I'm worrying about the dragon. Do you think he's going to be okay?''

''I don't know. We'll just have to wait and see.''

Not . . . terribly long. The voice was distant, and it was weak.

But it was there.

Karl didn't know whether to laugh or cry.

He settled for slapping his hands together. ''Okay, people, let's get to work.''

CHAPTER TWENTY-THREE:

Biemestren Revisited

It is a bad plan that admits of no modification.
—Publilius Syrus

Walter Slovotsky moved quietly through the dark night, slipping in and out of the shadows of Biemstren Castle like a wraith.

Two hundred yards to the west, a dozen peasant shacks huddled up against the outer wall like moss against a tree. Four hundred yards to the east was the outer wall's main gate. But this stretch of wall was empty, the grasses growing almost chest-high.

"Just a short way, Baron," he whispered to Furnael. The baron's breathing was heavy; he considered offering Furnael a hand, but decided that the old man's pride would be wounded.

This wasn't a job for an old man. On the other hand, complaining about Furnael didn't make sense; the baron, after all, was a manifestly necessary component of any plan to put the baron on the throne.

So? Who says I have to be logical all the time? I'm Walter Slovotsky, dammit, not Leonard Nimoy.

To his left, Henrad stumbled. Ahira's hand whipped out, caught and lifted him, setting Henrad back on his feet before the boy could fall.

Slovotsky shook his head. Henrad might be coming along well in his magical studies, but he'd be about as useful on a quiet recon as a belled cow. He kept looking behind him, as though he could see where Restius waited with the horses, or possibly what was going on a week's ride away at Furnael Keep.

Walter shook his head. That was going to be a bitch if the Holts and slavers were attacking with any kind of seriousness.

Karl me boy, I sure hope that you're every bit as good as everybody else thinks you are.

Granted, the defense had the edge in this kind of warfare, but it wasn't an insuperable one. Everything really depended on how many of the Holts were moving on Furnael Keep. Or *had* moved on Furnael Keep; it could actually all be over by now. Come to think of it—

Whoa. Methinks you'd better get your mind back on what you're supposed to be doing, Walter me boy. You're doing with your mind what Henrad is doing with his eyes.

Despite the silent complaining, he was pleased with how things were going, so far. Though it was obviously bad for morale for someone in authority to gripe openly, a constant stream of silent complaints helped Walter keep himself sane. Relatively sane, at least.

Besides, being impressed with his own abilities was something he still hadn't gotten over. In the old days, he was large and reasonably well coordinated, but it would have been difficult to think of himself as terribly graceful.

Spiderman, watch my smoke, he thought. Then: *Walter, Walter, remember Slovotsky's Law Number Seven: Thou shalt always cover thy ass.*

The castle guard wasn't set up badly, but whoever had set out the guards had been more capable at maintaining order than security: two-man watchfires were scattered evenly on the outer ramparts, touring sentries only on the inner curtain wall.

It didn't take a military genius to deduce a manpower shortage; the main gate on the outer wall was only lightly manned, and the northern bastion wasn't manned at all.

Still, that wasn't surprising, Walter decided. The bastion was supposed to be a strongpoint for an active defense of the castle, not a lookout tower. Pirondael—or the commander of the House Guard, more likely—expected to know in advance about any attack in force, and would man the bastion when appropriate.

Slovotsky nodded his approval. The commander of the

House Guard was right; any large force would have been spotted long since.

On the other hand, the ramparts overhead were silent and empty, which pleased Slovotsky as the four of them crouched in the dark at the base of the wall. Overhead, the massive stone merlons at the top of the wall stood invitingly.

Ahira beckoned to him. "Ready? Or do you need a rest?"

Slovotsky shook his head. "We human flies don't need rest."

"Eh?"

"*Do* it, Ahira, do it."

While Walter slipped into his suede climbing gloves, the dwarf reached over his shoulder and unfastened a long braided-leather rope from his rucksack. Ahira measured the merlon by eye, adjusting the size of his loop.

He swung the rope several times around his head and threw.

The loop settled raggedly around the stone merlon; Ahira twitched at the rope to settle it into place, then pulled it tight.

"You're on," the dwarf said, taking a strain on the rope.

The trick to climbing up a rope was to let the feet and the leg muscles do as much of the work as possible; only the foolish relied on the weaker shoulder muscles any more than absolutely necessary.

Walter Slovotsky swarmed up the rope like a squirrel up a tree. At the top of the wall, he lowered himself to the stone walkway and listened. That was one of the tricks of the trade: At night, the ears were every bit as important as the eyes. The whisk of a leather sole on stone could carry hundreds of yards through the dark.

Halfway around the jagged curve of the outer wall was the main gate, and there a fire blazed orange against the night. Walter closed his eyes, held his breath, and listened.

Perhaps the wind brought him faint murrmurings of the distant guards' voices. Perhaps not. In any case, there was nothing closer, nothing except for the night sounds of insects, and the distant sound of voices from the village shacks.

He reached over the merlon and tugged on the rope three times, waited a moment, then tugged twice again. In a few moments, Ahira was at his side. After pulling up the rope, and rigging a sling on one end, they lowered it and pulled Henrad up, then Furnael.

"What next?" Ahira said, as he coiled the rope and lashed it to his belt.

"Stay here for a moment," Walter whispered as he slipped away from the other three. It was still well before midnight, and there were hours of darkness left; best to use that darkness liberally, safely.

He found a stone staircase only a few hundred feet away, then went back for the others and led them to it, down the stairs, and into the tall grasses of the outer ward.

The slope was steep as they climbed quietly through the night toward the inner wall, slipping into the shadows.

Walter decided that Karl had been right: This would be a difficult slope to fight up. The defenders wouldn't even have to kill you to stop you; all they would have to do would be to get you to lose your balance and you'd roll down the grassy slope to the bottom. Certainly it would be nearly impossible to set up siege towers or ladders at the top of the motte.

Walter beckoned to Henrad. "Are you getting anything yet?"

The boy shook his head. "Nothing. I don't think there's a wizard in the area. Except for me."

Ahira snorted. "Don't put on airs, Henrad."

The absence of Pirondael's wizard surprised Walter for a moment, but only a moment.

Actually, it made sense; Furnael's wizard had deserted at the start of the war. Most wizards seemed to be abject cowards when it came to physical danger, although they often weren't. It was just that in any kind of combat situation, the other side's having an active wizard was such a huge disadvantage that any successful strategy necessitated killing the wizard.

That tended to discourage all but the more powerful wizards from getting involved in combat situations, and usually the more powerful wizards were far more interested in augmenting their own abilities than in using them.

"Henrad," Walter whispered to the boy. "Be sure you're ready to zap the hell out of any group of guards before they can raise a cry."

"Zap?"

I just plain gotta remember to persuade Andy to teach

these people more colloquial English. "Be ready to put them to sleep, then. Understood?"

"Yes, Walter Slovotsky."

The inner wall was a different sort of problem than the outer wall had been. Not only was its circumference studded with manned guard towers, but Walter could hear the slap of sandals as a guard walked his tour above.

This was one of the times that Walter almost wished Karl Cullinane were running this one instead of him.

He sighed. No, it was best this way; keeping Furnael Keep intact wasn't something that Walter would have wanted to try. Besides, Karl wouldn't have done this right—he would have tended toward silencing a guard or two, hoping to make it down the wall and into the fortress itself by speed alone, expecting to power his way through any opposition.

That would have been suicide here. This wasn't like a typical slaver camp, where the guards would usually sit in one place, waiting for eventual relief. That sort of thing was easy: All you had to do was hit an outer guard station just after it had been relieved, and you would have scads of time to get set up and move in.

This was different. It was like planning on jumping through the blades of a whirring fan without being cut into bloody little slices.

Not getting cut into bloody little slices is, after all, the key to a sound plan, he thought, suppressing a chuckle.

He told the others to wait at the foot of the wall, then slipped off into the night. Maybe the inner gate was up; perhaps they could slip in that way.

No good. The portcullis hadn't been lowered, but the whole area around the gateway was lit by dozens of smoking, flickering torches—too well lit. He could probably slip in, but that was too much to expect of the others.

Damn.

Ahira, Furnael, and Henrad were waiting where he had left them. Above, he could hear the slap of the sandals of an approaching guard, walking his tour on the ramparts.

Walter put his mouth to Ahira's ear. "Can't use the gate," he whispered. "So we've got to do it the hard way. The timing's going to be critical here. Get out the rope."

Unless he missed his guess, a guard walked by this part of

the wall at least every fifteen minutes, which left barely enough time. Assuming, of course, that there weren't extra sentries posted, or that a soldier on duty in the nearest tower didn't happen to step out into the night to clear his head and spot them. If that happened, Henrad's Sleep spell wouldn't do them any good, not after one quick shout.

As the guard's footsteps vanished in the distance, Walter nodded to the dwarf. "Do it."

Again, the dwarf unfastened the long braided-leather rope and adjusted the size of his loop. He whipped the rope several times around his head and threw.

It missed. Slovotsky raised an eyebrow. Missing when it counted wasn't what he was used to from the dwarf.

"Better do better, Jimmy me boy," he said.

Ahira glared at him and threw again. This time the loop settled down around the jutting merlon as though God Himself had slipped it on. One quick tug and it was tight.

Slovotsky swarmed up the rope and slipped to his belly on the rampart. Nothing.

Again, he tugged on the rope, rising to help Ahira up, then the two of them pulled the other two up. He led the others down a staircase and into the shadow of the wall of the inner courtyard.

Well, that's the easy part.

"Henrad," he whispered. "Locate her—and be quiet about it, boy."

"Yes, Walter Slovotsky." The apprentice wizard nodded. "Consider it done," he said, a trifle too smugly. Still, a short-distance Location spell wasn't supposed to be terribly difficult, not when the object of the search was already well known to the wizard.

As the boy quietly murmured the harsh words that could only be heard and forgotten, Walter glanced down at his amulet, which was hardly flashing at all.

Still, it was flashing, and there was no need to ask for trouble; he unlooped it from his neck and tucked it into an inner pocket of his blousy black pantaloons.

"She is . . . in a suite on the second story of the keep, directly opposite a guardroom. Beralyn is . . . awake, and irritated at the noise the guards are making across the hall. . . .

There is a female servant in her outer chamber, although she believes that the woman is sleeping on duty."

Walter turned to Furnael. "Do you know where this suite is?"

Furnael nodded, his face grim. "Yes. What are you going to do about the guards? Even if Karl Cullinane's accusations against Prince Pirondael are true, they're not to blame. It would be—"

"I'm not after their blood." *Did you say "Prince Pirondael," Baron? You're not calling him "my prince" anymore, eh? Good.* It looked, more and more, as if Furnael was accepting Karl's accusations against Pirondael. "Besides, they're essential to the plan—I *can't* kill them. Have some faith." He nodded to Ahira and Henrad. "Let's go."

After all the difficulties getting over the walls, getting into the residence tower itself was almost an anticlimax.

They waited in the shadows until nobody was in sight, then simply walked in through the arched front door and made their way quietly up the dark stone staircase.

Walter kept one of his throwing knives ready in his hand. Though he wasn't after any innocent's blood, if they were spotted, blood would be shed in any event.

And if somebody's going to bleed, I'd just as soon it not be little ol' me. It was only fair, after all: The rest of the universe consisted of millions and millions of people who collectively had millions and millions of gallons of blood; Walter Slovotsky had only his meager few quarts, all of which he continually put to good use.

The tower was quiet. That was the advantage of doing this in the middle of the night, after all: As long as they avoided anyone who could sound the alarm and wake the soldiers in the adjacent barracks, all they had to worry about was those few guardsmen on duty.

They reached the second-floor landing and crept into the hall. The door to Beralyn's suite stood open, the entrance room lit by a single oil lamp. The room across the hall was well lit. Walter could make out several voices talking quietly; there were at least four soldiers talking in the room, perhaps as many as eight.

He nodded to Henrad. "Once more, Henrad," he whispered, then turned to the dwarf. "Watch your timing, Ahira."

The dwarf raised an eyebrow. "Nervous, are we?"

"No, I'm not nervous," he whispered back. "What the hell do I have to be nervous about? I'm really calm about sneaking around inside a castle that's next to a barracks, both of which are inside two separate walls, all of which means that if anybody—*anybody*—raises an alarm I'll be dead within minutes, if I'm lucky. So what the hell do I have to be nervous about?"

"Damned if I know."

Henrad knelt on the floor, murmuring the words that could only be heard and forgotten, the rough syllables that vanished on the ear like a sugar crystal on the tongue, leaving behind only a vague memory.

As Henrad completed the spell, Ahira, his speed belying the shortness of his dwarf's legs, dashed around the corner and into the room.

Walter shuddered, waiting for the clamor of steel on steel or steel on stone that would alert someone, somewhere, that something untoward was going on, but . . .

Nothing.

He walked around the corner. Ahira had already relieved the seven sleeping soldiers of their swords and quietly stacked the weapons in the corner of the room. As the dwarf spotted him, he flashed Walter a quick smile.

Whew! Walter leaned back against the wall. That was out of the way. Next . . .

He beckoned to Henrad. "Help the dwarf tie them up, and bring them into position. Now it's Furnael's and my turn."

The dark archway into Beralyn's suite beckoned to them. Walter slipped inside, opening his pouch and removing several strips of cloth from it.

This was almost too easy. The serving girl was sleeping over by the window, starlight streaming in and splashing over where she sat back in the chair, fast asleep, her mouth open. He wadded a fistful of cloth into a gag, then beckoned to Furnael, pointing at the door beyond.

Furnael crept through the doorway and vanished from Walter's sight into Beralyn's sleeping room.

Walter rubbed his fingers together as he crumpled the cloth tight, then carefully pushed it into the serving girl's open mouth. Her eyes flew open; she gathered in a quick breath for a scream. He punched her in the solar plexus; she folded over like a blanket.

Within five seconds, she was fully gagged and tied.

John Norman, eat your heart out, he thought, then instantly regretted it. The poor girl was scared stiff; if this hadn't been necessary, it would have been an inexcusable thing to do to her. As it was, he wasn't terribly proud of himself.

Furnael pushed his way out through the curtains of the other room, carrying a lamp. "Beralyn is dressing; she will be along directly."

Dressing? *Damn* all women. This was something that could be done in pajamas, or whatever the hell Beralyn wore to bed. "Wonderful. She can come on up with Ahira." He hefted the bound form of the serving girl to his shoulder and walked out through the door.

The stairs up to the third floor waited for him. Walter hesitated for a moment, gathering his nerve.

Ahira tapped him on the shoulder. "If you need help—"

"Then we're already dead meat." He shrugged. "I don't have the slightest idea what you ought to do if you hear fighting sounds from upstairs, but make it good."

He crept up the stairway toward Pirondael's sleeping chambers, Furnael following along behind him. He peered out of the shadows. Two fully armored soldiers stood in front of the door, each with a spear in hand. They stood at full attention, although their eyes were glazed over, their shoulders stooped just a trifle.

Damn. Walter ducked back and hefted a throwing knife.

"No," Furnael whispered quietly, laying a hand on his shoulder.

There wasn't time to argue. Walter pushed him back and stood.

Pain sparked through his head like an explosion; the world went gray as he felt strong fingers prying the knife out of his hand.

No, he thought, *I can't—*

Through force of will alone, he kept himself from slipping away into the darkness.

He could hear Furnael rise and walk down the hall.

"I am Baron Zherr Furnael," Furnael said in a firm voice. "You will awaken Prince Pirondael and tell him I am here to see him."

"How—"

"*Now*, fellow."

Walter pushed himself to his feet and peered around the corner. One of the guards had vanished into the sleeping chambers, but the other, not looking at all sleepy anymore, stood between Furnael and the doorway.

Damn you, Furnael. Walter lifted a throwing knife, moved out into the hall, and threw, all in one smooth motion.

Later, he couldn't decide whether or not he had done it on purpose, but the hilt of the knife caught the guard directly between the eyes with a solid *thwock*; he collapsed like a marionette with its strings cut.

Walter caught his spear before it could clatter against the wall and lowered it to the ground, then quickly tied and gagged the guard before he paused to glare at Furnael.

The baron looked back at him impassively. *If this can't be done honorably,* his look seemed to say, *then it shall not be done at all.*

Up yours, Walter thought, resolving—assuming they got out of this alive—to spend some time with the baron and a baseball bat, before his own self-honesty made him admit that in the relief of getting out of this alive he'd surely be more glad than anything else.

Besides, where would I get a baseball bat?

Footsteps sounded from inside the room. "The prince will see you shortly," the other guard said, as he stuck his head out through the curtains.

His eyes grew wide; his mouth opened—

Walter caught him in the throat with a backhanded slap, then clapped both hands on the soldier's naked ears. Leaving the collapsing soldier to Furnael, he dashed through the curtains, already drawing another throwing knife, praying he wouldn't have to use it.

The prince, dressed only in a nightshirt, was fumbling

in the dark, trying to load a crossbow, when Walter rushed in.

Walter tackled him; and they rolled around on the thick carpet for a difficult few moments before Walter could get a proper hold on the larger man.

But finally he had one of the prince's arms twisted up into a hammerlock and the point of a knife barely pricking the skin over Pirondael's jugular.

"I think this counts as a gotcha, fatso," he said in English, then switched to Erendra. "I advise caution, your majesty— and silence."

He raised his voice fractionally. "All set in here, Baron." Walter frog-marched the prince over to the bed and pushed him face-down as Furnael entered the sleeping chamber and began lighting the several lamps scattered about the walls. "Search the bed for weapons, while I keep an eye on your prince."

The baron quickly pawed through the bedding, sweeping a dress dagger from the nightstand and onto the floor. "Nothing else, Walter Slovotsky."

"Good. Load the crossbow, please, then give it here."

Furnael slipped the bolt into the slot, nocked it, and handed it to Walter.

"Take a seat, Baron," Walter said. "The show starts in just a couple of minutes." He curled his fingers around the trigger as he let go of the prince. "You can turn over now, your majesty," he said merrily. He pulled a stool over next to the nearest wall, rapped on it to assure himself of its solidity, then sat down. "Now, I'm renowned for being one of the best shots with a crossbow that ever there was," he lied. "Matter of fact, back where I come from, an officious official once forced me to knock an apple off my son's head from a good hundred paces away . . . so, I wouldn't think that there's going to be any difficulty about putting this bolt through your throat if you cry for help, is there?"

The prince shook his head.

"I can't hear you."

"No," Pirondael whispered.

"No, no," Walter said. "Don't whisper. There's nothing that attracts attention like a whispering voice." He had to repress a smile when the prince looked at him as though he were insane. "Just talk in normal tones. Now: Karl Cullinane sends his greetings. Karl's a bit irritated with you for betraying us, and he sent the baron, Ellegon, and me to see about bringing back an explanation."

The prince's feigned look of surprise and shock came just a heartbeat too late.

"Then it's true." Furnael sucked air in through his teeth. "All along, I'd wished that there was another explanation."

"That counts as gin, shithead," Walter said to the prince, then switched back to Erendra. "Why, Pirondael?"

Pirondael spread his hands. "I do not know what you are talking about, Walter Slovotsky. I've . . . betrayed no one."

"Then how do you explain that the Holts knew enough to send assassins with dragonbane ahead? Other than our own people, there were only four who knew that we were expecting him: you, two of your soldiers, and Beralyn. None of the other three had any reason to betray us. You did. It didn't work, but," he said, eyeing the window, "Ellegon's irritated. He'll be along before morning to explain that in person." Walter leaned back against the wall. "So, we've got a bit of a wait."

"What did you say about the dragon?" Pirondael said, raising his voice just a trifle.

Walter ignored him as he turned to address Furnael. "You know why people don't like dragons, Baron?"

"No, Walter Slovotsky. I don't."

"It's not just that they're large and carnivorous, although that helps. But there are a lot of things in the world that are large and carnivorous, and—*I wouldn't move too far, Pirondael*—people don't fear them the way they do dragons.

"The real reason," he went on, as Pirondael folded his hands back in his lap, "is that dragons can read minds. They know what you're thinking, and if that's not enough, they can probe for everything you've ever done. Every dirty little secret, every private disgrace that you've tried to forget— every betrayal, Pirondael."

"I've betrayed no one, Walter Slovotsky."

Slovotsky shrugged. "Tell that to Ellegon. He'll eat you, if you've betrayed us. Too bad; the baron here would just banish you, load you up with gold, and let you and a small band hit the road."

"Banish *me?*"

"That's the other part of the deal that lets you get out of facing the dragon. You'd have to abdicate in Furnael's favor."

Pirondael laughed. "So. Now we know what this is all about." His face grew somber. "And I'd thought better of you, Zherr. I wouldn't have thought you a traitor."

"*Traitor?*" Furnael snarled. "You call me a traitor? I haven't breathed an unfaithful breath, Pirondael, not until I was persuaded you sold out my barony, my people, and my friends."

"Hah. Sold out *indeed*. Barony Furnael was already lost, Baron. I'd been forced to write it off to the Holts. It was dead. If the corpse could serve Bieme, then—"

"I *held!*" Furnael slammed his fist against the wall. "And would have held out forever, if need be. But you, you treated us like gamepieces on a board—"

"Save me your noble pretensions, Baron. Put yourself in my place—what would you have done?"

Furnael paused for a moment. "I don't know," he said softly. "But I would have kept faith with my people, Pirondael. As I always have."

"Honorable of you," Pirondael sneered. "Very honorable. I did what I thought best for Bieme, and I'm not ashamed of it."

"You wouldn't be." Furnael strode to the curtain over the doorway and jerked it from its hooks. "But you ought to be."

The bound forms of ten soldiers of the House Guard stood silently there, Ahira, Henrad, and Beralyn collectively brandishing more than enough sharpened steel to assure their silence.

Furnael spun the nearest of the guards about and slashed the rope binding his hands. "What do you say to this, Guard Captain?"

It's nutcutting time, Walter thought. This was what it all depended on. If the kind of soldier who would remain proudly on station on the losing side of a war didn't care about what kind of man he had pledged his life to defend, then everything was shortly going to go to hell.

But if Pirondael's guards *did* care, if it *was* important to them that their prince be a man of honor, and not the kind of sniggling opportunist that the prince had proved himself to be . . .

The captain stood and faced Pirondael, tears streaming freely down his grizzled cheeks. "I would have served you to the last, *your majesty*," he said, pronouncing the title like a curse. "I would have died protecting your body, pig." Wiping the tears away, he turned to Walter Slovotsky. "You mean to put Baron Furnael on the throne?" he asked quietly.

"If not, I've come a long way for damn little." Walter nodded. "He's got as good a claim as anyone. And he doesn't betray his people or his friends."

"And what would you do with this?" He jerked a thumb toward the prince.

"If he abdicates in Furnael's favor, it would be up to Prince Furnael, no?"

"Banishment," Furnael said. "If he abdicates."

"Generous." The captain nodded. He held out a hand to the dwarf. "Give me a sword."

Ahira raised an eyebrow. *Well?* his expression asked.

Furnael didn't wait. He jerked his sword out of his scabbard and threw it hilt-first to the captain, who caught it, then balanced it on the flat of his palms.

"I swear my loyalty to you, Zherr Furnael," the captain said, "for as long as you are worthy of it." He offered Furnael the sword.

"Keep it," the baron said. "And these others?"

The captain nodded. "They are my men, majesty. I wouldn't have them in my company if they weren't worth having."

"Then please unbind their hands, friend Ahira."

"*Excuse me.*" Walter raised a hand. "If you two will stop playing kiss-my-ring for a minute, we've still got an abdication to arrange."

The sword whistled through the air until the point rested just beneath Pirondael's chin, the hilt held firmly in the captain's hand. "I do not think there will be any problem," he said. "Will there, Pirondael?"

"N-no. I abdicate in favor of Tyr—" The prince went into a spasm of choking as the flat of the captain's sword slapped him across the throat.

"*No*. The choice is ours, not yours," the captain snarled. "Do you agree to that? Nod your head more briskly, Pirondael.

Good. Taren, procure paper and a pen, and fetch the Warder of the Seal. No explanations—just bring him."

Walter looked at Furnael.

The baron laughed. "If you don't want to trust Captain—what *is* your name?"

"Garavar, majesty."

"Not majesty yet. As I was saying, Walter Slovotsky, if you do not wish to trust Garavar, who will be chief captain of my personal guard, I'll be more than happy to listen to alternatives."

Walter laughed. "Then be on your way," he said, gesturing with the crossbow.

That was a mistake. He never knew where Pirondael got the knife. It could have been hidden in the bedding and missed by Furnael in his search; it could have been concealed somewhere on Pirondael's ample person.

Six inches of steel flickered through the air until stopped by Furnael's throat.

Walter centered the crossbow on Pirondael's chest and jerked the trigger. The bolt caught the prince's shoulder. Walter whipped one of his throwing knives through the air, relishing in the meaty thunk as it sunk into Pirondeal's chest, directly over the heart. A last knife caught Pirondael's twitching outflung palm, pinning it to the headboard.

He dropped his crossbow and rushed to Furnael's side. No good. There was no time to send for healing draughts.

Furnael was dead.

He crouched there for a long moment, until Garavar's shaking of his shoulder brought him back to the here-and-now.

Beralyn cradled the body in her lap, weeping silently, her husband's dead face hidden in her hair. Before, she had been able to face her husband's death almost casually, but not here, not now.

He glanced over at the bed. Pirondael's blind eyes stared glassily back at him.

Garavar shook his shoulder again. "What do we do now, Walter Slovotsky? Have you any good ideas?"

Walter stood, and forced himself to nod. *Shit. I'd better think fast. Technically, the heir is probably somebody like Tyrnael—or Thomen, maybe, if we assume that Pirondael actually abdicated in Furnael's favor. I guess we can wrap his hand around the seal long enough to stamp anything we want.*

But that won't do it. Tyrnael would probably have all our heads just on general principles, and Bieme doesn't need either a sixteen-year-old prince or some sort of regency.

"Yes," he said. "I have a suggestion. Pirondael abdicated in favor of whoever we choose, didn't he?" He took a deep breath.

Forgive me, my friend. "Now . . ."

CHAPTER TWENTY-FOUR:

The Defense of Furnael Keep

In war more than anywhere else in the world things happen differently from what we had expected. . . .
— Karl von Clausewitz

Karl Cullinane walked the ramparts, looking off to where the Holts waited. His eyes teared, partly from the glare of the setting sun, partly from the acrid smoke that the light breeze wafted his way.

"Belay firing," he called out, his sword picked up and echoed down the line of two hundred riflemen. Slowly, the ragged volley died out. "Clean and reload; oil patches, only," he said. "Aveneer, take over. Fire only at reasonable targets."

He turned and climbed down the ladder to the courtyard below, then walked over to where Ellegon lay sprawled on the dirt. The dragon's eyes were almost impossibly bleary, but they still glowed with life.

What is going on, Karl? Ellegon's mental voice was still weak, but growing firmer as every day brought the dragon more strength. Just today, he had been able to lift his head from the ground for the first time.

"Damned if I know," he said, reaching out and rubbing his fingers against the hard scales of the dragon's jaw. "They're redeploying a bit, but nothing much." Just the sort of idle shuffling of positions that would keep the defenders worried, but it didn't look as if the Holts were really getting ready for an assault, not yet.

It just didn't make any sense. After Tennetty's last recon,

270 THE SILVER CROWN

she had reported that the Holts were doing absolutely nothing, other than holding position. No building at all—no ladders, no siege engines, no beams being cut for shoring the walls of tunnels—nothing. Somewhere between thirty-two hundred and four thousand Holtish troops were sitting there, the nearest just out of rifleshot, all of them waiting.

Now I know how a candle on a birthday cake feels. But even so, even if Ahrmin is on his way, why the wait?

Why would the top Holtish commander be willing to let line troops stand idle, when they could undoubtedly be put to good use in the north after polishing off Furnael Keep?

What where they be waiting for?

I don't know. Maybe Tennetty would have some ideas?

Speaking of Tennetty . . . where is she?

On the northern . . . rampart. I've sent for her; she's on her way.

"Shh," Karl whispered. "Save your strength. Sleep, if you can."

Young dragons don't need much sleep.

"You don't look all that young right now."

Good point. The plate-sized eyes sagged shut.

Tennetty's slim form appeared atop the rampart; she bounded down the rungs to the bottom.

"You sent for me?" she asked, her index finger working its way under her eyepatch as if of its own volition.

"I was considering it—but Ellegon decided for me," he said, as he beckoned her over to the well in the center of the courtyard. He worked the crank and raised the bucket, scooping out a dipperful for Tennetty first, and then for himself.

The water was cool and wonderful as he tilted his head back, pouring it in his mouth, relishing the way the icy overflow ran down his beard and onto his chest.

That was the nice thing about now: Every sense was sharp, every sensation special, even the slightly metallic taste of Furnael Keep well water. Karl nodded softly to himself. It was easy to forgive your friends, at the end of it all.

"Move it, you," a merry basso sounded from the ramparts, as Aveneer brought the two hundred riflemen down from their full alert, passing out watch assignments for the night.

Karl nodded in approval. The Holts almost certainly weren't

going to try for some sort of tricky night assault, but there
was no sense in taking chances.

He turned to Tennetty. "You think we're going to get any
visitors tonight?"

She shook her head. "No. And I don't understand it. I
haven't seen any evidence of their building siege towers or
engines—or even ladders."

He nodded. "Me neither. It's like we're all waiting for
someone, or something. But I don't understand why."

"Ahrmin, of course . . . I can see that he'd want to be in
on the end." She fingered the amulet around her neck. "But
why would the Holts want to wait for him?"

"I don't know."

Tennetty cocked her head to one side. "Want me to find
out, Karl?"

"What say *we* find out?"

She shook her head. "I don't think you can sneak well
enough. Maybe Piell and me?"

"I've got a better idea; let's go talk to Andy." He walked
toward the nearest door into the keep proper and headed for
the suite that he and Andy-Andy were using.

She was seated in front of a flickering lamp that stood on a
wide wooden table; a huge leather book was open in front of
her as she carefully studied the words that Karl couldn't even
see.

He knew better than to interfere while she was studying, so
he waited until she lifted her head before he cleared his
throat.

"Karl." She smiled as she turned in the chair and rose to
her feet, stretching catlike in her gray robes. "Are they still
out of range?"

"Yeah. Funniest damn siege I've ever seen. How's your
invisibility spell these days?"

"Good enough," she said, then paused for a moment as
she sucked air in through her teeth. "You're planning on
taking a walk tonight?"

"Tennetty and I are, if you can manage it."

Tennetty raised her eyebrow. "Be still, my heart."

The tension between the two of them had evaporated in the
past days. A small part of it was that he needed somebody
around who he was used to working with; with Chak dead,

Piell occupied with his longbow squad, and Walter and Ahira gone, Tennetty was about the only one remaining from his original team he was really used to.

The big reason, of course, was simpler.

I'm not going to make it alive out of this one, he thought. There was no sense in taking hard feelings to the grave, not when the object of the anger was really a friend. Tennetty had had a horrible breach of judgment back in Enkiar, true, but she was a friend.

And death was a time to forgive one's friends, a time for gentle goodbyes.

"When are the two of you planning on leaving?" Andy-Andy asked.

He reached out and rubbed his thumb gently against her jaw. "About midnight, I thought. Give us some time to ourselves, before."

"Good." She smiled up at him. "I guess I didn't wear you out last night."

"Apparently not."

The conviction that his own end was near had brought a fierce passion to their lovemaking, and he didn't feel like stinting himself. Not when the end approached so quickly.

Maybe, if Walter and Furnael were successful in Biemestren, relief would be on its way, eventually. Hell, if they had actually gotten to Biemestren, and in the unlikely event that (a) they could put Furnael on the throne quickly, and (b) Furnael had ordered the House Guard to ride immediately, and (c) the House Guard had obeyed, and with alacrity, and (d) if they came in enough force to break through the Holtish roadblock on th west road, then relief could arrive in another week or so.

But that wasn't about to happen.

It probably wouldn't make a difference, or not enough of one. Since the Holts weren't building catapults and onagers, it was likely that already-built ones were on their way down the road.

Maybe that was it. But certainly Karl and the defenders didn't have forever. The Holts either knew or had to assume that the dragon was recovering within the walls; they and the slavers among them would have no desire to stall the assault until the dragon was recovered enough to fight.

He shook his head. Hell, they could take the keep by rushing it with siege ladders, if they didn't have a more elegant, a less costly way.

But maybe, just perhaps, the Holts would hold off until Ellegon got well enough to flee, if not to fight.

And then, beautiful, we can get you out of here. You, Thomen Furnael, perhaps Erek and Ranella. I'll give the orders, and see that it's done.

And then, he thought, lifting her from the chair, gathering her in his arms, *we'll give Ahrmin and the rest of those bastards a last run that'll make them wake up screaming for the rest of their lives.*

Tennetty cleared her throat. "You want me to put together a couple of kits? Crossbows, I suppose—can't use guns. . . . Andrea? Can you include the bows and everything in the spell?"

"Yes, but . . ." Andy-Andy pushed away from him. "I . . . can't keep you invisible for much time at all." She wrinkled her brow as she looked up at Karl. "Just a few minutes, if it's going to be both of you. Enough time to get out—"

"But not enough to get back in, eh?" He smiled. "Shouldn't be a problem. We'll leave just after dark, and coordinate our return with Aveneer. Tennetty, include a signal rocket in our kit, and two grenades each, plus fuses." He smiled at Andy-Andy as he jerked his thumb toward their sleeping quarters. "I'll be with you in a minute."

Andy-Andy smiled gently back at him and walked away, her spell book tucked carefully under her arm.

He turned to Tennetty. "There's something I've been meaning to talk to you about—"

"I know; consider it said." She eyed him levelly. "I'd better get us packed up for tonight." She started to walk away, then turned back. "It's all been worth it . . . hasn't it, Karl?"

You know, Tennetty, I've never heard you sound unsure of yourself before. I'm not sure I like it.

He forced a smile. "Count on it. Now get lost for a while."

*   *   *

Aveneer was waiting for them near the front gate. His eyes sparkled in the light of the torches as he shook his massive head. "It's not been my experience that generals do their own scouting, Karl," he said, "and I don't like the idea."

Frandred nodded, then shook his head. "Bad idea, Karl, bad."

Karl had never liked the way that Aveneer's second-in-command always had to say something twice. It reminded him of a retarded boy who had been his neighbor, long ago. Long, long ago . . .

"You think that man of yours is a better scout than I am?"

Aveneer nodded. "Possibly."

"He is, of course he is."

Karl nodded a false agreement. "Then fine, bring him up. One thing, though: Would he be able to tell a mobile gunshop from a mobile smithy?"

"No, but that's not relevant." Aveneer shook his head. "It wouldn't be his responsibility to decide, but to report."

"Right." He crooked a finger and beckoned Aveneer close. "And it isn't your responsibility," he whispered, "to tell me what my job is; it's your responsibility to carry out my orders. Understood?"

Aveneer pulled back and snorted. "True. But I'd be a bit careful, were I you. Eh?" He clapped his hand to Karl's shoulder. "You wouldn't want to get killed prematurely." He clasped Karl's hand in his. "Just in case you don't return, any advice?"

"Nothing much." Karl shrugged. "Except the obvious. Hold off using the grenades until the very last. You've got to get them bunched in order to get the right payoff. When they rush, I'd try for volley fire, instead of fire-at-will—you might be able to break the rush." He walked to the portcullis and looked out.

Perhaps five hundred yards down the road leading from the keep, the nearest of the Holtish encampments waited, campfires blazing away into the night. He slipped the heavy bolts on the man-high door that formed part of the base of the portcullis and then walked back to where Andy-Andy and Tennetty stood waiting.

He quickly stripped off his jerkin and leggings, then pulled a loose pair of shorts on over his shoes, belting the shorts tightly around his waist. That was a trick that Walter Slovotsky had taught him, long ago: On a recon, it was best to keep as little as possible between your skin and the air. It was almost as though he grew extra nerves; it was certain that he felt more vulnerable when creeping almost naked through the night.

Tennetty smeared the greasepaint over his skin, then strapped a crossbow across his back and handed him a drawstring-topped leather quiver, which he tied to his right thigh.

He looked at his swordbelt, debating whether or not it was right to take it. No, he decided; the crossbow and quiver were already going to be enough trouble to handle, and if this recon came down to swordplay, he was already in too deep.

He nodded to himself. Best to go as lightly armed as possible. He selected a Nehera-made bowie and belted its scabbard around his waist, thonging the knife into the scabbard. Logical; he wouldn't need the saber, but a knife could be handy.

To hell with logic. He belted on the saber.

Tennetty had already armed herself and stood ready, her fists clenching and unclenching.

Karl turned to his wife. "Do it," he said.

Andy-Andy began to murmur the words of the spell, the harsh, flat sounds that could only be forgotten, never saved in the mind.

The world slowly went gray around him, until it settled into a total black. That was the trouble with a simple invisibility spell: It made its subject totally transparent to light, and that included his retinas. Transparent retinas couldn't react to light.

But this wasn't a simple invisibility spell; Andy wasn't done. Her hand reached out and touched his forehead, the fingertips sliding down until she touched his eyelids.

The pressure of her fingers increased as the words of the spell finished.

She released his lids; he opened his eyes. Two feet away and a foot below his eye level, he could see the dark discontinuity that marked where Tennetty's eye was.

Karl looked down. He could see right through himself, all the way down to the outline of his bootprints in the dirt.

He reached out and took Tennetty's hand.

"Let's go," he whispered. They would have to touch each other; in the darkness outside the keep, he wouldn't be able to see her any more than the Holts could see him.

They stepped out through the door and into the night. Down the road, eager-eyed sentries had perhaps already noted the open door, and were probably waiting to see if this time it meant that somebody was leaving the keep, trying to slip away.

But they had been keeping watch for five nights now, and every night Karl had ordered the small door opened, then closed several times, both when Tennetty was trying to sneak away for a quiet recon and not. By now, the watchers were probably persuaded that this was simply intended to spook them.

Karl and Tennetty walked swiftly down the road.

By the time they had faded back into visibility, they were far down the road, well concealed in the trees.

The main Holtish camp spread out in front of them. Despite the greater size of his force, the leader of this expedition had followed the same general plan as the leader of the last one. He had split off three cavalry units to camp separately opposite the keep's other walls, and even put his main camp on the same ground his predecessor had chosen.

But that was where the similarity ended. This Holtish general was much more security-conscious. There were twelve watchfires spread around the camp's perimeter, each manned by at least twenty guards. And even within the camp there was added security: The inner portion of his main camp was a corral-like compound, perhaps forty yards across, containing what Karl was sure was the powder magazine, as well as several boxy travel wagons—one of them a wizard's wagon, no doubt.

There was something else in that corral as well, something that scouts hadn't reported seeing. But it was almost hidden between the wagons and covered by a tarpaulin, and all he could tell was that it was longer than it was wide, which didn't do a damn bit of good.

"That . . . thing in the compound wasn't there last night." Tennetty looked at him. "Do you think we could get in there?'' she whispered, her words barely carrying the few inches to his ear.

"Not and get out, that's for sure."

"I wasn't talking about getting out. If we could blow up their magazine, scatter the powder, the morning dew would finish the job for us."

A nice idea in principle, but it just wouldn't work. The interior of the camp was clearly too well guarded—he wouldn't even be able to get within throwing range. Besides, unless it was very well thrown, a grenade probably wouldn't break open the barrels containing the Holts' reserve supply of slaver powder.

He shook his head. "I don't think even Walter could get in there." Damn. He lifted his amulet. It was flashing red, though; clearly, the Holts had added a wizard in the past few days, as well as whatever that thing under the tarp was.

He looked up at the overhanging branches of the dying oak. It might be possible to get about twenty, maybe twenty-five feet up, and that might give a decent view of whatever was going on in the camp. "How's your tree-climbing?"

"Better than yours. And quieter. Give me a hand up." She quickly stripped off her weapons and boots. Karl cocked and loaded both crossbows, then set them carefully on the ground before boosting Tennetty up to an overhanging branch.

Silently, she climbed, while Karl kept watch. She would be almost invisible to anyone looking, but only almost. Off in the distance, Karl could hear something moving through the field. He hoped that Tennetty could hear it, too, but loosed his sword in its scabbard in case she couldn't.

The sound grew closer; a whisk of leather on grass.

Great. Patrolling Holts weren't what he needed right now, but it looked as if he was going to get them anyway. If he was lucky, as they passed by his position they'd be discussing whatever strategy the Holtish general was planning for the morning.

He wasn't lucky. Two Holtish soldiers, each armed with a slaver rifle, walked by, only yards from where Karl huddled in the shadow of the old oak's projecting roots. It seemed for a moment as though one of them looked directly at him before the Holt's gaze swung by, but perhaps he was mistaken.

In a few minutes, they were gone.

Tennetty dropped lightly from an overhanging branch. "Unless they've got another cripple with them, he's *there*. I saw him coming out of the magazine with a wizard."

"Ahrmin?"

"Who else? He was showing the wizard that ram."

"Ram?"

"The . . . thing near the powder magazine. Ahrmin had the covering off for a moment. It's a ram, a damn large one."

That was strange. A ram attack, intended to breach the keep's walls, ought to be accompanied by some other sort of attack elsewhere; by itself, the ram and its crew would be too vulnerable to concentrated fire from the defenders. So where were the onagers and catapults or the siege ladders?

A chill washed across him. "Describe this ram."

"Strange-looking thing. Like a long metal sausage, about twice as long as you're tall. It's mounted on a cart. I guess they're going to have some sort of rigging for horses to propel the thing, but the wagon it's on is rigged for pulling, not pushing." She shrugged. "And why it has a hole in one end . . ."

A hole?

Omigod. "That's not a ram. It's a cannon." Which explained what the Holts had been waiting for. A cannon could shatter the walls, or, firing chainshot or grapeshot, quickly reduce the defenders on the walls to bloody hunks of flesh. The Holts had been holding up the attack, waiting for this to arrive.

His heart thudding in his chest, he forced himself to breathe slowly. He would have to see that Andy-Andy was smuggled out, and not tomorrow, but tonight. The cannon that they had waited for had arrived; the Holts would attack in the morning.

But would she go? And who could he trust to smuggle her out of here? *Damn* Walter Slovotsky for taking Ahira.

Tennetty. It would have to be Tennetty.

"What is a cannon?" Tennetty whispered.

"Like a big rifle. Except that it can knock down walls."

"Knock down—I see." She nodded sagely. "How do you counter a cannon?"

"You spike it—" He caught himself. Maybe? No. There

were ample guards around, and a wizard within the compound, likely there either to assist in the attack or to keep the slaver powder from picking up water from the air and self-detonating. "Or you do what Chak did, except on a large scale. Without enough powder, a cannon is useless."

She nodded wisely. "Then we'd better get to it, no?"

Ridiculous. Absolutely ridiculous. There wasn't a chance in a billion that the two of them could get through the Holts and into the magazine, and there wasn't a chance in a million that a large group could.

But a group didn't have to. Only one had to, if that one knew what to do. If in the noise and confusion, one man could break through to the magazine or have just enough time to spike the cannon, that might buy some time for Slovotsky to put Furnael on the throne and bring relief to the keep.

At the very least, it would force the Holts to switch strategies, and spend some time building ladders or siege engines.

"Karl, we may never get another chance at him. We've got to—"

"Don't tell me what we have to do. Ahrmin is secondary, dammit. The cannon's the first priority. Listen," he said. "Get back to the keep—"

"No. You can't do it yourself."

"Damn right, Tennetty. Bring back as many people as you're sure you can smuggle out without being seen. No guns; we're not going to have time to reload, and even if we pull this off, they're going to need them in the keep. But load up with grenades. And all of the smith's hammers and a dozen spikes."

"And if we can do that . . . ?"

"The magazine and the cannon first. Then we kill the little bastard."

"Fine." She smiled, and turned to leave.

He caught her arm. "One more thing: Bring my clothes. I don't want to die half-naked."

It felt as if it took forever for Tennetty to get back. By the time she arrived, seven others in tow, Karl had made and rejected a thousand different, useless plans for getting in and out of the Holts' camp all by himself.

Seven others. That was all she had brought back. Karl

didn't admonish her; she knew better than he did how many she could sneak out of the castle.

But she could easily have picked a worse seven: Piell, Firkh, Hervean, Rahnidge, Thermen, Erek . . . and Aveneer.

"I thought I left you in command," Karl said to the red-bearded Nyph, as he handed Aveneer his share of the grenades. It worked out to nine each, with two extras, both of which Karl appropriated for himself.

"You did. And *I* left Valeran in command." Aveneer shrugged. "I've spent far too much of my life away from the center of things. Figured that this one time I'd make absolutely sure I don't die of old age."

Karl shrugged. There was nothing that could be done about that now, even if he didn't want Aveneer and his battleaxe around.

Which he very much did. "Fine," Karl said. "First thing, we've got to be sure that we take out the wizard." He lifted his amulet. "This won't provide much protection, but it's all that we've got—"

"No." Tennetty looked over at him soberly. "Andrea sends a message: The wizard is hers. When she hears the sound of the first grenade going off, she will—how did she put it—'brighten her fire.' The Holts' wizard will see that as a challenge."

Ellegon, relay— He caught himself. He was out of range, and there wasn't a damn thing that he could do. Except— "My orders stand. If you see the wizard, take him out. Understood?"

Tennetty looked him square in the face. "Even if that means missing the magazine? Or the cannon?"

He grabbed her by the tunic. "You challenging my orders, Tennetty?"

She raised her palms. "No. I'm asking what they are. Think about it."

Andy . . . He forced himself to keep his harsh whisper under control. "Get the magazine and the cannon. No matter what."

Accepting his tunic from Tennetty, Karl drew it on and belted it tightly around his hips with a length of rope. After inserting the fuses in the detonators and the detonators in the grenades, he carefully tucked them into his tunic, their iron sides cold against his belly, then buckled on his swordbelt, with the pouch tied tightly to its right side.

"Keep an even spacing," he said. "Not too close—if a shot hits you in the wrong place, you're going up, complete with grenades."

Tennetty smiled. "Right, right. Do we get to it or not?"

There had been a time, long, long ago, when a younger Karl Cullinane wouldn't have been able to face the idea of walking into the lion's mouth.

But that was long, long ago. He looked from face to face, trying to come up with the right words.

He couldn't find any.

"Follow me," he said.

On hands and knees, they crept through the waist-high grasses in the dark, Tennetty and Piell armed with crossbows in addition to their grenades. With a bit of luck, perhaps all nine of them could get to the Holts' outer perimeter before they were spotted.

Their luck was not in; when they were still a good fifty yards from the outer edge of the cleared area that marked the Holtish camp, a harsh voice called out a warning; a shot rang out, a bullet hissed overhead.

Piell rose, his crossbow discharging. The bolt caught the watchman in the chest; he screamed hideously. Hervean rose to his feet, a sizzling grenade in his hand.

But the Holtish guards reacted quickly; Piell and Hervean were cut down by a flurry of gunfire, Hervean's grenade exploding while still in his hands, miraculously not triggering any of his or Piell's remaining grenades.

Already on his feet and on the run, Karl struck the tip of a fuse on his swordbelt buckle and sent a grenade hissing toward the Holts. It landed in between three of them and exploded, sending bodies and pieces of bodies flying into the night.

An explosion on his right shook him from his feet. As he rose, he pulled out another grenade, struck it, threw it, then another.

Three Holtish swordsmen came at him. Karl drew his saber

and parried the first's lunge, letting the rush carry the man past, while he speared the next one through the throat.

The third one smiled as he lunged for Karl.

The smile vanished as he went down, a crossbow bolt transfixing his neck. Tennetty laughed as she sent another grenade hissing off into the Holts. Karl drew one from his tunic and threw it into the watchfire, not bothering to strike it. It blew almost immediately, turning the fire into a shower of sparks and flinders.

Karl couldn't see what had happened to most of the others; all except Tennetty and Aveneer had been carried away from him.

"This way," he shouted, as the three of them worked their way farther into the camp, Aveneer using his axe like a scythe to clear the way, Karl and Tennetty lighting and throwing grenades one-handed, their swords weaving like snakes.

The flat of his sword parallel to the ground, Karl speared a Holt through the chest, then kicked the body off his wet blade before turning to cut down one on Tennetty's back.

Less than a hundred yards in front of him, the Holts' wizard stood within the inner camp, halfway between the magazine shed and the cannon.

Lightning issued from the wizard's fingertips, crackling off into the night.

Andy— "No!" He fought his way toward the wizard, but a heavy blow hit him on the right side, just above the waist, knocking him down before he heard the rifle's crack. As he tried to get to his feet, a booted foot caught him in the chest, knocking him back, half out of breath.

Instinct brought his sword up, slipping the saber's tip up the other's thigh and into his groin, Karl lurched away, giving his saber a savage twist before he leaped to his feet. Another Holt was bringing a rifle to bear on Tennetty; Karl booted the weapon out of the man's hands, then caught him by the hair, the Holt's body spasming twice as he absorbed two shots meant for Karl.

He drew his saber across the Holt's throat before sending him on his way, then decided that it had been too long since he'd set off a grenade, and quickly lit off two.

Thunder echoed the grenades' explosion.

Now I'll get the wiz—

Where *was* the Holts' wizard? Where he had stood but moments before, there was nothing, nothing but a small crater.

He felt Tennetty pulling at his arm. Momentarily, the screaming and the shooting rushed around them like a stream around an outthrust rock.

"I took out the wizard," she shouted. "Hope you don't mind."

There wasn't time to thank her. "I'm going for the cannon. Cover me."

She fended off two attackers as he dashed toward the cannon, dropping his sword and drawing the spike and hammer from his pouch.

A heavy weight landed on his back; he thrust back an elbow, then swung the smith's hammer around, feeling the Holt's skull cave in like an eggshell.

Spiking the cannon took only a second, but as he dropped his hammer and stooped to retrieve his sword, a sharp blow to his back knocked him down to the ground. He clawed inside his tunic for another grenade, but they had all bounced away in the dark, and the weakness in his side and back was spreading.

There was another explosion somewhere off to the rear, but that wouldn't do any good. The magazine was ahead, not behind.

He started to crawl toward it as thunder shattered the sky into rain.

A dark mass crashed into him from the side; blindly, his hand clawed at the other's face, only to encounter an eyepatch. "Tennetty!"

She smiled weakly at him, her mouth working, but no sound issuing from between her bloody lips as her eyes sagged shut.

I'm sorry, Tennetty, Rahff, Fialt, Erek, Aveneer, Chak—all of you—

But *rain?* It wasn't rainy season—

Andy. It was a goodbye from Andy, her way of telling him that she had survived. The Holts' wizard wouldn't have started a rainstorm, even if he could have; you couldn't reload in the rain, because the powder would get wet. And the Holts were under attack; they would want to reload. Now, they couldn't—

No, they couldn't, could they? Real gunpowder would become wet and useless in the rain.

But slaver gunpowder had to stay safely under cover, or it would turn back into superheated steam.

The powder would get wet. His fumbling fingers tore at Tennetty's tunic until he found a grenade. He struck the fuse against his thumbnail and flicked it toward the magazine shack.

The powder would get wet. The explosion tore off one wall of the shack, sending the barrels inside clattering.

He gathered Tennetty against his chest as he heard the crack of splitting wood . . .

. . . and the largest explosion of all, that shattered the world into white-hot sparks of pain that quickly went black.

CHAPTER TWENTY-FIVE:

Arta Myrdhyn

What though the field be lost?
All is not lost; th' unconquerable will,
And study of revenge, immortal hate,
And courage never to submit or yield.

—John Milton

For a long time, there was nothing. Nobody was there . . .
and no body was there.

And then there was a spark, and the spark thought: *So this
is what being dead feels like.*

"I doubt that you have nearly enough information to decide that yet, Karl," an airy tenor voice out of his past said.
"Although if you ever do find out for certain, I would be
most grateful if you would let me know. If you *can* let me
know, that is. It's something I have wondered about for . . .
for a long time." Deighton chuckled thinly, a hollow sound.

There was no question; the voice was Deighton's. Professor Arthur Simpson Deighton, Ph.D. Lecturer in, though not
practitioner of, ethics; gamemaster, wizard.

The bastard who sent us all across.

"My parentage is not at issue here. And I won't accept the
blame for the second time, Karl. As I recall, you had a knife
to my throat." A thin chuckle echoed through the empty
universe. "Although I would gladly have done it simply for
the asking . . . as you may have surmised by now."

*Where are you, Deighton? Hell, where am I, for that
matter?*

"Matter, Karl, has rather little to do with it. Would you settle for illusion? It will be quite persuasive, I can promise you that."

What the—

"I'll take that as an assent."

There were no loud sounds or bright lights. The universe simply came back, until Karl Cullinane was sitting in a wooden chair at the battered mahogany table in Room 109 of the Student Union.

The room was as they'd left it on that long-ago night: books and coats piled against the wall and on the extra chairs; pens, pencils, paper, and dice scattered around the battered surface of the old mahogany table. He looked up at the overhead lights. Strange, so strange to see fluorescent lights again. No flicker, just a steady light.

Slowly, gingerly, he got to his feet, waiting for his wounds to start hurting.

But they didn't. He felt fine, except that he wasn't himself, not the self he should have been, not here. While he was wearing jeans and a slightly tight plaid shirt—just as he had way back then—he was still himself from the Other Side, not the skinny Karl Cullinane of This Side.

He flexed his right biceps in the sleeve; the fabric split along the seam.

"And yes, if you prick yourself, you will bleed," the directionless voice said. "But it is all illusion. Have an illusionary cup of coffee, and perhaps a phantom cigarette. You may feel better."

He looked down at the table. A white porcelain mug of coffee sat steaming next to a battered half-empty pack of Camel Filters.

"Drink up, Karl."

He shrugged and picked up the coffee cup, then took a cautious sip.

Good Colombian beans, gently roasted, well laced with rich cream and sugar. Karl had once thought coffee an acquired addiction, but one that could be broken with a bit of abstinence. He now knew he was wrong: This was absolutely delicious. He picked up the cellophane-wrapped pack of cigarettes and extracted one, snickering at the Surgeon General's warning.

I don't suppose us dead folks have to worry about whether

something is hazardous to our health. He stuck the filter
between his lips. "Light?"

"As I told you, you are not dead. Still, an illusory cigarette is harmless. Enjoy." The end of the cigarette flared into
flame.

Karl inhaled the rich smoke . . .

. . . and doubled over in a spasm of coughing. He threw
the cigarette away.

"I said it was harmless, not unirritating."

"Fine." He wiped his mouth with the back of his hand.
"Deighton—or should I call you Arta Myrdhyn?"

"Either will serve."

"Why don't you show yourself?"

"If you'd like." Across the table from him, the air shimmered momentarily, and there he sat, just as Karl had seen
him on a night more than seven years before. A thin, stoop-
shouldered man in a tan wool suit, puffing on the bulldog
briar pipe that was responsible for the burns that marked the
pockets and arms of the suit.

Deighton removed the pipe from his mouth and touched it
to his lined forehead in a brief, mocking salute.

"How have you been, Karl?" He puffed a cloud of smoke
into the air.

Karl considered lunging across the table for Deighton, but
decided against it. This was either some sort of very real
dream or it was Deighton's turf. Either way, jumping Deighton
was unlikely to get any results.

"I've had friends die because of you, Arta Myrdhyn," he
said.

"True." Deighton nodded slowly, gravely. "True enough.
And I assure you that I'm as aware of that as you are.
Including Jason Parker, by the way. It was rather nice of
Andrea to name your son after him." His face grew pensive
for a moment. "I . . . truly didn't mean any of you any
harm. And I truly would tell you everything, Karl, if there
weren't sufficient reasons not to."

"What do you want?"

"We had an agreement, Karl Cullinane." The pleasant
demeanor vanished, as Deighton's eyes turned icy. "You
agreed to keep my sword for your son, hold it for him until
he was ready to use it. In return for that promise, you were

allowed to use it against that young fool Thyren. But you didn't keep your promise, Karl.''

Karl pushed himself to his feet. "Not my son, bastard. You keep your filthy hands off of him.''

"*Sit down.*"

Karl gathered himself for a leap—

—but found himself sitting in the chair.

"Illusion, remember? My illusion, not yours." Deighton puffed at the pipe for several seconds. "I'll offer you another deal: Fetch the sword for Jason, hold it for him until he's ready for it, and I'll send you back.''

Karl dialed for a calm voice. "I thought you said this was an illusion," he said, pleased to find that he could talk calmly. "How can you send me back?"

"Right . . . now, I guess you would call it?—right now, Karl, your body is lying on the battlefield, a knife's edge from death. Normally, I couldn't communicate with you across the barrier between This Side and the Other Side, but this is . . . a special circumstance. While you're not on This Side at all, you're not fully on the Other Side. Does that make sense to you?''

Deighton cocked his head to one side as he steepled his fingers in front of his chin. "I couldn't bring you back from the dead, and I wouldn't push you over the precipice, but I will . . . use my best efforts to hold you on the side of life, for the time being. If, that is, we have an agreement.''

"No deals." Karl shook his head. "No deals, Art. You're not going to play around with my son's life the way you have with mine," he said, instantly resolute. He was surprised at himself. There had been a time when he had had difficulty with commitment, even when it was only a matter of committing himself to a course of study.

But that had been long, long ago.

"Yes," Deighton said, studying him closely, "there have been some changes. It is clear is nothing I would be willing to do would make you change your mind." He rose to his feet. "Well, I suppose that is that," he said matter-of-factly, tossing his pipe aside. It vanished.

The room started to melt away, the colors running together. Karl braced himself for the final darkness. *Goodbye, Andy . . .*

"Oh, don't be so melodramatic." The room solidified

again. "You may dispense with the heroics for now. Save them for when they're appropriate. As they will be. I still have to send you back," Deighton said, shaking a finger at him, "although you really ought to be more careful. It's unlikely I'll be able to do even this little for you next time we meet."

"Next time?"

Deighton nodded. "Once more, Karl Cullinane. Once more."

Suddenly, Deighton stood at his side. The old man stuck out a hand. "Be well, Karl Cullinane. Take good care of that son of yours. He's awfully important, as you've suspected."

Karl didn't take the hand. "I will take care of my son, Deighton, whether you want me to or not."

"I'd expect no less."

"Just tell me one thing, please—why?"

"I can't tell you. Not now."

"Will you ever?"

"No." Deighton caught his lip between his teeth. "I'm sorry, Karl. I can't explain it to you right now, and I doubt I'll have the opportunity the next time we meet." He clapped his hand to Karl's shoulder. "Be well, my friend."

"You're no friend of mine!"

Deighton looked surprised. "Of course not. But you are one of mine. It is my fond hope that you will do me a great favor, the next time we meet. Until then, be well."

"Wait—"

"One more thing: Ahrmin isn't dead. He got away again. While I can't blame you for this one, you really ought to have been more thorough in Melawei, Karl."

Deighton smiled genially. "Be well."

The room melted away.

CHAPTER TWENTY-SIX:

The Silver Crown

Uneasy lies the head that wears a crown.
—William Shakespeare

"Karl," Andy-Andy's voice called to him, sweeter in his ears than anything he had ever heard. It occurred to him that she had been calling his name over and over again—for minutes, or was it hours?

She sounds worried. His eyelids weren't heavier than twin Volkswagens, so he opened them. It didn't make much of a difference: The room was dark, and it was far too much effort to focus. He was stretched out on a down mattress, the heavy blankets piled on his chest threatening to interfere with his breathing.

"Karl," she said urgently, "can you hear me?"

"Of course I can hear you," he tried to say, but the words came out as *glmph.*

He can hear you perfectly well. Ellegon's mental voice was firm. *Karl, don't talk. Just use your mind—assuming you have one. I'll relay.*

Fine. Got to tell her about Deighton—

Save that for later.

But—

But nothing; you've been dreaming about nothing else since they brought you within range. I know it all.

Ellegon—

Shut up and listen. You're the luckiest human that ever there was. As far as blood goes, Andrea thinks you're down more than a quart, so you have to take it easy. We pulled five bullets out of your hide; none of them hit anything vital. And not only did you fall into the cannon's blast shadow—that's what saved your life—but Andrea got to you with the healing draughts quickly enough to save everything except most of three fingers on your left hand. You've been hovering on the edge for eleven days now, and we've all been worrying about whether or not you were ever coming out. Happy?*

His eyelids had increased in mass until they were much heavier than Buicks, so he let them sag shut.

Tennetty, Aveneer, Erek—did they—

Tennetty's fine, Karl. She cracked some ribs, that's all. Although once we figured out that you were going to be okay, she did have some words about you pawing around inside her tunic. Says if you want to do that again you should ask really prettily.

Ellegon, you're not telling me about the others. Did any of them—

No. None of them made it.

His fists started to clench, but he didn't even have the strength to do that. *The Holts and the slavers—*

Chased all to hell and gone. After the explosion, Valeran led a rifle company out after them. The Holts couldn't use their own guns, not with Andrea keeping up a light drizzle; Valeran captured about two hundred, killed more than three times that number, and sent the rest running. Now go back to sleep.

The next time he woke, light was streaming in through the mottled glass window, splashing warmly, brightly on the bed.

Andy-Andy was next to him, sitting on a low stool, her face only a couple of feet from his. She smiled at him as she reached out and took his hand.

"Hello there," she said, her calm, level voice belying the exhaustion written in her face. The dark shadows under her red-rimmed eyes showed that she clearly needed a night's sleep.

"Hi." Lifting and dropping his hand to pat the mattress next to him wasn't quite impossible. "Get . . . in."

"Really?" She brightened. "You're getting better quickly, but not that quickly."

"No. Sleep."

"Maybe later. Would you like some broth?"

I've already sent down to the kitchen for the food. Andrea, I've got to tell him.

"It can *wait!*" she hissed.

That is a matter of opinion. Mine differs from yours. Karl, Walter wants you to know that Pirondael did abdicate, just as you wanted, but Furnael didn't survive through Biemestren.

Furnael was dead. That meant that Thomen was now the prince? A bit young, but Beralyn might be a decent regent.

Guess again. Thomen is Baron Furnael; his mother will be regent, but only of barony Furnael.

Wait. If Pirondael abdicated in Zherr Furnael's favor, then—

But he didn't. What Prince Pirondael agreed to do was to abdicate in favor of Captain Garavar's selection. As far as Garavar and the rest of the House Guard are concerned, that pretty much settles it: Garavar picks the next prince, and if the rest of the barons don't like it, they can try to revolt.

Who's this Garavar person?

Officially, he's a guard captain in the House Guard. Unofficially, he's the Biemish commander-in-chief, although that'll have to be ratified by the new prince.

Great. So who is the prince? Some—

You.

Very funny.

I thought so, too. But Captain Garavar of the House Guard is here along with all of the House Guard except for a skeleton force that's waiting at Biemestren castle, and Garavar and the two thousand House Guardsmen don't think it funny at all. Matter of fact, he's pretty damn impressed with the firepower your majesty is bringing to the throne, including one spiked slaver cannon, a few hundred real gunpowder guns, a dozen hand grenades, and—ahem!—one slightly damaged dragon. Dowager Baroness Beralyn has dispatched messengers to the remaining barons, pledging barony Furnael's loyalty to your majesty, and explaining that you and five hundred men just scattered two regiments of Holts and slavers all to hell—which ought to impress them.

This is all crazy, you know.

That is entirely a matter of opinion. If I were you, I'd try to get used to it. Now go back to sleep.

But—

That wasn't a suggestion.

None of it made any sense to him.

Sleep, on the other hand, did.

Sleep, food, and rest gradually brought back some of his strength. Within three days, Andrea decided that he could have visitors, as long as they didn't tire him.

Walter Slovotsky was the first. "Hey, Prince, how you doing?" he asked, manifestly pleased with himself. As usual.

Karl pushed away the bowl of soup that Andy-Andy was trying to force on him. "No more beef stock. I want a beef*steak*. Thick one. Pan-fried. With butter, lots of it. And corn—on the cob. And maybe some deep-fried chotte—"

"*Whoa*, hero." She laughed, kissing him lightly on the forehead. "Take it slow." She gave him another sisterly peck.

Karl quietly resolved to even the score for that, and shortly.

Sex. All this one thinks about is—

Shh.

Andy-Andy rose to leave the room, stopping for a moment to whisper to Walter that she wanted him to make the visit short.

"Well," Slovotsky said, shaking his head, "I'll keep it as short as possible; there's a lot to catch up on."

"Think about it." Her face stern, she held a hand in front of Walter's face and murmured a few harsh syllables. Sparks arced from her thumb to her forefinger. "Just a few minutes, I said."

"Right. Just a couple of minutes. One minute. Thirty seconds—whatever you say." Slovotsky waited until the door shut behind her. "Whew!" He shook his head. "I'll be happy to get back to Kirah. *My* wife isn't deadly." He threw a hip over the edge of the bed. "How long you figure you'll be laid up?"

Karl sat up all the way, his head spinning only slowly.

"Another couple of days and I'll be on my feet. Probably be quite a while before I'm back to par, but . . ." He eyed the fresh bandages covering the still-painful stumps of the three missing outer fingers on his left hand. "It could be worse."

"Good. I'm going to send Garavar in here in a couple of minutes." Slovotsky snorted. "I'll tell you, there was a time when I regretted getting him and the House Guard to go along with Pirondael's abdication—I'd planned on showing him an upright Karl Cullinane, not a comatose one."

"What is this nonsense about my being a prince?"

"Not nonsense. Bieme's all yours—unless *you* abdicate. Which I wouldn't suggest. There've been enough changes—"

"But why *me?*" *Dammit, Walter, this isn't my sort of thing, and you—*

"Garavar went along with it because there had to be somebody, and your name was the one on the table." Slovotsky shrugged. "I pushed for you because the only way I can think of for this war to be ended is for the Holts to sue for peace quickly. And that wouldn't happen with some revenge-minded baron on the Biemish throne.

"Which is where you come in. After word percolates through Holtun of your defeat of two regiments of combined Holtish and slaver troops, you're going to be the most feared man in the Middle Lands. If the Holtish don't come to the peace table, my guess is that with Andy making sure that the Holts can't use their guns, Valeran's improvised brigade can go through them like shit through a goose."

"But I'd intended on ending the war—"

"In your own way." Walter spread his hands. "Which might or might not work. This will. Whatsamatter, don't you want the crown?"

Karl clenched his fists. "Don't give me that—"

"Then fine. Give it to Thomen, and let Beralyn rule as regent. That'll be a fine gift to Furnael's son."

"Now, wait—"

"Or let the barons fight over which one gets it. They *might* settle it quickly enough so that Bieme doesn't necessarily lose the war. Bieme might even win, Karl—and instead of Bieme's being chopped up and sold to Pandathaway on the installment plan, it'll be Holtun that gets the axe."

"Not while I'm alive, it won't."

Slovotsky nodded. "And not while you're prince, either. Here's one hell of a chance for you to make some changes, Karl. Go ahead and use it." He turned to the door and raised his voice. "Garavar! He'll see you now."

Garavar was a large, grizzled man of about fifty. His features were regular, and his hands of normal size, but he had something of Aveneer's expression around the eyes, the same look of eagles.

"Your majesty?" he said, as he walked slowly into the room, an aged wooden box in his hands.

Karl sighed. Walter was right. He was stuck with it, for now. But not forever.

Of course not forever. You're not even going to live forever.

Good point.

Thank you.

"I am Karl Cullinane," he said carefully.

"I am Garavar, of the House Guard. With the others, I have been . . . managing as best I can, waiting for you to be able to take over your duties."

"Fine." Karl swung his feet over the edge of the bed. "Give me a hand, both of you. Walter, get me some clothes. There's work to be done."

"Andy-Andy said—"

"If I'm prince, then I outrank her, no? Move. Captain," he said, forcing himself not to waver as he pushed himself to his feet, "I'll want a staff meeting tonight. Frandred, Valeran, Beralyn, my wife, Tennetty, plus you and anyone from the House Guard you think needs inviting. In the meantime . . . Ellegon, are you flying yet?"

Just short distances. I . . . still have a ways to go. And the same goes for you—

"Shut up. Captain, tell Valeran I want a recon of the slaver camp on Aershtyn, and I want it yesterday."

The warrior nodded gravely. "Yes, your majesty. You intend to send a detachment up Aershtyn?"

Karl snorted as Walter helped him on with his breechclout and leggings, then slipped a clean tunic over his head. "I plan on *leading* a detachment up Aershtyn, Captain."

"With all due respect, princes don't—"

Kneeling to slip Karl's boots on, Walter threw back his head and laughed. "With all due respect, Captain, this prince is going to do whatever the hell he damn well pleases. Get used to it." He belted Karl's saber around his waist. "Better give him what's in the box."

Garavar opened it. Inside lay a circlet of silver, studded with diamonds, rubies, and emeralds. "You could wear a simple cap of maintenance, if you'd prefer, but—"

"This will do for now." Karl took the crown and set it on his own head. It didn't feel steady there; he had to hold himself up straight to make sure it didn't slip off.

Probably I can improvise some sort of bobby pin, but . . . first things first. "Captain Garavar, as of now, nobody owns people in Bieme. Anybody who thinks he owns anybody else—"

"Ta havath, Karl." Slovotsky chuckled. "Garavar's already had that explained to him, complete with ruffles and flourishes. No point in bothering with any proclamations right now; no matter how you yell and scream, there aren't going to be any changes, not until the war settles down. Hmm . . . what *are* you going to do about the former slaves?"

"Sharecropping is a step up, no? *No*, not sharecropping," he decided, remembering little Petros' fierce devotion to his scraggly field. "Better: We'll give the former slaves some of the barons' land, and allow the barons reasonable taxation privileges."

I'll soon be known as Karl the Tyrant by the barons, but that's their problem. Government needn't worry about the strong and wealthy; they could always take care of themselves. "Give me your arm," he said. "I've got work to do."

CHAPTER TWENTY-SEVEN:

Goodbyes

*Why is it, Maecenas, that no man living is content with
the lot that either his choice has given him or that
chance has thrown to him, but each has praise for those
who follow other paths?*

—Horace

Andy-Andy and Tennetty standing at his side, Karl said
goodbye to Walter and Ahira at the keep's gates.

Their mounts and their packhorses were champing at their
bits, possibly because of the way that Ellegon was eyeing
them interestedly.

"You sure you don't want an escort?" Karl asked. "If
you'll just wait a couple of weeks, I can send Ranella with
you—and I could send a company with you as far as Biemestren
right now."

*Karl, since when does putting something off make it not
happen?*

*I don't know. But how can I say goodbye to either of these
two?*

*Briefly and matter-of-factly, if you don't want to nauseate
a recovering dragon.*

Sitting uncomfortably in his pony's saddle, Ahira shook his
head. " 'Tis best done quickly, eh?"

Adjusting a rifle in its saddle boot, Slovotsky shrugged.
"Seems that way to me, too. Hey, who knows? Endell might
turn out to be a real drag; I may get so bored in a year or so
that I'll need to get back into harness. Hell, we might even

still be Home when you and Ellegon show up to pick up the kids.''

''I'd like that.''

''Karl.'' The dwarf looked down at him. ''I have to say this again: If you ever need either of us . . . you'll know where to find us, Karl. Come if you can; send word if you can't. This isn't goodbye—just so long.''

I need you two now, he thought. But he couldn't say that. Not in front of everyone.

Damn. He reached up and shook hands first with Ahira, then with Walter. ''I'll miss you, both of you.''

Slovotsky snorted. ''*Tell* me about it.'' He clasped hands briefly with Tennetty, then vaulted from the saddle to kiss Andy-Andy thoroughly, whispering softly in her ear as he held her close.

You're supposed to be jealous.

Shut up, Karl explained.

Walter's all-is-well-with-a-universe-whose-center-holds-Walter-Slovotsky smile seemed a bit forced as he climbed back up to the fore-and-aft-peaked saddle, making sure that the packhorse's leads were still tightly bound to it.

Andy-Andy walked over to Ahira, threw her arm around his waist, and buried her face against his thigh, not saying anything, while the dwarf ran gentle fingers through her hair. She turned away, her face wet.

''Watch your butt, Karl. Or Andy's; it's much prettier,'' Walter Slovotsky said as he and the dwarf turned their horses around and rode them slowly through the open gate, the three packhorses trailing behind. ''And remember Slovotsky's Law Number Twenty-nine: 'It ain't over 'til it's over, and maybe not then, either.' ''

Karl watched them for a long time, until they had vanished around the bend.

Finally, he turned to Tennetty. ''Once we hit the slavers on Aershtyn, you want to hitch a ride Home with Ellegon and take over our raider team?''

''No.'' Idly, she fumbled in her pouch, pulling out her glass eye, holding it up with thumb and forefinger, considering it in the daylight. ''We're going to have to rush this

Aershtyn raid, so that you and Ellegon can take off soon enough to get back to the valley before Gwellin leaves.''

''Oh? Why is that?''

''You're going to see if you can persuade Daherrin to take over the team, instead of going back to Endell. Gwellin wouldn't go for it, but I think Daherrin might.''

''So, you want Aveneer's team instead?''

''Frandred's team, now,'' she said firmly. ''Granted, he'll give every order twice, but that won't hurt anything.''

''So what are you going to do?''

She tossed the glass eye high into the air, then let it *thunk* into the palm of her hand. Tucking it back in her pouch, she adjusted her eyepatch and smiled up at him. ''I'm going to watch your back. Somebody's got to make sure it doesn't sprout knives.''

How about me—

''*You?*'' Tennetty spat. ''You who can't even dodge a quartet of clumsy crossbowmen? You're going to watch out for Karl? Who's going to watch out for you?''

Ellegon didn't answer; he just lowered his massive head to his crossed forelegs and closed his eyes.

Andy-Andy smiled her approval.

Karl turned away from all of them for a moment, forcing his shoulders not to sag, though even his cap of maintenance seemed heavy.

But it wasn't really the cloth cap or this absurd title that weighed on him. Karl had long ago taken on a task vastly more important, far more difficult, than governing a two-bit principality, and neither a manipulating wizard nor a crippled slaver was going to stand in his way. There were going to be some changes made, no matter what.

Karl. All the playfulness was now gone from Ellegon's mental voice; it was gentle but serious. *Do you think that Walter and Ahira don't know that? Do you think that they aren't committed to it? Taking a vacation isn't the abandonment of a vocation, Karl.*

I know that.

And so do Walter, Ahira, Lou, Andrea, Tennetty, and all the rest. They're every bit as committed as you and I are, my friend. Gentle fingers stroked his mind. *The phrase is: ''and we mutually pledge to each other our lives, our fortunes,*

and our sacred honor.'' And we *shall* keep the flame burning.*
Ellegon sent a gout of fire roaring into the sky. *In more
ways than one.*

   ''Fine by me.'' Karl Cullinane straightened his shoulders,
then wiped his eyes before he turned back to the others.
''We've got a lot to do. Let's get started.''

EPILOGUE:

Ahrmin

Fortune is like glass—the brighter the glitter, the more easily broken.

—Publilius Syrus

Ahrmin looked around the Aershtyn camp, shaking his head ruefully. The slave drive to Pandathaway had to start within a matter of days, or it surely would never leave. It was a certainty that Karl Cullinane would be sending a force up the slopes of Aershtyn to steal the slaves; Ahrmin had no intention of being around when that happened. Under other circumstances, he would have wanted to try to ambush Cullinane, but not this time. This was Cullinane's moment; best to let him win. There would be another day.

Just one more time, Karl Cullinane. . . .

It was even possible that Cullinane and that damned dragon of his would somehow manage to ambush the drive en route to Pandathaway. Ahrmin had no intention of being around for that, either. Let Fenrius take the caravan to Pandathaway; Ahrmin would travel more quickly by himself.

He shook his head. The assault on Cullinane at Furnael Keep had been a disaster, but Ahrmin had survived disasters before. The trick wasn't simply to survive, but to turn the setback into an advance.

Things didn't work out as well as you must think, Karl Cullinane, he thought. Until now, Cullinane had been able to move freely about, magically protected from being Located; the only place in the Eren region in which he ever could surely be found was that blasted valley of his. And that had been too well defended.

But now it was different. Cullinane was pinned down in Bieme; that would make him more vulnerable, not less so. Let him wear a crown for a year or two; a crown could be separated from a head as easily as the head could be separated from its shoulders.

We aren't done with each other, Karl Cullinane, Ahrmin thought. *You have won two battles, that is all.*

The third battle and the war will be mine.

"Fenrius," he said, "saddle my horse. I want an escort of twelve men ready to leave before nightfall. You will bring the chain to Pandathaway; I will meet you there."

"Yes, Master Ahrmin."

The next time we meet, Karl Cullinane, you die, he thought, completely certain that it would come to pass.

Ahrmin smiled.

ABOUT THE AUTHOR

Joel Rosenberg was born in Winnipeg, Manitoba, Canada, in 1954, and raised in eastern North Dakota and northern Connecticut. He attended the University of Connecticut, where he met and married Felicia Herman.

Joel's occupations, before settling down to writing full-time, have run the usual gamut, including driving a truck, caring for the institutionalized retarded, bookkeeping, gambling, motel desk-clerking, and a two-week stint of passing himself off as a head chef.

Joel's first sale, an op-ed piece favoring nuclear power, was published in *The New York Times*. His stories have appeared in *Isaac Asimov's Science Fiction Magazine, Perpetual Light, Amazing Science Fiction Stories,* and TSR's *The Dragon.*

Joel's hobbies include backgammon, poker, bridge, and several other sorts of gaming, as well as cooking; his broiled butterfly leg of lamb has to be tasted to be believed.

He now lives in New Haven, Connecticut, with his wife and the traditional two cats.

The Sleeping Dragon and *The Sword and the Chain,* the first two novels in Joel's *Guardians of the Flame* series, are also available in Signet editions, as is his science fiction novel, *Ties of Blood and Silver.*

DISTANT REALMS